DANA SCHWARTZ is a television writer and the creator of the number-one-charting history podcast *Noble Blood*. As a journalist and critic, Schwartz has written for *Entertainment Weekly, Marie Claire, Glamour, GQ, Cosmopolitan, Vanity Fair,* and other publications. She lives in Los Angeles with her fiancé and their cats, Eddie and Beetlejuice. Her books include *Choose Your Own Disaster* and *The White Man's Guide to White Male Writers of the Western Canon.*

also by
dana schwartz

Anatomy: A Love Story

*The White Man's Guide to
White Male Writers of the Western Canon*

Choose Your Own Disaster

And We're Off

immortality

a love story

dana schwartz

PIATKUS

PIATKUS

First published in the US in 2023 by Wednesday Books,
an imprint of St. Martin's Publishing Group
First published in Great Britain in 2023 by Piatkus

1 3 5 7 9 10 8 6 4 2

A CIP catalogue record for this book
is available from the British Library.

HB ISBN 978-0-34943-339-4
TPB ISBN 978-0-34943-340-0

Printed and bound in Great Britain by
Clays Ltd, Elcograf S.p.A.

Designed by Devan Norman

Papers used by Piatkus are from well-managed forests
and other responsible sources.

MIX
Paper from
responsible sources
FSC® C104740

Piatkus
An imprint of
Little, Brown Book Group
Carmelite House
50 Victoria Embankment
London EC4Y 0DZ

An Hachette UK Company
www.hachette.co.uk

www.littlebrown.co.uk

For anyone living
ahead of their time

"It is not everyone," said Elinor,
"who has your passion for dead leaves."

—JANE AUSTEN,
SENSE AND SENSIBILITY

immortality

prologue

prologue

THE SQUARE WAS FILLED WITH PEOPLE WHO had woken up at dawn to see blood. They surrounded the wooden stage where the guillotine had been built, elbowing one another and pressing their bodies forward, each person trying to get as close to the action as possible. Those lucky few who had managed to get to the front of the crowd waved handkerchiefs—when the heads began to roll, they would try to dip the handkerchiefs in the blood. Souvenirs. An heirloom they could pass on to their children, and their children's children. *See? I was there*, they would say, unfolding the bit of cloth. *I saw the Revolution. I saw the traitors lose their heads.*

The morning sunlight reflected off the white stone of the courthouse. Even though his hands were bound, Antoine Lavoisier managed to fix the cuffs of his shirt. He had worn his plainest work shirt to court that morning, a simple flax-colored thing; it was what he wore in his laboratory, knowing that it might get stained with sweat or one of the hundreds of chemical solutions he kept in glass vials. His wife, Marie-Anne, had threatened to throw it out a dozen times. Antoine had worn it today, hoping to prove to the judge and the braying crowd outside that he was a man of the people. For all the good it did, he might have worn silk brocade.

"Please," he had told the judge. (That cursed word had almost caught in his throat; if the circumstance hadn't been *quite* so dire, his nature would have made it impossible to beg.) "Please," he repeated, "France needs my work. Imagine what I can do for the nation—for the *Republic*—if I have more time to continue my scientific studies. I've already achieved so much in the study of oxygen. Of hydrogen, the science of combustion! At least let me return to my apartment to organize my paperwork. There are years of calculations. The possibilities for—"

The judge interrupted with a hacking, phlegmy cough. "Enough," he said. "The Republic needs neither scholars nor chemists who have stolen from the people. And the course of justice cannot be delayed any further." He struck his desk with a gavel. "Guilty."

Lavoisier sighed. "Pity," he murmured to himself, too softly to be heard above the shouts and jeers from the gleeful crowd. Officially, Antoine Lavoisier had been charged with tax fraud and with selling unsuitable tobacco, swindling the common people by adding water to weigh it down. But he knew as well as anyone that he was really on trial for something else: being an aristocrat and an academic. For having spent the previous decade of his life with his wife, holding salons in their apartment with intellectuals and artists, events where Marie-Anne served tea and repartee and biscuits made by their servants.

France was changing, *had* changed, faster than Lavoisier had believed possible. There was a bloodlust in the air, a frenzy for something that was called justice but looked like cruelty. Half a dozen of his friends had already lost their heads over meaningless criminal charges that appeared in the middle of the night. The rest of his friends fled to London or Italy. The Lavoisiers had had their chance, too, to run away to England, but they weren't able to leave their experiments. Their laboratory. They were *so* close.

Now it was too late.

Just a few months ago, Lavoisier watched as the queen herself was taken through the streets of Paris on the back of a cart, transported like so much lumber in an open cage so that loyal citizens of the Republic could see her face, could throw their rotting fruit and cabbages at her. Lavoisier had to force himself to look; the last time he had seen the queen, he had been a guest at Versailles, demonstrating a new form of chemical combustion for King Louis and his court. The queen had been wearing yellow satin, and her hair was powdered and teased a meter high, dotted with ostrich feathers and pearls. She had been laughing, he remembered that. She laughed when he'd made the small explosions—the smoke first blue, and then green, and then purple, meant to dazzle and amuse. Her face was young and her cheeks had high color.

The day they took the queen to the guillotine, Lavoisier saw that her face was drawn and lined. She looked like a woman decades older than she really was. Her hair had gone stark white and so thin that he could see her scalp in places. Her eyes, Lavoisier observed as the cart passed, were empty and blank. It was as if she had died already, a long time ago.

A guard with a bayonet pulled Lavoisier toward the stage.

Some of the onlookers tried to trip him, or get in a blow as he walked past, but Lavoisier barely noticed, so focused was he was on scanning the thousands of faces for his wife, Marie-Anne.

"There!" he shouted.

The sun lit her from behind, her hair giving her a golden halo. She stood near the wooden steps of the platform, her eyes determinedly scanning the crowd, and her mouth straight and tight. The guard looked back at Lavoisier in confusion, not sure what he had shouted about.

Just then, Marie-Anne saw her husband, and she started swimming her way against the current of bodies to get to him.

The guard jostled Lavoisier, trying to force him along.

He resisted. "Surely the Republic's justice can wait long enough for me to kiss my wife farewell?"

The guard sighed but paused and let the pair embrace. Marie-Anne whispered in her husband's ear. No one noticed her pressing a small vial into his palm.

The guillotine's blade was brown with blood. There had already been two beheadings that morning, and the straw onstage was matted and red. Someone held a basket, ready to catch Lavoisier's head when it tumbled from his neck. Others held their white handkerchiefs aloft, hoping for blood splatter.

Marie-Anne Lavoisier didn't watch her husband ascend the small wooden steps onto the stage. She didn't want to know if he would shake, or if his legs might give out beneath him. There were even some stories of the condemned soiling themselves.

And so instead, she moved briskly through the crowd, away from the center of the square, toward their apartment, where she would gather as much of her husband's research material as she could before the vultures came to scavenge whatever valuables they could claim. The new regime was seizing everything it could. Marie-Anne comforted herself with the notion that no matter who stole her husband's papers, they almost certainly wouldn't understand them.

She ducked down a small alley. Her footsteps were swift and sure. The crowd behind her inhaled in excitement. Words were shouted that she couldn't make out. And then there came the unmistakable sound of a blade cutting through the air. Marie-Anne Lavoisier said a quick prayer for her husband, and for her country, and continued on.

1

"THIS IS GOING TO HURT. I AM SORRY ABOUT that." Hazel Sinnett didn't feel as though there was any use in lying.

The boy bit down harder on the piece of leather she had brought for that very purpose and nodded. A young girl had come to Hazel's door the night before and begged her to come, describing the way her older brother's arm had broken weeks before, while he was working at the shipyard, and the way it had healed wrong: twisted and impossible to move. When Hazel arrived at their dingy flat near Mary King's Close first thing in the morning, she had found the boy's arm swollen and hot, the skin bruised yellow and green, and tight as a sausage casing.

Hazel prepared her equipment: a scalpel to cut open the arm and let out the worst of the infection, the needle and thread she would use to sew his arm back up, and then the strips of cloth and pieces of wood she would fashion into something to keep his arm in place once she re-broke and reset it. That last part was going to hurt the most.

The patient was named Martin Potter, and he might have been around her age—sixteen or seventeen maybe—but his face was already browned and set like an adult's. Hazel imagined that he had been working the docks at Leith since he was ten.

"It's Martin, isn't it? I'm Hazel. Dr. Sinnett. *Miss Sinnett*," she said. "And I'm going to do everything I can to make this better."

Martin nodded with a gesture so small it might have been a shiver.

The sound of children laughing and stomping upstairs disrupted the tense, nervous silence. Martin removed the leather strip from his mouth. "My brothers and sisters," he said almost apologetically. "There are eight of us but I'm the oldest. You would have met Rose already. She's the one that came to fetch ye. She heard there was a lady doctor who didn't take much in terms of payment."

"Eight siblings! Your poor mother," Hazel said. "There are only three of us. Me and my two brothers."

Hazel realized what she had said even before the words had fully left her mouth. There *had* been three of them: George, Hazel, and little Percy. George, the golden child, athletic and strong, smarter than Hazel and genuinely *kind*; Hazel, who always found a new way for her mother to criticize her; and Percy, the spoiled princeling who had basically all but become their mother's poodle.

But there *weren't* three of them. Not anymore. George had died a few years ago, when the Roman fever swept through the city, one of thousands who perished before they even understood what the sickness was. He had been so *young*, so strong, so *healthy* that even when he first got sick, Hazel remembered wondering whether he'd be well enough for ninepins on the lawn that very weekend or whether she'd have to wait another week for him to get his energy back. But then, quick as the sickness came, it took him. One morning, Hazel woke to the sound of their mother shrieking in heaving sobs. And George was cold.

Her throat used to tighten whenever she thought of George. She would need to turn away and take deep breaths to stave off the tears that came prickling at her eyes. But in the years since, his memory had become like scar tissue, healed over again and again until it was shiny and smooth to the touch, and almost never hurt. Permanent, but the pain wasn't so sharp. Jack's death was still an open wound. She couldn't think of Jack now. Not while she was working.

"Are you ready?" Hazel asked. Martin's arm, swollen and askew, was more than distraction enough. Hazel mentally flipped through the pages of the books she'd memorized about the proper placement of arm bones and the ligaments connecting the muscle. Hazel lifted the scalpel. "Are you ready?" she repeated.

The knife entered just below the elbow. Instantly, the wound began to weep thin yellow liquid. The infection that had been making Martin's arm tight and hot. Martin winced.

The pus kept coming—pints of it, it seemed, without any additional prodding from Hazel. "I'm going to need a cloth. Is there a rag I can use?"

Almost as soon as Hazel asked, there was the sound of stomping down the stairs. Two young girls with dark brown curls matted to their heads raced toward Hazel, both carrying squares of dishwater-gray cloth. The girls looked to be twins, no older than eight.

"I brought," one of the girls said, holding up the fabric for Hazel.

The girl's sister elbowed her sharply in the ribs. "No, *I* brought!"

Hazel graciously took both cloths and immediately put them to use soaking up the liquid still leaking from her incision. "Thank you, girls." She said, "Is this your brother?" The twins nodded but they remained with their tiny mouths agape, unable to tear their eyes from their brother's broken arm. Martin noticed, and pulled the leather piece from his mouth with his good hand.

"Sue, May—get out of here. I told you that you was meant to stay upstairs, remember?"

The girls acted like they couldn't hear him. One of the girls—Sue, maybe—extended her index finger, readying herself to poke her brother's injury.

Hazel swatted her hand out of the way before it made contact. "Your brother is right. You're going to need to go back upstairs if you want Martin to get well."

The girls giggled in place, undaunted by the yellow pus that had slightly abated but also thickened into greenish clumps. Hazel decided to try a new strategy. "Girls," she said, fishing in her pocket and pulling out a few coins. "Would you be able to get me one orange for your brother? It's very important for Martin to have an orange if he's going to get well. Can you do that for me?"

Spellbound as the girls had been by the surgery, the coins in Hazel's hand dazzled them more. They snatched the money so quickly it was as if they'd expected her palm to close, and then, without giving her enough time to change her mind, raced out the door to their task.

The room returned to relative silence. Hazel finished pressing the infection from the cut and washed the wound with water and the small bottle of alcohol she'd stolen from her father's collection. "All right," Hazel said, "next we sew up the wound."

There were several drawbacks to being a young woman working as a surgeon, but there was also one advantage: years of her childhood had been spent on embroidery—on mastering the neat, orderly stitches that would, her mother had assured her, make fine gifts for her future mother-in-law one day—and that meant she was a prodigy when it came to stitching wounds.

Her older brother had been tutored in Latin and history and mathematics; when it came to science, Hazel was forced to listen at doors, learning through borrowed workbooks and lessons that George passed along. Hazel's own lessons were in violin and piano. She was taught French and Italian. And she was forced to sit, for hours and hours, as the solarium filled with the still and stifling heat of late afternoon, *sewing*.

When she had dressed in her brother's clothing and sneaked into the lectures at the Anatomists' Society under an assumed name, pretending to be a boy, she was at the top of the class in every subject. But it was her stitches that forced even the famously strict and impassive Dr. Straine to acknowledge her skill.

"Well, yes!" one of the boys in class had scoffed after Straine admitted that Hazel's work on the dead rabbit she had been assigned was impeccable. "He's got these tiny hands, like a girl! I'd rather be worse at stitching and have bigger hands, *if you know what I mean*." The rest of the class had laughed until Straine shot them all a deadly look. Hazel stifled her own giggle.

ARTIN'S ARM WAS STITCHED UP IN SECONDS,
the line tidy and even. Hazel smiled at her work.
It probably wouldn't even leave a scar. Martin spat out his
leather. "Are we done, then?" he asked. "You did it, yeah? I'm
better now?"

"Not quite."

Martin looked down at his arm. "But I'm all sewed up!"

"Your arm was broken quite severely," Hazel said, pressing gingerly up from his elbow. "In several places, from the feel of it. If we don't reset it now, you might never be able to use your arm again. Or it might have to come off altogether."

Martin clenched his eyes shut. "Just do it, then."

Hazel braced herself against the table, gripped his arm tight. She would have to position herself at the correct angle if she was going to be able to re-break the bone. Hazel took a deep breath, and exhaled hard while she pulled, summoning all the strength she could muster for one well-placed burst of force.

The crunch echoed through the small room.

Before Martin could scream, Hazel reset the arm firmly in place, where it could heal correctly. Both their foreheads glistened with sweat. Martin's hair hung wet down at his ears, and a stain was blooming at both his armpits.

"That's it, then," Hazel said. She wiped the scalpel off on her apron and deposited it back into her bag before she turned to the work of wrapping Martin's arm. "But you're not to move this arm for a week at the earliest. Change the dressing on the bandage over the stitches if it looks yellow, but not before, and tell your mum that you're absolutely not to go to the shipyard for another month. There's no work you'll be able to do anyway."

Martin moved his arm slowly at the shoulder to test the tightness of the ties. "Ain't got no mum," he said, still looking at his arm.

"What do you mean? All of your sisters, the girls?"

"Mum died with the twins. Is'a miracle they came out okay as they were. Tried to get a midwife when she was having them, but Mum said she had been through it all half a dozen times already and knew what she was doing. Besides," he added, "not like we could afford a fancy doctor." He looked at Hazel with something halfway between gratitude and suspicion. "So, I take care of us. All of 'em. I can go a week without work, but no longer."

At that moment, Martin's two younger sisters reappeared at the door. One of them held a small, perfectly round orange in her palm, purchased for a penny from one of the carts lining High Street. "We got it," said one girl. "We got the orange. Very important."

"Very important," her sister echoed.

"Yes," Hazel said. "Will you do your brother and me a big favor and peel it for us?"

The girls eagerly accepted their task, using their tiny fingernails to dig into the flesh of the orange and peel its skin away. When the fruit inside was exposed—slightly lopsided and dripping juice from its messy excavation—one of the girls held it aloft in her hand and offered it to Hazel like a jewel.

"Now, here's the hardest part," Hazel said. "You're going to need to divide it into thirds, and help your brother eat his third without letting him use his hands. Do you know what thirds are? Enough for the three of you."

In answer, the girls began their work. Martin gratefully

opened his mouth to allow one of his younger sisters to feed him a segment.

"Can't remember the last time we had an orange," Martin said, letting some of the juice run from the corner of his mouth and down his chin.

"Well, good food will help you heal," Hazel said. "That's what this is for." She pointed to the small pile of coins she'd left on the table. "So you can rest for a week at least."

Martin's face contorted and he moved as if to push the coins away, but he only lifted his right arm an inch before he winced in pain and lowered it to his side once more. "I don't accept charity," he said, his voice suddenly colder and more frightful than it had been moments before, when Hazel was holding a blade to his skin.

"It's not charity," Hazel said. "It's treatment. What's the point of me coming here and fixing your arm if you're just going to ruin it tomorrow with a day of work at the docks?"

Martin clenched his teeth. His sisters were in a corner of the room, sticky with orange juice, sharing segments of the fruit and sucking on the peel. "I'm not going to thank you for that," he said finally, tilting his head toward the money. "But thank you for fixing the arm."

"You're welcome," Hazel replied simply. She finished packing her black leather medical bag and gave a small bow to Martin, and then to his sisters. "Ladies," she said. And Hazel Sinnett exited their flat and reemerged onto the streets of Crichton's Close, walking briskly toward her next appointment with the still-rising sun at her back. There was another bonesetting to do, and two tooth extractions, and a case of syphilis to treat. And Mrs. Bede's baby would be due any day now. There was work to be done.

Notes from Hazel Sinnett,
A Treatise on Modern Medicine (Unpublished)

Though the speed at which the Roman fever seizes its patients varies, the presentation of symptoms is—perhaps comfortingly—routine. First, patients report a few days of weariness, but an inability to sleep, and feverishness. Soon, the pustules (buboes) appear on the body, typically the back, upper arms, and legs.

The buboes fill with blood and become red-purple, and eventually burst. Contrary to popular opinion, Roman fever is *not* so named because it originated in Italy (earliest cases were identified in London and Bavaria) but because when the buboes burst, the shirts of patients become stained with a blood pattern that resembles multiple stab wounds, akin to Julius Caesar being stabbed on the steps of the Roman Senate.

Though neither cure nor prevention has been identified, *wortroot* has been proved in my practice to ameliorate the symptoms and stave off death. I have applied wortflower root in a salve and administered it as tea, and will report on the more efficacious course of action. Will also remain abreast as to literature on whether the Roman fever can be prevented via inoculation. (Do not yet feel confident enough to test it on patients nor self.)

Wortflower tea: dry and powder several stems of the wortflower plant, steep in hot water with honey and lemon. For salve: powder the dried herb and add oil and warm candle wax.

Additional treatment for the Roman fever: cardamom seeds and warm milk in the evening, for strength.

2

AZEL SINNETT DREAMED OF FINGERS. BONY, spindly fingers, with knuckles knobbed like walnuts and gray-green flesh peeling off in thin strips. Sometimes the fingers weren't attached to any hands at all: sometimes they were like living things, set on a flat table, twitching like insect legs. Sometimes in her dreams, she saw Dr. Beecham's fingers, the way they had looked when the famed surgeon pulled off his leather gloves for her at the Anatomists' Society to reveal the truth of what he hid beneath: swollen digits, some purple and black, sewn onto his hand.

Fingers that had fallen off and been reattached. A pinkie finger that looked like it never belonged to him in the first place.

No. She never woke up from her dreams panting or crying out, with sweat dampening the hair to her forehead. She never felt her heart racing. She never talked or shouted in her sleep. Her lady's maid, Iona, never had need to rush in with a cool cloth and soothing cup of tea. Hazel's nightmares didn't scare her any longer.

One night, she had dreamed of a single index finger, with bone visible at the knuckles, still dripping blood, pulling itself toward her like an inchworm. When she woke up, Hazel was thinking of the stitches she would have selected to reattach it to a hand.

She no longer had time for fear or horror at blood or decay: working as a surgeon meant every second mattered more than the last. A mere instant, the time it would take to recoil or stifle a gasp, might mean the difference between life and death. She had work to do. And in the past few months, she had been very, very busy.

"Easy there!"

Hazel pulled her plate of toast from the table, rescuing it from where Iona's belly had almost knocked it to the floor. The young woman was five months along now—Hazel forced her to submit to regular examinations and consultations—but Iona still didn't seem aware of the damage she could cause when walking through close quarters.

"Hmm?" Iona said, spinning around, knocking an empty plate to the floor. Mercifully, it spun and settled, unbroken.

"No, no, I'll get it!" Hazel said, seeing Iona begin to reach down to pick it up.

"It's this blasted belly," Iona said, rubbing it absentmindedly. "Already the size of a shoulder of mutton. And to think I'm going to get even bigger. How many months you say I have to go now?"

"Four," Hazel said. "And I'm not going to want you working at Hawthornden much longer, do you hear me? Bed rest soon, especially if the little darling continues to grow at the rate he's been doing so far. I'm delivering this child, so you'll do as I say now."

"Charles says all the babes in his family are hearty types. Come out with full sets of hair and full sets of teeth," Iona said, depositing herself at the table in the chair next to Hazel and letting out an *oof*.

"Lord have mercy," Hazel murmured.

"And," Iona said, "I'll work at the house as long as I well like, miss." She hadn't even had the child yet, and she was already addressing Hazel like she was a mother, never mind the fact that they were all but the same age. "Who else is going to keep you fed when you're working late in the night?"

Hazel grimaced. "These hours are only until I finish my treatise. Then I'll start keeping normal hours."

"Aye, your *treatise*." Iona rolled her eyes and bit into a piece of toast. Hazel had talked of little else for the past few months: her lofty goal of developing a new, updated guidebook on anatomy and basic household treatments, complete with her own illustrations.

The idea was a book of anatomy written in the style of a household manual, the type of book anyone with the ability to read would be able to understand, with diagrams of the human body and its components and advice on home treatments. *Dr. Beecham's Treatise on Anatomy; or, The Prevention and Cure of Modern Diseases* was a masterwork in the field, of course; it was the achievement of a lifetime (or *several* lifetimes, Hazel reminded herself), but it was also a tome thick enough to kill a man if it fell upon him from a high shelf, and nearly impenetrable for anyone without a specific interest in physiology. Hazel's book would be different—influenced by the manuals for proper etiquette and entertaining that seemed to just appear as if by magic in a young woman's sitting room as soon as she turned fifteen.

Common people have bodies, Hazel reasoned; *there's no reason they can't understand how those bodies work. And so many of them cannot afford doctors, or the ones they can afford are charlatans or else poorly trained.* Hazel understood with genuine clarity that a straightforward guide to effective home remedies could save lives.

The problem, of course, was that as noble as her intentions were, Hazel had inadvertently begun a staggering undertaking. A book meant to identify common ailments and their treatment could take years if she was thorough, and on top of that, Hazel wanted detailed diagrams and descriptions of the major systems and organs of the body. The drawings of the organs in Beecham's book were neat as sewing patterns: Hazel had been shocked when the first corpse was opened in front of her and she saw what truly existed beneath our skin, the wet and dark and bleeding mass of flesh. It was frightening to know that that was all we were, that the human soul existed somewhere in that putrid, writhing soup. But it needn't be frightening. It could be explained, and she could be the one to explain it, with drawings and diagrams and language that read the way people talked.

Since Jack's trial and hanging, it had become nearly impossible for medical students to get fresh bodies. Hazel was forced to work from old notes, diagrams she had drawn back when she was studying for the Royal Examination. Of course, in the end, she hadn't taken the test at all. She had followed Dr. Beecham to his surgical hall, watched him attempt to "transplace" an eye from a living patient into another man, and then try to take the beating heart from Jack Currer's body. She had stopped the doctor, but it wasn't enough. She hadn't done enough to save Jack's life. Jack was gone.

Just thinking of Jack now caused an electric shock to run up from Hazel's stomach, as though she had swallowed something metallic and alive. She missed him so much she could feel it in her bones, a longing like hunger through every part of her. She missed the way his arms felt around her, the way he smelled, the way the scruff on his cheeks brushed her skin when he kissed her forehead and she just wanted to pull him close, close, closer forever. Jack was gone—he was gone and what good did it do to think of him? He was a hole in her stomach, a longing that she couldn't fill but whose piercing heat seemed to dull when she worked, when she focused on the task at hand.

Assembling her notes. Reading her notes. Copying her notes so that the handwriting was legible. Identifying the gaps in her study. Slowly, methodically, illustrating the system of veins that delivered blood through each limb: drawings for the arms, the legs, the hands, the feet. In those vast and expansive hours after Iona had brought Hazel her dinner but before she knocked at the laboratory door with breakfast—when the candles were still burning and the only thing that filled Hazel's mind was rendering the veins that traced their way down the thumb from a preserved hand she had ordered from Paris, in which hardened wax tracked the vessels that once carried blood—Jack might almost have been there, outside, riding a horse or sleeping in Hawthornden, there safe and close enough that she could call him.

From a raging fire that threatened to turn Hazel's world to ash, the longing instead dampened to a small flame, a flickering candle visible only in the corner of her eyes. *You can't speak to him now, but he's there if you need him,* the candle said. *He's just there, only just out of view.* That was the real way she survived losing Jack: by pretending that she hadn't lost him at all, and that at any moment she might walk up to the big house and see him smiling up at her over tea, see the way his canine teeth extended past the others and overlapped, see his messy hair, which had always contained a hidden pocket of sawdust. Turn Jack from a memory into something that needn't even concern her—that was the trick. That was the magic she could pull off only when the full power of her focus was entirely on her writing.

Her work was too important to allow for distractions. She knew that to be true, and if she kept repeating it to herself, maybe one day she would just about believe it.

Hazel flipped a broadsheet newspaper on the breakfast table and rubbed the ink between her hands, imagining the cost of the materials and the use of the press that would one day allow her to publish her own book. The ink stained her fingertips black. It was a welcome break from the stains they usually bore—the maroon and brown of dried blood.

Iona gasped and Hazel leapt to her feet. "What is it? Is the baby all right? Are you feeling any cramping or pain?"

Iona was staring at the paper, pointing at a line drawing on the front page. "Is that the Princess? It is! It's Charlotte! What's it say, Hazel?"

Hazel sank back into her chair and pulled the page closer to her. Iona could read, but that was a slow and laborious process, and Hazel had long since given up on badgering her to practice. ("Maybe you fine ladies have time to read your novels all day, but some of us have work to do," she had scoffed once.) Novels did not interest Iona; gossip about the

Princess of Wales did, the future Queen of England and only child of the Prince Regent. "It says here," Hazel said, her heart rate still recovering from her panic moments before, "that Princess Charlotte has chosen to end her engagement with William of Orange."

Iona looked genuinely heartbroken. "No!" she said. "They were a beautiful couple! And she's not getting any younger. If she doesn't have a baby soon, who knows if she'll even be able to."

"She's not much older than us! She's, what, twenty-one? I think she has plenty of time, Iona."

Iona rubbed her own belly knowingly. "Less than you think, miss. Does it say why? Was he a philanderer? I bet not. I bet someone else caught her eye. Duke of Gloucester, I reckon."

Hazel couldn't help but laugh. "I don't know. It doesn't say. I think it must have had something to do with her illness. Maybe she wasn't well enough to travel to Holland. And why, might I add, do you even care? Good Scottish girl that you are, I've heard you curse the name of the King and Prince on more than one occasion, when you thought no one could hear you."

Iona blushed but her expression didn't otherwise falter. "Aye," she said loftily. "I can dislike the King and England for all they've done to us, and still like the Princess."

"Whatever you say."

Everyone did seem to like the Princess; it wasn't just Iona. All the frustration with and resentment of the monarchy—the pity and revulsion people felt for poor, mad King George and the outright dislike of the buffoonish Prince Regent—dissolved when it came to Princess Charlotte.

"You've met her, haven't you?" Iona asked. She was prompting an anecdote that Hazel had already recounted on more than one occasion but which Iona never seemed to tire of.

"Yes," Hazel said. "Briefly, when I was in London. Before George died. The last time my mother took me to buy new dresses there. I wasn't *officially* out yet, and so I didn't attend any balls, or any of that sort of thing. But Mercer Elphinstone—a girl from Edinburgh I had spent some time with—she was friends with the Princess. She was hosting a tea, and I met the Princess there."

"And?" Iona said, exactly as scripted, her eyes as wide as saucers.

"*And*," Hazel continued, "I remember her being very beautiful, and very fashionable, and very kind. She was in the high-waisted gowns before the rest of us, and looked marvelous. And she was in *drawers*, if you can believe it—I remember being able to see the lace edges peeking out from under her dress. Quite scandalous. I recall my mother telling me afterward that she had used the wrong fork for her salad course and I found it so funny I was in fits of giggles all the way back to Edinburgh. That there was a correct fork for salad at all, that the Princess would use the wrong one, and that people like my mother would notice."

"And yet," Iona said slyly, "you always have me set the table with correct forks, miss, and you always know the right one to use."

"Well," Hazel said, dabbing at her lips with her serviette, "I suppose some things become habit." It was true, the lessons her mother had drilled into her brain through hours of repetition when she was a child still had their hold on her.

After George died, her mother's etiquette lessons stopped abruptly—her mother had fallen into a deep melancholy, scarcely leaving her room and scarcely talking to Hazel at all for more than a sentence at a time. From that point on, Hazel raised herself, dressing in whatever clothes she could find or chose to have made, educating herself from the books in her father's library. Her manners, then, were half-formed and strange. She knew most of the proper lessons for a girl of her class, but found that some of the manners had been overwritten, like sentences written over each other on parchment, in the years she spent more or less alone.

Still, she chose the proper riding habit and matching hat to make a house call that morning at one of the fashionable white-stone manors over in Edinburgh's New Town. Some things, she supposed, just couldn't be helped.

The ride was short enough, and before the sun had even reached its apex, Hazel trotted onto the stone streets of the New Town. Nearly a century ago, the wealthy had become fed up with the narrow streets and the stink of too many people stacked on top of one another in the city center surrounding Edinburgh Castle. And so, a second city, New Town, had sprung up in neatly manicured squares, rows of manor houses with clean white brick and neo-Grecian columns. The two Edinburghs were separated by Princes Street Gardens. Where there was once a loch thick with sewage and all manner of waste, there were now stretches of elegantly groomed grass, park space in which only those who paid a steep annual fee were allowed to partake, although there was talk of opening it to the public. Hazel liked the idea, and not just because she could imagine how much it would scandalize her mother.

When Hazel began making house calls, she was mostly calling on the working poor in Edinburgh, those who would never be able to afford a private physician and who, in their terror at the possibility of ending up at one of the abysmal poorhouse hospitals, were willing to enlist the young female surgeon of whom they had heard rumors. However, in recent months, Hazel had been making the journey on horseback to New Town more and more frequently.

After Hazel had learned the truth about Dr. Beecham's medical practice in Edinburgh—that he was making his living by abducting resurrection men and beggars and children to steal body parts for his wealthy clients—he disappeared from the city. From those who didn't know the truth—and no one knew the truth except for Hazel and Jack—the rumors came fast and freely: The doctor had fallen in love with a woman in Sweden. He had been summoned to treat Tsar Alexander in Russia. He had died while on a ship bound for India.

Hazel did know the truth: if Beecham was immortal, as he claimed, then he could live only so long in a single place without the consistency of his appearance raising questions. He needed to disappear once every generation, reemerging with a new name or, if it had been long enough, with a story about being a previous Beecham's distant relative, and hoping anyone surviving remembered only a passing resemblance to the doctor they once knew.

There was no telling where he was. He could be anywhere in the world. Finding him would be impossible. Forcing him to face a semblance of justice for the people he had killed, doubly so. For months, Hazel had fantasized about the different things she could have said to Dr. Beecham, the way their final conversation at the Anatomists' Society could have gone. Was there a combination of words she could have said to unlock his empathy, the way a key opens a door? Could she have persuaded him to face justice? Was there something she could have said to help him understand that what he was doing was cruel, that the physician had no right to sacrifice one human life to benefit someone else?

Thinking about it for too long made Hazel's stomach knot up in anger. She told herself that the best thing she could do now was help the people in her city.

And now, with Beecham gone, many of his wealthy former patients were left with no one to treat them. Or, at least, no one *respectable*.

Physicians were easy enough to come by, young men who graduated from the university's medical school or who came up from London in top hats, bearing pristine leather cases printed with their initials. But surgery was a different animal. Those men—well, surgeons were practically butchers. And they'd sell your secrets for a snuff of tobacco.

Still, in some cases, a butcher was necessary.

Somehow, word had gotten around that Lord Almont's *niece* was adept and able to treat common maladies, and that her stitches were small and even and left almost no scar. A female surgeon was, to put it mildly, a curiosity. But if you're going to invite someone into the private inner rooms of your home, well, it may as well be someone who runs in the proper circles. They might not know how well Hazel was trained in medicine, but they could at least comfort themselves with the fact that she knew the appropriate gloves to wear to the opera. Besides, her reputation was already muddied, and who better to trust with one's own less-than-savory secrets than someone no one would bother to listen to?

And so, to Hazel's shock more than anyone else's, quiet requests began to come to Hawthornden for Hazel Sinnett to be the one to deliver their children and their grandchildren, to confidentially inspect their nether regions after encounters with mistresses and not tell their wives, and to pull the teeth from their mouths that had become black and cracked.

Which was how Hazel found herself in the private parlor of Richard Parlake, the Earl of Hammond, inspecting the pink, foul-smelling mouth of his beloved son and heir, Richard Parlake III.

The younger Richard, a squirmy boy of about twelve, was not happy to have a woman operating on him. He was sullen, refusing to make eye contact when Hazel entered and refusing to take off his hat. He kept it on even as Hazel gestured for him to sit on the plum-colored sofa and open his mouth. When she walked behind him to examine the offending teeth, she "accidentally" knocked the top hat from his head and onto the floor.

"Whoops," she said, kicking it under the sofa. It was a simple-enough case: two teeth cracked and already loose.

The elder Richard Parlake, a man who prided himself on his mane of shoulder-length silver hair, took it upon himself to stand over Hazel's shoulder, all but reaching into his son's mouth with her to direct her fingers toward the appropriate tooth. "It's this sugar," he declared, nodding his head at his own wisdom. "All this sugar the young boys today are putting in their tea. Turns teeth black, but no one listens to what I have to say on the matter."

Hazel offered a small grunt in affirmation, trying to reach behind the man to grab the pliers from her medical bag, which she had set on the small table beside them. "If you might step aside, Lord Parlake . . ."

He ignored her. "I've been telling Dickie—haven't I been telling you, Dickie?—it's *sugar* that's going to be the death of all of us. If men of Edinburgh followed the diet of the Highlands . . . Now, *they* know a proper diet. Meat! None of this sugar. None of this *sugar in their tea.* I can hardly stand it. We're supposed to be men of dignity and not, you know, women." He glanced at Hazel apologetically. She pretended not to hear him and continued peering at his son's rotting teeth.

Sensing the conversation getting away from him, the earl leaned closer. "How goes it, Dickie?"

The boy had his mouth held open. He gave a gargled sound in reply to his father.

Lord Parlake patted his son heartily on the back, almost forcing the cloth Hazel had put into the boy's mouth to dislodge and choke him. "Good lad," the earl said merrily, unaware of the chaos he'd caused.

"Sir, I'm going to need you to stand *several steps away.* I need the light to make sure I pull the right tooth," Hazel said. Her patient, Dickie, turned his wide eyes toward her in gratitude.

The earl murmured something but acquiesced. Still, his pride bruised, he called to Hazel, "You know, we had a letter in to *Dr. Ferris* to treat Dickie. Have you heard of Dr. Ferris? Supposedly the finest surgeon in Europe. Treating George III himself! He was the one we were *supposed* to have here pulling Dickie's teeth. Man's such a genius I imagine he'd find a way to keep the teeth in the mouth."

Hazel had indeed heard of Dr. Ferris. It seemed every year or so, there was a new, incredibly pompous physician from Denmark or Germany or Russia who would arrive to their little isle bearing a medical bag and a reputation for genius.

In Hazel's opinion, their brilliance seemed limited to an extraordinary ability to separate fools from their money. They were the type of doctors who charged hundreds of pounds to tell people to eat more potato skins, or else, to eat *fewer* potato skins, and who then spent more time waltzing around balls held in their honor than they did in operating rooms. Hazel could picture Ferris now: sixty years old, probably, with a potbelly from all the feasts people threw for him and all the wine they gifted him, the type of doctor who had a powdered wig and soft hands.

"What a shame he couldn't make it," Hazel said.

"Indeed!" the earl huffed. "I imagine my letter was lost en route to London."

If the doctor were half as acclaimed as the earl seemed to believe, Hazel seriously doubted he would ever have bothered to come to Edinburgh to pull two teeth, a job that any halfway decent barber could handle and that even a terrible barber had fairly good odds at managing.

Hazel had Dickie lean back a little farther so the light from the window would help her to see the teeth she'd be pulling. The gums seemed relatively free from infection. Hazel held the pliers delicately in her hand, and, quick as a fox changing direction, she gripped the first offending tooth and twisted. Dickie shouted, but before the sound left his mouth, Hazel had gotten a good enough grip on the second tooth. One more twist, and she was done, with the two teeth rattling in her palm and Dickie rubbing his jaw in shock.

"See, it smarts for a second, but I bet those teeth were bothering you for a while," Hazel said quietly to the boy. "That's the thing about this sort of thing: a sharp bit of hurt now to save a lot of hurt adding up over time." She turned to his father. "Two shillings, please, sir."

Like most wealthy people, the earl found it distinctly unpleasant to hand over money for a service provided to him. He dropped the coins in Hazel's palm with a grimace. She closed her hand around the money and the small black teeth. They had pointed roots, still dotted with red blood.

"Soak a rag in wine and hold it to the gums tonight and tomorrow," she instructed. "Send someone to fetch me if the bleeding hasn't stopped by dawn."

"Yes, yes," the earl said absently. Dickie moaned. And Hazel shook the teeth and the coins in her palm, already mentally drafting an entry for her treatise on the mechanics of pulling teeth.

3

AWTHORNDEN CASTLE, HAZEL'S FAMILY home, was built of stone on a cliffside overlooking a small stream, several miles beyond the din and grime of the heart of Edinburgh's Old Town, visible like a smoking chimney in the distance. Sheets covered most of the furniture, dust gathering in their folds. Spiderwebs had claimed the front parlor, and Hazel found it wasn't worth the trouble to keep them at bay. Now that she was alone, Hazel kept half the rooms in the castle unlit and unheated—no use wasting the candles or firewood.

Over the summer, Hazel's younger brother, Percy, had been accepted at Eton down in England—a *fine* school, their father said in his letters when he heard the news—and Lady Sinnett, not willing to be several days' ride from her precious little boy, had decided to abscond permanently to a town house in Slough, where the school's gray towers were visible from her window. It was almost enough for Hazel to feel sorry for Percy.

Hazel had assumed word of her underground medical

practice would eventually reach her parents—her mother in London and her father on Saint Helena, where he was still stationed as a captain in the royal military—but weeks passed, and then months, and no rebuke came.

Maybe working as a surgeon wasn't a bigger scandal than Hazel refusing Bernard's proposal last year. From that point on, Lady Sinnett had come to see Hazel as a lost cause, a willful waste of a daughter. An embarrassment, really. No one would want to marry a girl who spent her days lancing boils and slicing open limbs, treating patients in the underbelly of Edinburgh's impoverished and unfashionable Old Town, where the smell of urine and coal smoke hovered low in the air.

If her reputation was already ruined, Hazel thought, well, so be it. Little harm it did to *continue* to ruin it.

Lady Sinnett had barely offered a goodbye to her daughter when she entered the carriage, which was already sagging under the weight of her three massive valises, strapped to the roof. Hazel's mother had been wearing black ever since the death of her eldest son, George, and though it was a sweltering day in August, she wore a gown of thick black velvet crepe and a veil over her face. While her horses whinnied, Lady Sinnett eyed Hazel coldly. She lifted her veil, disembarked, and took a few ginger steps toward her daughter, and for a moment, Hazel wondered if her mother was going to kiss her.

"Your shoes are stained," she said simply. "Dirt." Hazel looked down at her boots. The dirtied boots were the ones she had worn to sneak into the graveyard with Jack, to steal bodies to bring back to her laboratory for study. She hadn't thought to scrub the dirt from them. She always imagined that she and Jack would eventually be going back to the kirk-yards.

Before Hazel could come up with a suitable response, Lady Sinnett had gotten back aboard and closed the door of her carriage, and Hazel watched as it disappeared down the tree-lined drive.

From that day forward, Hazel was almost entirely alone at Hawthornden Castle. (Cook stayed on to prepare meals for Hazel, though Lady Sinnett had pleaded with the woman to join the rest of the household staff down in England. "I was born in Scotland and I'll die in Scotland," Cook had said. "Nothing good can come from me trying to cook with vege-tables grown in English rocks or skinny cows eating English weeds.") Hazel's lady's maid remained, of course, but she was pregnant with her first child, and Hazel had insisted that Iona spend many of her days resting in the cottage at the top of the road, where she lived.

Hazel didn't mind Hawthornden Castle half-shrouded and cold. Besides, she spent so little time in the castle any-way; when she wasn't making house calls in town, she was working in her laboratory.

Hazel had built the laboratory piece by piece, bringing in furniture and torches and books until it was comfortable enough that she could go days without leaving its confines while she worked on her writing, meticulously recording every symptom she identified and every treatment she ad-ministered. The laboratory had once been the Hawthornden Castle dungeon, dug into a cave beneath the hill on which the house perched. Inside, the air was cool and thick with the smell of damp and dirt. Only one high window allowed a sliver of natural light in, and so Hazel surrounded her table with dozens of candles so she could read late into the night.

She brought her favorite chair, covered in faded red cloth, down from her bedroom so she could read, and took an oil painting of their family from her father's study to set on a shelf. It was commissioned when George was still alive and Percy was still a baby. Her mother appeared almost happy. (Hazel hated how she herself looked in the portrait—twelve years old or so, hair in tiny curls that she remembered as being tight and itchy on her scalp.)

When midnight struck on the day Hazel turned eighteen, she was reading a medical journal about the possible detriments of bloodletting on cholera patients. She looked up at the chiming of the clock and saw her family's faces in oil paint looking down at her. It was almost as if they were there with her, wishing her a happy birthday.

A letter arrived from her father the next week (postage service from the islands was notoriously difficult, he wrote in preemptive apology), and a drawing of a cat came from Percy the following week. (She and Percy had never owned a cat, nor had they ever spoken about any particular fondness for them, and so the choice of creature seemed a little indiscriminate, but Hazel still pinned the drawing above her desk to look at it while she worked.)

The letter she had truly been waiting for wasn't from family at all. Hazel was waiting—had been waiting, for *months*—to hear from Jack, the only boy she had ever loved. Jack Currer, who lived at the theater and worked by night as a resurrection man, digging up dead bodies and selling them to doctors who needed bodies to study on. Jack Currer, who had taken her on midnight digs to kirkyards, who had kissed her in a grave, who had made the heart in her chest feel as though a fist were clenched around it and all the air in her lungs had turned to lead. Jack Currer, who was framed for murders that Dr. Beecham had committed, sentenced to death, and hanged in Haymarket Square. And who maybe, *maybe*, Hazel hoped with a small hidden part of herself, had found a way to survive.

It was ludicrous, Hazel knew, to think that the tiny vial of purple-black liquid Dr. Beecham had given her could make a man immortal. It was against every one of the scientific principles she had been taught, every lesson in every book. The human body was not designed to last forever—it was meant to decay, to consume and expend energy, and then to relieve its godly soul to an eternal resting place in heaven. There was no elixir, no *tonic*—as Beecham called it—that could undo mortality.

And yet.

And yet Beecham still lived.

Beecham, who had appeared to Hazel as a man in midlife, should have been at least a hundred years old. That's only if what he claimed was true, Hazel reminded herself when she found her mind wandering to flights of fancy. Maybe Beecham was just a madman. Perhaps he had figured out a way to transplace young, healthy body parts into the bodies of those who ailed, patients who were willing to pay for new eyes, new livers, new hands. But that didn't mean Beecham actually *was* the *original* Dr. Beecham—born a hundred years ago—and not his grandson, as people believed. And it certainly didn't mean that Beecham was going to live forever, or that he knew a way to allow a man to survive a hanging.

(Even now, less than a year later, the memory of her

conversation with Beecham was beginning to fade. Had the tonic been purple, or had it been gold? Had the stopper been cork? Had he promised immortality against all harm or just immunity to disease? The strongest memory that remained to her was just a feeling: frenzy and terror flooding her brain and turning her vision blurry, that sense of standing on the bow of a ship as the ocean rolled beneath her feet.)

A few months ago, a letter arrived, unmarked and un-signed, in handwriting she had convinced herself looked familiar.

My beating heart is still yours, and I'll be waiting for you. *I'll be waiting for you.*

At the bottom, the sender had scribbled the words: *in Amer-ica*. Hazel kept the letter inside her corset, pressed against her breast for weeks, until the paper began to disintegrate at the edges and the ink became cracked. It *had* to be from Jack. It *had* to be. What else? Was it some cruel prank? A random so-licitation?

Some days, Hazel was certain that Beecham's tonic had worked and Jack was alive somewhere, making a living for himself in the New World, a place where men of low birth could seek opportunity. Some days she clenched her teeth and told the other part of herself that she was acting like a foolish little girl, not the surgeon to whom people entrusted their lives.

Even on the days when Hazel *did* feel certain Jack was alive, dwelling somewhere in America, questions loomed: How was she supposed to find him? America was a vast na-tion on an even vaster continent. If he was in America, why wouldn't he write another letter, telling her where to find him? Telling her that he still *wanted* her to come find him.

No. Those were foolish thoughts. Jack was dead.

Hazel knew the truth deep in her gut, even if she let her imagination run away from her occasionally. No other letter from him had come. She didn't even know if that first letter was his to begin with. Jack had been found guilty and hanged. She had been in love, real love that gave her goose pimples and made her grin for no reason. She had gotten love, and that was more than plenty of people got on this planet.

Better to be grateful for that, to accept that it was over, and go on serving the people of Edinburgh who needed help and didn't have the means to pay for it. She was learning and getting better every day, her knife work becoming more confident, her diagnoses coming quicker, and with more certainty. This was what she was made for, why she had spent hours as a child on the floor of her father's library, studying books no one else bothered to read until she understood the human body the way a person could understand a new language. Royal Examination or not, she was a surgeon, finally. Working, treating patients, learning more every day about the miracle of anatomy and the infinite variations of the strange plagues and injuries that affected it. There was no use crying for the memory of a boy she once loved.

Still: she wished she remembered his smell.

There was one problem with having ruined her own reputation with scandal: Hazel was lonely.

Sometimes, if she didn't have a patient and if Iona was on a day off, Hazel would go an entire day without speaking to anyone, without opening her mouth. By the afternoon, she would feel that if she did speak, her voice would come out like a croak. It hadn't always been like this: as a child, she had had George, and then Bernard, who was at least willing to indulge her monologues and smile politely when she got excited about something. And then there were her classes, with fellow students to sweat beside and laugh with when Straine's back was turned. Maybe they had never known the real her, but Hazel knew them, and they had been her friends, in a way. They had quizzed each other about valves of the heart and components of blood and shared theories on which knives to use for which amputations.

Now she had no one to share ideas with except her own notebook.

Hazel had memories from childhood, back when her father was still in Edinburgh, of people coming to dinner at Hawthornden. She would hide between their legs and listen to the adults talking about books and poetry and symphonies. They had all sounded so sophisticated, speaking in an impenetrable language that had just seemed impossibly *adult*. Where were the salons now? Were there dining rooms in fashionable New Town town houses where people were still meeting and talking about Walter Scott and Goethe and Byron?

In the middle of the night, that terrible hunger clawed at Hazel's belly: the thought that, yes, surely the scions of society were still meeting—smart, interesting people, their laughter as effervescent as champagne—*somewhere*, and that Hazel, in her disgrace, simply wasn't invited. She would be invited in to pull the Parlake boy's teeth, but if someone else happened to be calling on them that day, she would be ushered out the back entrance.

When Hazel was digging graves with Jack, the very notion of "disgrace" had seemed so abstract, as distant as the moon. Now a small part of her understood what she had sacrificed in her impulsiveness. Jack was dead, and she was by herself.

If she had married Bernard, she wouldn't be a surgeon, but she would be a guest in those dining rooms. She would have friends, and conversation. There would have been people to share her ideas with.

For now, her ideas were hers alone. Her thoughts on human anatomy became pot after pot of ink spilled into her scribblings that would become her treatise. Most of the time, Hazel was busy and focused, her brain buzzing with electricity and determination. But in moments of quiet, she would imagine the parties surely happening across town without her, and she would remember Jack, and wonder if she had doomed herself to be alone forever.

The Edinburgh Guardian

10 March 1818

Her Royal Highness the Princess Charlotte of Wales has broken her engagement with William, Hereditary Prince of Orange. Princess Charlotte is the only daughter of the Prince Regent and only legitimate grandchild of King George III.

Sources close to the Princess speculate that the marriage has been called off at least in part because of the Princess's ill health. In 1814, Princess Charlotte suffered from a debilitating case of Roman fever. The illness has been lingering, and the Princess has yet to resume normal public appearances, although raucous and adoring crowds have seen her outside her residence, Warwick House, and on carriage rides in St. James's Park.

As heir presumptive to the throne, Princess Charlotte surely understands the importance of selecting a suitable husband and providing the eagerly awaiting country with an heir.

4

The evening after she pulled Dickie Parlake's teeth, Hazel was reading in bed when she heard a knock echoing through Hawthornden. She sighed. Naturally, the earl had *already* decided to send someone. No doubt he had seen a dab of blood on his son's serviette at dinner and shouted at the footman to fetch her straightaway.

"I told him it would be fine until morning," she mumbled to no one as she pulled her robe around her and lifted the candle from her bedside table. Iona was out for the evening; the castle was empty and so there was no one to open the front door but her. The knock continued, faster and louder. Poor servant, she thought. Out on the steps, she knew, was some poor footman sent to ride for an hour in the cold up to her house, in pitch blackness, probably freezing half to death. She would have to persuade him to come inside for a cup of tea to warm up before they went back to Hammond House in her carriage.

Surely, Hazel thought, Lord Parlake had told the footman

that it was an *urgent matter* and that the servant *needed to fetch the lady doctor right away!* but Hazel knew there was nothing wrong with Dickie's mouth. The teeth had come out cleanly; there was nothing that couldn't wait for the time it took for a pot of tea to boil. She was happy to stitch the gums if it kept the earl from worrying, but it would only cause the boy more pain when the mouth would certainly heal fine to begin with.

Hazel's resentment toward the earl and his son grew with every step down the staircase. Calling on her this late at night when she'd specifically told them that no problem would require her until morning . . . forcing her out of bed at this hour . . . the entitlement of these people. Maybe she would give the messenger a cup of tea or dram of whisky and send him on his way, to tell the earl that she would be there *tomorrow morning*, as was reasonable.

The candles in the front hall had burned almost to the nub. It was close to midnight. When her mother and Percy first left for England, Hazel had reveled in the silence, the *freedom* to read or sew or study in any of the sprawling rooms of the home at her leisure. But usually after supper, when a cup of tea went cold and she found that she needed to bring the extra blankets up from the cupboard to keep the chill from reaching like a hand around her bones, Hazel admitted that the house could be lonely. But loneliness, like frost, usually melted in the morning sun.

The knocking continued, and as the sound echoed in the high ceiling of the hall, something tightened in Hazel's gut. All her annoyance, her planned self-righteousness, dissolved instantly, like sugar candy in water. Something made the hairs on the back of her neck prickle, and Hazel was suddenly wide awake.

"Please."

There was a voice calling from the other side of the thick oak door, almost inaudible, the murmur of someone desperate and exhausted.

Hazel pulled the door open to reveal a woman, no older than she was, but so small that at first Hazel took her for a child. She was five feet tall, at most, with small sharp eyes. The initial impression was that of a mouse. Brown curls spilled from beneath the woman's bonnet, and it took Hazel a few seconds to realize that her hands were covered in blood. "Please," the woman said, her voice no louder than a whisper. And then she fell forward into Hazel's arms.

As small as the woman was, there was no way for Hazel to get her into the bedroom on the second floor, let alone the guest rooms on the third. Hazel went into her mother's sitting room and pulled the blue-black settee into the front entryway before helping to lift the woman onto it so that she could lie down.

As Hazel removed the traveling cloak from the woman, she gasped. The woman's stomach was distended, swollen and round as a melon. Pregnant, Hazel thought. And from between her legs, there was a wet river of blood, already soaking through her drawers and chemise.

The woman's eyes fluttered closed. Her eyelashes were so pale, they were almost white.

And her face, too, was bloodless. It reminded Hazel of a death mask.

There had been no horse outside, no carriage. The woman must have walked here from God knows how far, in the cold and dark, tripping over the roots and twists in the path that led to the castle's front door. It was a treacherous walk by daylight; Hazel couldn't imagine the terror of doing it alone, on a moonless night, stumbling and losing so much blood all the while that her vision might have been going blurry.

"We need to get you out of that dress. Here"—Hazel pulled off her own robe—"we'll put you in this." She helped the woman peel herself out of her dress, and then her chemise. Both were stained with blood and sweat and coated in mud up to the knee.

Hazel sucked in her breath when she saw how much blood coated the inside of the woman's thighs, fresh and bright red. "It's going to be okay," Hazel said, as much to herself as to her new patient. "What's your name?" She used a clean cloth to wipe the sweat from her forehead; Hazel was surprised to find there was no fever. Both the sweat and the skin beneath were cold as the dead.

"I can't have this baby," said the woman in a small voice. She shook her head back and forth, and tears raced down her cheeks. Hazel could make out freckles beneath the dirt. "I can't. I can't. I can't."

"It's going to be okay," Hazel said again. "Just, please. Tell me your name."

Again, the woman shook her head. Tears filled her eyes. "I can't tell you my name." She began to shiver, even though Hazel had started the fire roaring in the grate and the room was almost stiflingly warm. "I'm so scared I'm going to die."

Her eyes were wide, and Hazel noticed that her pupils were black and round as tea saucers. She had thought that it was a sign of the woman's fear, but the longer Hazel looked at the woman's eyes, the more she realized there was something strange in the way they didn't seem to catch the light, the way her pupils seemed to vibrate and quiver.

"Did you take something?" Hazel asked, trying to suppress

the wavering in her voice. "Did you take anything—any tinctures, any herbs?"

The woman answered in her sobs. "I can't have his baby. I can't have his baby."

Hazel swallowed hard and continued to pat at the woman's forehead with a damp cloth. "Please. I just need to know what you took. I'm going to help try to make you better."

The woman clenched her eyes shut and whispered, "Calomel. There was . . . some mercury. And . . . and pennyroyal leaves."

Hazel knew the names instantly. They were all treatments that women passed among themselves like shadows, vials hidden beneath sleeves and under coats. The type of medicine that came to shops with no names and only back-alley addresses; from men with no teeth, who charged too much money for thimblefuls of tinctures poured from dusty bottles and for the promise not to tell the authorities. Treatments that poor women spent their meager savings on; that rich men procured for their daughters and mistresses.

Calomel. Mercury. Pennyroyal.

Taking a single dose of just one of those would have been enough to keep this woman in bed for a week, on her back while the cramping moved through her. Taking all three . . . Well, she must have been desperate, Hazel thought. Beyond desperate. Terrified to the point of madness.

No wonder the woman refused to give Hazel her name: a charge of intentionally inducing miscarriage would cause a woman to be locked up for life. Hazel looked at the woman's belly, tried to gauge how far along she was. Hazel couldn't tell, but she knew well enough that if this woman got caught, the penalty might even be hanging.

"I just couldn't have his baby," the small woman said again. "He forced me . . . I never would have . . . I couldn't . . ."

"Shhhh," Hazel said, brushing the dampened hair from her face. "Quiet now. You're safe here. I'll take care of you."

The woman's eyes closed, her eyelids fluttering with their veins visible and pink, and Hazel feared the worst until she heard the faint heartbeat beneath the woman's breastbone. A faint but persistent patter, a rope holding her to this world in spite of all the pain it had caused her.

Through the night, Hazel had kept the woman on the settee in the front room, afraid that if she moved her more than a few inches, the luck or mercy that had kept her alive up until this point would abandon them. Every few hours, Hazel pressed a cup of cool water to the pale woman's lips and tried to get her to drink. Even with the fire roaring, the woman's shaking continued, her skin cool to the touch. Hazel had wrapped the stranger in the quilt from her own bed.

Charles and Iona came to Hawthornden the next day, their exuberance dissolving like smoke when they entered the main hall and saw the grim scene before them. Hazel sent the footman to the kitchen to begin preparing tea, and told her lady's maid to fetch fresh bed linens, and they both obeyed silently. It wasn't until both Iona and Charles were back from their tasks, helping watch over the unnamed woman, that Hazel felt comfortable enough to finally get some sleep.

Iona and Charles stayed at the house, communicating silently in the way a married couple can, taking care of Hazel while she took care of the patient.

"You need to eat, miss," Iona said, offering Hazel a slice of brown bread. "Here, just the crust, then. With butter."

"Hot tea," Charles murmured before he tended to the fire in the entryway to keep it warm. The tea he brought her was thick with honey and sickly sweet; Hazel drank it eagerly anyway.

"You know, I always thought of honey in one's tea as a sort of moral weakness," Hazel said, draining her cup. "And now I can't seem to remember why. It's *good*, isn't it? Do people know that? Honey makes the tea taste *so* good."

"Aye, I think people know, miss," Charles said, refilling the cup and adding a generous spoonful of honey.

"Well, *I* didn't," Hazel murmured, turning back to the notes she had made, documenting the condition of the patient at every hour. The woman never gave her a name, and so Hazel began referring to her privately as Mary.

For two days straight, Mary remained on the edge of death—unconscious and barely able to eat or drink the spoonfuls that Hazel held up to her pale-white lips. On the third day, a morning where the sun rose in the sky yellow as an egg yolk, the woman finally roused enough to sit up. The stranger still wouldn't tell Hazel her name, and so she remained Mary, and she also refused to answer any of the other questions Hazel had asked: Where do you live? Where do you work? The one question she really wanted to know the answer to, Hazel knew well enough not to raise: *Who got you pregnant, and did he hurt you?*

From the fear in the woman's eyes, the way her eyes darted around the room like a caged animal's, Hazel guessed it was someone powerful. The master of a house she worked in, a foreman—even, Hazel thought, listening to the murmurs of the woman praying in bed one morning, a priest. It wasn't uncommon for men of the cloth to have children out of wedlock. Some were even brazen enough to give their children their last names.

Whoever it was, Hazel knew he had hurt this woman, and when Hazel imagined this woman returning to wherever it was she was from, Hazel herself prayed that the man wouldn't be there, and that he wouldn't have any power over her.

"I can't pay you," Mary declared one morning, a week after she first arrived. By then, Hazel and Charles had been able to help Mary up the staircase to one of Hawthornden's guest bedrooms. Hazel had entered the room, carrying a saucer of tea. Now that the color had returned to Mary's face, Hazel found that she really did look like a mouse—with small, round features and pale eyelashes.

"I assure you," Hazel said lightly, depositing the saucer on the dresser. "I don't charge for tea in my home."

The woman's eyes darkened and she looked toward the window. "For any of it, I mean. I only came—I was desperate, you know. I heard there was a woman in the manor on the hill, that's you, I suppose, who treated people. But I don't have much."

"I wouldn't take it even if you did." Hazel took a deep breath and sat at the corner of the bed. "The things you took, to get rid of a child, there are people who will get you in trouble for that, do you understand? I know you can't tell me where you work, or live, but are there people who knew you were pregnant?" Mary's mouth became a hard, tight line. She nodded. "Better to say nothing," Hazel said. "And if anyone asks, you can tell them that you lost the child. It happens every day."

Mary was suddenly seized by terror. "My landlady—she was the one who told me where to find the medicines. Where to buy them."

"Is she a trustworthy sort?"

"Well, she took a fair bit of coin to give me the information," Mary said.

Hazel tried to force her lips into something that might resemble a comforting smile. "You'll be fine," she said. "The most important thing is you're well. Be sure to continue with mild food only—porridge. No cheese or meat for a few weeks. Once you feel ready to return home, just know if the bleeding comes back, you know where to find me."

From the hallway, Iona watched the entire exchange through the half-open door. She was wringing a cloth in her hands. When Hazel left, shutting the door gingerly behind her, Iona came up close. "This is dangerous, miss," she said.

Hazel knitted her brows together in mock confusion. "I don't know what you're talking about. She's hardly contagious."

Iona breathed in deeply through her nose. One of her hands rose, almost involuntarily, to her pregnant belly and then fell. "If it's after the baby's quickening, it's a hanging for the woman, and a hanging for the doctor as well. I remember a hanging in Grassmarket for an—" She swallowed hard, forcing herself to say the word. "—*abortionist*." She shuddered. "Not even a few years back. They're *criminals*."

Hazel laughed. "Honestly, Iona. I'm not a criminal. I haven't the stomach for it, you know that." Iona didn't laugh. Hazel continued. "I simply treated a woman who came to my house asking for help. Is that a crime, now?"

The dishcloth in Iona's hands continued to twist. "It's dangerous, is all. People start getting suspicious, and asking questions. People already ask questions, you being a lady and all. I hear the whispers."

Now it was Hazel's turn to be surprised. "What whispers?"

Hazel knew that there was gossip about her—of course there was. How else did people like the Earl of Hammond know to call on her? But she had imagined the gossip confined to drawing rooms and boxes at the theater, the type of places where people like her cousin Bernard and his new wife preened for one another. They were the people she had spent a lifetime with, at various parties and lunches and teas. To them, she was a curio, and probably always would be.

But there was something unsettling about gossip that made its way to someone like Iona—the notion that there were people talking about her in the markets or pubs in Edinburgh. Strangers who knew her and didn't know her. Who might twist her in their minds and turn her into something she wasn't.

Iona didn't make eye contact. "People say it isn't right. A lady being a doctor, is all."

Hazel fixed her face and raised herself an inch taller. "People have been talking for a long time, I think. And I'm sure they'll continue to talk. And it won't make a lick of difference when it comes to what I do. And now, if you'll excuse me, I have notes to make on the patient I'm treating."

Hazel walked past Iona and down the stairs, back to the foyer and out the front door, toward her laboratory entrance underneath the house. Iona remained upstairs, watching Hazel leave.

The Edinburgh Guardian

21 March 1818

PRINCESS'S WEAK HEALTH
FRIGHTENS NATION

All of Great Britain remains in a state of fear and anxiety upon hearing reports that Charlotte, Princess of Wales, is yet again in ill health. Several years ago, the nation held its breath when the Princess was confined to her chambers, suffering from the sickness known as the Roman fever. Now, reports from the Palace suggest the Princess has once again withdrawn to Warwick House and is unable to make public appearances, though crowds of well-wishers have appeared at her window.

The Princess's popularity among the common people of the city is thanks in part to her politics: Princess Charlotte has been a close ally of the minority Whigs, the progressive party which advocates for labor reform and workers' rights. Her political leanings have occasionally put her at odds with her father, the Prince Regent, who identifies as a conservative Tory.

She is the only legitimate grandchild of King George III, and the line of succession depends on her, though the Princess broke her engagement from William, Hereditary Prince of Orange, for reasons sources believe to be due to her illness.

We pray for her swift recovery and return to health.

5

THE NEW TREATISE WAS TAKING UP MOST OF Hazel's time; it managed to soak up the hours she didn't spend eating or sleeping or treating patients.

Looking back, Hazel could curse herself for the notes she had taken last year, back when Jack brought her corpses to dissect. She had been so giddy with the thrill of it, the newness and the strangeness, that her notes were haphazard and lacking.

Why hadn't she drawn clearer diagrams, then? Why were her ink lines so thick and sloppy? Now she made it a habit to keep a clear and organized diary of all her patients, their symptoms, and the treatment she recommended:

Martin Potter. Broken arm, swelling and infection, requiring draining and resetting of the bone.

Robert Parlake. Blackened teeth, requiring pulling.

"Mary." Poisoning, self-inflicted: calomel, mercury, pennyroyal. Requiring charcoal broth, liquid diet, rest. Tea of anise and poppy. Mulberry for sleep.

It had taken ten days, but eventually Mary became strong enough to raise herself from bed and join Hazel on a walk down by the stream: she had leaned heavily on Hazel's arm, her legs unsteady as a newborn foal's. It was another two days after that before Hazel felt she was strong enough to leave Hawthornden. Hazel had packed Mary a small satchel of bread and cheese, and insisted that she take their carriage back to her home.

"It's too much," Mary had said, shaking her head.

"Nonsense," Hazel replied. "What's the purpose of spending two weeks nursing you to health if you're going to exhaust yourself on the walk back to the center of the city?"

Mary had just blinked her pale eyelashes then, and she snatched the parcel of food from Hazel's arms as if scared Hazel was going to think better of the offer.

"Good riddance to bad trouble," Iona had murmured as they watched the carriage crest the drive.

As her list of patients grew, so, too, did Hazel's inventory of ailments and remedies for her treatise: cupping for paroxysms; millet bread and dates to treat an excess of black bile; rue and dill for yellow bile; for lupus, mallow and nettles; hot wine to treat inflamed tonsils; salt fish, fennel, and cumin for fever. If someone was waking and needed rest, she would give them mulberry and lettuce. If someone needed to be roused, she would use thyme and catmint.

And on and on it went.

Once Hazel had compiled enough cases, she would organize them and index them by category. Eventually, she hoped, it would be enough to interest a publisher, even if she understood it would probably never be published under her own name. She probably wouldn't even be afforded the privilege of the author who wrote *Sense and Sensibility*, who was at least identified as "A Lady." The idea of a woman writing a novel might be embarrassing for her family, but it was no scandal. But a novel and a medical text were different animals, and the willingness of men to allow women in professional spaces would extend only so far. *Let them publish it anonymously*, thought Hazel magnanimously. *It doesn't matter if I don't get the credit, so long as the valuable work is out in the world.* She repeated those thoughts to herself like a stern lecture, in order to dispel the nagging truth she knew deep down: in actuality, it would drive her mad to see her work published and praised while she herself received none of the acclaim.

Two gentle, familiar knocks on the door brought Hazel back from her own thoughts. Without waiting for Hazel's response, Iona opened the door and entered, bearing a breakfast tray. Morning already. Hazel had worked all night. Again.

"Tea, and toast, miss," Iona said, lowering the tray on the desk while Hazel quickly pulled papers out from under it. "And Cook made blackberry jam."

"Goody," Hazel said, surprised at how the small pleasures of life, the promise of fresh blackberry jam, immediately lifted her mood. The toast was burnt at the edges, just the way she liked it. "Thank you, Iona."

The maid dipped her head. "And a letter for you." Hazel looked down and noticed the parchment on the tray, beautifully thick and sealed with crimson wax. Iona waited expectantly. "Aren't you going to open it? It came this morning from a footman in livery lined in gold. Fancy carriage. Charles hasn't stopped talking about it. Wheels as high as a horse's back."

In one swift motion, Hazel broke the letter's seal and opened it. "It's from Mercer—the Comtesse de Flauat. She and the comte are hosting a—" Hazel stopped reading, folded the letter, and put it away in one of her skirt's pockets. One of the advantages to female dress in her profession, she found, was the use of external pockets; Hazel would sometimes string two or three above her petticoats for her pens, ink, notebook, needles, and scalpel. Dried herbs were scattered throughout.

"An invitation to what, miss?" Iona said. "Surely you must go! It's been an age since . . ."

"Since I've been invited to any society event, you mean."

Iona blushed a deep crimson. "I just mean, it's a good sign, if a woman like the comtesse is inviting you to her home."

"Or it's a sign they're having me as entertainment. Perhaps gossip is thin this season."

"Surely that isn't true, miss. You're friends with Miss Elphinstone—I mean, the comtesse."

Iona was right: Hazel and Margaret Elphinstone—whom everyone called Mercer—used to be friends, or at least the type of acquaintances who stood together at parties and gently touched each other's arm to signal that something ridiculous was happening. But their correspondence had fallen off since, well, since George's death. When Hazel and Hawthornden had descended into mourning, most of her friendships and all her correspondence had fallen to the wayside. And then Hazel had become fixated on the Anatomists' Society and passing the Medical Examination—everything else was an afterthought. She had written Mercer a congratulatory note when she had married the French comte, but with all the time Mercer spent in London, it must have been years since they had seen each other in person. Hazel remembered her as delightfully loud and vivacious, the first to demand that the boys hovering shyly at the edges of the room escort the women to dance, and swift to steal a bottle of champagne.

"What's she inviting you to, then, miss?" Iona prompted.

Hazel pulled the letter out from her pocket with a sigh. "It's a private performance of an opera, at her home." As she scanned the words, she unsuccessfully tried to keep the excitement from creeping into her voice. "It was an opera she saw when it premiered in London for the first time last March—by Rossini—*The Barber of Seville.*"

Iona laughed. "An opera? About a barber?"

"And she's invited Luigi Zamboni and Geltrude Righetti-Giorgi—" Hazel lowered the invitation. "Oh, Iona. Well, now I'm afraid I'm going to have to go."

"Friends of yours?"

"*Celebrated* singers, Iona. Meant to be brilliant. Voices that could make you cry on hearing them."

"Then it's settled! I'll lay out a dress for you."

"Well, don't say *that*. It's not that simple. They're going to whisper." Hazel paced the floor. "Of course," she added, "they're going to whisper if I'm *not* there too—that's the terrible rub, isn't it?" She turned on her heel. "I should go, shouldn't I?"

Iona nodded. "After all, when have ye ever cared about whether people are whispering about you?"

Hazel grinned.

"I do think you'll be glad to get out of the house and see your friends, miss," Iona said. "Just be sure to, er, scrub the blood from your wrists before you do."

Hazel did scrub the blood from her wrists, and the blood that had crusted to brown beneath her fingernails. She stayed in the bath so long the water ran brown. After she dried off, she brushed her long hair—it *had* gotten long, almost to her waist, she would need to cut it soon—and got dressed. Knowing Mercer, it would be a fashionable event, populated with Frenchmen who had left their home country after the fall of Napoleon but hadn't abandoned their haughty sense of superiority and style.

In her daily work, Hazel preferred cotton stockings and stays beneath her dresses, but tonight she would be wearing stockings of silk and a corset she could don like battle armor.

Iona helped her into her favorite chemisette—gauzy white fabric with a high ruffled collar—and then finally, her dress. For years, mourning had turned Hazel's mother into a ghost, nearly silent and entirely self-regarding, who came as close to ignoring Hazel as feasibly possible. Which meant that, for years, Hazel had worn dresses that were hand-me-downs or seasons old, with her mother too distracted to order Hazel new gowns and Hazel too young to know how.

But there was one dress that her mother had selected for her with care and attention. Months ago, back when Lady Sinnett had anticipated that Hazel would soon be engaged to Bernard and that she would be swirling around the social circuit on his arm, Lady Sinnett sent Hazel's measurements down to Mrs. Thire on Fleet Street in London. "You'll need at least something fit for a baroness," Hazel remembered her mother sniffing. The engagement never happened, but perhaps her mother had forgotten about the order because just a few weeks ago, the box arrived, wrapped in purple ribbon. Hazel had simply deposited it, unopened, beneath her wardrobe. She hadn't had occasion, or the heart, to open it. Now she pulled it onto the bed, blew the dust from the lid, and gingerly removed the paper that covered the fine fabric below.

It was a ball gown in marigold, orange-yellow bright as a setting sun. The fabric shimmered as it caught the light of the candle flames. The cap sleeves were puffed and sheer, so delicate Hazel touched them only with her fingertips. For half a heartbeat, Hazel's mind went back to the green dress in the back of her closet, the one she had already worn to a dozen social appearances. It was a simple dress—beyond reproach, even—comfortable as a chemise.

But then the marigold dress glittered in the candlelight and Hazel couldn't help herself. She shimmied into the fabric, cool as water against her skin, and pouted her lips in the mirror. There was no rule that said a woman surgeon couldn't also wear beautiful things, was there?

Devoting herself to a profession didn't mean that she couldn't also prove she was as capable of wearing a gown as any of the French women who deigned to flit around Edinburgh.

She had to admit to herself, as she turned and swirled the skirt in front of the glass, the effect was shocking. After weeks of wearing nothing but black cotton gowns and men's trousers, she had forgotten that she could almost look pretty—that the color in the dress could bring out the pink in her cheeks and the amber in her eyes. Iona's husband, Charles, nearly stumbled over his own feet when he saw Hazel come down the stairs.

"Would you mind calling the carriage round, Charles?" Hazel said, pulling her cape over her shoulders. The cape wasn't as fashionable as a modern dress coat, but Hazel couldn't bring herself to part with it. "I don't think it's prudent to ride to Edinburgh in this dress."

Charles shook his head and raced out the door to alert the coachman.

IN THE BACK OF HAZEL'S MIND, SHE HAD entertained the abstract possibility that her cousin Bernard Almont and his new wife, Cecilia, might be present at the party that evening, but seeing them in person, stepping gingerly one after another from their carriage as they arrived in front of the comtesse's estate, Hazel hadn't anticipated the way her stomach would knot into itself and her tongue would suddenly become dry. It was hard to swallow. If another carriage hadn't come behind her, blocking her into the drive, she might have told the coachman to turn around and take her home. It was too late for that. She was here, wearing a *Thire* dress, for God's sake, and she was going to hear the opera. Bernard shouldn't have the power to stop that.

The stares from mingling party guests seemed to burrow through Hazel's skin. Hazel willed herself to keep her head high and her shoulders squared. Maybe they were just struck dumb by her dress.

Hazel spotted an old friend of her mother's sweeping toward the entrance. "Hello, Lady Bridgers, so lovely to see you again," Hazel said.

Lady Bridgers's face twitched in recognition for an impossibly brief moment before she turned away.

The same pattern repeated itself with two more party guests, men and women Hazel had once known and socialized with. There seemed to be a universal understanding that her rebellion was dangerous, possibly contagious. Conversations halted as soon as Hazel came within earshot; Hazel knew that she had been the subject of their gossip.

And so, as Hazel made her way inside, she veered toward

the champagne and turned her attention to Mercer's elegantly appointed manor. It was a historic beauty—a stone building first constructed in the sixteenth century that had expanded outward, with turrets and a walled garden and a courtyard that glittered with torches. Inside, the sound of horses and carriages disappeared, replaced by the clinking of glass and laughter. Bernard and Cecilia had disappeared somewhere into the crowd. Hazel downed a full glass of wine before she even tasted it.

There, across the ballroom, Hazel saw a floating shock of black hair. Her heart pounded. He was here. Jack had come for her. His back was turned, and though he was wearing an embroidered jacket that Hazel had never seen him in, his limbs were long and lithe as she remembered, the hunch in his posture and the curve of his neck exactly as she had seen them in her dreams. Her mouth was suddenly dry and the blood became audible in her ears. Jack was here, at Mercer Elphinstone's party, and in another moment, he would turn and she would see the smile that had played in her mind a thousand times and he would reach his hands out and pull her close and nothing about the pain of his loss or the loneliness of the past few months would matter at all because she would be with Jack again.

Jack turned and Hazel held her breath in anticipation.

It wasn't him.

It was a stranger with a long, thin nose and wide, deepset eyes at least thirty years Hazel's senior. A perfectly good-looking stranger with long limbs and black hair, but a stranger nonetheless.

She had been foolish. It was illogical and silly, letting her fantasies run away with her. Whether or not Jack had survived his hanging, he was gone. And waiting for him to show up again was just prolonging her pain. Every time the wound of his loss began to heal over, Hazel would peel the scab away and let the bleeding begin anew.

She needed to grow up.

Blinking back tears, Hazel spotted her host through the throng of pastry-colored dresses.

"Mercer!"

Margaret Mercer Elphinstone turned toward Hazel. Her dress was white and flowing, and might have looked casual, had it not been for the elaborate lace Medici collar that fanned out behind her neck, and the fact that she wore the dress with a gilt and gemstone comb in her tight curls and several heavy strings of pearls. Her face was smiling, but it was a smile that covered a gentle confusion. "Hazel!" she said brightly, but her eyes kept darting around the room. "I—I didn't expect you to come."

"I couldn't miss the chance to hear the opera."

The comtesse's face relaxed. "Of course." She leaned in and kissed Hazel twice on both cheeks. "I'm delighted that you're here. I've talked of you *endlessly*, ask Charles, truly, our honeymoon became a *bore* with how often I remarked on my dear friend Hazel Sinnett, and have you heard of Hazel Sinnett, and *surely*, I told you about Hazel Sinnett." Mercer stepped back and clutched a hand to her chest. "And that dress! Has no one told you it's considered rude to upstage the hostess?"

With Mercer's attention, Hazel could feel the room thaw toward her. She smiled back at the hostess. "As if anyone could ever upstage you, Mercer."

Mercer did a small spin and let her own dress fan out

around her. "I thought my dress was lovely until I saw your dress, and now I'll have to order one in that color. What is it? Orange? Yellow?"

"Actually, I believe it's marigold." A voice from behind Hazel had answered, and Hazel turned to see Bernard standing rigidly, and alone. "Miss Sinnett," he said.

Out of sheer habit, Hazel felt her hand lift. Bernard took it and kissed it, and as quickly as she could, she returned her hand to her side. She hadn't seen him in months, not since he had all but sent Jack Currer to his death, out of jealousy and cowardice. He wrote Hazel letters she hadn't opened before they were thrown into the fire, and the few occasions on which he had arrived to Hawthornden to call on her, Hazel gave the footman strict instructions to tell him that she wasn't welcoming visitors. Eventually, Bernard gave up, and a few weeks ago, Hazel had seen the announcements in the papers that he had married Cecilia Hartwick-Ellis, a perfectly fine girl who had been eyeing him and his title for years.

It was strange seeing him now, in his formal jacket, his hair combed, smelling of pomade. In spite of everything, it was *odd* that she wasn't here with him, that she hadn't arrived on his arm and wouldn't be spending the evening with him refreshing her drinks. It was a habit, the two of them together. A pair since childhood, they had become comfortable and easy as one's favorite pair of house slippers. Only a true betrayal had been strong enough to break that bond and leave their years of companionship torn and tattered. Sour and ruined.

Once, Hazel had looked at him and seen her future—yes, a future that eventually became a yoke, but a future inevitable as a sunrise. Now she looked at him and felt bile rise in her throat. Everything about his face was wrong and awful: his nose bulbous, his eyes too close together, his collar ludicrously tight around his neck. Hazel hated him. It wasn't until Bernard cleared his throat that she realized she had been standing before him, silent and seething, for a full minute.

"I was, um, sorry that you missed the wedding. My father insisted on hiring fifty violinists for the reception. The cake was topped with candied sugar. I know you always liked candied sugar."

Hazel remained stony, unable even to bring herself to turn her face into a scowl.

Bernard continued: "We thought perhaps your mother, Lady Sinnett, would have come, but—"

"Still in mourning, I believe. Isn't that right, Hazel?" Mercer cut in mercifully.

Hazel nodded stiffly. The formal mourning for her brother George ended years ago, but Mercer had always understood the strange isolation and lingering grief that descended over Hawthornden. Hazel mouthed a thank-you to Mercer, who grabbed at her elbow. "Now, Mr. Almont, if you'll excuse me, I simply must introduce Hazel to my new husband."

As soon as they were beyond Bernard's eyeline, Mercer released Hazel's elbow. "Dreadful boy, I always thought. Terribly pleased you aren't saddled with him. Besides," she added, her eyes twinkling. "Far less interesting than a life in medicine."

Hazel smiled.

Mercer moved closer. "I've been dying to ask you. We've all heard the stories. Is it true you wore your brother's clothes? How many people have you operated on? Do you faint when you see blood? Do you still dress as a man?"

"Yes, dozens now, no, and almost never."

Mercer blinked. "Astonishing."

Just then, a tall boy with curly hair whom Hazel didn't recognize came bounding up behind the hostess. "Comtesse! Darling!" He spoke with a French accent.

"Claude," she greeted him politely. "Might I introduce my friend, Miss Hazel Sinnett."

The Frenchman—Claude—nodded absently at Hazel but then quickly did a double take, staring at her with wide eyes. "Is she ze one—"

"The very same," Hazel said.

"Aha!" Claude laughed and grabbed Hazel's hand to kiss it. "Mercer, ma chérie, you make ze most fascinating friends. Ze female surgeon, ze Princess . . ."

Mercer rolled her eyes. "Ah, it always comes back to the Princess with you, doesn't it?"

"Is she really ill? And why did she break ze engagement with Le Orange?"

"Claude, I have told you a dozen times, she and I haven't so much as exchanged letters since I got back from my honeymoon. You know as much as I do. But I will say, she was never keen on the Prince of Orange. Her mother hated him, and you know how Charlotte despises defying her mother, especially in a case when it would *so* please her father."

Hazel surprised herself by chiming in. "Do you think the Princess will marry for love, then?"

Mercer exhaled. "No," she said. "When the Princess marries, it will be for *pragmatism.*"

Claude grabbed two flutes of champagne from a passing tray. "Well, she better make it quick. I hear ze Englishmen are hungry for an heir."

Mercer grabbed one of the glasses. "We *have* an heir. Charlotte's grandfather is King now, and her *father* is next in line for the throne, and *then* Charlotte will be queen after that. She has plenty of time to have a baby."

With artfully arched brows, Claude made eye contact with Hazel and they silently communicated the same sentiment: Charlotte's father, the Prince Regent, was the man truly running the country while George III was in his state of madness—and he was publicly loathed.

The country wanted young, liberal Charlotte. And they wanted her line, as quickly as possible.

A woman in a chartreuse bubble of a dress elbowed her way into the conversation. "Is she quite ill, do you think? I've heard the Princess is on death's door again and that she's refusing to see her physician."

Claude scoffed. "Well, can you blame her? Zhose doctors, always poking and prodding, cutting and draining. As bad as ze sickness itself."

"Charlotte has always been willful," Mercer said. "But I'm afraid I don't know any more about her condition than the weekly papers. *And* because this is *my* party, I say that there shall be no more speaking about the Princess. Or politics." Turning out to face the rest of the room, Mercer raised her voice and her glass: "Hello, all! The concerto will start soon, but first, everyone outside to the front lawn for a little surprise!"

The crowd followed her instruction, and caught in the current of silks and satin evening dresses, Hazel trailed out the front door and onto the front lawn. She tried to identify faces—people she used to know, girls she used to attend etiquette classes with, maybe even boys she had sat beside when she was pretending to be a boy herself in Dr. Straine's medical classes—but the faces all dissolved and swam together in the darkness.

For a moment, they all stood together, the party guests, hungry and impatient, tittering and wondering why they had been herded out into the chilly evening air. But only for a moment. There came a strange sizzling sound, and then an eardrum-shattering pop, and the lawn and the estate and all the faces were illuminated by the dazzling glow of fireworks.

The crowd erupted into applause; Hazel joined them. She couldn't help it. It was extraordinary—bright white, blinding, fire made into something that glittered like the diamonds on her host's comb. Hazel pulled her attention from the sky to look at the expressions on the faces of the people next to her, how they gazed upward with the joy and innocence of children. Hazel grinned.

The fireworks display lasted for five minutes, and when the final burst exploded in the air, the people erupted into cheers. Through the fog of gunpowder, Hazel caught a glimpse of Mercer. She was beaming, on the arm of her husband, the comte, a tall Frenchman with a mustache that curled up on the ends. "And now," Mercer shouted, "back inside for the *real* show!" She glided through the doors and Hazel made to follow her, but a hand landed on her elbow.

She attempted to jerk her elbow away before she realized that the hand belonged to a policeman. Buttons gleamed on his navy coat, and his boots were high. He was a tall man, at least six feet, with a face and bald scalp both beet red. Hazel realized that he wasn't merely a policeman; he wore the hat of a high constable, with a well-polished bronze badge.

"Miss Hazel Sinnett?" the red-faced constable asked.

Something yellow was crusted in the corner of his mouth. His breath smelled stale and foul.

She nodded.

"I went to your house. Hawthornden. Quite a castle," he sneered. "I was told I would find you here."

Hazel's heart pumped fast. The blood grew loud in her ears. Whom had he spoken to—Iona? Charles? The man's grip tightened on her arm. "And why," she said, steadying her voice, "would you need to find me here?" The air around them had gone still and the smell of the man's breath was stifling. Something was wrong. Something was very wrong.

People in the crowd seemed to become aware of the interaction; Bernard pulled away from Cecilia and moved toward Hazel and the high constable.

"Pardon me, Constable." Bernard cleared his throat. His eyebrows furrowed, meeting in the middle of his forehead. "This is my *cousin*. Niece of Lord Almont. Surely you know well enough to take your *hands* off a lady."

Hazel was equal parts mortified and grateful. She kept her eyes glued to the constable's purple fingers still wrapped around her upper arm, refusing to give Bernard the satisfaction of looking at him.

"Aye," the high constable said, shifting his body square with Bernard. "It wouldn't matter to me if she was the Princess of Wales. This woman is under arrest for murder."

A laugh left Hazel's throat like a bark. She couldn't help it. "*Murder?*" She spat, "Murdering *whom?*"

Bernard blinked a few times. "Surely, there's some sort of misunderstanding. To think a *lady* is capable of—"

The constable ignored Bernard and yanked Hazel away, up the path toward a waiting carriage, high and black. Hazel glanced back at the party. Cecilia had come to stand next to Bernard, whose eyebrows remained pulled together in confusion.

"Come on, you," the constable grunted, pulling Hazel faster, farther away from the party of blank-faced strangers and acquaintances standing together and staring.

It was then that Hazel stumbled over the hem of her beautiful marigold dress, elegant satin hand-sewn, ordered from Mrs. Thire's in London. She heard the edge of it rip. Ruined. But what did it matter? A strange man had his hand around her arm and was shoving her into a carriage, claiming that she was being arrested for murder, taking her somewhere in the middle of night. Still, hearing the dress rip was enough to jolt Hazel from the abstract dread of the entire scenario, and she felt her eyes wet with tears.

The smell of gunpowder from the fireworks was strong and metallic in the air. With a shout, the high constable bade his horses trot down the dirt road, toward the Old City. Behind them, the smoke from the fireworks was still hovering, thick and white near the ground around the estate, illuminated by the torches and candles, opaque. The party shrank behind them in the distance, and Hazel, speechless and paralyzed by fear, turned her attention to the darkness of the road ahead of her, her mind racing but no thoughts finding purchase.

6

AZEL SAT IN THE HIGH CONSTABLE'S carriage, her hands locked in irons, watching the dark landscape whip past. It took until they were already back onto the main road before she was able to slow her heart rate enough to think clearly, and a few minutes after that until she gathered the presence of mind to lean her head out the window to get the attention of the high constable sitting atop and driving the coach. The wind whipped her hair around her face, and her voice felt tight and thin in her throat. "Can't you at least take these irons off? I'm not a murderer."

He ignored her, and the carriage continued on, rattling down the cobblestone street. From what Hazel could tell, they were headed north, but she wasn't certain in the dark. Hazel contemplated her escape: the door was locked from the outside, but could she fit out the window? Almost certainly not, and even if she could, how far would she get in these irons? The constable was twice her size.

After a few more moments of agonizing silence, she leaned

out the window again. "Excuse me. Can you at least tell me whom I'm meant to have murdered?"

The moonlight glinted off the constable's bald scalp. Yet again, he refused to turn back to look at her, but after a second's hesitation, he cleared his throat. "I assume you know a woman by the name of Florence Fitzpatrick," he said, bile dripping from each syllable.

Hazel's panicked brain, electrified with fear, raced through the names of every person she had ever met in half a second. She had never made the acquaintance of anyone called Florence Fitzpatrick. This was a mistake, then. One tiny thread of terror slackened and relaxed inside her. This was all a misunderstanding. A mistake. It would be sorted out. "I don't," Hazel said, her voice strangely high-pitched and echoing in her ears. "I don't know that person. You are mistaken."

The high constable snorted. "Mmmhmm," he said.

It had to be a mistake. She methodically combed through her memory. The name was completely foreign to her, but even more reassuring, not a single woman had died in her care in the past few months. Back in January, she had removed a tumor from a man named Billy Barber—she had cut into his belly, where a hardened lump of flesh the size of an orange had risen, and to her horror, his organs were dotted with buboes, black and hard. She had removed the first tumor and sewn the wound closed, but he died a week later. That couldn't be what they were referring to. Hazel had comforted his weeping widow and sent flowers to his burial.

Maybe they were just taking her somewhere for questioning. Maybe in the next few minutes they would arrive at the estate of the Lord High Constable himself, he would give her a cup of tea and take the irons off her wrists, and they would all have a laugh about the misunderstanding.

And then Hazel saw it, high on the hill, tall as a medieval fortress, and she knew she wasn't going to a manor home for tea: Calton Gaol. It was a prison built of stone with turrets that loomed above Edinburgh's New Town. It had opened just a few years prior, and Hazel remembered pointing it out to Percy on one of their rare trips to town together. From a distance, the imposing structure, the tallest in the area, perched high across a grassy knoll, looked like a castle, and Percy, his hands sticky, had pointed to it and asked Hazel if the King lived there when he visited Scotland. There had been carts rattling around them that day, shopkeepers sweeping their stoops, and merchants shouting about the price of fish.

Hazel had to lower her face down close to Percy's to speak to him. He must have been four or five at the time. "No, Perce," she had said. "That is a place where very bad people go when they hurt other people. And we never need to worry about that." They also certainly didn't need to worry about the King coming to visit Scotland—their monarch hadn't bothered to visit Scotland in nearly two centuries—but Hazel didn't bother Percy with that.

What else had they done that day? It was so hard to remember. It must have been before George died, because Hazel couldn't recall a time when she and Percy would have spent the day together in town after their family had become shadowed by mourning.

The carriage wheels hit a particularly rough bump and Hazel jerked from her seat, banging her head on the roof. "Ouch!" she shouted.

"Quiet back there," came the reply from the constable,

who punctuated his order with a hard *thwack* on the carriage roof.

Hazel sat back. This was all a misunderstanding. One born, no doubt, of all the dangerous rumors about her. She was a woman who had turned down a marriage, and now lived alone, cavorting about unsupervised and acting as a surgeon. Of course, people would view her with suspicion. A disreputable figure. A threat, even. But Hazel didn't know any Florence Fitzpatrick, and she certainly hadn't murdered one. She closed her eyes and tried to repeat to herself that everything would be sorted out. Her uncle, her mother, her father. They were prominent people—*titled* people. People who would be able to help her and probably cause a good deal of embarrassment for the new Edinburgh Policing Force.

The carriage lurched up the road, and in the darkness, Calton Gaol became just a looming shadow. Everything would be sorted out, Hazel told herself. Everything would be fine.

After they pulled through the gates, a guard appeared and pulled Hazel from the carriage. "Quite a fine dress," the guard said, rubbing his thick fingers over the fabric at Hazel's shoulder.

She jerked herself away.

"My, my!" He coughed, the sound of it thick with phlegm. "Feisty, aren't we?" Inside, Hazel was thrown into an empty stone room and told to change into a plain white cotton shift. Mercifully, the guard had removed her irons, and he shut the door behind her to give her a moment of privacy.

The room was damp and smelled of rot and human waste. Hazel nearly gagged as she pulled on the dress she had been given: scratchy and rough, with brown stains that made Hazel certain she wasn't the first one to be wearing it. When she was finished, the guard returned and clamped the irons back on her wrists.

"I need to write a letter," Hazel said, finding her voice as the guard escorted her down a long hallway. "Several letters, in fact."

The guard coughed again. "I don't handle any of that. I'm just to put you in your cell."

"My *cell*? Surely you can't put me in a *cell* without at least explaining what I'm here for!" Hazel repeated to herself that it was a misunderstanding, surely it was a misunderstanding, but tears were prickling at her eyes.

The coughing guard took a handkerchief from a breast pocket and spat into it. He examined the spittle, then folded the handkerchief and put it back in his pocket. "I'm just the night guard. I don't handle any of that."

"Well, it must be *somebody's job* to handle that."

"Aye," the guard said. "But they don't come until morning." With that, he pulled a brass key from a ring on his belt and opened the door to a small room. With only the torchlight from the hallway, Hazel could make out just a small cot and a chamber pot. "In you go."

Numb, Hazel obeyed. The smell had only gotten stronger the deeper they went into the bowels of the jail. What was meant to be her room smelled so strongly of mildew and iron it nearly made her eyes water. "You can remove the irons at the very least, can't you?" Hazel asked.

Backlit by the torches, the man was just a shadow now, his face invisible in the gloom. "'M afraid I don't have permission to do anything like that," he said. He coughed again, and it sounded almost apologetic.

"What *do* you have the permission to do?" Hazel asked, hating the tightness and fear in her voice.

In answer, the guard closed the door and turned the key.

Hazel sat on the cot—really just a piece of canvas pulled across a wooden frame—and felt exhaustion and confusion flood her system. In the darkness, listening to the *plonk* of water somewhere in the distance and the faint sound of screaming, Hazel Sinnett allowed herself to cry.

7

THERE WAS NO WINDOW TO THE OUTSIDE world in the cell. The only indication Hazel had for whether it was morning or night was the change in the light that came through the small square bar on the cell's heavy wooden door. Twice a day—it seemed to be twice a day, at least—a pimple-faced guard arrived with a tray of bread and a cup of water.

How long had she been in the cell? It was already impossible for her to tell, but even more worrisome was the fact that Hazel had no idea how much longer she *would* be in the cell. No one had told her *who* Florence Fitzpatrick was, or how Hazel was supposed to have killed her. Hazel could feel herself beginning to go mad.

There had been one mercy—the high constable came into her cell one day and presented Hazel with a piece of parchment and a pen with a dull nib. "I have to watch you write it," he said. Hazel didn't argue. She ripped the parchment into thirds and quickly wrote three letters on each of the pieces.

The letters' intended destinations were different, but the content of each was the same.

> Please send help. I have been arrested by a High Constable and brought to Calton Gaol on false charges. I have little room to write and no word on when I will be released.—Hazel Sinnett

She folded the letters, being sure not to smudge the ink, and wrote their intended recipients on the outside: her mother in London; her father on Saint Helena; and her uncle, Lord Almont, just down the hill in the New Town.

Almost as soon as she finished the last stroke on her uncle's address, the high constable pulled the letters away from Hazel. "You will send them, won't you?" she said. "I'm allowed that right, at the very least, am I not?"

The high constable just blew air through his nose and left, closing her cell door with a heavy thud and letting the jingle of the locking key echo in the air.

Hazel had very little hope that her letters to her parents would be much help—it would take days for the letter to arrive in London, let alone for a letter to make it onto a ship to be safely delivered to her father's island command, but her uncle's letter could make a difference.

Any minute now, she thought to herself that evening. *Any minute now.*

By the next morning, nothing had changed: no one had stormed into the jail, telling them that they had made a mistake. Maybe the letter hadn't reached her uncle yet; surely, if it had, Lord Almont would have sent help.

Hazel's hope shrank with every passing hour, with every

new meal the pimple-faced guard brought her. Four meals had passed since she wrote to her uncle, and then five and then six. By the seventh meal of bread and water, Hazel was telling herself that they had never sent the letters at all. By the tenth, she believed that her uncle *had* read her plea, and decided to ignore her. Surely Iona knew she was gone. Besides, everyone at that party had seen her arrested. Maybe Bernard hated her more than Hazel knew. Maybe he had convinced his father that rotting in prison was all Hazel deserved.

Not long after she had written the letters, Hazel noticed that her vision began to darken at the edges. She wished she had her notebooks to record her symptoms as they came. She tried to remember them and repeat them to herself: blurred vision, stomach cramps, sweating so severe it left her so cold that her teeth were chattering when she woke in the morning. For a few mornings in a row, Hazel found that she was too weak to raise herself from the cot at all: the guard would deliver her food and remove the previous meal, uneaten.

It was a fever; she knew that much. She needed nourishing food, and good rest, and clean water, and she had none of that; all she had were these cold walls and this hard, flat cot, and the time trapped in her own head to tell herself that she needed to survive, needed to get better. "Am I at least permitted a doctor?" she moaned into the darkness. It had taken all her strength to summon those words, and still Hazel heard that they left her mouth scarcely louder than a whisper. No one in the jail heard her; or no one chose to respond.

Hazel would not die here. She repeated that simple phrase to herself over and over when she was too weak for any other thoughts to fill her mind: I will not die here. I will not die here. Five words. Five syllables. A phrase she could hold tight to when the world around her was spinning and cold. She would not die here. She had come too far to die of a fever.

And one morning, she woke, still wet with sweat, but her limbs weren't sore and heavy. Her eyelids no longer burned when she closed them. When she heard the guard slide the breakfast tray into her cell, she realized that she had an appetite, for the first time in days. She crawled over to the bread and plucked small bites to feed herself. It wasn't much, but it was something.

Hazel hadn't realized, but the pimple-faced guard had been waiting outside the door. "Here," he whispered, sliding her another piece of bread. Hazel devoured it like it was nothing more than air.

The next morning, when the pimple-faced guard was delivering the bread and water, Hazel jerked upright on the cot. She looked at him clearly for the first time: he was at least a foot taller than Hazel, and he carried it with the grace of a drunken goose. His neck was long but narrow as a spool of thread. If she hadn't been the one locked in a prison cell, Hazel might have pitied him.

"You know," she said. "You can use witch hazel. On your face. And honey to calm the . . ." She patted at her own cheek. If the young guard blushed, it was impossible to tell through the redness of his already inflamed face. "It'll help keep the swelling down. And help the redness." The guard blinked at her but didn't say anything back. Still, from then on, every now and then, her meals included a bite of cheese.

Hazel was running out of ways to pass the time. To keep herself from going mad, she studied the lines on the wall, the cracks that ran up the floor, and the knots in the wood of her cell's door. When she was lying in her cot, she closed her eyes and tried to picture a human body and dissect it in her head. Here's the sternum. Here were the lungs. Beneath that the stomach, the liver, the gallbladder. She counted every bone in the human hand a hundred times. She ran through every ailment she could think of and then tried to name them in alphabetical order. If she distracted herself enough, she wouldn't think too much about the hunger. Already, her hip bones were becoming prominent, she could feel them through the fabric of her dress when she was lying down on the cot. Her hair had become so matted that she could no longer run her fingers through it.

It was while Hazel was trying to picture every blood vessel that ran through the upper thigh that her cell door swung open.

It was the high constable.

"Is that it?" Hazel croaked. "Am I being released? Did you talk to my uncle?"

The high constable coughed in reply. He jerked his head, and motioned for Hazel to follow.

Her legs were weak and unsteady after spending days barely moving, but Hazel did her best to keep up with him, through the winding hallway of the jail, past countless doors with barred windows. From behind some of them, Hazel heard moans or crying. Still, other doors were silent. Hazel wondered whether the cells were empty or worse. The constable led Hazel up a staircase into a large, empty hall, where a sliver of natural sunlight came through a window. The light caused Hazel to dissolve into a fit of sneezing.

"Just through here," the constable said, when Hazel had finally finished sneezing and blinking.

"Am I being released?" Hazel asked again. She looked around. The pimple-faced guard was standing nearby. He made eye contact with Hazel and shook his head slightly. Her stomach sank.

The constable led Hazel through the hall and into a small antechamber.

Hazel blinked. The room was completely different from anything else she had seen in the jail—it might have been the well-appointed sitting room of a town house, with patterned yellow wallpaper, a large fireplace, and an assortment of wooden chairs. And then Hazel realized the man in a powdered wig and robe sitting at the top of the room was a judge.

"Is this a trial?" Hazel said. "Surely I'm permitted a barrister."

The judge sneered. "Merely a hearing, *miss*." The word ended on a snakelike *hiss*. "And someone in your position is lucky to get even that. *And* I remind you not to speak to your betters before you're spoken to."

Hazel managed to swallow her rage, and grinding her teeth, she lowered into a deep curtsy that would make her mother proud. "Of course, my lord. My sincerest apologies." This was the rare position where her knowledge of decorum could be used to her advantage. Already, she saw the judge's face soften, but only briefly.

"Bring in the witness," he called, not looking at Hazel. Hazel turned.

At first, she didn't recognize the woman. Her pale hair was tucked beneath a bonnet, and since Hazel had seen her last, her figure had regained some of its shape. It was the pale eyelashes Hazel recognized first, so light they might as well have been white.

"Mary," Hazel said quietly.

The woman shivered, and looked at her feet. Mary. The woman Hazel had nursed back to health from the brink of death.

The judge cleared his throat. "Please state your name."

"Florence Fitzpatrick," she said, her voice barely more than a whisper.

The judge sat higher in his seat. "And, Mrs. Fitzpatrick, is it *true* that this is the woman whom you sought out to procure an illegal abortion?"

The woman—Florence—said nothing.

"It's not true," Hazel said. "Tell them it's *not true*. She came to me sick, and dying, with the baby in her belly already gone. I saved her *life*."

"*Silence!*" the judge bellowed. "Mrs. Fitzpatrick, we have spoken to your landlady. We know you were with child, and you inquired about means to murder your own infant. Your husband has instructed that justice be served. Now, I ask you once again: Is this the woman who procured your illegal abortion?"

Florence began to shake, her eyes glued to the floor.

The judge continued. "Perhaps you need reminding. Your husband has ensured that if you cooperate with Justice on this matter, mercy will be shown for your own actions. Mercy, that, in my opinion, you do not deserve."

Florence, still shaking, gave a small nod of her head. "Is that a yes, Mrs. Fitzpatrick?"

The word came out so quietly that Hazel, only a foot away, could barely hear her. "Yes," Florence Fitzpatrick whispered.

The judge banged the table with his hand. "There we have it. You may go, Mrs. Fitzpatrick."

Hazel stared at Florence, boring into her with her eyes, willing her to turn to at least look at her. Hazel saved this woman's life, and in return, she had damned her. She never looked up. Still staring at her feet, too ashamed to look Hazel in the eyes, Florence let the constable escort her back into the hall.

"It's not true!" Hazel called. Blind rage and terror had made her forget every rule of decorum. "It's a lie! I've been imprisoned here on a lie!"

The judge looked down at her as if she were a bug crushed under his boot. In a frenzy, Hazel ran toward the pimple-faced guard who was standing at the door. "Have any of my letters been sent? Tell me that, at least! Please fetch my uncle, Lord Almont, down in the New Town."

The pimple-faced guard looked down at Hazel. "I'm sorry," he whispered.

The judge continued to shout, but the world went blurry around Hazel. The constable grabbed hold of the irons binding Hazel's hands and pulled her out of the antechamber, back into the hall, and then down the stairs back into the belly of the jail. It was almost with relief when Hazel was back at her own cell and she was able to lie flat on the cot to wait for the world to stop spinning. But then the sound of the key in the door jerked her back to reality, and Hazel Sinnett understood well and good just how much trouble she was in.

43 George 3 c.58:
Lord Ellenborough's Act of 1803

Whereas certain other heinous offences, committed with intent to destroy the lives of His Majesty's subjects by poison or with intent to procure the miscarriage of women . . .

. . . Be it therefore enacted by the King's most excellent majesty . . .

. . . That if any person or persons willfully, maliciously, and unlawfully cause and procure the miscarriage of any woman, then being quick with child . . .

. . . The person or persons so offending, their counsellors, aiders, and abettors, knowing of any privy to such offence, shall be and are hereby declared to be felons, and shall suffer death.

Applicable in England, Wales, and Ireland, and in Scotland under provision 6 Geo. 4 c. 126

8

I T WAS DAYS SPENT IN THE DARK. HAZEL LOST all sense of time, and all hope that the letters she had written to her family were even delivered. Horace— she had since overheard that that was, in fact, the pimply-faced guard's name—continued to deliver bread and cheese to her twice a day. On one occasion, he brought her a pear. "Don't tell," he whispered, sliding it across the floor. It was mealy and tasted of grass but Hazel still sucked it to its seeds.

Sometimes, Hazel pounded at the door, demanding to speak to someone, for *anyone* to listen to her. Other times, she just sat on her cot, staring into the distance, wondering what it would feel like to be led up the wooden scaffolding at Grassmarket. There were always crowds for executions: surely they'd be there, shouting and jeering at her, calling her terrible names for the crime they thought she had committed. Would Hazel get a chance to say a final word? Would her legs shake and reveal her fear?

The bodies of hanged criminals were the only legal corpses permitted for dissection—Hazel knew after her drop from the gallows, there would be another grisly scene below: boys elbowing one another, each trying to get hold of the body they knew would fetch a pretty penny from a studying physician. Had Jack been among them once? Had he wrestled with other poor boys over the bodies of hanged criminals before he met Munroe and decided it was simpler to go to the kirkyards at night and dig instead?

The damp in Hazel's cell was overpowering. Some days, the moisture held in the air thick as a wool blanket, and on those days, it was so hot that all Hazel could do was lie flat on her cot and pray for the time to pass more quickly. Perhaps this is how it had been for Jack, when he was imprisoned before his hanging. Hazel was thinking about him more and more frequently lately, trying to conjure the memory of how his skin had felt under her fingertips, and how his dark hair had flopped over his eyes. He had been so kind to her, and to everyone. She found herself unable to remember specific things he had told her, but she remembered the way she felt when she had been with him: like he actually cared about her, and wanted her to be safe and taken care of.

Jack spent his last days in a prison cell. Had the hours become meaningless for him too? Did he also go from terror to resignation in mere moments? Hazel would listen to the footsteps approach and disappear in the hallway beyond her cell door, certain that each time *this* would be the moment when guards would enter and bring her toward her death. She wondered whether she would take the tonic that Dr. Beecham had first offered her now, when death seemed not only likely but imminent—would she swig from a vial that promised an unknown but indefinite future? She still wasn't sure.

Today was another stiflingly hot morning. The bite of

cheese Horace brought her with her tray of breakfast had been wet with the sweat of condensation. The shift Hazel was wearing, itchy, and with a smell that reminded Hazel of the stables, stuck to her legs and her underarms. The air felt heavy as it entered her lungs. She wished she had a book.

And then, after an eternity and a moment, they came for her.

There was a knock on the cell door, and electricity ran through Hazel's body. Before she even had the chance to sit up, the door swung open with a heavy creak. It was the prison guard who had brought her to her cell for the first time so long ago. Was it weeks? Months? Hazel's memory had become slack, and shapeless as gas. The guard stood still as a statue, filling out nearly the entire doorframe. His mouth was a thin, straight line, and before he uttered a single word, Hazel understood that she was supposed to leave with him.

So, this is what it feels like to march toward death, Hazel thought, following the silent guard through the hallway. Neither money nor family influence was able to save her, and she had discovered, minute by anguishing minute in her cell, that she had fewer friends than she once believed. Hazel was going to be hanged. Perhaps if she were a poet, not a surgeon, she might be capable of comforting herself with some lyrical thought about the fleeting nature of life or man's cruel purpose on the planet. But exhaustion and hunger had drained the poetry from her brain. She was tired and frightened, and when the fleeting thought of conjuring some "last words" passed through her mind, none came to her.

She had read that when King Charles I was beheaded, he insisted on wearing two shirts to his execution because it was a cold day and he didn't want anyone to see him shivering and mistake it for shaking in fear. Katherine Howard, one of the doomed wives of Henry VIII, asked for a block to be brought to her prison cell at the Tower of London so that she could practice laying her head upon it. The idea was that when the moment finally came, and teenage Katherine was on display in front of the hundreds of people who had come to see her head severed from her body, she would be able to rely on instinct and make the entire thing look natural. Elegant, almost choreographed, maybe.

Hazel would not be beheaded. She was being hanged like a common criminal in a market square.

The rocks Hazel had hidden in her undergarments ground unpleasantly against her skin. Even in the heat of the day, and pressed against Hazel's body, the stones somehow managed to stay cool to the touch. Hazel had spent the past several days filling her dress and stockings with rocks in every way she could conceive of without being caught. Her time in prison had left her emaciated—even without a looking glass, Hazel could tell that from the way her knees now knocked together and the way her brown hair left her scalp in clumps. Hanging was a swift death, Hazel knew, but only if the force of the fall broke the victim's neck. If the victim was too small or too light for gravity to do its work, they would be strangled by the rope, slowly and painfully. The goal with the rocks was to weigh herself down however she could to ensure that her death would be swift.

When she was sure that the guard was looking straight ahead, Hazel grabbed a smooth rock the size of her palm from the floor and slipped it into the space between her shift and her stays, where it clinked against the ones she had already collected there. Maybe once they got to Grassmarket, she would be able to find rocks flat enough to fit into her shoes.

The guard quickened his pace. Hazel followed, and as she walked, she tried to keep her breath calm and deliberate; that would be important. She didn't want to appear nervous when she finally made it to the scaffold. Let them say what they would about Hazel Sinnett, but they would say that she went to her death bravely, with her head held high, posture straight and nose pointed to the sky in defiance.

From the dim interior light of the atrium, the guard led Hazel toward the main door of the prison. The outside world. Maybe her last time seeing the sun, Hazel thought absently. She wished she could have told her mother and her father goodbye. She hadn't seen her father in years—when she pictured his face now, it was the version that existed in the portrait in their home. She had looked upon it so often that it had overwritten her own memory. She would have wanted to kiss Percy on the cheek, to tell him to be good, to be kind to their mother. She would tell Jack she loved him. But maybe she would be seeing Jack soon enough.

"Here," the guard said as they stood before the door. He wrestled a ring of jangling metal keys from his jacket and swung it around until he secured the right one. With a snap that reminded Hazel of a breaking bone, he unlocked the irons around Hazel's wrists. She supposed the irons belonged to the prison. She also supposed she would go to the gallows tied in ropes. She was still wearing the simple shift they had given her in the cell. For a moment, she wondered if they might return the dress she had been wearing that night when they took her from the party, the dress of gold fabric that shone in the candlelight. She imagined a body dropping from the gallows in a beautiful evening gown and almost smiled at its ridiculousness. Where was that dress now? Probably in the trunk of one of the guards' wives, or daughters. *Good,* Hazel thought. *Let someone else enjoy it.* She wouldn't need it where she was going.

When the prison door opened, Hazel almost collapsed to her knees. The shock of it—the light, the chill, the feeling of wind hitting her cheek. In her time in prison, a rash of red bumps had spread across her face. It felt itchy and tight in the sun.

The guard looked uncomfortable; his weight shifted awkwardly between his feet. His expression was oddly flat and dark. "No one consults me on anything anymore," he said, apparently to himself.

"I'm sorry?" Hazel said.

He looked down at Hazel as though surprised she was standing there. "Well," he said. He shooed her as one might a stray cat. "Go on, then. Get."

Hazel stumbled over her own feet on the cobblestone path that led to the street. The cart that she imagined would take her to Grassmarket wasn't there; aside from a high black carriage that looked like it belonged to the judge or a magistrate, the road was empty.

"Do I . . . walk?" Hazel asked.

"You think yer funny, do ya?" the guard replied. "'Walk,' my arse." He coughed a few times.

Hazel looked around. There was nowhere for her to go. Certainly, no one had ever taken a black varnished carriage with gilded accents to their own execution. Was the cart she was meant to ride in behind it? Hazel took a few tentative steps forward, feeling the rocks grinding uncomfortably where she had hidden them. Her steps were awkward and slow; she tried not to let the rocks fall from her shift to the ground.

The door of the black carriage opened, revealing a young man wearing a powdered wig. "Come along, Miss Sinnett. I'm afraid we don't have all day!" He spoke with a crisp English accent. He consulted a pocket watch and scoffed in frustration. "Surely your natural gait is faster than that! Hip hip!"

Hazel blinked, but obeyed and walked faster toward the black carriage, letting the hidden rocks fall past the hem of her dress to the ground. The man in the wig helped lift Hazel up to the seat beside him in the carriage.

"We'll have to get you a bath by the end of the day, that's absolutely certain," the stranger said. He plucked at the white dress Hazel had been given in prison and shivered in distaste.

The world, which had been spinning since Hazel heard the knock on her cell door, was beginning to slow.

"I take it I'm not going to be hanged, then," she said.

The man shook his head and gave a small rueful smile. "No." He patted the roof of the carriage, and it began its lurching progress down the street, down the hill, and away from the jail. "Other arrangements have been made."

9

IS NAME WAS GASPAR PHILIP PEMBROKE, and he was a steward in the royal household. Within an hour of riding in a carriage with him, Hazel learned his opinions on Scottish cooking (abysmal), the state of the roads from London to Edinburgh (an embarrassment), and his opinions on the waltzing ability of the guests who had attended the Congress of Vienna (better than he anticipated). His clothing was strangely formal and old-fashioned— very few men were still wearing powdered wigs, and those that were, were old men who resented having to give up the fashion of their youth. Gaspar appeared to be in his thirties. Every aspect of his appearance, from his perfectly polished shoes to the white powdered hair, was fastidious. He seemed like the type of man who would wake up several hours early to brush the lint from his trousers and steam the creases from his stockings.

"I apologize," Hazel interrupted finally, as their carriage rattled past fields of horses and Gaspar was pontificating on whether the Scottish crossbill had a sweeter song than its

English counterpart, "but can you tell me what exactly is going on here?"

"Ah." Gaspar adjusted himself slightly. Hazel noticed he took great pains to keep the impeccably tailored sleeve of his jacket from rubbing up against the filth and grime on Hazel's dress. "We're going to London."

"London."

"London. Yes."

"But—" Hazel stopped. A thousand questions had flooded her head at once. This morning, she had been in a prison cell awaiting her own hanging. And now she was riding. In a carriage. To London. "Am I still . . . ?" Hazel raised her wrists in a pantomime of the irons that had been on them just hours ago. She jerked her head to the side and stuck her tongue out like a hanged corpse.

Gaspar flinched. "The short answer to that is no."

"What's the long answer?" Hazel asked.

Gaspar sighed and the ruffled scarf at his neck fluttered. "The long answer is no, at the mercy of His Royal Highness the Prince Regent."

"How is that possible? The Prince Regent?" *Had* her letters gotten through to her uncle? Even if they did, it seemed impossible that the Prince Regent would have involved himself in the troubles of a Scottish viscount. "Wait a moment. If I've been released, why are we going to London? I want to be at Hawthornden Castle. We've passed it." Hazel turned around in the carriage to try to see whether the smoke from Edinburgh was still visible in the distance. "Go back! I have a household to run. A medical practice. My treatise! I've been working on a treatise—a sort of *manual* of medicine and anatomy, and my papers will be all over my laboratory."

Hazel sucked at her teeth, imagining the fragile parchment crumbling or becoming damp and mildewed. "I have to go *home*," she said finally, hating the whine that managed to find its way into her own voice.

Gaspar arched an eyebrow. "The only reason you are not awaiting the sharp drop of the gallows, Miss Sinnett, is because the Prince himself has summoned you to London. I assure you, whatever little *papers* you're working on are now the least of your concern."

"Tell me then. Why am I being summoned?"

Gaspar sighed again, and thudded the roof of the carriage, signaling to the driver that they should stop. "My trousers are wrinkled, my hair is flat, and my feet are swelling. And I suppose after whatever they put you through in that wretched jail, you'll be wanting a bite to eat. There's no reason I can't explain things to you over supper."

THE INN WHERE THEY STOPPED OFF THE MAIN road was small but comfortable, with a fire roaring in the grate in the corner of the room, and only a few other lonely souls occupying the seats near the bar. Gaspar chose a table in the corner, and spread a serviette on his stool before he lowered himself onto it. "I suppose this will do," he muttered.

The smell of roasting meat was making Hazel's mouth water. When the innkeeper's wife brought two mugs of beer to the table, Hazel drank hers in a single breath. The fish pie came out moments later. Hazel had never tasted anything so delicious in her life; years of formal parties and banquets prepared by expensive cooks—nothing came close to the first bite of fish pie at that small inn off the main road heading down to London. It warmed her from the inside out. With each bite of it, she felt the sensation return to her fingertips and the warmth to her cheeks. She imagined it was like the first deep breath after drowning, and Hazel licked the potato from her fork when she had cleaned her plate, all of her childhood governess's careful etiquette lessons dissolved like mist. Gaspar pushed his half-eaten plate toward Hazel without a word.

She finished his supper gratefully.

When Hazel was finished, reclining and feeling as sated as she had in weeks, Gaspar dabbed at his lips with his handkerchief and turned to her. "I'm sure you're aware that Princess Charlotte of Wales has been in some ill health."

Hazel began putting the pieces together in her head. "She had the Roman fever, didn't she? And she . . . broke off an engagement."

"Yes," Gaspar said. "Even though the Princess is *well* aware that the Prince of Orange would make a perfect match both politically and diplomatically. I digress. The Princess had recovered from the Roman fever. And the court celebrated. But in recent months, her health has, once again, become . . . delicate."

The hair on the back of Hazel's neck stood at attention. "The Roman fever came back? There's never been a confirmed case of a patient succumbing again after recovering. That can't be right. She can't have the Roman fever *again*."

"She doesn't," Gaspar said crisply. "Or rather, she *probably* doesn't. It's impossible for me to say."

"Surely, she has a physician. Surely the King and the Prince have *hundreds* of physicians. What do they say?"

"And now you've arrived at the crux of the matter," Gaspar said. "The Princess is refusing to see a physician. Any physician. She has confined herself to her chambers and is refusing to open the door to admit anyone but her lady's maid. She refuses to speak to His Royal Highness the Prince Regent or Her Royal Highness the Princess of Wales. She's even turned away Her Majesty the Queen. She claims she is contagious. She refuses food, and wails through the night. The impression I have been given is that she's quite ill, and yet no one has been able to examine her. As you can imagine, the situation has become quite desperate."

"I see," Hazel said slowly. "But what am I doing here?"

"The Prince Regent was hoping that they might try a different tack." Gaspar smoothed the folds of his collar. "The physicians that have been previously employed by the royal family, as you might imagine, have the pedigree and *experience* that one expects. As such, they are, perhaps, less suited to the private examinations of a young princess. London had heard rumors of the viscount's niece working as a surgeon"—here, Gaspar eyed Hazel up and down—"and the Prince Regent believed it possible that the Princess might be more willing to see a physician of her own sex. About her own age. Perhaps she might even see you as a friend. I was tasked with retrieving you."

"But I'm not a physician," Hazel said, her heart sinking even as she said it. "Not officially. I never took the Royal Examination." She felt the fish pie become lead in her stomach. Perhaps this was all a misunderstanding after all, and she would be taken back to the jail.

To Hazel's relief, Gaspar merely shrugged. "As I said, the situation has become quite desperate."

"They knew the charges against me, then? Am I . . . free?"

Gaspar cleared his throat and rose, pulling a few coins from his pocket and depositing them on the table without letting them clink. "Consider yourself in the service of the royal household," he said. He then leaned in close to Hazel and whispered so quietly she would later wonder if he had said anything at all. "Royal Court might be a friendlier prison, but it is a prison all the same." He pulled away from Hazel suddenly, and the mask of gentility returned to his face. He grinned merrily at the innkeeper and his wife, and swept out of the inn, his jacket tails, half a century out of date, flapping behind him.

10

THE CARRIAGE RIDE DOWN TO LONDON LASTED four days. Most of that time was occupied by Gaspar loudly espousing his opinions on whatever popped into his head at the moment. Their first night, Hazel was able to purchase a new dress for herself. (Gaspar had forbidden her from buying a pair of trousers in addition: "We're going to the Royal Court!" "Well, I wasn't going to wear the trousers while curtsying to Her Majesty the Queen!")

Their stop in York was even more exciting for Hazel: the village shop had a copy of a German medical journal, which she gleefully studied for the next several hours of their journey.

"Do you read that?" Gaspar asked, glancing over her shoulder.

"An essay about the liver's ability to regenerate? Yes, of course I read it. I'm *reading* it."

"No," Gaspar said. "I mean—you read German?"

"Oh. Yes. German, Italian, French, and Latin."

Gaspar raised an eyebrow. "And are all women in Scotland as accomplished as you are?" he said.

"Many," Hazel said. "The English seem to have it in their minds that we're—I don't know—running naked through fields and throwing mud at each other for entertainment, subsisting on ditch water and slop. Admit it! You'll read Hume and Sir Walter Scott, and still, you'll believe that we're all barbarians."

Gaspar blushed. "Not . . . *all*." Eager to change the subject, he pointed at Hazel's German journal. "Did your tutors teach you medicine too? Are women doctors just roaming the streets in Edinburgh?"

"No," Hazel said. "And I wouldn't even have got the tutoring I did if my father hadn't had an open-minded approach to education. He had me learning alongside my older brother, George. Same tutor, same lessons. Trying to best each other by getting better marks. I suppose the competitive spirit never leaves one, does it?"

"But you didn't answer my question!" Gaspar said. "How does a woman go about becoming a surgeon?"

"She doesn't," Hazel replied. "She dresses up in her brother's clothing, gives a false name at the anatomy school, and pays the entrance fee. And then when she's found out, and she's thrown out of class, she hires a resurrection man to sell her bodies to study from."

"Pardon me—what sort of 'bodies' are being sold?"

"Dead bodies, Mr. Pembroke. Corpses. Dug up from kirkyards."

Gaspar had gone green, and looked close to vomiting. "You—you studied *dead* bodies? Dead? Already? From the ground?"

"How else would I understand the human body well enough to operate on it?"

"I don't know!" Gaspar spewed. "Books, I suppose!"

"Mr. Pembroke, I assure you, you would not want a surgeon with a knife standing over you who had only learned from a book. Books are sterile and cold. Drawings help some, yes, but you learn quick enough it's impossible to understand the human anatomy unless you're actually looking at it."

"I suppose you're right," Gaspar murmured. "But . . . did you *really* purchase them from kirkyards?"

"Sometimes," Hazel said, "I even helped to dig them up."

Gaspar made the sign of the cross and retched.

B Y THE TIME GASPAR AND HAZEL'S CARRIAGE finally arrived on the bright streets of Mayfair in London, Hazel's joints were stiff and aching. Gaspar directed Hazel toward her new apartments on a fashionable block, around the corner from the Princess's lodgings of Warwick House on Pall Mall. The room was pleasant and bright, with a large window facing the park, a pitcher of water on the dresser, and a thick quilt on the bed.

"Any bags, m'lady?" the maid asked.

Gaspar looked a bit sheepish. "I suppose—perhaps—we should have stopped at your home in Edinburgh to gather a few things you might need."

Hazel dismissed him with a brush of her hand. "It's no matter at all. I'll have my things sent down to me. There are a number of books I need as well. And my treatise! Iona can send down my treatise. I can keep writing!" She paused and turned back to Gaspar. "Do you have any idea how long I'm going to be here?"

"I imagine," he said, "as long as it takes to return our Princess to good health."

They stood there for a moment with nothing left to say, the pause before the inevitable goodbye. What was the appropriate farewell for a stranger with whom you had just spent the better part of a week, rattling together shoulder to shoulder in a carriage?

Gaspar cleared his throat. "Well, Miss Sinnett, I'm certain I'll be seeing you. At Warwick, or Buckingham, or Kew. The like."

"Yes," Hazel replied. "And thank you for bringing me here."

"I'm a steward in the service of the royal household. I was simply doing my duty." With that, he bowed low, and turned toward the door.

"Wait!"

Gaspar turned back, and Hazel continued. "I'm sorry, I just— Your wig. And your jacket. They're from decades ago. I admit it's been a little while since I've returned to London, but is that the fashion now?"

Gaspar gave Hazel a small, sad smile and shook his head. "No."

"I have to know. It's been driving me mad with curiosity. Just an affectation, then?"

Gaspar raised his fingers to his powdered wig and brushed them across it. "As royal steward, I serve the King, His Majesty George III. As you are no doubt aware, our King suffers tremendously." Hazel knew, of course. The stories of the King's madness were common knowledge by that point, that he would spend days raving and shouting nonsense, mumbling, unable to hold any single thought in his mind at any given moment. It was the reason why his son, the Prince, was acting as Regent. "Sometimes," Gaspar continued, "the King loses himself in time. I find that the King is comforted when he sees the fashions of his youth. It helps him feel as though he knows where he is." He lowered his head in another bow and left Hazel alone in her room to settle in.

Hazel bathed, brushed out her hair, and wrote to her family to let them know of her change in location, and to Iona requesting she send down her things as soon as possible. When she delivered the stack of letters to the maid attending outside Hazel's door, Hazel had no doubt that this time, her letters would actually reach their intended destinations.

The sound of the shutting door echoed and then disappeared, and then Hazel let the silence expand around her. There was yellow afternoon light streaming in from the window, and silence. It was a strange feeling, being alone in a comfortable room so suddenly, like stepping on land for the first time after weeks on a rocking ship. A week ago, she had been miserable and sweating on a pallet in a dingy prison cell, her nervous system frayed and electrified as she waited for her execution to come at any moment. Now, she was sitting on a bed with goose-down pillows, awaiting an audience with Princess Charlotte of Wales.

Her circumstances were better, certainly, but Hazel was still uneasy. She had always been an independent child. By virtue of an absent father and a mother who disappeared into herself, from a young age Hazel felt, perhaps naïvely, that she was responsible for herself and her own circumstances. If she wanted to attend Dr. Beecham's lectures, she needed to find a way in herself; if she wanted to study bodies, she needed to procure bodies herself.

And so, being the victim of such an extreme change in circumstance beyond her control left Hazel feeling unmoored and uneasy. Her room was comfortable—she was watching the sun set over the park through her window, and listening to the pleasant sounds of evening conversation and birdsong drifting through the breeze—but she couldn't dismiss the sense that something was wrong. It was as if she were in a carriage and the doors had been locked from the outside, and though its horse was trotting along at the moment, Hazel knew that at any second it could bolt and send her careering.

Her sleep that night was immediate and deep, but when she woke, it was with the memory of a dream that consisted only of laughter. Laughter like pealing bells but a chilling, mocking laughter. Fortunately, by the time she bathed and dressed for the day, the dream of the cruel laugh had dissolved entirely from her mind.

A Complete Map of Britain's Royal Families, from 1066 to Present Day
by Sir Alberic Twistle-Wick-Alleyne (1814)

... The royal House of Stuart ended in 1714, when Anne, Queen of Great Britain, died without a surviving child. (Though she had seventeen pregnancies, no children survived infancy.) The Act of Settlement 1701 had stipulated that no Catholics could succeed to the English and Irish Crown, and so the next King of England would be Anne's second cousin, George I of the House of Hanover, whose mother had been a direct descendant of King James I.

𝕿𝖍𝖊 𝕳𝖆𝖓𝖔𝖛𝖊𝖗 𝕱𝖆𝖒𝖎𝖑𝖞 𝕿𝖗𝖊𝖊

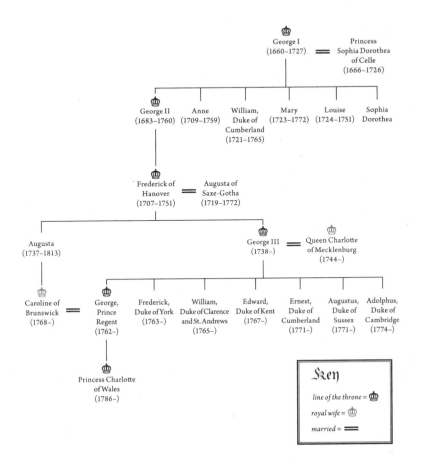

11

OU CAN'T GO IN."

"What do you mean?"

"She's not well enough to see visitors." Princess Charlotte's lady-in-waiting was a small woman, at least two inches shorter than Hazel, with dark hair and a pert, upturned nose. Her eyes were sharp, and though one side of her mouth was curled upward into a permanent half smirk, she stood with her arms crossed in front of the door to Princess Charlotte's private rooms at Warwick House, looking very, very serious.

Hazel had arrived at the Princess's residence—a three-story stone house at the end of Pall Mall—earlier that afternoon, hoping to at least make an initial introduction to the Princess. She waited downstairs for an hour before the lady-in-waiting finally arrived and told Hazel to wait some more while she went and checked to see if the Princess was willing to receive her. As it turned out, the answer was no.

"I apologize for the inconvenience," the lady-in-waiting with the upturned nose said. Her voice had a pleasant, throaty quality. "But Her Royal Highness needs her rest. She's unwell."

"If she's unwell, then it's all the more reason I should attend to her." Hazel squared her shoulders and straightened herself up to her full height, all too aware that the temporary clothes that had been waiting for her in London were ill-fitting and that she didn't yet have her medical bag with her. "I'm the doctor."

The lady-in-waiting's eyes narrowed slightly. "The female doctor. Yes. I heard about you." She sized Hazel up. "I imagined you would be . . . older. Twenty-five at least."

"It's a blessing for my mother's sake I'm not. Could you imagine if she had a daughter *twenty-five years old* and still unmarried? She would hurl herself into the Channel."

There was a moment of silence, and then the lady-in-waiting smiled, cracking her steely façade. "Miss Eliza Murray," she said, extending her hand. "Nineteen years old and still unmarried."

"Hazel Sinnett. Pleasure."

Hazel decided instantly that she liked Eliza Murray. Something about Eliza's face—maybe it was the way one side of her mouth was slightly crooked—made her look like she had a secret, and that, if you were lucky, you might be on the receiving end of it.

Eliza took a step closer to Hazel. "I still can't let you into the Princess's rooms, but there's a chance she'll be more congenial to visitors in the next few hours. She's usually in a better mood after supper. You're welcome to wait. I can send for tea."

"That would be wonderful, thank you."

Hazel waited in the front room of Warwick House for the rest of the afternoon. A servant brought out tea, and then—possibly out of pity at seeing Hazel still waiting as the sun began to set over Pall Mall—supper. A few months ago, Hazel would have found herself fidgeting and impatient, tapping her toes or drumming her fingers along her leg, but the hours spent in a cell made time pass differently now. She was content sitting with her own thoughts, mentally writing the next chapter of the treatise she would work on when her trunks arrived from Edinburgh.

"So why are you unmarried, then?" Eliza Murray asked Hazel an hour after she had finished her supper. Eliza was strolling back into the main room and carrying a box to deliver to the footman. "Not many men interested in a woman who can cut them to bits with a knife?"

Now Hazel laughed. "Not too many, no."

"Probably for the best. What sort of man would want his wife running around, sawing off legs and the like?"

"A very, very rare sort of man," Hazel said, and her mind turned again to Jack. In her memory, she saw him in the graveyard, illuminated only by moonlight. His hair was thick and dark and tousled, and he smiled at her and extended his hand. He had made her feel like home. Her heart ached and Hazel blinked away the fantasy before it would hurt even more. "And how about you? Why is a lady-in-waiting to Princess Charlotte still unwed?"

Eliza's mouth twitched slightly but she didn't blush. "There might be a certain suitor. And an offer of marriage. I suppose if the Princess had accepted the Prince of Orange's offer and gone to live in Holland for half the year, I would be out of a job and I would have said yes to a husband. But . . ." Eliza trailed off.

"But she turned him down."

Eliza looked at the door leading to the Princess's rooms. "Yes. Her health."

"Of course."

Eliza lowered herself into a brocade chair beside Hazel. "That's not to say I have fully limited my prospects. I have *many* suitors."

"I had no doubt. You're lovely."

Eliza smiled like a child with a secret. "The boy who offered?" she said, looking up at Hazel through her eyelashes. "A *man*, really." She continued without prompting. "A lieutenant, under Prince Frederick Augustus of Prussia."

"A foreigner, then," Hazel teased. "Tall, dark, and handsome?"

Eliza thought for a moment. "Tall, yes. Fair, not dark. And I think people do tend to find him handsome, yes. In a roguish, Continental soldier sort of way."

"And have you given him your answer yet?"

"*Elizaaaaa.*" A voice like a tinkling bell called from the Princess's rooms. A summoning.

Eliza stood. "I should go. And to be frank, so should you. Maybe try again tomorrow?" Eliza nodded politely to Hazel, and walked quickly toward the source of the call, disappearing behind the Princess's door.

The next day, Hazel arrived at dawn. She sat in the Princess's foyer with several books she'd brought, and read through the entire day, while servants politely dropped off trays with tea at regular intervals.

Eliza greeted her. "She's not going to let you see her today, so there's really no point in waiting," she said.

"I have tea and books," Hazel replied. "I'm perfectly happy here as I would be anywhere."

By the evening, when Hazel was squinting by candlelight at the tight printing on the page in front of her, she decided it was once again time to return home.

On her third day at Warwick House, Hazel brought three books and a full sheet of parchment. She figured as long as she was here, she might as well continue working on a new chapter of her treatise, even in isolation from its other component parts. But Hazel had been working for less than an hour when she heard the creak of a door. She turned, expecting Eliza, perhaps to tell Hazel that she was wasting her time yet again—but, no; in the doorway, wearing a silk dressing gown, with her long curling brown hair falling loose past her shoulders, stood the granddaughter of King George III and the future heir presumptive to the throne of Great Britain, Princess Charlotte of Wales.

It was a face Hazel had seen thousands of times in newspaper etchings and portraits but only briefly in the flesh. Her skin was impossibly unblemished and milky white, like rising bread that had just been floured. Her nose was curved like a finch's beak, and her eyes were small and round. They rolled around the sitting room until they landed on Hazel.

"You're here again," she said. "They told me you were waiting."

"I am," Hazel replied. She wondered if she should curtsy. It was just the two of them in a hall falling into shadow, and one of them was in her nightclothes. A curtsy was surely the correct thing to do, but still felt somehow wrong. The Princess waited, and for a fraction of a second Hazel wondered whether she had made the wrong decision, but then the Princess sighed and turned, leaving the door ajar behind her.

"You can come in," she called back. "But I'm not letting you *examine* me."

"That's fine," Hazel replied, bounding toward the bedchamber. "I don't have any of my equipment with me anyway."

Though it was morning, the heavy curtains of the room were

drawn, keeping the bedroom in a dim, candlelit twilight. Still, even in the gloom, Hazel could see that the room was sumptuously appointed, with surfaces covered in so many different colors and varieties of thick and patterned fabrics, Hazel couldn't identify them quickly enough to count them. The wallpaper was green and richly textured, patterned with vines and leaves. A tapestry hung behind the massive four-poster bed, and buried within it, under a mountain of pillows, was the Princess, who had returned to a state of repose.

She stroked a small dog the size and shape of a cream puff resting placidly in her arms.

"Good, Edwina," Princess Charlotte cooed to the dog.

Eliza Murray sat in a chair in the corner of the room with her embroidery. She didn't look up when Hazel entered.

Hazel cleared her throat. "Perhaps—Your Royal Highness—you could begin by telling me your symptoms."

Charlotte flopped onto her side. "What *aren't* my symptoms?" she moaned. "I'm tired of being ill, I really am. I'm young; I should be able to *live my life.*"

"Fatigue?" Hazel prompted.

"Fatigue, nausea. Headaches—terrible, terrible headaches. So awful I can hardly leave bed. Eliza knows. Tell her, Eliza."

Eliza raised an eyebrow but didn't look up from her embroidery.

"Any rashes?" Hazel asked.

"Yes. No. No, no rashes, not really. But I'm *swollen*, it feels as though my entire body has expanded somehow. My skin too tight over everything on the inside."

"Is it painful?"

The Princess gently deposited her dog onto the floor—Edwina scampered out the door—and then pulled her duvet over her head. She answered from below the duvet: "Yes! Terribly! Sharp pain in my stomach almost daily, and that's in addition to the pain I get in my head. It's a miracle I'm able to leave the house at all."

Hazel was almost certain she knew what was wrong with the Princess, but it would be impossible to be sure unless she could examine her. She raised a hand and took a step forward, the way one would approach a skittish horse. "Might I see if your forehead is hot, ma'am—"

"No!" Charlotte swatted Hazel's hand away. "I told you. You can't touch me. Too many doctors have *touched me. Prodded me.* It's bad enough I'm supposed to do what my father says, I refuse to be a pincushion for that parade of short, ill-mannered men who smell like . . . tobacco and gin. It's been years of that and I've only got better on occasion and it never stuck anyway."

"I understand," Hazel said.

Princess Charlotte arched an eyebrow. "Do you?"

"I do," Hazel said. "They seldom teach doctors how to talk to the people they're supposed to treat. They learn on cadavers and those can't complain."

"I question how much they 'learn' at all. My father has brought in a dozen doctors, and none have been able to figure out what's wrong with me. Which of course makes him furious because he can't make me marry if I'm not able to leave bed."

"I'll find out what's wrong with you, ma'am."

Now Princess Charlotte arched both eyebrows. "I wish you the best of luck, Doctor," she said breezily before turning away from Hazel and pulling the blankets tight around her.

On cue, Eliza deposited her embroidery on the chair next to her and rose. "I'll see you to your carriage, Miss Sinnett," she said.

The sun had set, and the moon was a faint, dim crescent in the distance, but Pall Mall was illuminated by gas lamps that stood like soldiers in an even row down the side of the street. The Princess's home was at the far end of a street that was lined on either side by row houses in white stone, and the effect of the lamplight in the evening fog reflecting against the façade of the buildings was a little ghostly. A decade ago, they were the first gas lamps in London, a small bubble of sickly yellow light pressing against a darkness illuminated only by pinprick candlelight in the distance. In another decade, maybe every street would have gas lamps. Perhaps a decade after that, the streets would be illuminated by electricity. What color cast would that light give on the cobblestones? Hazel wondered. What new shapes might the shadows be that those lights threw onto the city streets?

Hazel was approaching her carriage when she heard a shrieking laughter echoing from up the lane where the border of the light ended. It was a laughter that sounded like the one in her dream. From around the corner, a group of strangers became visible, now half-illuminated by the yellow of the gas lamps. There were six or seven of them, all laughing and pulling at one another and swaggering down the street. Their voices carried—they were men and women, drunk on wine or happiness or something even stronger. And though the details of their clothes were difficult to make out in the dim lighting, even from a block away Hazel could tell that they were dressed for a party. And on their faces, every single one of them wore a gilded mask shaped like a rabbit.

Hazel was transfixed. She watched as one of the mask-wearing women grabbed a man by the hand and pulled him through a small, almost invisible door in the brick of the row houses across the street—a door that seemed to lead *between* the houses. Hazel hadn't even noticed it until the woman opened it and went in. The rest of the group in their finery and rabbit masks followed through quickly, the echoing of their laughter disappearing with them. Hazel had squinted from the far side of the street, but she had only been able to make out darkness through the door.

"Who are they?" Hazel asked Eliza, awestruck by the group that had appeared and disappeared like a figment of her imagination.

"The Companions to the Death. It's a secret society, but the secret part seems to be lost on them. A literary society, they claim, but mostly a society for drinking themselves to death and impressing each other with more expensive parties."

"I imagine it's an exclusive group," Hazel said.

"Put it this way: it helps if your great-great-grandfather was a Plantagenet, but you'll have better odds if you're famous."

"Famous?"

Just then, another mask-wearing figure appeared at the far end of the street. From behind the gold mask's rabbit ears, Hazel could see he had thick, dark brown hair. He strolled slowly but purposefully down Pall Mall, oblivious to the presence of Hazel and Eliza tucked behind the carriage at the opposite end of the street. As the man got closer, Hazel noticed he was effortfully walking to conceal a limp. He approached the hidden door and knocked in a strange rhythm:

Knock.

Knock-Knock.

Knock.

Knock-Knock.

Eliza gestured with her head toward the figure and whispered to Hazel, "Have you read *Childe Harold*?"

"That's not . . ." The door swung open, and the latecomer slipped inside. "*Lord Byron?*"

Eliza rolled her eyes. "The very same. They collect celebrities. Everyone who matters to art and culture and society tries to become a member. The Prince Regent thinks he's ruling this country. He's wrong. The decisions are being made by the people behind that door."

"Is Princess Charlotte a member of the exclusive club, then? The Companions to the Death, or whatever they're called?"

"Are you joking? Any club that involves Romantic poets disappearing down hidden alleyways isn't the type of place for a future Queen of England in the process of making a respectable marriage."

"Still," Hazel said, "aren't you the least bit curious to know what they get up to in there?"

"Drinking and congratulating each other on their collective brilliance. Mystery solved. Good night, Hazel Sinnett."

Eliza closed the carriage door, and Hazel watched her re-enter the Princess's house as the carriage began rolling down the street. The sound of the woman's laughter was still vibrating in her head. That night, Hazel dreamed of rabbits. Her first day at the anatomy school in Edinburgh, they had been given a rabbit to cut open, to study its organs and the way blood flowed through its tiny body. In her dream, she was back in the classroom, and the rabbit under her scalpel had a golden face. When she tried to cut it open, it leapt from the table, and escaped out onto the street.

15 May 1818
No. 4 Clarence Road
Windsor

Dear Hazel,

I am aghast. Aghast and despairing. I do not understand why you
would think it amusing to write now informing me of the fact that you
have apparently been imprisoned (?) and nearly brought a shame
onto our family from which we would never recover. (Do you not
think you had already made quite enough of an effort in that regard?)
    I am relieved, at least, that the mess has been sorted and to
learn that you are safe in London. I am, as you know, in Berkshire
where Percy has been excelling beyond all expectations at Eton.
If you ever find yourself near, please do stop by for tea (so long as
you are willing to apologize first for the unspeakable damage you
nearly did to our family).

                                        Your mother,
                                        Lady Sinnett

12

ERCIFULLY, IT TOOK ONLY FIVE DAYS for Hazel's trunk to arrive from Edinburgh. Gaspar knocked just as a footman was leaving it in the foyer. Today, both his jacket and his trousers were piped with red thread. His powdered wig was as impeccably coiffed as ever.

"Ah," he said, sidestepping the large trunk. "I see your things made the journey safely."

Hazel flung the trunk lid open. In less than a moment, she was elbow deep. *Yes, good. Fine.* There were her notebooks, and the pages she had been writing her treatise on—thank God—and her good stays and shift, and her favorite scarf. But—

"Where's my medical bag?"

Hazel began flinging things from the trunk. "It's a large leather bag. Worn. Fairly cracked. It used to be my father's."

"Is it sentimental, then?" Gaspar said, using a finger to lift and examine the hem of one of Hazel's dresses, which she had managed to throw halfway across the floor. Hazel's display of emotion was clearly making him uncomfortable.

"No. I mean, *yes*, but that's not the problem. All my medical equipment is in it. My scalpel, my saw, my scissors, my—"

"Yes, yes. Fine." Gaspar twitched as if Hazel's words had been worms she was dangling before him.

"Are you . . . scared of doctors, Gaspar?"

"I'm not *scared*, thank you. I just find the conversation—" He searched for the appropriate word, and then found it. "—unnecessary! No need to go on about—scissors, and the like." He shivered. Hazel smiled. For a reason she couldn't quite explain, she found his barely concealed fright of surgery endearing.

"Anyway," Gaspar continued, "I will get it sorted out. I'm sure we can purchase those *things* for you in London. It's a big city, you know."

"Yes, I'm certain. But equipment is highly personal, and if I'm—"

"I assure you!" Gaspar said loudly. "I will sort it out." He straightened his cuff links. "And perhaps don't mention this small—*small, and easily remedied!*—hiccup to the Prince Regent."

"Did you say the Prince Regent?"

"Yes," Gaspar said, sighing. "Once again, I've been sent to fetch you. I'm to take you to Kew. He's requested an audience with you."

Hazel quickly scanned over her dresses, all in various states of wrinkled disrepair, having traveled across the whole of England, and then having been thrown on the floor.

Gaspar noticed. "This one will have to do," he said, picking up a rather hideous navy blue dress Hazel's mother had bought her to wear at the ceremony when her father was promoted to his captaincy. She hadn't worn it since, and recalled it being nightmarishly hot and itchy beneath the arms. "It's the only half-suitable one among the bunch."

"I can't wear that to meet the Prince. I don't even know why Iona packed it—I haven't worn it in ages. The hem is probably too short. It itches. I'll look like a grown woman dressed as a child for some sort of farcical performance."

Gaspar patted the dust from the dress's skirt. "I actually find it quite fetching."

Hazel held up one of her newer dresses, a simple flax-colored shift she often wore while working in her laboratory. "Can't I just wear this?"

Gaspar looked as if he had just been slapped.

THIRTY MINUTES LATER, HAZEL WAS IN THE hideous navy dress, in a carriage with Gaspar on the way to Kew, one of the royal family's many estates near London. "Be sure to compliment him on the gardens," Gaspar said. "And the furnishings, he picked out many of the furnishings himself. And *curtsy* when you come in. *Low.*" A sudden look of terror seized him. "You do know how to curtsy, don't you? Please tell me you know how to curtsy; we don't have the time for me to teach you."

"Yes," Hazel said. "I know how to curtsy. Would be easier if I were in a dress that allowed me the full use of my limbs, but I'll manage." She tried to rotate her shoulder and heard the tiny tear of a ripping seam somewhere. She lowered her arm quickly.

"I don't understand what you're complaining about. The dress looks marvelous. You might almost pass for a lady."

"I am a lady, Gaspar."

"No ladies I know have run around kirkyards in trousers."

"Perhaps," Hazel said, looking straight ahead and trying not to smile, "that just means you need to meet more ladies."

Gaspar blushed so red he matched his cravat.

The gardens at Kew were vast and expansive, so manicured Hazel imagined they must have a staff of hundreds to keep them looking so orderly and maintained, with the tulips all blooming in unison and facing in the same direction, the hedges sharp, and the grass lush. Their carriage crossed a small bridge over a bubbling pond. Hazel looked down to see large, flopping koi fish in the water.

"First we greet the King," Gaspar said, not breaking his stride. Hazel tried to keep up, following the back of Gaspar's wig through the palace's massive entrance foyer, down a seemingly endless hallway that ended, finally, at a small wooden door. Gaspar knocked. No answer.

"Sire?" Gaspar said. Still no response. He twisted the knob so slowly it barely creaked and turned to Hazel, whispering, "Just curtsy quickly. Do not ask any questions. Do not *say* anything to the King at all. Curtsy, and do not turn your back on him. We show our respect, and then we leave." Hazel nodded her assent, and Gaspar gently pushed the small door open.

The room was stiflingly warm, and small, appearing even smaller because all four walls were covered in the same emerald-green brocade wallpaper; it had a claustrophobic, disorienting effect, exacerbated by the heat and the sparseness of the room—aside from the large four-poster bed, the bedroom contained almost no furniture. The smell of mildew and death was pervasive. Hazel had to resist the urge to cover her mouth and nose with her sleeve. Gaspar bowed low, and only then did Hazel realize that King George III was present at all. He was a small, crumbling man, chewing at the air and revealing bright pink gums. Gaspar stared at Hazel, and she remembered herself and curtsied. "Your Majesty," she said, remembering only after the words had left her mouth that she wasn't supposed to say anything at all. But the King did not react. His eyes swirled in their sockets and his mouth opened and closed soundlessly. Gaspar tugged at Hazel's arm, and the two of them walked backward from the room and back into the hallway, where they both exhaled in the cool air.

"A bad day," Gaspar said, more to himself than to Hazel. He straightened. "And now we see the Regent."

Down two more hallways, up a flight of stairs, and down a third hallway, Gaspar finally led Hazel into a bright sitting room with large windows overlooking the garden, where the Prince Regent was standing on a pedestal, posing for a portrait.

From the portraits she had seen of him, Hazel expected the Prince Regent to be relatively handsome. He was not. His figure was like a lump of clay that had been squeezed in the hands of a child, and he had styled his hair sweeping forward, toward his face, but the combing had been too aggressive—there were comb-mark tracks of bare pink scalp visible between the over-creamed lines of greasy hair. Small, watery blue eyes gazed out from a face red and swollen as a roasted sausage.

"Excellent, sir," the painter said from behind his easel. "*Very* dignified."

Hazel stifled a laugh. Gaspar elbowed her, and she lowered

into a deep curtsy. One of her best; her mother would have been so proud.

"Your Royal Highness," Gaspar said, rising from his own bow, which had been so low his wig nearly slipped from his head. "May I present Miss Hazel Sinnett, niece of Lord Almont."

The Prince Regent fidgeted like a toddler, and Hazel noticed that the Regent was wearing a girdle that had been laced to defiance against his midsection.

"Yes, well, how do you do?" he said gruffly.

"The physician," Gaspar prompted gently, "to treat the Princess. Your brilliant idea, if you recall, that the Princess would be more amenable to a doctor of her own age and sex. An idea that has *already* proved itself a success, sir: Miss Sinnett has been permitted into the Princess's chambers already."

"Yes, yes. Of course. The physician. My brilliant idea." The Regent puffed his chest out and hopped down from the pedestal. "That's enough of the painting today, I think," he said to the artist.

The artist tried to protest. "Sir, I—"

But the Regent ignored him. He undid his collar and in a single swift motion, removed his girdle with a heaving sigh. "A Prince must be fit and slim!" he declared to no one. Turning to Gaspar, his eyes narrowed. "Have you always had such fat legs, Gaspar?"

"Yes, I believe so, sir."

Hazel had known that she disagreed with the Regent's politics: he was a staunch Tory, a man who favored war and the powers of the aristocracy. But being in the same room as him, she found there was something instantly unlikable about him, an energy to his posturing and the sneer of his upper lip that set Hazel on edge. Like the rest of Great Britain, she would be grateful when it was Princess Charlotte on the throne.

The Regent sized Hazel up as one would examine a bug before lowering one's boot onto it. "So, the female physician. Ugly little thing, aren't you?"

"I suppose you did not bring me here to treat your daughter because of my looks, Your Royal Highness," Hazel muttered, not breaking eye contact.

The Regent swaggered over to her and stood too close. He leaned in even closer, and every fiber of Hazel's being wanted to take a step back, to retreat, to drop her head and her eyes, but she resisted. His breath was foul, like animal fat gone bad. "Let me be incredibly crystal clear about one thing, *Miss Sinnett*," he said, and Hazel's stomach clenched.

She hadn't been sure he was paying attention to her name; he had seemed, well, *silly*. But now he was staring straight into her eyes, and Hazel became aware of just how much power he had, and the fact that his words were now deadly serious.

"The Princess's health is of more importance to this nation than you could ever conceive. We have had brilliant—brilliant!—experts examine and treat her. You are an experiment. You are a footnote. I expect you will fail, and when you do, I will see you returned to whatever hovel you call a castle in Scotland to live out the rest of your life pulling teeth and setting broken donkey legs. And if you do *anything* to hurt the Princess or worsen her condition in *any way*—you will be *begging* for disgrace." The Regent turned on his expensive heels. "Good day, Miss Sinnett. Good day, Gaspar."

Hazel would have laughed—the abruptness, the shock of

it all—if she hadn't noticed that her hands were shaking. "I'll need some equipment, then," she said to Gaspar. "Surgical tools. And some herbs."

Gaspar seemed shaken by the Regent's remarks too. "Yes, yes. There's an infirmary here at Kew. Take what you need and send a note along if you require anything else."

"Thank you."

Hazel left the room, headed toward the infirmary, trying to anchor herself and stop herself from shaking. She would treat the Princess. She wouldn't fail. She had proved to herself and to Dr. Beecham and to Dr. Straine that she could hold her own at the school for anatomy. And now she would prove herself once again, because she didn't want to know what would happen to her, or to her family, if this time, she didn't.

ERHAPS SHE SHOULD HAVE EXPECTED IT OUT OF a royal palace, but the infirmary at Kew was beyond Hazel's wildest dreams. Her breath caught in her chest when she entered and saw the vast array of surgical tools, all glistening and lined up, beckoning for Hazel to reach out and claim them. On shelves above the workbench were neatly organized jars of dried herbs and medicines, lined up in alphabetical order beside strips of cotton and alcohol. Some of the names on the jars were completely unfamiliar, remedies Hazel had never even heard of, let alone seen in person or had access to. But there were books here as well—a miniature library that Hazel was certain without even checking would inform her of which of the powders were meant to be mixed into a poultice to stop bleeding and which would be brewed into tea to fight lethargy. Her heart quickened at the thought of all the information hidden between the cracking leather covers of the books, and she reached out a hand to open the first book in the stack, a discussion for the treatment of melancholy, written in French.

Hazel pulled herself away after reading just the first chapter, promising herself she would return to finish it, and to finish all the other books that were there, too, beckoning her with the promise of new things to learn, of ways to become a better surgeon and physician. But she was here today with a mission, and so she set about remaking her lost medical bag, collecting a new pair of scissors, a new scalpel, a sharp needle, and a spool of strong black thread. She was just examining a small saw when she heard someone clearing his throat behind her.

She spun and saw a man with his arms crossed over his chest. He was impossibly tall, probably six feet, but what she noticed before that was how broad he was, with strong shoulders and a wide chest. With his frame and blond hair, Hazel would have guessed that he was a farmer, someone who spent long hours in the sun doing manual labor. But the details of the rest of his appearance came through slowly: he was dressed like a gentleman, in a well-tailored jacket; he had a neatly trimmed mustache; and he wore spectacles. Round metal spectacles that framed his eyes, which were the color of honey on toast.

"What do you think you're doing here?" the blond stranger asked. He spoke with a faint accent Hazel couldn't quite identify. His syllables were precise but oddly rounded. "If you're a thief, just leave what you've taken. I'd rather not call the guards, but some of this equipment is quite valuable, and I would prefer not to go through the hassle of replacing it."

"I'm not a thief," Hazel spat. The stranger raised an eyebrow, and Hazel realized her arms were full of things she had taken from the infirmary. She dropped it all onto the workbench with a clang. "Gaspar said I could come here," she said.

"Ah," the man said, taking one step closer. He didn't smile. "And did Gaspar also tell you that you could take—let's see—my scalpel, scissors, saw, and thread?"

Hazel took a step to try to block the workbench from his vision. "Hypothetically. If I were taking them. It would be because I didn't know they were yours. And I needed them."

"That thread won't do to sew a dress." He lowered his voice to a mock whisper. "It's for skin, not skirts."

"I was summoned here *as a physician* to treat Princess Charlotte. I'm sure she can afford far more qualified seamstresses for her gowns."

The stranger took another step forward, and Hazel tried to block him, but he feinted left and then went right and grabbed the pair of scissors from behind her. He snapped them twice in the air. "A fellow physician should know how important one's own tools are."

"I am well aware. I was brought here from Edinburgh and I sent for my things, but my medical bag didn't arrive. And the stakes of my treating the Princess have been made quite clear to me, and I preferred to get started sooner rather than later."

The stranger cocked his head. "Funny," he said.

"What's funny?"

"I don't believe I heard an apology in there."

Hazel's blood boiled. He looked scarcely older than she

was, maybe five years her senior, and yet he was talking to her as though she were a child. She knew he was right; she *should* apologize. But instead she said, "And are you going to apologize for implying that I was going to use surgical equipment to sew a dress?"

He breathed out through his nose: not quite a laugh, but his brown eyes glittered a little bit, either with amusement or contempt. Hazel felt her cheeks flush.

"Okay," the man said after a moment. "I apologize." His mustache really was impossibly straight. He must have to examine it every day to trim it for errant hairs. And it was undignified for an *adult* man to be blond, wasn't it? Blond hair was for toddlers with rosy cheeks, not tall, broad-chested men with unidentifiable accents who made Hazel's mouth go dry when they stepped closer to her.

Here was where she was supposed to apologize back, to return his instruments and ask him politely if there were any extras about, but she found herself rooted to the floor and unable to speak.

As if reading her mind, the man walked over to a cabinet at the far end of the room and opened it. "There is extra equipment in here. You're welcome to use it if you wish."

Hazel remained silent, still frustrated for reasons she couldn't articulate and then even more frustrated that in being *kind*, this stranger undermined her right to be upset. Something about this man just made her *cross*. Why was he so *polite*?

"So, it seems ladies in this country don't apologize *or* say thank you," the man said lightly.

Just then, the door at the top of the room swung open. A harried-looking footman caught his breath and doubled over, holding on to the doorframe. "Dr. Ferris," he panted, "you're needed in the bedchamber."

Before Dr. Ferris could respond—*the* Dr. Ferris?—or react, an old man in his nightclothes burst past the footman and into the infirmary. "I detest these festivities, but I simply must put on a good face and attend!" he said, pirouetting toward Hazel. "Lady Marlborough, how marvelous you look." The man's hair was wild, and his eyes were round and wide, with the whites visible on all sides. Hazel noticed that his skin was red and inflamed, the way one's might be after a night of heavy drinking. She also noticed that this strange man, caught in a fit of delusion, was the man she had curtsied to earlier that afternoon: the King of England.

Dr. Ferris slid between Hazel and King George III.

"Your Majesty," the doctor said, sinking into a deep bow. "If I might escort you into the *dining room*." He gently held the King's arm and began walking with him out of the room. The King walked along with the doctor, but gave an apologetic look back at Hazel. Hazel smiled, and King George smiled back.

"You're free to take the surplus from the cabinet," Dr. Ferris said before he stepped beyond the doorframe. "But please do not take my personal equipment."

"I won't," Hazel said quietly. And she listened as the footsteps of the two men disappeared down the hallway, the sounds of Dr. Ferris's comforting murmuring getting quieter and quieter.

13

AZEL FOUND HERSELF IN A NEW, COMFORTABLE routine. She would wake up, get dressed, and head over to Warwick House, where the servants would greet her with a cup of tea and a comfortable place to sit while she waited for the Princess to decide whether she would let Hazel see her that day. Without a medical bag, Hazel had wrapped all the borrowed equipment from the Kew infirmary in a piece of canvas and carried the whole bundle with her. She had yet to use it.

Most afternoons, while the Princess was napping, Hazel played whist with Eliza, who was a fierce competitor.

"I grew up the youngest of four girls," Eliza said. "I learned not to pull my punches when it came to card games."

"I have brothers," Hazel said.

"Ah," Eliza said. "See, if you had sisters, you would know that women can be wily. Like now when I was distracting you with conversation so I could get away with *this*." With a flourish, she snapped her winning card onto the table. "My game, again."

"I think you have an advantage. You're far more well prac-
ticed in this game than I am."

"Well, then I'm doing you a favor playing you now and not
betting anything while you learn to improve."

Hazel learned that Eliza was not only a ruthless card
player but the Princess's lady-in-waiting for nearly two years.
Her father was the third son of a baron, and his prospects for
inheritance were minimal. "The goal is to find a suitable husband for me before I'm doomed to remain the spinster aunt
for the rest of my life. Two of my sisters are already married
with children. I have *three nephews!*"

"And how has the marriage market been for you?" Hazel
asked. "Have you given your answer to your Continental
lieutenant?"

Eliza offered a small crooked smile. "There is *talk. Letters*
and possible declarations of love."

Hazel raised her eyebrows. "On his end, or yours?"

"Oh, his end, of course. He's completely besotted. You'll
be able to see for yourself; he'll be at the Regent's ball at
Buckingham House a week from next."

"A ball?"

"Yes, you're coming, aren't you? The Regent keeps throwing them in the hopes that one of these days the Princess's
health will improve enough to allow her to dance and meet
someone and fall in love and finally pick a husband. Of course,
he's secretly hoping she'll change her mind about Orange."

"She won't?"

Eliza guffawed. "Have you seen the Hereditary Prince
of Orange? Weedy, miserable thing. Sour-faced. Terrible
dancer. Plus, he looks like he's about twelve."

"Not like your first lieutenant."

"No," Eliza said, unable to contain her smile. "Nothing like him at all."

Hazel grinned. "And for the first time all day, I have beat you at a game of whist!" She revealed her hand of cards.

"No fair! I was distracted . . . keeping you up to date on the essential social gossip!

"If it makes you feel better," Hazel said, "you beat me about forty-five times in a row before this. The odds of probability were that I would have to win one hand eventually."

Eliza smiled and gathered the cards neatly. She cocked her head toward the Princess's closed door. "I'll go check on her."

A few minutes later, Eliza poked her head out of the room. Hazel stood. "I'm sorry," Eliza said. "She doesn't want to be seen today, but she did say to tell you that her symptoms today were pain in her stomach, a headache, and chills. She also says her urine has gone darker than normal. Does any of that help you?"

"I don't know yet, but it might. Anyway, thank you," Hazel said.

"For a whist champion, anything."

WHEN IT CAME TO WORKING ON HER TREATISE, Hazel found it nearly impossible to focus on writing in her room. It was too bright, too *light*, too cheery. The air was stagnant and hot. Something about the way the sun shone through the sheer white curtains caused the words to become stuck in her pen. It was altogether too unlike the laboratory where she worked in Edinburgh, which had been dark and smelled of wet stone and earth.

On a day where the Princess and Eliza had dismissed her as soon as she walked in the door, Hazel found herself unable to write more than half a sentence at the small desk by her bed, so she decided she would take her parchment and ink down to the infirmary at Kew, where she recalled an unvarnished wooden bench and table and absolutely no bright windows.

It was empty, and just as comfortingly organized and tidy as it had been the first time she visited. Hazel settled onto a wooden bench and spread her pages out before her. As it turned out, it wasn't that hard to pick up from where she had left off back in Edinburgh. Hazel felt as though she had only been writing for moments when she looked up through the thin window at the top of the room to see that the light had already shifted to the golden orange of afternoon. She was working with intense focus on labeling a diagram of a heart she had already drawn.

"The left ventricle has blood going *to* the body, not returning from the body," said a soft voice over her shoulder. Hazel jumped to standing and nearly spilled a pot of ink. "Sorry, I'm sorry," Dr. Ferris said, raising his hands as if to protect his face. "I was curious to see what you were working on."

Hazel tried to calm her own racing heart, pounding at the surprise of the intrusion. "What are you *doing* here?"

"This is . . . my infirmary," he said.

"It's the palace infirmary. You work at the pleasure of the Crown, same as I do."

"Is that so?" the doctor said, cocking his head. "You know what I do, then." He said it as a statement, not a question, and Hazel was suddenly aware that she was alone, unchaperoned, with a man in a room where anyone might walk in on them. That was the thing she would have been worried about a lifetime ago. Before she dressed up as a man to study at the Anatomists' Society. Before Jack. She couldn't think of Jack now. Hazel straightened her papers and moved her body to block her work from Dr. Ferris.

"Yes, I do," she said. "Treating King George III, God help and save him."

The corner of Dr. Ferris's mouth lifted into a smirk. "Admit it," he said. "You're a little impressed."

"Of *you*? Why should I be?"

He cocked his head. "First in my class at Uppsala University at sixteen. Youngest ever chief minister of surgery at Saint Göran Hospital in Stockholm. Already published in the *Journal of the Royal Society of Medicine* and the *New England Journal of Medicine*. Twice in that last one. Fellow of the Royal College of Surgeons of England. Fluent in Swedish, French, English, Latin, German. Oh, and Danish. The personal physician to the King of Great Britain and Ireland at twenty-four years old. Should I go on?" Hazel rolled her eyes. Dr. Ferris continued: "Can I see what you're working on, there? Maybe I can offer some help? A reminder of what the left ventricle does?"

"I *know* what the left ventricle does."

"I'm sure you do," Dr. Ferris said. "But it's wrong there, on your diagram. The left ventricle is from the perspective of the patient, not the doctor. The patient's left side."

Hazel looked down at her drawing. Infuriatingly, he was right. "I know which one the left ventricle is," she said, and then immediately regretted it because she sounded like a petulant child.

Dr. Ferris scrunched his face up. "Do you, though?"

Hazel grabbed her pen and quickly scratched out her

writing. "An error in my marking. Not in my thinking. There's a difference. Sometimes you *know* something in your head but you just write it down incorrectly. That's all."

The doctor ignored her and went to the medicinal supplies to gather some herbs. He lowered a large, porcelain tub from a high shelf and slowly removed its lid. Hazel craned her neck to see what was inside.

"Leeches!" she said.

"Yes, of course." Dr. Ferris shrugged. "As good a way as any to align the humors."

"Yes, yes, I know, I just—" Hazel shivered involuntarily, and Dr. Ferris clocked it.

"Curious," he said. "A doctor who doesn't know her left from her right, and who's squeamish. Very curious."

"I'm not squeamish. I've cut off two legs and broken twice as many arms. Removed a bullet from a femur and a sword from an ear *and* both times the patient survived."

The doctor's mustache bristled, and he lifted a single thick, brown leech onto a finger and slowly moved it toward Hazel. She flinched involuntarily. The doctor deposited it back in the tub with the others. "If you say so," he said lightly. He picked up the entire tub of leeches and walked up the stairs and out of the room. There was a buzzing in Hazel's head and her ears were hot. She corrected her diagram of the heart but then found that she wasn't able to do any more writing the rest of the day.

A WEEK LATER, HAZEL WAS DRAWING A DIAGRAM of the trachea when Dr. Ferris appeared behind her again.

"Dr. Ferris. Do you always bother young women when they're trying to write?"

"Only when they're in my infirmary. I brought you tea." He deposited a mug on the table, careful not to set it upon any of Hazel's papers.

"Thank you, Dr. Ferris," she said as coldly as she could manage.

"You can call me Simon."

"I'd rather not."

"I would much rather you did. Otherwise, it will feel far too familiar when I call you Hazel."

"First, you will not call me Hazel. Even though you seem to think it appropriate to come disturb me while I am working here *alone,* you will not delude yourself into thinking we've reached any level of familiarity."

Ferris dropped into a mock bow. "As you wish, Miss Sinnett."

"And second, I don't even recall us ever being properly introduced. How do you even know my name? Have you asked about me?" The last question slipped out of her mouth before she had a chance to stop it.

"Well, *Miss Sinnett,* you might find it interesting to know that there are not many female doctors in Great Britain and even fewer who have been invited to treat the Princess. Your reputation, as they say, precedes you."

"And what is my reputation?"

He made a show of running his eyes up and down her frame. "Intelligent. Stubborn. Well connected, but a scandal to her family. I believe I recall hearing something with a prison in Edinburgh. Good with a needle and thread when it comes to stitches. Terrible handwriting. Thin legs."

"You have not heard that!"

"Oh, haven't I?"

"Well, I've heard about you, as well, Dr. Ferris. They say you're overindulged, arrogant, and another in a long line of precocious medical celebrities too thrilled with their own fame to bother to be any good at their job."

"A 'celebrity'! I thank you, Miss Sinnett."

"It was not intended to be a compliment, Dr. Ferris."

"Simon."

"No."

Simon von Ferris sighed and put his hands into the pockets of his large overcoat. "This is the problem. I came here with a cup of tea, hoping to make a good impression. Somehow we fell off course."

"I believe you insulted me a few times," Hazel said.

"I think what you English mistake for insults are merely honesty. We're much more honest in Sweden. You disguise your insults in politeness. It's much crueler."

"You're finally wrong about something," Hazel said. She took a sip of the tea that Simon had brought; it was strong and tasted like vanilla. She smiled. "You're right about the English in general. But I'm not English. I'm Scots."

"So, we are both foreigners here," he said. "May I join you?" He gestured at a wooden chair next to Hazel's bench. "At least for the cup of tea. And then I promise, I will let you work in peace."

Hazel nodded and Simon sat, content. From one of the many pockets of his overcoat, he pulled an apple and took a large bite with relish.

Hazel laughed. "Did you have that in your coat the entire time?"

"Of course!" Simon said after he swallowed. "One never knows when one might need a snack." He patted his pockets. "Filled with secrets and supplies."

"So that's how someone becomes the personal physician to the King of Great Britain: preparedness."

"That, and understanding how to talk to royalty. They're a species unto themselves." He took another bite of the apple.

Hazel turned so that her body was facing his completely. "Wait. Maybe you can help me."

"More than the tea?"

"With the Princess. She refuses to let me examine her."

"Ah," Simon said. "Yes, I am well aware of the Princess's patterns. She refused to unlock the doors to Warwick House to let me in when they sent me to try to figure out what was wrong with her."

"Just out of curiosity," Hazel said. "What do you think is wrong with her?"

He took another bite of his apple. "God if I know. Could be anything. Am I helping yet?"

"No, but I think you might. How do I talk to royalty, then? It doesn't seem as though she despises me, but I haven't got the chance to really look at her. And I can't have a hope of figuring out what's wrong with her until I can do an actual examination."

Simon paused for a moment and put a finger to his lips while he was thinking. "Have you ever been duck hunting in Venice?"

"Venice?" Hazel didn't want to tell him that she had never left Great Britain, and so she just said, "No. Not yet, I mean."

And then, to Hazel's pleasure and surprise, he just continued talking, without any of the condescending horror of something like *Oh, it's marvelous, you simply must go.* Maybe he was right about English politeness. "You have to get up before dawn," he said. "*Before* before dawn, when the ducks are still asleep. And there are hundreds of them in the lagoons there. Thousands maybe. But you can't start shooting until you've settled into place. And you wait there. Quietly, not moving, for an hour maybe, until the ducks start waking up. And then you find that because you're already there, they're accustomed to you. And then you can shoot."

"Are you comparing treating the Princess to . . . shooting ducks?"

"Only incidentally, but I recognize that the metaphor might not be perfect."

"I already show up every day," Hazel said. "I've spent hours reading in her foyer. I don't think the problem is that she's uncomfortable with me."

"Well, then maybe you need to turn it into a game? Or perhaps," he said, "you simply need to ask her. Has no one told you that being a royal is miserable? They spend all day locked in their gilded cages, waiting for someone to treat them like a real human being and not a piece of porcelain. It's a terrible existence."

"It's hard for me to muster up my sympathy for the people with more money and more land than they know what to do with," Hazel said.

"So you're a revolutionary?" Simon asked.

"Not necessarily," Hazel said. "But I've spent too much time reading the news in Scotland to consider myself a devout monarchist."

"Very wise," Simon said. "I see you've finished your tea. I'll take your cup, and allow you the quiet to do your writing."

"I meant to ask," Hazel said as he reached down and lifted the cup and saucer. "Are the leeches working? On the King?"

Simon shook his head. "No more and no less than anything else. I've learned as I've spent time with King George that even someone without much sympathy for the monarchy will find themselves having sympathy for the man. Good afternoon, Miss Sinnett."

The doctor took long strides toward the door. Hazel had wanted to be alone to work, but now that he was leaving, she found that she wanted him to stay. "Wait!" Hazel said. "I forgot to ask. You've been in London longer than I. Have you ever heard of the Companions to the Death Society?"

Simon cocked his head to the side and ran a finger through his mustache. "Yes. Marie-Anne Lavoisier and her cadre. They like the young and the beautiful and the brilliant. I expect they'll come calling on you any day now."

The name Marie-Anne Lavoisier was familiar to Hazel, but she couldn't quite place it. Hazel wondered which of the figures under rabbit masks she had been that night, running through Pall Mall. "So, I assume you've been invited?" Hazel asked Simon before she could stop herself.

Simon smiled. "I much prefer nights in, and getting a good night's sleep. Drinking tea and reading a book and to bed by nine." He left the infirmary, and though he had taken the cup with Hazel's tea dregs, she could swear that she still smelled the dark, tannic black tea and vanilla long after he was gone.

THE NEXT MORNING, HAZEL WALKED TO WARWICK House carrying three books, a fresh pen, and several

clean sheets of paper. If she would be spending her time waiting for the Princess to be willing to see her, at least she would
be able to use her time productively.

Hazel also brought with her the borrowed medical equipment from Kew, wrapped in a roll of canvas.

When Hazel's trunks had arrived without her medical
bag, she immediately wrote to Hawthornden, asking Iona
to send it along. A few days later, her beloved bag had come,
but Hazel nearly cried when she opened it: the leather was
sopping wet, and the bag's inside was fuzzy with green-gray
mildew. Somewhere on the journey between Edinburgh and
London, her bag had fallen in a puddle and remained there.
The smell was enough to make her gag.

The clasp was rusted and broken. The notebooks she had
kept inside were transformed into useless pulp.

The smell of mold had lingered in her room for days, even
after she had thrown the entire bag away.

Hazel had meant to buy a new medical bag, but she hadn't
found something quite right yet. Before it had been ruined,
her old medical bag in Edinburgh was *perfect*: used enough so
that the leather was soft but not falling apart; large enough to
carry everything she needed but not unwieldy. She spent an
afternoon scouring shops, and the results had been dispirit-
ing. She found a dozen medical bags, each one slightly wrong
in its own way, and all three times the price and nowhere
near as good as the one she used to have.

And so: a canvas roll. For now.

Hazel carried her books in her arms, and she was deciding
which of the books she would begin with when something
caught her eye: a small puff of gray fur lying in the sun, directly in the road.

"Well, hello there," Hazel said, approaching.

The dog had no collar around its neck and no lead, and it rolled onto its back, wriggling in the dust, either unaware of or undisturbed by the fact that a carriage could speed past at any moment. Hazel went closer and saw that the small gray dog, more fluff than animal, was the one she had seen lounging in Princess Charlotte's bed: Edith, or Edwarda. *Edwina*. "I don't think you should be outside all alone, little one," Hazel murmured.

On cue, the Princess appeared in the doorway of Warwick House, her hair undone and wearing only a dressing robe. "Edwina!" she called, distraught. "Come to Mummy!"

The dog's ears pricked up upon hearing her name, and she leapt to all fours, wriggling as if to run farther afield and keep the game going. Before Edwina had the chance to flee, Hazel scooped her up, and arrived at the steps of Warwick House moments later.

"Oh, thank *heavens*!" Charlotte said, tearing Edwina from Hazel's arms. The dog licked her mother's face happily. "I looked everywhere when she wasn't in bed this morning. I looked everywhere and then I thought she might have run out with the footman and I just didn't know what I was going to do if she was gone."

She cooed to the dog in her arms, alternating between chides and words of affection as she strode back toward her bedchamber. She didn't thank Hazel, but she didn't close the door behind her either.

And so, Hazel followed behind, and rather than taking her usual seat in the hallway, she took a seat at the breakfast table in the Princess's room. Eliza burst into the room moments later, her hair disheveled and sweat clinging to her forehead.

"Oh, you *found* her. I was scouring the kitchens."

"She was outside," Princess Charlotte purred, never breaking her attention from the dog in her arms. "And Miss Sinnett found her."

"Oh, well, what do you know," Eliza said. She plopped down in the chair opposite Hazel. The Princess was back under the covers, immersed in her own world with her puppy curled onto her chest and licking at her face. Eliza sighed and turned to Hazel. "Cards?"

Morning became afternoon. Hazel had just lost her third game of whist in a row to Eliza when Princess Charlotte was rousing from a nap and ringing for the maid to bring her tea.

It was a lazy afternoon. The Princess was at ease, grateful to Hazel for returning her dog (even if she hadn't said as much), and comfortable enough with her to at least allow her to sit in her private room. It was a nebulous calculation, made on nothing but intuition, but Hazel decided that the time had come to try to get the Princess to open up to her. She would try a new tactic.

Hazel rose from the table and cleared her throat. Princess Charlotte raised an eyebrow, and Hazel lowered into a small curtsy. "Your Royal Highness, can I be honest for a moment?"

Eliza watched from the corner of the room, her face unchanged but concern creeping into her eyes. Charlotte just shrugged.

"Your father has made it very clear that I need to be able to diagnose whatever is ailing you. If I don't, I'm worried he'll make it difficult for my mother and my brother. *More* difficult. They've already had to deal with the scandal of my refusing an engagement and dressing as a man to study anatomy, and if the Regent thinks I betrayed the Crown, we'll probably have to, I don't know, flee the kingdom. Live on Saint Helena."

"You broke an engagement?" Charlotte asked.

"Last year. My cousin. I had feelings for someone else." And just like that, the thought of Jack came back in a wave that Hazel couldn't stop. She was back at the graveyard with him, in the grave they had just dug, pressing their bodies close together with the smell of earth around them, listening to each other's breath and feeling each other's heartbeats. Back in the Princess's room, the skin on Hazel's arm rose up in goose pimples. "Five minutes, ma'am. That's all I'm asking. Just five minutes, and I can write a report to Gaspar for the Prince Regent."

Hazel held her breath.

"Okay," Charlotte said. "Five minutes."

Eliza looked genuinely surprised. "I'll go ask for a fresh batch of tea."

"No, stay," the Princess said. "Miss Sinnett can go ask for the tea, and she'll examine me when she's back."

HAZEL HADN'T BEEN EXPECTING TO FIND AN obvious giveaway in the Princess's symptoms, but at least now she had something to work from. Charlotte's forehead had been warm, her temperature clearly elevated. A fever, that much was obvious, as was the fact that the Princess complained of fatigue and blurred vision. But the rest of the Princess's examination was completely clear. Her heartbeat was normal. There was no swelling or rashes. There were scars on her back, remnants from the Roman fever that she had survived, but none of the markings were fresh, thank God. The Princess complained of a pain in her stomach, but Hazel felt no stiffness or swelling there.

Altogether, there was nothing in the examination that explained why a twenty-two-year-old woman would be bedridden with a fever for weeks on end. Still, Hazel wrote it all down dutifully, adding the examination to her notebook of observations. She was making progress. Strangely, as she got in her carriage to return to her apartments that evening, the thought entered her head that even though she didn't have the answer yet, she wished she could tell Simon von Ferris about the examination she did that day.

14

A T ELIZA'S INSISTENCE, HAZEL AGREED TO get a new dress for the Regent's ball. "I'm sorry, but you cannot keep wearing what you've *been* wearing," she said, plucking at Hazel's skirt one day. "This hem is an inch too short and the bust is six months out of date."

"I don't even know if I'm going to the ball, Miss Murray," Hazel said. "I have a lot of work I should be doing. I'm here to be treating the Princess, not . . . I don't know . . . doing quadrilles."

Eliza gave her a quick withering look and rolled her eyes. "You're supposed to be treating the Princess, and she'll be at the ball. Done. This is basically in your job description. I don't know why you make it so difficult for me to try to help you have a chance at enjoying yourself."

"Wait. The Princess is going to the ball?" Hazel hadn't seen Charlotte outside her bedchamber, save for the few times they took a promenade around the park nearby. "I wouldn't think her health allows it."

Eliza's mouth became a tight, thin line. "Even Princess Charlotte knows when she has to compromise with her father. He wants her to settle on a husband and be done with it, health be damned." She leaned in, and Hazel mirrored her. "If you ask me, he'd rather just have her married to the Prince of Orange and out of the country for good."

"Why would the Regent want the *Princess* out of the country? She's the most popular royal by far."

"Exactly," Eliza said. "Haven't you noticed the way people line up for her? Cheer her name?" Hazel had. Nearly every day when she arrived at Warwick House, there was a gaggle of well-wishers nearby, shouting up and sending Charlotte best hopes for a quick recovery. "And you've met the Regent. Not to ever speak ill of His Royal Highness"—a smirk—"but there's a man who likes his praise exclusively for himself. The faster Charlotte is out of the country with a husband, the faster people will focus on him, and the faster she has a son, the faster people can forget about her altogether."

"So, she'll be marrying into her own obsolescence."

"Every woman marries into obsolescence," Eliza said. "The things that make us celebrated as young women—being charming, and being coquettish and being clever? In a married woman and mother, all of that becomes desperate and embarrassing, like wearing too much rouge. Even our educations serve no purpose after we're wed. Charlotte and I were tutored in languages and music for the sake of becoming accomplished enough to attract husbands. We'll marry, and become matrons, and then we will raise our sons to make decisions on our behalf."

Hazel recalled the feeling of Bernard proposing to her, of knowing that if she accepted, the rest of her life would follow a narrow and constricted path. Day after day of wearing the right dress and making the right social calls and bearing children and watching as every day, the memory of what she once loved about surgery and human anatomy became fainter and fainter.

"I suppose that's why I have no intention of ever getting married," Hazel said. The thought had just materialized, fully formed, as she said it. She wouldn't get married. She had found a love once, but Jack was gone, and now Hazel would live only on her own terms.

"That's well and good for a female surgeon," Eliza said. "I suppose you're a rare bird in that regard. But Princess Charlotte doesn't have that luxury. Her marriage is a major diplomatic and political event. Bearing an heir is her primary duty to the Crown."

"And so, sick or not, she goes to her father's ball."

Eliza nodded. "Although I can usually find a way to sneak her out of these sorts of things early."

"Okay," Hazel said. "I'll be there." If nothing else, Hazel thought, it would be another chance to observe the Princess, to watch her in public, and continue to note her symptoms. Perhaps treating her would be like duck hunting after all. Hazel would have to wait and watch as the clues that might lead to a diagnosis slowly revealed themselves.

Eliza was still studying the dress Hazel was wearing, frowning as she felt the fabric of the sleeve between her fingers. "You'll go to Mrs. Thire's for a new dress. That's not open for discussion. I'll personally make sure she finishes in time for you."

"I actually had a Mrs. Thire's dress made!" Hazel said in surprise, delighted she could offer something that would please Eliza. "My mother sent my measurements down last year."

"You did?" Eliza said. "Well, that's easy enough, then. Wear that. I have to imagine it's heaps and bounds better than the dresses you've been wearing here. No offense."

What had happened to that dress? She wore it that night at Mercer's house, the evening she was arrested. They had taken her to the jail on the hill in that dress, and she had been wearing it when they forced her to change into the stiff, cotton shift for female prisoners. They probably still had her beautiful marigold dress there, crumpled up into a ball, mildewing in the damp and neglect. "I . . . actually don't have it anymore," Hazel said. "I, uh, lost it."

Eliza blinked slowly. "All right," she said. "In that case, we're back to our original plan. Probably for the best anyway; a months-old dress is embarrassing enough. Worse if you've already worn it out once."

"'Once'?"

"You're in London, my dear Miss Sinnett. Perhaps in Edinburgh, the tartan and simple shifts are considered charming, but you'll see. I'm protecting you. These people will eat you alive if they get the chance."

"And a dress from Mrs. Thire will prevent that?"

Eliza twirled a strand of hair around her finger. "A dress from Mrs. Thire will distract them so you can get the first blow."

Being friends of a friend of the Princess had its advantages: the very next day, Mrs. Thire's atelier squeezed Hazel in for a last-minute fitting with Mrs. Thire herself in a small but handsomely appointed shop with white columns on a fashionable corner near Soho.

"This will have to be quick," Mrs. Thire said by way of greeting, ushering Hazel toward the back of the atelier. "Every young thing in the ton wants a new dress to catch the eye of some dashing soldier, now that they're all back from fighting Napoleon." She spoke with pins in her mouth. "You. Miss Hazel Sinnett. Hawthornden Castle, Edinburgh. I have your measurements somewhere. I never forget a customer." She sized Hazel up with her eyes disapprovingly. "An inch less in the bust now, and we'll need more fullness in the skirt to help disguise those horribly skinny legs. Come." And without Hazel uttering a word, she was swept onto a pedestal so Mrs. Thire could commence with more detailed measurements using a piece of thread she pulled from one of her skirt's many hidden pockets.

Mrs. Thire was a tall woman, around forty years old, but it was difficult to tell exactly. Her dark skin was clear but she had a line forming between her eyebrows that conveyed a sense of intensity and focus. Her curls spilled from her bonnet, and Hazel could see a single streak of gray hair, framing Mrs. Thire's face. The woman studied Hazel with a look of concentration.

"Pink isn't your color," she said. She spoke with a soft accent from somewhere in the Caribbean islands.

"Oh," Hazel replied.

"Blues. Greens. Jewel tones. Bring out your lovely flush. You need to eat more. Drink a glass of champagne at the ball when you get there to get some rosiness in your cheeks." Mrs. Thire spoke as though she were dictating a letter. Hazel wondered if she should be taking notes. "Stay here." She swept away, leaving Hazel standing alone on the pedestal in the back of the room, still wearing the dress she came in with but somehow feeling very, very naked.

Moments later, Mrs. Thire returned carrying a heap of midnight-blue fabric. "We don't have time to do custom, I'm afraid," she said. "But I think this will look lovely. Try it on."

"Here?"

"No, the colonies. *Yes*, here. Hop to it."

And so, feeling more than a little self-conscious, Hazel pulled off the dress she was wearing to her stays, and let Mrs. Thire pull the dark blue dress over her head.

"Yes," Mrs. Thire said. "Yes, this will do much better." And without waiting for Hazel to respond, Mrs. Thire had begun pinching and sewing, lifting the bodice so it fit directly on Hazel's waist and bringing in the bust. Her hands moved so quickly, adding small stitches, pinning in places, that it took Hazel nearly ten minutes of watching Mrs. Thire in action to realize that on her left hand, she only had four fingers. Instead of a pinkie, she had a small pink stretch of scar tissue, shiny as a burn. It was an old wound, Hazel saw, judging from the way the scar tissue had faded to white along the edges, likely from an injury years ago.

"There," Mrs. Thire said, pulling the dress over Hazel's head before she had even had a proper chance to look at herself in the mirror. "I'll do the tailoring, and have it delivered to your apartments next week."

"Thank you," Hazel said. She reached for her purse to pay Mrs. Thire for the dress, but Mrs. Thire waved her off.

"Nothing," she said. "Consider it a gift."

"No," Hazel said. "No, please. I insist."

Mrs. Thire kept her hand raised. "It's a pleasure to be able to dress interesting women, Miss Sinnett. Let alone interesting women who are serving as the personal physicians to the Princess of England." She smiled and Hazel saw a flash of something behind her eyes that didn't entirely look like kindness. She stared too long without blinking, still sizing Hazel up even though she was off the shop's measuring pedestal. "Lovely meeting you in person, Miss Sinnett."

Bells on the top of the atelier's door rang merrily as Hazel walked out onto the street and back toward her carriage. Though the day was warm, she felt a sudden chill she couldn't shake.

THE DRESS ARRIVED THE MORNING OF THE REGENT'S ball, hand-delivered by a footman who hopped off the back of a carriage carrying a large ivory-colored box. The thin paper inside was like spiderwebs, and though Hazel hadn't thought much of the dress when she tried it on at Mrs. Thire's atelier, when she slipped it over her head that afternoon and studied herself in the looking glass, she had to admit there was something magical about it. The dress was blue, but dark as a night sky, woven through with silver thread that glistened as she moved, like starlight. Though the cut had seemed standard—the sleeves were capped at her shoulders and the waist sat high on her bust—when Hazel put it on, she felt transformed. Other gowns had left her feeling like she was playing dress-up: this one felt like her.

Mrs. Thire really was a genius, Hazel thought, swirling the skirt of the dress and watching the way the silver embroidery caught the light from the window. The material was thin and silky, running over Hazel's skin like water. Her last thoughts as she exited her apartments and caught one last glimpse of herself in the mirror: she wished Jack were able to see her in this dress. She wished he had seen her in any fine dress at all. He fell in love with her half-coated in mud, exhausted and blood splattered. In another universe, they would have been able to go hand in hand to a dinner party, with nothing to worry about and no nightmares chasing them. Just the two of them, the pleasure of being clean and wearing fine clothes and of smiling at each other across a crowded ballroom like sharing a secret.

By the time Hazel arrived at Buckingham House, the party was already full, with carriages lined up and down the street and guests in their hand-sewn finery spilling out onto the lawn. In the ballroom, the band was playing something lilting and up-tempo, and the sound of the violins was swirling through the mansion, past the crowds of strangers to Hazel, where she stood wondering where she should go not to feel out of place. There must have been fifty people in the foyer alone, grouped in small clusters, tilting their heads together to gossip. The sound of whispers and the snap of unfurling fans punctuated the music like percussion. Neither Eliza nor the Princess was anywhere to be found. The only face Hazel recognized was Mrs. Thire herself, who was standing close to a woman dressed in French fashion. Hazel waved, but Mrs. Thire offered only a tight smile and nod before returning to her conversation.

And then Hazel saw another face she recognized: Simon von Ferris, standing by the table with the food, and looking as though he'd rather be anywhere else. He was wearing all black, with only a pop of his white shirt visible at his collar.

Hazel approached him. "Dr. Ferris."

"Miss Sinnett."

"I must say," Hazel said, "I'm a little surprised to see you here. I wouldn't have expected this to be your type of evening."

Simon leaned closer so that he was almost whispering in her ear. "And what would you have expected my type of evening to be?"

Hazel pulled away, breaking the electric charge between them. She looked around to see if anyone noticed how close they had gotten; no one was paying them any attention. "What was it that you said the other day? Tea and a good book and an early bedtime."

"In a perfect world," Simon said. "But royal physician is more of a political position than anything else. I have to make my appearances. And I've found that I can be quite good at them. I'm a natural when it comes to charming the upper class."

Hazel choked on a small goat cheese tart. "You have to be kidding me. You were standing over here alone like a petrified child when I came in."

"Maybe I was just waiting. Biding my time."

"For what?"

Simon was silent for a moment. He lowered his eyes to take in Hazel's midnight-blue gown embroidered with silver. "A new dress," he said.

"Is that a compliment?" Hazel said.

"Just an observation."

"Well, for a man of science, I would have expected your methods to be more precise. You've seen me on only, let's see, three occasions. You would have no way of knowing that my dress is new. Conclusions must be drawn from observable factors."

"Ah," Simon said. "You're mistaken. There are a number of

observable factors." He studied the fabric intently, and Hazel felt a flush rising over her cheeks. "The stitches are impeccable, not torn or snagged. The hem is entirely unstained. And there are creases, there"—he ran a finger a centimeter above Hazel's stomach—"and there"—and her upper thigh—"that indicate it was recently pulled from a box. Ergo: new dress." His hand had hovered above her body, almost but not quite touching her dress, but she could feel the electricity of his skin through the fabric. And it lingered after he pulled his hand away.

"Once again," Hazel said, "a male doctor's arrogance has got the better of him. There's no way to know if the dress is *actually* new, or if I merely take excellent care of it. Perhaps I keep it in a box between wearings."

"And then there's the way you're standing in it," Simon said.

"What do you mean?"

"Women always stand differently in a new dress. Taller. Shoulders back. You're glowing. You look beautiful and you know it."

"That is not a scientific observation," Hazel said.

"Isn't it?" Simon replied. "And anyway, there's one way to tell for certain whether it's a new dress or it isn't."

"And what is that?"

"See how it looks when it's dancing." He kept his face so serious, without even a flicker of a smile playing behind his eyes. "Will you do me the honor? For the sake of science?" Simon extended his arm for Hazel to grab. She did and her silver silk gloves were thin enough that it was almost like holding hands.

She could feel the eyeballs on the two of them as they entered the ballroom. Simon didn't seem to notice. He kept his eyes straight ahead and his posture perfectly erect.

"So, is it?" Simon asked as they took their position.

"Is it what?"

"A new dress."

"Yes," Hazel said. "It is a new dress. But your methodology in determining that was still just a lucky guess."

Hazel and Simon faced each other, ready for the dance to begin, and he smiled, wide enough for dimples to appear on his cheeks.

The dancing was interrupted when a group of men arrived at the entrance to the ballroom and everyone turned to look. There was a small fleet of them, probably half a dozen in matching Prussian uniforms: bright red jackets, high boots, and tight white trousers. Their leader was obvious. Though he wasn't the tallest or the most handsome, he had an air of command about him. He stood at the front of the group like a bird at the tip of a flying V formation, with one hip cocked jauntily out to the side. So many medals festooned his jacket that Hazel wondered how he could have found the time to possibly win them all.

"The Prussian prince, I imagine?" she remarked to Simon.

"Frederick Augustus. One of the younger sons of the Prussian heir. A fixture in court since they feted him after the Battle of Leipzig."

He cut a dashing figure, it was impossible to deny, with his hair swept forward and a curling sneer on his lip. The Prince of Orange—Prince Charlotte's former fiancé—was a weedy boy standing in the corner of the room, looking, as Eliza had described, like a prepubescent child. Orange couldn't even grow a mustache; it was just a few pathetic wisps on his upper lip, more a shadow than anything else. Prince Frederick Augustus, in stark contrast, looked like a *man*. No wonder Princess Charlotte had been so quick to end her engagement with the Prince of Orange at the first hint of a fever; Hazel couldn't blame her.

Hazel watched as Prince Frederick Augustus sauntered over toward Eliza Murray, bowed deeply, and kissed her hand. She curtsied and then repeated the greeting to a tan boy with curly hair standing shyly right behind the Prince. Hazel imagined this was Eliza's first lieutenant, and her assumption was proved correct when Eliza came over, escorted by the curly-haired boy.

"Miss Sinnett, may I present you with Lieutenant Otto Anhalt. Lieutenant, this is Miss Hazel Sinnett, a physician treating our Princess Charlotte."

Otto bowed. "The pleasure is all mine."

Hazel smiled at Eliza, hoping that she conveyed his approval. He seemed perfectly nice enough, and relatively good-looking, with a full head of hair and all his teeth.

When Otto rose, he turned to Simon. "Perhaps we can get the ladies some refreshments."

"Absolutely," Simon said, never taking his eyes from Hazel. The men left.

"What do you think?" Eliza said to Hazel. "He's handsome." She said it as a declarative statement, as much to herself as to Hazel.

"He is," Hazel said as reassuringly as she could.

"I think I'm going to marry him," Eliza said. "His service with the Prussian prince is ending next month and he's returning home. He asked me to go with him. His family has an estate, and he does well enough as a soldier, but his family has money. He brings in something like five thousand pounds a year." Hazel didn't reply immediately, and Eliza searched her eyes before just continuing to speak. "It's not as though I can just stay with Princess Charlotte forever. As soon as she's well, she'll get married and move to a new household with a new staff and I'll be even older with even fewer prospects. *No* prospects. I like Otto. I like him quite a bit, and I think that in time I might even love him. He's very kind. *Very* kind. And funny! And he's been very patient with me."

"I think," Hazel said, "he sounds lovely."

Eliza was smiling when the men came back with glasses of champagne.

"Will the Princess be coming this evening?" Otto asked. "I heard she would be attending."

Eliza shook her head. "She's been too ill. Headache this evening." She didn't make eye contact with Hazel. "If you'll excuse me," she said, and slipped through the crowd.

"Have you determined a diagnosis yet?" Simon murmured to Hazel.

"No," Hazel replied. "But I did examine her finally. No distention. No pox, thank God. Not the Roman fever again. She had a fever, and complained about stomach pain and pain in her head. There was redness and swelling around the eyes."

"Headaches and redness around the eyes could be yellow fever. An excess of yellow bile?"

"I thought that, but her skin tone was rosy. Not jaundiced at all. Red if anything."

"Scarlet fever, then?"

"Tongue was completely normal. And no sore throat or swollen glands."

Simon thought for a moment. "Vomiting?" he asked. "Could be typhus."

"No vomiting," Hazel said. "At least none that I know of. The fever is too low for typhus. And it wouldn't explain the stomach pain."

"Pregnancy?" Simon asked with an arched eyebrow. "That would account for the aching and exhaustion."

Hazel shook her head. "She's too closely watched. Miss Murray is with her every moment of the day, and I'm sure her father has the footmen reporting to him as well. A man wouldn't be able to get within a square meter of her. Perhaps it's a disease I haven't seen before. Something rare, perhaps. The thought that really frightens me is that there's something growing beneath her skin that I can't see."

She hadn't said that out loud before, but the fear of it had been keeping her awake at night since the day that she examined Charlotte and found so few physical symptoms. Back in Edinburgh, Hazel had cut open patients and seen tumors as big as oranges, black and pulsing on their organs. What if something was poisoning Charlotte from the inside, and she was missing it? There would be no way of knowing for sure without operating, and she wouldn't ever risk operating on the Princess without already knowing for sure.

It was shockingly enjoyable to talk it out, she realized, thinking aloud in the company of another physician. She hadn't had the chance to talk about medicine or surgery with *anyone* since her brief time at the Anatomists' Society, and back then, there hadn't been real cases to talk about; they were bleary-eyed students excitedly comparing notes on their diagrams. And Hazel hadn't even been Hazel at all, she had been George Hazelton (or had it been George Hazleton?), wearing her brother's clothes. It was nice to be herself, to ask for advice, to have a conversation about medicine with a man who treated her like a peer and not like a peculiarity or a spectacle.

"Hmmm." Simon brought a finger up to his mustache. He brushed it absentmindedly, something Hazel noticed he did when he was nervous or thinking. "There was something an instructor of mine told me in Uppsala, back when I was in medical school. He said that if you hear four hooves galloping in the distance, you should think 'horse' before you think 'camel.'"

From across the ballroom, Hazel watched Prince Frederick Augustus and his men laughing and drinking with their arms draped across each other's shoulders. Eliza stood nearby, gracefully sipping a glass of wine next to Otto.

"So, you mean to say," Hazel said, "that when you're dealing with a medical question that seems confounding, it's more likely a common ailment displaying uncommon symptoms."

"Precisely."

The band began an up-tempo waltz, and without warning, he pulled Hazel in close by the waist, so suddenly she gasped. "This is how the dance begins, yes?" Simon asked.

"I believe so," Hazel replied, and without another word, the two of them were twirling among the throng of dancers.

As a dancer, Simon von Ferris was stiff and formal, his body simply too tall to allow much of what Hazel would have called grace. He never let his posture shrink, never let his elbow drop below precisely where it was meant to be. Simon was so deep in concentration on getting the steps right that Hazel didn't think he was aware of the attention that he was receiving from the ladies on the edges of the ballroom. Hazel watched their eyes flicker over Simon's figure, and saw as they opened their fans to hide their whispers. They wanted him, Hazel realized. When she looked back at Simon's face, he was looking only at her.

The dance ended and the clapping was interrupted by an off-key fanfare announcing the arrival of the Prince Regent. He entered wearing a sour expression and bright red jacket, Gaspar at his side wearing his old-fashioned powdered wig as always. The Regent puffed his chest out and scanned the crowd, apparently unhappy with what he saw, even though the courtiers were bowing low and putting on their most obsequious smiles. He turned to Gaspar to ask something Hazel couldn't hear. Gaspar responded with a shake of his head, and the Prince Regent stormed away, without a single dance.

His entrance and abrupt exit let the air out of the party like a deflating balloon. The energy in the room evaporated, and it was less than an hour later that the rest of the guests began filing out. (Frederick Augustus and his friends seemed unaware of any tension; they were stacking champagne glasses and laughing as the stemware collapsed and shattered on the ground.)

At the edge of the dance floor, Hazel pulled Eliza aside. "Did Charlotte ever consider Prince Frederick Augustus as a husband?"

Eliza shook her head, and looked around to make sure no one had overheard them. "No, God no! Why? What have you heard?"

"Nothing!" Hazel said. "I was just wondering. Him being a prince and all. The appropriate age. And seeming quite . . . you know, sociable."

Eliza shook her head again. "No. Not all princes are *princes*, of the caliber to marry the future Queen of England. Europe is *littered* with princes. Frederick Augustus is relatively low ranking. Not the oldest son. Cadet branch of his family. But that wouldn't even be a problem if it weren't for his reputation. He's a *cad*. Rumors of two children out of wedlock and a dozen heartbreaks in his wake. No," Eliza said, "he's a soldier and he'll traipse around Europe making women fall in love with him until his father forces him to settle down for a paltry inheritance. There is an exceedingly limited number of potential suitors available to Princess Charlotte, a fact of which she is well aware. Besides, I think he's already engaged. To some Austrian duchess or another. Poor thing. That's why he's leaving next month and Otto is going home. Frederick Augustus has finally run out his father's patience and he's being shipped off to his bride. She'll have to spend the rest of her life watching him gamble through their fortune." Eliza and Charlotte turned to watch the prince kiss up the arm of a giggling blonde. "Charming," Eliza said. "Now, if you'll excuse me, I have to make sure the Princess gets her infusion before bed."

The party was dissolving around them, and Hazel turned to say goodbye to Simon, to thank him for the dance and for the advice with Charlotte's diagnosis and for altogether making the evening far more pleasant than it would have been without his company, but he was gone. He had disappeared into the crowd, or left while Hazel was talking to Eliza.

It left Hazel feeling like the evening was an unfinished melody, a song played until its final stanza and then suspended, the tension of it palpable.

Behind her, Buckingham House was lit by lanterns in the windows, a ghostly bubble of light against the inky black grass of St. James's Park that extended, velvety, before it. The evening was pleasant, and Hazel decided she would walk home, first through the park and then following the dark ribbon of the Thames until she reached her apartments. She was energized when she arrived, buzzing from the cold night air and the red wine she had drank. Scenes from the evening replayed in her head as she undressed, neatly folding the dress that Simon had known was brand new.

A smile extended across her face. In that moment, Hazel became sure of something that had up until that point been only a nagging question, a suspicion. She finally knew what was wrong with the Princess. Her diagnosis was certain, and she saw it, in that moment, with complete and utter overwhelming clarity.

Hazel was so caught up in her thoughts about Princess Charlotte that she almost didn't notice that an envelope had been placed on her pillow.

No one was in the room, and no one had been outside on the street. She wondered when it was delivered, and *how* it had been delivered so intimately.

The envelope was thick and bloodred, and sealed with red wax stamped in the shape of a human brain. It was addressed in red ink almost invisible on the envelope but for the way it glistened in the candlelight.

Her name was on the front of the envelope, written in perfect script: *Miss Hazel Sinnett.*

15

THERE WAS NO LETTER INSIDE THE RED
envelope, just a slip of paper with no signature, written in the same perfect and even script as Hazel's name. It was a poem and a riddle and an invitation wrapped in one, and Hazel read the lines first to herself, and then out loud so that she could feel them in her mouth.

Where there once were six but claimed seven
And a great lion is white
If you can Pierce the veil, find the mind
Eleven p.m., Thursday night

It was an invitation to the Companions to the Death, she was almost sure of it; or at least, an invitation contingent on her ability to solve its riddle. (For a fleeting moment, Hazel was titillated and scandalized in equal measure with the thought of Lord Byron himself having come into her bedroom to deliver the invitation.)

As for actually figuring out where the rhyme was leading

her, Hazel imagined it would have been easier if she were more familiar with London geography. There was probably a white lion sculpture somewhere of marble, maybe six of them of varying sizes. Or maybe "six" was a street address, and she was looking for Number 6 on a Seventh Avenue, or something of the like.

It was intriguing, but before Hazel could spend too long wrestling with it (*surely there's a city map lying somewhere around here*), another letter was delivered, this time in person.

Gaspar bowed deeply when he handed her the letter, and though Hazel greeted him warmly, when he rose, his face was stony. "The Regent is not a patient man," he said.

Hazel broke the royal seal on the envelope and quickly scanned through the letter's brief lines.

Miss Sinnett.

I was much dismayed to find the Princess not present at the revelry tonight. If Charlotte is too unwell to attend the fete that will be thrown to honor Sir Robert Mends on his promotion to Commodore in three weeks' time, consider your position terminated.

His Royal Highness,
George, Prince Regent

Gaspar studied Hazel's eyes as she read. "Are you in trouble?" he asked hesitantly. "The Regent . . . didn't seem happy."

"If I had to guess," Hazel said, "the Regent is a man who is never happy. I'm not in trouble. I've merely been given a deadline."

"And . . . that's not going to be trouble?"

"No," Hazel said. "Not when you know what you're doing."

HARLOTTE WAS IN A FOUL MOOD THE NEXT morning when Hazel arrived. She stormed into the Princess's bedchambers above Eliza's protests. "She's resting! She doesn't want company! She doesn't even want *me* in her bedchamber!"

The curtains were drawn in the Princess's room, and it was oppressively warm, with a fire roaring in the grate despite the pleasantly sunny spring day outside. The bedroom had become a damp, humid cave, and Hazel offered only the briefest curtsy out of courtesy before standing square before the Princess and saying, "I know what's wrong with you."

The Princess had been lying on a small barge of pillows with her arm draped across her eyes to block out any of the light remaining in the dim room. Suddenly, she sat up and looked at Hazel.

"What do you mean? I mean, what is it?"

"I know what's wrong with you," Hazel said once more.

The two women held each other's eyes for a beat before Charlotte reclined again. "Well, that would be a surprise. My father has had a dozen of the world's top physicians come through, and they've treated me for everything. Headaches and humors out of order. I've been leeched and drained and cut. Whatever cure you have planned for me, I won't promise to go through with it until I hear what it'll be. So, what'll it be? A tonic? Cupping? Don't tell me bleeding; they've tried bleeding, and I despise it. Makes me hungry."

Hazel shook her head. "No need for any of that," she said.

"Oh?"

"No," Hazel said.

The Princess fluffed her pillow. "Well, then I would love to hear how you're planning on healing me."

"I won't be healing you," Hazel said. "Because there's nothing wrong with you at all. You've been faking it."

Princess Charlotte's mouth opened and then closed again. She clenched her teeth and glanced around, Eliza was out: it was just the two of them in the room, the silence broken only by the crackling pops of the fireplace. Hazel refused to break eye contact.

Finally, the Princess spoke. "Why would I fake an illness?" she said softly, her face a blank mask.

"Because," Hazel said, careful to keep her voice even, "a princess who is ill can postpone a wedding to the Prince of Orange, and then cancel the engagement altogether. And then if a princess finds herself too ill to find another husband, maybe she can even put off getting married altogether." Hazel's heart was pounding; she was watching the Princess's face carefully, but Charlotte remained fully impassive. "Because maybe the princess is in love with someone she can't be with. And if she fakes an illness, she won't have to go to dinners or parties or balls and see that person about to marry someone else. If she's ill, she can remain in bed, with her curtains closed to the world, and stay in that place where there was the hope of being with the person she loves."

The part Hazel didn't say to the Princess was that she knew what it was like. After Jack's death, Hazel retreated into her work, into the dungeon laboratory below Hawthornden, where days and nights blended together. Time passing felt like a betrayal of him, of his memory; that she should live to see more days without him, that she should go on when he was gone. Hazel didn't feign illness; she began her treatise. She had hidden in her work because every time she was out in the world, she wondered what it would have been like if Jack had been there at her side.

Princess Charlotte smoothed her blanket on the bed carefully, looking at her hands. "What are you going to do?" she said quietly, finally.

Hazel exhaled. She moved to the seat next to Charlotte's bed, where Eliza usually sat to read to her. On the table was a copy of *Sense and Sensibility*. "I read that!" Hazel said.

Charlotte smiled. "One of my favorites," she said. "I've read it a dozen times. Have you read the others the author has written?"

Hazel shook her head. "I admit, I never quite went in for fiction. I mostly read medical texts, and the history books I used to borrow from my father's library. My mother had that one lying around, though. I don't actually think she read it. In fact, I'm certain she never read it. I cut the pages."

"I always saw myself as Marianne."

Hazel struggled to distinguish the book's two sisters in her memory. "Romantic, and impetuous," Hazel said.

Charlotte just smiled. "But learns how to be sensible in the end," she said.

"How long were you planning on being ill for?" Hazel asked.

"I don't know," Charlotte says. "How long does heartbreak last? Because I'm not faking it, Miss Sinnett. Not really. I feel it as real as any illness. The pain in my heart and in my stomach. The way my entire body feels ready to betray me at a moment's notice, how I might burst into tears at the sight of anything: flowers, or a mother and child, or strangers embracing. It's as real as any of the illnesses my father's doctors have diagnosed me with, except there's no tonic I can take to cure it. There is nothing a physician can do to make me feel better."

"No," Hazel said. "There's nothing I can give you to take away the pain." If there were, Hazel thought, she would have taken it herself long ago.

Charlotte sat up in bed and turned so that she was facing Hazel, eye to eye. She raised a perfectly manicured eyebrow. "Are you going to tell my father?"

"How about we make a deal?" Hazel said. She reached into her pocket to fish out the letter she had gotten that morning from the Prince Regent. "I won't tell him about your 'illness' if you'll find yourself with enough energy to muster attending"—she consulted the letter—"the party for Sir Robert Mends's promotion."

"And what about after that?" Princess Charlotte asked.

"I don't know," Hazel replied honestly. "It buys us some time, though, doesn't it? Maybe I'll find the cure for a broken heart between now and then."

Charlotte smiled and wiped a tear from dropping. "I admit it's something of a relief, to have you know. Eliza was going to faint from exhaustion from having to fetch a fresh hot water bottle before every time you wanted to feel my forehead." She lowered her eyes to the ground and saw a crimson envelope on the embroidered rug. "What's that?"

The letter from the Companions to the Death had fallen

from Hazel's pocket when she retrieved the Regent's letter. Hazel hastened to pick it up, but Charlotte beat her to it.

"Ooooh," the Princess said. "A riddle, is it? 'Where there are six but claim seven / And a great lion is white ...'" What are they doing at the Seven Dials?"

"What?" Now Hazel was surprised. "What in heaven's name is the Seven Dials?"

"It's, well, it's a corner. There used to be a big tower, with six sundials there, in the center where the streets meet. Near Covent Garden."

"If there are six sundials," Hazel said, reeling, "why is it called Seven Dials?"

"Well, I don't actually know," Princess Charlotte said, shrugging. "I guess the tower itself was considered the seventh. 'Where there are six but claim seven.' They took the tower down some years back, I think, but that's the reason the area is called Seven Dials. But you already know this, of course. You got the invitation."

"No," Hazel said. "I didn't know it!"

"I thought you were supposed to be intelligent to be a physician."

"I'm better with the map of a human body than I am with London city streets, I suppose," Hazel said.

Charlotte shrugged. "If you say so."

"What about the rest of it? Is there a lion statue there, too, then?"

Charlotte scanned the poem again. "'Great lion is white.' Great White Lion Street is one of the streets there. Pierce was the architect. Designed the tower. Famous sculptor. I'm surprised you don't know this stuff, feels very obvious to me."

"Humor me," Hazel said. "What about the last part—'find the mind'?"

"I don't know. Maybe some sort of signpost or drawing. But the rest of it couldn't be clearer."

"I'm gleaning that."

Charlotte grinned and rang a bell hanging on the wall near her bed. Moments later, a maid opened the door and entered with a small curtsy.

"Tea for me and for Dr. Sinnett, please, Susan," Princess Charlotte said. The maid curtsied again and slipped soundlessly out the door.

"It's just Miss, actually," Hazel said. "I'm a surgeon. And, to be completely honest with you, I never actually passed the Royal Examination."

"You went to anatomy classes, didn't you?" Charlotte asked. Hazel nodded. "It's like I told you before," Charlotte continued. "A dozen men with spectacles and more royal certifications than they knew what to do with poked and prodded me for months on end, and not one of them actually figured out what was wrong with me. Royal Examination be damned. You're a doctor, Hazel Sinnett, whatever else you want to call yourself."

16

ROM THE BIRD'S-EYE VIEW, SEVEN DIALS WAS
made up of converging streets all coming together,
dividing the map into triangles. Though it was only
steps away from the gleaming white stone of Covent Garden,
the second Hazel turned down the narrow lane toward her
destination, she could feel the air change. This was a place of
beggars and thieves, where women with kerchiefs wrapped
around their heads coughed into their sleeves and the sound
of crying children echoed from the thin-walled apartments.
Leering men were gathered on the empty plinth where Hazel
imagined the tower and its sundials once stood, and Hazel
pulled the collar of her cloak up as high as she could to block
her face while she walked fast.

She had assumed that the riddle was from the Companions to the Death, but it was also possible that this was some
sort of trap. The note could have been sent from dangerous
people, trying to use her to get to the Princess or punish her
for having gotten out of Calton Gaol. (It was also possible, Hazel reasoned, that for all their social status, the Companions

to the Death could still be dangerous.) Hazel was a woman alone, walking through a dark neighborhood to an unknown destination. If she had been a stranger, she would have called herself a fool.

But charlatans and constables rarely went in for poetry, she reasoned to herself as she walked. And she kept a scalpel in her pocket just in case, as ready for use in self-defense as it was for surgery. And there was something driving her footsteps more forcefully than reason: curiosity. Hazel would never have been able to sleep if she had ignored the letter. Something strange and interesting was happening in the city, and now she was desperate to become a part of it.

She had left her apartments at half past ten, when the night was already dark. At least the area around her residence had been lit with gas lamps. Here, the only light was the flickering reflections of candles in windows and pubs with lanterns above their doors.

All in all, it didn't seem like the type of neighborhood that a distinguished social club would frequent, but, yes, there it was, Great White Lion Street, and just a few feet from the corner was a black door, highly polished as a mirror and well maintained, with a gilded doorknob that looked out of place in the shabby surroundings. Above the black door there was a small swinging wooden sign, so small that Hazel wouldn't have noticed it if she hadn't been looking for it. It was a sign with no words, just a symbol, the same symbol that had been pressed into the wax to seal her invitation: a brain.

This was the place. It had to be.

She knocked tentatively and then tried the doorknob. It was locked.

It *had* to be the place. Dismayed, Hazel tried again. Still locked. She pulled the invitation from her pocket and compared the seal to the symbol on the sign: exactly the same design of a brain, its two lobes clearly demarcated, laced with a few bold swirls. It *was* the place. And yet, the door was locked. Hazel looked around. Was there another riddle she needed to solve? She sighed and leaned against the wall. A passing beggar gave her a toothless smile, and Hazel wondered whether she should just go home. Church bells nearby rang out, hollow, metallic clanging: eleven times in a row. As the sound of the final ring was evaporating in the night air, Hazel faced the door and tried the knob one last time. This time, the knob turned easily. The door unlocked at eleven o'clock, on the dot.

Hazel pulled the door open, her greeting and thanks for whoever had unlocked it already on her tongue, but to her surprise no one was there. The door opened to reveal nothing more than a staircase, descending into blackness, with no torches or candles visible. By three steps down, the light from the street had faded completely; the stairs led completely into the dark.

For a breath, Hazel hesitated. But only for a breath. She had disguised herself as a man and dissected corpses, dug graves and stolen bodies, faced an immortal doctor who had threatened to cut the heart out of the boy she loved. She had been in love, and she lost him and learned how to be alone again. Hazel could handle a dark flight of stairs.

Still, she took the steps gingerly, aware that she didn't know how long she might be falling if she happened to lose her balance.

A gust of wind swept the door shut behind her as soon as she was past the threshold, and without warning, the darkness became complete.

If this was a trap, Hazel thought, it was too late for her to turn back. They had trapped her. The only way out was forward.

Hazel rested her fingers on the scalpel in her pocket.

It was getting colder now with every step, and Hazel could no longer hear the shouts and laughter coming from the street; the only sounds were her footsteps and the distant drip of water somewhere. Instinctively, Hazel extended both her hands in front of her so that her fingertips would know before her face if the stairs ended in a sharp turn or brick wall.

Her ears pricked at every sound. Was someone sneaking up behind her? Hazel almost turned, but then forced herself to continue on. If she turned, she realized, she might become disoriented in the dark.

"You're not going to be able to sneak up on me," Hazel said aloud, her voice distorted strangely by the stairwell.

There was no reply.

And then, after Hazel had descended what felt like a hundred stairs, just as she was deciding whether she should turn back, a sliver of light appeared in front of her. A room, brightly lit with candles, and a shadowy figure standing in a doorway.

"Welcome," the female voice said. "How glad we are that you made it."

Hazel felt as though she were sleepwalking. She followed the voice and the sliver of light into what appeared at first glance to be a pub. But, no, it wasn't a pub. Though there were tables, and about a dozen people sitting around them, they weren't sitting on barstools or benches: they reclined on overstuffed leather chairs and settee couches upholstered in fine velvets. Most of them were chatting or talking, barely acknowledging Hazel's arrival.

Hazel's eyes adjusted to the new light and she saw that nearly every available inch of wall space was covered by paintings. More paintings, unhung, sat on the floor, resting at an angle against the walls, in some places stacked three deep. On the ceiling, a chandelier twinkled with the light of a hundred candles. A fireplace burned cheerily behind an ornate grate, with an antique silver pistol mounted above.

Hazel turned her attention to her hostess, a woman of about thirty-five, with a sharp, intelligent face. The woman raised a clever eyebrow. "I am Marie-Anne Lavoisier," she said in a voice like water running over rocks.

After Eliza had mentioned the name, Hazel went back into her books to remind herself why it sounded so familiar. "Lavoisier . . ." Hazel said. "The *chemist?*"

The small bubble of fear that had been inflating in Hazel's chest began to release.

Marie-Anne gave a small, humble nod of the head. "The very same. And I'm sure you've discovered who we are by now?" she said.

"Companions to the Death," Hazel said. "A clever name. The name that Cleopatra and Marc Antony used for their drinking society."

The seated cohort behind Marie-Anne had been distracted, but a few faces turned toward Hazel, pleased, and Hazel swelled a little with the pride of answering a question correctly.

"She's a surgeon *and* she's read Pliny the Younger," Marie-Anne said. "How charming."

"I assume it's gallows humor on your part," Hazel continued. "Cleopatra and Marc Antony renamed their society only when Octavius's invasion was inevitable. When death was at the gates."

Marie-Anne smiled without showing her teeth. "Indeed." She swept her arm toward the vast room behind them, and Hazel noticed that in addition to the portraits filling the walls, there were stacks of books covering nearly every flat surface: tables, bare stretches of floor, even balancing on a tea tray, being used as a plate for a few bites of shortbread cookies.

"Am I being invited to become a member, then?" Hazel asked Marie-Anne.

"Possibly," she replied.

A Black man wearing a large fur hat swept up behind Marie-Anne and threw his arm gregariously around her shoulders. "Are you going to introduce me to this beautiful woman, or do I have to do everything myself?" he chided her before extending a large calloused hand to Hazel directly. "Benjamin Banneker. Mathematician. Astronomer. Naturalist. Privately, I'm also something of a poet." He spoke with a broad, friendly American accent. Hazel liked him immediately.

Hazel smiled and shook his hand while a voice called from the back of the room: "Stop calling yourself a poet, Banneker. One of these days someone will believe you." The second man swaggered to standing, and Hazel knew who he was without introduction. The dark curls swept over his forehead and his curled lip were famous.

"Oh, come off it, Byron," Banneker called back. "Not everyone writes poetry in order to become famous."

"No," Byron retorted. "Some get into it to make the rest of us look better. Thank you for that, by the way."

"Excuse my *friend*," Banneker said to Hazel. "He believes fame excuses a lack of manners."

"Quite the contrary, Banneker," Byron said, swaggering forward. He eyed Hazel but then lost interest and returned his attention to Banneker. "I believe fame turns a lack of manners into charming idiosyncrasy. Really, it's a gift I give to high society. I come in, do or say something outrageous, and the rest of them get to spend the rest of their lives *preening* on about the *simply audacious* behavior of Lord Byron. It's the real reason I get invited to those parties."

"You are invited to those parties," Banneker said, "because you are sleeping with the hostesses."

Byron grabbed a piece of shortbread that was resting on the cover of a book and deposited it onto his extended tongue. "That too," he said, grinning. He nodded at Hazel and returned to his table, where he drained a waiting goblet of wine.

"Your ego is a distraction," said a small man sitting at Byron's table. He spoke with a thick French accent. "Imagine what you might have to say if your talent weren't wasted getting women to forgo their marital vows to get into bed with you."

"And who says that's not a worthwhile pursuit, *François*?" Byron sneered the man's name. "Poetry is born out of lust! Emotion! Sentiment! See, that's your problem. You're moralizing again. You *always* moralize."

In her entire life, Hazel had never been in a room quite like this one. It reminded her in some ways of the salons her uncle used to hold at Almont House in Edinburgh, where he would invite authors and politicians to lecture guests, and Hazel—too young to be allowed to attend—would hide beneath chairs or behind couches to hear what was happening. To feel as though she were a *part* of a world filled with ideas and philosophy and art. But her uncle's drawing room had been stoic and dignified, guests sitting quietly in their hard-back chairs and clapping on cue. This was something else entirely, the type of place where people spoke loudly and passionately. She liked it immensely.

"Ignore him," Banneker said, ushering Hazel toward a table and pouring her a glass of wine. "I usually do." There were two other people already sitting at the table, in the middle of a game of cards: a man with a high ruffled neckline that reached his chin, and—

"Mrs. Thire!"

The seamstress smiled at Hazel. "Hello, Miss Sinnett. I heard the midnight-blue dress looked divine on you."

"I had no idea you were involved in . . . this."

Mrs. Thire shrugged and ran her long fingers along the fanned cards in her hand. Hazel noticed again that her left hand was missing its pinkie finger. "The whole point of a secret society, in theory, is to be secret."

Banneker pulled a chair up to join them. "And no one knows more gossip than the woman who sews everyone's dresses."

Mrs. Thire lowered her cards onto the table with a flourish. "Is it my fault that people want to tell their secrets to someone they don't think is listening?" To her cards companion, the man with the ruffled collar, she smiled. "I win. Again."

The man in the ruffled collar rolled his eyes.

"Antoine is bitter because he hasn't won a hand in a year,"

Mrs. Thire said. "And he likes to think he's so much smarter than me." Antoine—in the ruffled collar—silently frowned. "It's true!" Mrs. Thire said of his pout, and Hazel realized that Antoine was mute.

From somewhere in the room, the notes of a pianoforte played beneath the sound of conversation. The candles seemed to flicker in rhythm. The room had a *scent*, a specific smell that felt familiar to Hazel, but she couldn't quite place it. It was the smell of the earth before a thunderstorm, before it started raining, but when the air was thick with electricity.

Banneker squared his body toward Hazel's. "So, you've already met Mrs. Thire. And Antoine there—hello, yes. And you met me, Marie-Anne. Byron, unfortunately . . . Who else? Let's see . . . Ah! Lewis!"

Over the next hour, Hazel made the acquaintance of another half dozen members of the Companions to the Death, a group that included two members of Parliament, a finance minister, and a woman named Élisabeth, who Hazel gleaned was a former court painter at Versailles. ("Marie Antoinette's personal portrait painter," Banneker whispered. "But *don't* ask her about it. Just makes her upset.")

And the Companions, Hazel learned, collaborated on projects that were prestigious and exciting. Lord Byron had helped write the lyrics for an opera for one of the members, a celebrated French soprano. Another of the members had been the chief architect for the remodeling of the palace at Kew, and had enlisted Marie-Anne as a chemist to help dye the wallpaper of the King's chambers a color that no one else would have.

"How was it that you and your husband actually discovered the nature of combustion?" Hazel asked Marie-Anne when she had managed to dislodge herself from another introduction and talk to the famed chemist one-on-one. "What sort of setup, I mean. To prevent the fire from igniting the equipment?"

Marie-Anne laughed. "Well, fire prevention was something we became masters of only *after* Antoine had burned off both of my eyebrows. Both! They never grew back the same, but at least they grew back."

Hazel laughed and Banneker elbowed his way into the chair next to her.

"Tell me more about the treatise you're working on, Miss Sinnett," Banneker said. "I don't mean to boast, but I *did* manage to complete several very well-regarded almanacs, and if you have questions about publishing, I'm sure I can oblige—"

Byron turned. "Yes, Benjamin. I'm sure out of *all of us here*, she'll most want the publishing advice of an American farmer."

"Cruelty doesn't suit you, Byron," the Frenchman at Byron's table said. "It makes your complexion sallow. Perhaps if we can't appeal to your goodness, we can at least appeal to your vanity." Byron spun his attention back to his table, leaving Banneker with his mouth still hanging open from a delayed attempt to respond to Byron's insult.

"How long have you been in the Companions?" Hazel asked Banneker, attempting to diffuse the tension.

Banneker visibly relaxed. "Now, let's see. Decades, at least." He looked off into the distance, as if lost in memory. "I first came to France before the Revolution. To meet Antoine, of course. That must have been, what, 1771? I was calculating a solar eclipse, and the Lavoisiers were the only ones in Europe with the right equipment. It was like a miracle, coming from the Province of Maryland, where I had to build everything by hand out of wood and twine and whatever spare parts I could manage, and then seeing *their* laboratory. Gilded! The amount of glass alone! I thought I had died on the voyage over.

"I returned to Maryland to settle my affairs, but from that moment on, I knew I would not stay in America. Or the colonies, as it had been then. I stayed on my farm through the revolutions in France and then the revolution in America, and—oh heavens, must have been 1804 that I left America for good and found Marie-Anne in London." He leaned in close to Hazel. "It was easier for me than most. I never married, never had children. That complicates things. I was a man of science simply trying to do my work, but in a country enslaving and killing people who look like me. I knew without a doubt that the future would be kinder to me than the present."

"The future—living in Europe, you mean," Hazel said.

"Detestable," Mrs. Thire chimed in. "That America pretends to be a child of the Enlightenment and they still have people working as chattel. As property. They demanded liberation from the British Empire—for what? For freedom? If they had still been colonies of England, slavery would have been banned there a decade ago, same as the rest of the Empire."

One of the Whig politicians whose name Hazel couldn't recall pounded a walking stick on the ground. "Hear, hear! Thank heavens for Mends and the West Africa Squadron, that's all I have to say. We'll be sending him back out with our best ships and best men."

Banneker noticed Hazel's furrowed brow. "It's a British squadron of ships stationed off the coast of Africa, to intercept slavers," he murmured. "Won't do anything to stop the slavery that is *still* happening there, but at least it does something."

"Abolition is the goal," Marie-Anne said. "First, we have to secure a Whig majority here. Our conservative government will always feel that our trade relationship with those slavers in America is too valuable to jeopardize. We'll need more weapons in our diplomatic arsenal, so to speak. When Princess Charlotte is on the throne, this will all be much easier."

There were murmurs of agreement.

"Miss Sinnett," Banneker said, "I'd be fascinated to hear your opinion on a simple matter. Why do you think it is that women in Philadelphia are already studying in medical schools but it's not yet permitted in Britain?" He looked right at her, straight into her eyes, expectantly.

Hazel thought for a moment. "A young country has fewer traditions. Fewer rules. The social rules we've established here, in England and Scotland, have been in place for centuries. We're settled in our ways. They're rewriting the rules as they go. Although from what I've read, I'd venture to say they're not quite so distanced from English traditions as they might seem to think."

"Yes! Well said!" said one of the Whigs.

"Every American thinks of themselves as a grand adventurer," another of the politicians remarked. "Without a monarchy, they're left to feel as though each one of them might be a king of their own making. Or queen, in this case."

The conversation continued, and a warmth began to radiate from Hazel's belly. It was a rare gift, Hazel thought, to be surrounded by intelligent people who actually cared what you had to say.

From the time Hazel was a child, she had accepted that her life was meant to be lived on the periphery. Her family's status was respectable but not spectacular; they might be granted access to important people, *famous* people, the people making decisions, but the Sinnetts were not those people themselves. But beyond that, Hazel was a woman. Governesses had taught Hazel that if women were to influence the world at all, it was through the ability to help and support their husbands. Women might be present at dinner parties, but unless the subject landed on the price of dress fabric or the choice of colors for curtains, they were expected to be silent.

If a woman had any hope at all of living in the rarefied world of art or poetry, it was to be beautiful enough for a man to choose her as a muse. A muse was celebrated, sure, praised and feted, but she existed entirely at the mercy of her artist, who was placing her high on a pedestal so small it didn't allow her to move more than a step in either direction lest she fall.

Hazel was aware that her family name and her negligent mother had left a crack in the system that she had exploited in order to become a surgeon, but it was a thin and narrow crack, too precarious for Hazel to believe her own position was secure, let alone imagine another woman able to follow behind her. Hazel's existence as a female surgeon was an oddity that society seemed willing to tolerate for the time being, and nothing more.

But this room, the Companions . . . they promised an entirely new future. A different society. Here, the women drank openly and swore, and beat men at cards. Marie-Anne was the *leader*, respected not because she was beautiful or charming but because she was brilliant. Women were not objects on a shelf waiting to be selected for marriage; they were as much a part of the society as the men at their sides.

A plate of shortbread passed by, and Hazel gratefully accepted a biscuit. It was impossibly buttery, and dissolved to nothingness on her tongue in an instant. She took another.

And just as Hazel was settling into her leather seat, from across the room came the screech of wood on wood and then the thud of a chair hitting the floor. Byron had stood up and shoved his seat to the ground, caught up in an argument with the Frenchman. "Just like you to dismiss feelings just because you can't measure them!" he shouted.

"The world is measurable, much as you seem loath to admit it," his companion with the French accent replied. "Even a poem is measurable. Meter, rhyme, pacing. Do you diminish your own art by pretending as though it's assembled at random? Mere *feeling* devoid of skill?"

Byron spewed, "But *beauty* is not measurable. The sublime is not measurable. I'm sorry, *Voltaire*, that you can't come up with a pithy line to explain what happens to the soul when it beholds a mountain. Or, yes, a beautiful woman."

The Frenchman shook his head. "You're a fool, Byron. And you will continue to fumble through this world blind to everything but your own ego until you recognize that."

Without warning, Byron pulled the silver pistol that was mounted above the fireplace, cocked it, and before Hazel could scream, fired it directly into the chest of the man still sitting across the table from him.

17

HE SOUND OF THE GUNSHOT HAD QUIETED the room. Byron blew the smoke from the pistol and deposited it back onto its mounting. The Frenchman had fallen from his chair and was clutching at his bleeding shoulder. Hazel sprang into action. "I need clean cloth and a basin of water! Scissors, thread, and a needle. And surgical tongs. Quickly! Or tweezers. Does anyone have tweezers?"

She wished she had brought more than her scalpel, but how could she have known her medical equipment would be needed? She rushed over to the Frenchman's side and tried to staunch the bleeding with her hand. The bullet had gone straight through him, below his right shoulder, and mercifully the entrance and exit wounds had missed his vital organs. But he was already losing blood. The man was pale, his lips flapping soundlessly, his wig slipping from his head. If she couldn't sew the wound closed quickly enough, she might need to amputate the arm entirely. No one else in the room seemed the least bit concerned that a man had just been shot in front of them. Byron was sitting again, his boots up on a table. "Please!" Hazel shouted. "Somebody, a needle and thread at least!" To the dying man, she whispered, "You're going to be okay."

"You heard her," Marie-Anne said with nowhere near enough urgency. "A needle and thread for our physician."

Mrs. Thire obliged, and walked over to Hazel, giving her what she needed, and Hazel set out to work as rapidly as she could. She used her own dress to staunch the bleeding, and then set about repairing as much of the shredded tissue as she could. Byron watched her work from the corner of his eye, but Hazel paid him no attention. Her focus was on closing the open veins, and stopping the internal bleeding, and then sewing up the wounds on both the front and back of his shoulder. "You'll be okay," she whispered to the man periodically to comfort him. He winced when her needle entered his flesh, but otherwise, he showed no signs of being in pain. His eyes remained clear and open. He blinked, watching Hazel work. When she finally finished stitching his wounds, she held his left hand in hers and gave his a comforting squeeze. "You're going to be okay," she said one final time. She realized then, that like Mrs. Thire, his left hand had only four fingers.

The Frenchman rose and moved his shoulder. "Well done," he said, swinging his arm in big circles. "Feels like everything is more or less in the right spot."

"You really shouldn't be moving it like that," Hazel said. "You . . . you were just shot. You lost a lot of blood. You need to rest."

Mrs. Thire came over and examined the stitches. "She really did do an excellent job. Even stitching. Small. Probably won't scar."

"Feels wonderful," the Frenchman said, still swinging his arm.

"You really need to stop that," Hazel said.

"Look," Byron called over Hazel's head. "I'm sorry I shot you, all right? But you *know* I get excited about this sort of thing."

The Frenchman didn't look angry at Byron at all. In fact, he smiled. "See? When you fail to find a way to win an argument through *reason,* you resort to violence. Much of the problem with what we're seeing in Russia at the moment."

"Oh, don't compare me to those backwater Orthodox peasants!" Byron replied. "Banneker, you've been there. What's it like? Terrible? Cold? Starving?"

"Actually," Banneker said, wiping some blood from the bottom of his boot. "I found it quite cosmopolitan. At least in Saint Petersburg."

"I remind you *all,*" the Frenchman said, "I was an honorary member of the Russian Academy of Sciences by the empress's *personal command.* I think I have a few of her letters here somewhere. . . ." He lifted a tall stack of books onto the table that had been at risk of being stained by the expanding pool of blood on the floor and began rummaging through them.

"I'm sorry," Hazel said. "Everyone needs to stop talking about Russia for a moment. This man was *just* shot."

The room stared at her, and all at once, Hazel was able to place the peculiar smell in the room. It was a scent from sitting across from Dr. Beecham in the study of the Anatomists' Society in Edinburgh. A smell of electricity in the air that lingered at the back of one's throat. Hazel looked around at

Marie-Anne, Benjamin Banneker, and Byron; they were all missing the smallest finger on their left hands.

Hazel tried to recall Banneker's story. What year had he said he came to Europe? How old had he been then? Byron, Banneker, Lavoisier . . . "You're immortal," she whispered. "You've all done what he did—what Dr. Beecham did."

Banneker clapped Hazel on the shoulder. "Well done, you," he said. He looked around at the assembled group. "I think that's a record, isn't it? Putting two and two together before we even finished a bottle of wine?"

"It's cheating," Byron said, shortbread crumbs spewing from his mouth. "She knew Beecham. She had context. Makes it easier."

Banneker scoffed. "I had to pull my heart full out and put it back before you believed it, Byron."

"As if Byron had ever been enticed by the offer of anyone's heart," the Frenchman said.

"You know Beecham?" Hazel asked. "Is he also a member of the Companions to the Death? Is he the one who came up with the . . . formula? The tonic?"

The society members looked at one another. Finally, Marie-Anne cleared her throat and spoke. "It's a *Tincture*," she said. "And, *no*. Did he tell you that? Hah! He was like a puppy at the elbow of my Antoine's laboratory. Didn't know the difference between hydrogen and hotcakes when he arrived in France. My Antoine discovered the formula for the Tincture. Beecham was one of our early students. Left soon after to pursue his own ends."

"Is Beecham still traipsing around Scotland?" Mrs. Thire asked. "It's been ages since I heard from him. He used to send a card at Christmas."

Marie-Anne sighed. "Same story, again and again. Off to find himself in some new city before he reinvents himself as his own grandson. Simple, pedestrian goals." She turned to Hazel. "Antoine and I knew that what we—what *he*— created was something with incredible potential. Longer lives lead to wisdom. An ability to see the patterns of history. To understand human nature and its consequences. And that, Miss Sinnett, is why we started the Companions to the Death."

"For *artists*," Byron said, half-mocking with a self-important tone.

"For the future," Marie-Anne corrected. "To preserve the greatest minds of a generation. Of every generation. To create a cohort with the talent and ability to steer the future of culture and politics for the better."

"And Beecham?" Hazel asked.

Marie-Anne sighed. "Beecham was . . . undisciplined in certain regards. Selfish. Too eager to make money and to cultivate his own acclaim." She drummed the fingers of her left hand on the table slowly and deliberately. Hazel's eye was drawn to Marie-Anne's missing pinkie finger. "The privilege of immortality," she said, "requires sacrifice."

Byron waggled his own four-fingered hand at Hazel. "An initiation ritual."

Hazel looked around at the group in front of her, examining them one by one.

She approached the silent man with the high ruffled neckline and a face she had seen in history book etchings. "Monsieur Lavoisier," she said. "It's an honor."

Antoine Lavoisier nodded his polite assent.

"My father had a book in his library summarizing your

work on oxygen," Hazel continued. "I can't say I understood it all, but I found it incredibly compelling all the same."

He smiled.

"Is that what the tonic—er, Tincture is, then?" Hazel asked. "An alchemical compound of oxygen and helium? Or does it require electricity? Is it galvanism, then? Because combined with certain chemical properties, I—"

"Enough of that," Marie-Anne said, interrupting. "Antoine and I learned early that the nature of the Tincture would not be revealed. Not even to the Companions."

Byron took a swig from a goblet. "No matter how many times I ask."

"It is a burden that we alone carry. And so, yes, Byron, no matter how many times you ask, we will not curse you with knowledge that in truth, should belong only to God."

"Byron thinks he's a god already," Banneker added.

"It's not like I would *sell* it, or whatever you think I would do. Bet it in a card game and use it to pay off gambling debts. I just want to know," Byron said, pouting.

Marie-Anne swirled a finger around the rim of her glass. "Knowing how to create the Tincture would only cause temptation. Not to sell it, no, not at first, but to share the knowledge with a loved one. A family member on the verge of death, a lover sick and dying before their time. A stranger, even, close to the end. Our numbers must always be few and *discreet*. Only Antoine and I know the formula, and only Antoine and I *will* know the formula."

"Except Beecham," Hazel said.

Marie-Anne raised her eyebrows.

"Beecham knows the formula. He knows how to make the, Tincture, or whatever."

"Yes," Marie-Anne said, her lips tight. "Me, Antoine, and Beecham." She didn't sound pleased about it.

"Am I to be the *only* one here who goes uncelebrated?" the Frenchman called suddenly. He fingered the stitches on his shoulder. "She'll sew me up but not ask my name. So, the brutish nature of Scottish manners has *not* been exaggerated."

Hazel turned. "My sincerest apologies, Mr. . . ."

"François-Marie Arouet, at your service. Also known as—"

Hazel's eyes went wide. "Voltaire. Voltaire! *The* Voltaire. Surely not. I can't believe I just performed surgery on . . . *Voltaire*. I'm rambling now. Forgive me. It's just, I thought you were . . ."

"Aye, well, that's the thing about our little Tincture, isn't it?" Voltaire said. "Immortality has forced me into an early retirement."

Byron gleefully pounded a fist on the table, shaking the stacks of books. "It's immortality twice over! Imagine how many people are going to read me when I die tragically young, forever beautiful and all wasted potential. That's the problem with poets: we're never appreciated in our time. It's only when we're in an early grave and the full extent of what we *might* have been able to do becomes visible that people even begin to care. And of course, by then it's too late to reap the financial benefits. I think I'll have my death be soon. Height of my powers. And the obituaries had better be fawning. I want *weeping* in the streets!"

Voltaire was still studying Hazel's stitching on his shoulder. "Marvelous. Such tiny stitches, Miss Sinnett! I don't even think this is going to scar—and you *shot* me, Byron! It's very impressive work. Very impressive."

Marie-Anne Lavoisier smiled. "I had a feeling it would be." She refilled Hazel's wineglass. "As you've gleaned, Miss Sinnett, our numbers are very few. And entrance to our little social club remains incredibly exclusive. Only those who we truly feel will *contribute* to creating positive change in the world are allowed past our threshold and into our elite circle. Immortality is a gift. The most precious commodity, desperately sought by kings and emperors in vain. But one tiny consequence is the slight tendency to sustain injuries over a long life."

She lifted her right hand, and Hazel noticed that several of the fingers had stitching around the base. Fallen off and sewn back on, just as Dr. Beecham's had been.

Byron pulled off a boot and sock and wiggled a foot gone gray, poorly reattached at the ankle. It was swollen and dead. "I'm still limping!" he complained. "People are saying I have a clubfoot."

"It is not my fault!" Mrs. Thire cried. "I'm a seamstress, not a surgeon."

"In the distant past," Marie-Anne said to Hazel, "we had a surgeon among our number."

"Beecham," Hazel said.

Marie-Anne nodded. "It's a very particular skill, and challenging: the ability to reattach flesh, cauterize veins, minimize scarring, maintain blood flow. You possess rare gifts, Miss Sinnett. We think you can help us, and we think we can help you. More than we already have, I mean."

"What do you mean?" Hazel said.

"The Companions to the Death are at the heart of London court and society. It was we who heard the rumors about you, and suggested to the Prince Regent that perhaps his daughter might prefer to be treated by a young, female surgeon close to her age. That's what we do," Marie-Anne said. "Influence things. Make them better. Move things forward."

"Why me?" Hazel whispered.

"You're famous," Byron said, as if it were obvious. "Only female surgeon in Britain."

Marie-Anne gave him a stern look. "You, Miss Sinnett, are a woman out of time. Imagine what the world will be for a woman in fifty years. In a *hundred*. Women will be celebrated as surgeons, not working in scandal, alone. A woman won't need to marry to have a place to live, to be able to participate in society."

"Dr. Beecham said the same thing to me last year," Hazel said. She knew enough not to add that Beecham had offered the Tincture to her, or that he had given her a vial.

"Did he, now?" Marie-Anne replied. Her face was impassive. Marie-Anne was a woman who held her emotions close, but there was a small twitch at the corner of her mouth, and Hazel understood enough to infer that there had been a falling-out between the Lavoisiers and Beecham. "We are offering you, Miss Sinnett, a rare invitation to join us. Help us with our minor repairs. Live forever exactly the way you were *meant* to live."

"Are we going to do the finger now?" Byron asked. "Or later? I don't want to be put off my appetite, and I'm worried the blood spatter will stain these shoes. I'll leave."

"Go upstairs if you wish, George," Marie-Anne said. "Sit in the laboratory. No need for you to make such a fuss." From a pocket swung around the hip of her skirt, she removed a long knife with a black handle. It glistened in the candlelight. "Would you like a glass of wine before we begin, Hazel?"

The buzzing in Hazel's ears was back. "No."

"Good. We'll be quick, then. Antoine, be a dear and fetch the Tincture from upstairs, love?"

"No!" Hazel said louder than she meant. "I don't want to join your . . . I mean, I don't want to be immortal."

Silence. And then Byron erupted in laughter.

"Whyever," Marie-Anne said, "not?" Her face was still a mask, but the twitch at the corner of her mouth was threatening to become a frown.

Hazel didn't know if it was cowardice or prudence; perhaps it didn't matter. But the thought of taking the Tincture—of living forever—gave her the sensation of standing on a rocky ledge atop a very, very tall cliff and being told to jump.

Hazel's mouth had gone dry, and she felt the room's eyeballs on her. "I don't want to live forever." No one said anything, and so Hazel continued. "It's too . . . *permanent.*"

"The only thing that's permanent is death," Voltaire said. "Life changes constantly."

"I would get bored. I know I would. Eventually," Hazel said.

Benjamin Banneker smiled reassuringly. "Bored? Of travel and reading? Of science and discovery? A dullard might get bored with infinite time, but I do seriously doubt that *boredom* would be possible for someone like you, if you'll forgive the presumptuousness."

"I don't want to watch the people I love die."

"You will *always* have to watch people you love die," Marie-Anne said. "Do you think mortality protects you from that?" The knife was sharp; Hazel saw the light flicker off its edge.

"Can I think about it?" Hazel asked quietly.

Byron guffawed. "No! We are giving you a once-in-a-lifetime opportunity that *anyone* in London would cut off their left hand for"—"Left pinkie at least," Voltaire muttered—"and you're dallying about?"

"Yes," Marie-Anne said. "You can think about it."

Byron almost knocked his goblet off the table. "She *knows*!" he spewed. "She could tell anyone! I say we make her take the Tincture or we . . . I don't know, we kill her. At least tie her up and leave her down here or something."

"Honestly!" Voltaire said. "You'll scare the poor thing."

"She's not going to tell," Marie-Anne said.

Hazel found it unsettling to hear them talk about her as if she weren't standing feet in front of them. Just then, Antoine returned from a set of stairs in the back corner of the room that Hazel hadn't noticed. He carried with him a small vial of purple liquid, thick as ink.

"Too late," Byron said to Antoine. "She's not going to do it."

Hazel's voice came back to her. "I'm not going to be immortal now," she said. She glanced around the room, at the brilliant artists and scientists gathered in one place. She didn't want to be immortal, but she didn't want to lose this: the collection of great minds talking about art and science. Being down here, in the comfortable room hidden beneath London, was the first time she had forgotten her loneliness since Jack's death. "But Lord Byron is right. I do know. And I am willing to help. I'll perform surgery and do the repair work that you need."

Banneker broke the silence. "Our first honorary member," he said. "Do we still cut off her finger?"

"No," Hazel said, answering for herself. "We don't. She needs the dexterity of all her fingers available to her."

Marie-Anne didn't smile, but she didn't look angry either. "It's decided, then. Hazel Sinnett: welcome to the Companions to the Death."

18

BY THE TIME HAZEL CLIMBED THE LONG set of stairs that led back to the streets of London, the first light of dawn was beginning to creep across the sky. She felt electrified, *alive*, her brain asking a thousand questions and reaching a thousand conclusions all at once. It was real, then. It was all real, and she was at the heart of it. She knew it hadn't been a dream—everything that happened with Beecham last year—of course it wasn't, but it had all been so wild and sudden and preposterous that Hazel never allowed herself to fully accept it.

But here she was. A secret society of immortals, the most famous academics and artists and philosophers in Europe. And they had invited Hazel to join their number. Sort of.

As she walked across the cobblestones glossy with rain—*Did it rain while I was down there?*—a familiar ache returned, the longing for Jack. If he were here, she would have been able to tell him everything. They would have been able to stay up all night, to walk every corner of this strange city together, loping through the alleys of London while they talked about everything that had happened. Who else could she tell? The problem with learning about immortality, the *Tincture*, was it made someone sound mad if they tried to describe it. Jack had been the only one Hazel had truly been her full self with. He was the only person with whom she could share every part of herself and who listened and accepted her with full understanding. He had seen her and he had loved her.

But then where is he? The nagging voice in the back of Hazel's mind hissed cruelly. *If he is alive, then why hasn't he written in the months since he disappeared with a city, an address? Why hasn't he come and found me?* Even if Jack was alive, the truth was he was still gone, and so the ache remained.

She couldn't return to her apartments: there was simply *too much* going on in her head to be contained by that small, simple room. The streets were still quiet, but if Hazel paid attention, she could feel London beginning to come to life around her. The smell of fresh-baked bread rose like steam from the windows of bakeries, and birds were tittering around the inky wet grass of the park. Hazel ignored the walking path and strode straight across the lawn itself, ignoring the way the mud and damp began to creep up the hem of her skirts.

She hadn't even known where she was walking, but somehow as the sun was just beginning to crest the horizon, Hazel found herself at Kew, walking through the silent gardens and toward the infirmary.

The Palace was still fast asleep. Hazel gave a nod to a yawning guard and entered through the gate. It was a few steps down into the infirmary, and the temperature dropped several degrees as she entered. It was dark and cool as a cave, and the neat jars of herbs glittered on their shelves. It was perfect.

Except the bench where she worked was taken.

Simon von Ferris was sleeping, his notebooks splayed out around his head like a halo. His cheeks were rosy as a child's, and his blond hair, usually so impeccably combed, was ruffled and messy. Hazel smiled and stepped closer to him; she wasn't going to wake him, but there was something strangely exciting about seeing him sleep. It was intimate, the evenness of his breath, the small dot of drool on the page of the book stuck to his cheek.

As if sensing her presence, he woke with a start, scattering paper.

"Good morning," Hazel said.

He blinked and righted himself. "Is it?"

"Morning? Almost. Good? Well, I'm not quite sure. Were you working all night?"

Simon began to gather himself, straightening his collar and smoothing his hair down with his palm. "We have a mad King and he's only getting worse. I work almost every night."

Hazel was going to excuse herself, to apologize for the intrusion and leave him with his books when Simon set his perfect, honey-brown eyes on her and said unexpectedly, "I was dreaming of you. And here you are."

He rose.

Perhaps if Hazel hadn't been awake all night, she would have been thinking clearly. Maybe if her exhaustion weren't overwritten by excitement and novelty and new people and new experiences, she would have had room in her head to remember propriety. But Hazel wasn't thinking clearly. And so, when Simon von Ferris told her that he was dreaming of her, she took a step toward him and halved the distance between them.

"Was it a good dream?" she asked.

"Yes," he said. "It was. A welcome respite from work too." Simon attempted to smooth his hair and straighten his collar. "I've been reading so long the words are all but blotches on the page."

Hazel leaned over to read the cover of the nearest book over Simon's shoulder. "*Poisons of Europe, and Their Antidotes*?! Do you think the King has been poisoned, then?"

Simon hid the book at the bottom of the stack. "No. It is just an idea I had. Some extra reading as a way to research possible treatments. It would be impossible for the King to actually have been poisoned, of course, but since some of the symptoms are similar, I thought . . ." He trailed off.

"Why would it be impossible for the King to be poisoned?" Hazel asked.

"He has two tasters for every meal, eating a bite and taking a sip of everything that passes through the King's lips. In the kitchen, there are three chefs who watch each other. I oversee his menu personally. Even the sugar he puts in his tea is tested."

"Probably not poison, then," Hazel agreed.

"Perhaps not all madness has a physical cause," Simon said, more to himself than to Hazel. "Or perhaps the cause is not one we are yet able to comprehend. But we continue on regardless. New treatments. New remedies."

"Is it bad, then?" Hazel said. "The King's condition, I mean."

Simon nodded. "Getting worse. There used to be moments of clarity, where he knew himself, but those moments have gone from rare to, well, to never. There have been bouts of violence, but most of the time, he's just speaking. Murmuring to himself or talking at full volume. For hours, sometimes even days straight. Saying the walls are moving on him. Nonsense like that. Like a child. It reminds me of things my brother used to say when he was young. Babbling."

"You have a brother?" Hazel asked.

"Two," Simon said. "And a sister. All much younger. I helped to raise them."

Hazel thought of her brother George. "You must miss them," she said.

"I do," Simon replied. "Very much. I miss much about Sweden."

For the first time, Hazel noticed how tired Simon looked. His eyes were bloodshot, and the bags beneath his eyes were swollen and purple. Simon was so pale and the hollows beneath his cheekbones were so severe that he looked like a corpse. Even so, he was still impossibly handsome, so good-looking Hazel had to remind herself that he actually *was* a physician and not a stage actor pretending to be one.

Hazel missed the feeling of being able to touch someone, of being touched. After Jack's death, she had tended to and protected her loneliness as if it were the flame of a small candle. Now she felt the flame burning her from the inside out.

Almost involuntarily, she felt her hand rise toward Simon's face.

But before her hand reached him, Simon wrapped his arms around Hazel's waist and pulled her in toward him. They were so close now that she could feel the heat of his body. Simon's eyes shifted from Hazel's eyes to her lips, and then her neck, and then back to her lips.

And then the two of them pressed together into a kiss.

The world disappeared. All that existed was the air shared between them, the taste of tannic vanilla tea and butter cookies and Simon, Simon's tongue pressing into her mouth and his arms pulling her tighter against him. She could feel his chest, broad and firm, against hers, through the layers of dress and jacket and jacket and shirt.

And then Simon pulled away. "Forgive me, Miss Sinnett. Perhaps I forget myself." He moved to gather his papers and books.

Hazel's heart was pounding. Her blood felt thick and her brain was buzzing.

"I should be off to bed," Simon muttered.

If Simon wondered whether Hazel had been out all night, or why she was in the infirmary that early, he didn't ask. Instead, he merely gathered his books and deposited them neatly into his handsome leather medical bag. (Hazel couldn't help but to admire it.) He paused as he passed Hazel on the way out, hesitating and seemingly unsure whether he should kiss her again, but his reason got the better of him, and he swept out of the infirmary without another word, the scent of vanilla tea following in his wake.

Hazel had to lift her hand to her lips, to let her finger linger where Simon's lips had been just moments before, to convince herself that it was real. Simon von Ferris had kissed her in the infirmary, before sunrise.

But then, like a cloud passing over the sun, the memory of Jack came to Hazel.

She saw him in her mind, clear as if he were with them there in the infirmary: the boy with long limbs and messy hair and toothy smile. She felt *guilty*, as if she had betrayed

Jack by kissing Simon, and betrayed him again by *enjoying* her kiss with Simon so much.

She shouldn't feel guilty, she knew that. Jack wasn't here. He had been hanged, and if he survived, he had left her without a forwarding address. He had no claim on her.

A brilliant, handsome, famous doctor had kissed her and she had kissed him back. There was nothing she owed to Jack Currer, even if his memory persisted like moisture in the air after a storm.

The exhaustion of having been awake all night was finally beginning to settle onto her like a blanket. She should have followed Simon's example and gone to bed, but Hazel was already at Kew, and instead of thinking about Simon or Jack, she forced herself to read several chapters in a book she found on the infirmary shelves that made reference to Antoine Lavoisier's work before she returned to her rooms. She fell asleep still in her clothes and didn't wake up until the servant was ringing for dinner.

The London Encyclopaedia of Scientific Persons, 1814 Edition, Edited by R. M. Karmel, C. R. S. Stewart, and Z. Fraser

Antoine Lavoisier
(b. August 26, 1743; d. May 8, 1794)

Antoine Lavoisier was a French chemist famous for his identification of oxygen and hydrogen, and for his theory on chemical reactivity. Lavoisier aided in the introduction of the metric system in order to establish scientific consistency.

Prior to Lavoisier's work, the scientific community believed in the phlogiston theory to explain combustion. The false theory was the belief that an element known as "phlogiston" was released during burning. Lavoisier disproved the theory by establishing that combustion occurred when elements were combined with oxygen. Lavoisier's oxygen theory of combustion also became the foundation of his discovery of conservation of matter, which states that matter can neither be created nor destroyed within a fixed system. In 1768, the King of France awarded him a gold medal for his work examining street lighting in Paris.

Lavoisier's wife, Marie-Anne Paulze Lavoisier, drew many of his experimental diagrams. As Lavoisier did not speak English, his wife translated scientific articles and books for him. Together, they wrote the first comprehensive list of the elements.

For his role as a financier and public administrator with the *ferme générale* for the royal government before the Revolution in France, Antoine Lavoisier was executed by guillotine.

19

HE INVITATIONS BEGAN ARRIVING AT HAZEL'S apartment nearly every day: bloodred envelopes with her name in perfect script, delivered with her breakfast trays. They contained invitations, often to the Companions' clubhouse at Seven Dials, but also to dinner parties and operas, and private evenings at the theater.

"It seems you've found quite a social life for yourself in London," Eliza commented when Hazel had to excuse herself from Warwick House before supper to make an early curtain time. Hazel just smiled back. "Are you going to tell me anything about the Companions at least? A tidbit I can gossip about later behind your back?"

Hazel shrugged on her coat. "They drink," she said. "Heavily."

It was true: they drank heavily. Not just wine (brought from Italy) but also absinthe (Germany) and beer (Belgium) and sparkling champagne (France). The protection of immortality, it seemed, allowed them to do *everything* heavily. A dinner party with the members of the society might involve a

dozen courses: game meat stuffed with chestnuts and cher-
ries, steaming loaves of brioche and salted butter, chilled as-
paragus soup, apple and pear tarts, ice cream served in cold
silver dishes eaten with tiny spoons, and, finally, intricate
sugar sculptures in the shape of a copse of trees or birds mid-
flight, brought out at the end of the meal to much *oooh*ing and
*ahh*ing. It was strange, Hazel thought to herself, how quickly
the extraordinary became commonplace. How depressing it
was that what had once been thrilling now elicited nothing
stronger than mere satisfaction. The Companions were then
forced to go searching for something even *more* extraordinary than before in order to feel ever-fleeting moments of
pleasure and surprise. The thought made Hazel both grateful and relieved she had declined the chance to join them in
their eternal life.

Which was not to say that the time spent with the Companions wasn't enjoyable. Far from it; it was, perhaps, the
first time in Hazel's life where she felt she was surrounded by
an entire collection of people who were as passionate about
life and learning as she was.

Most evenings at Seven Dials ended in poetry readings,
Byron making a show of faux reluctance but then happily
opening up his notebook and standing before the group to
deliver an excerpt of whatever he was currently working on.

Hazel didn't particularly care for Byron, with his vanity
and the way he was his own favorite topic of conversation,
but even she had to admit that his poetry was beautiful.

One afternoon, the group had convened for tea at the
home of the French painter Élisabeth Le Brun. The entire
house was beautifully appointed; Hazel had never been to
Versailles, but she imagined that before the Revolution, it

had been something like this: patterned wallpaper and mirrors with gilded edges reflecting the light of glittering candles, and tasteful porcelain knickknacks scattered on every surface.

"Miss Sinnett," one of the Whig politicians—Mr. Lewis—said to her while waiting for his cup of tea to steep. "I wonder if I might trouble you to perform a bit of surgery on me." He lifted his left hand, which was heavily bandaged, and slowly unwrapped the fabric. The hand was already missing his pinkie, but Hazel saw that the first two fingers on the hand were purple and swollen as sausages, and bent at unnatural angles.

"Honestly!" Élisabeth called across the room. "Put that away. We're at tea."

"My apologies, Madame Le Brun," Mr. Lewis said, rewrapping his hand. To Hazel, he whispered: "I'm afraid some shrapnel is still in the wound. Hunting accident. Last autumn."

"I can take care of that," Hazel said. "Perhaps you could be by my apartments tomorrow morning?" She would have much preferred to perform the surgery in the infirmary at Kew as opposed to her own small, comfortable, but simple room, but she was a guest at Kew herself. She hardly had the authority to invite another person into a royal palace.

Marie-Anne sat up straighter. "Your *apartments*? Don't be foolish, dear. Come to the laboratory."

"The laboratory?"

And that was how Hazel ended up the next morning following Marie-Anne and Mr. Lewis down into the clubhouse at Seven Dials. But rather than settling onto one of the plush settees or overstuffed leather chairs with which Hazel had become well acquainted, Marie-Anne approached one of the bookshelves in the back of the room, by the fireplace.

"About time we showed this to you," she said, and she pushed the bookshelf aside as easily as if it were on wheels. It *was* on some sliding mechanism, and as it slid aside, it revealed another room.

A laboratory.

But not *just* a laboratory.

The most incredible laboratory Hazel had ever seen.

Glass and copper and a thousand living plants that Hazel could identify and another thousand that she couldn't. They were underground, beneath street level, Hazel knew, but somewhere there was a skylight in glass far, far above them, bathing the room in warm white light. And where the sunlight didn't reach, there were gas lamps, the flames dancing in perfect glass orbs.

Off to the side of the room, Antoine Lavoisier was looking intently at clear liquid in a bulbous bottle, which he was gently heating above a small blue flame. He was, as always, wearing a high ruffled collar that reached his chin.

"Hello, darling," Marie-Anne said. Antoine waved, but didn't look up from his experiment. "Will this serve?" she asked Hazel.

"Yes, this will serve quite well," Hazel said, eyeing the surgical bench beneath a shelf of herbs and clean white bandages. Hazel went closer to the bottles of medicine. One of the glass bottles contained something purple and viscous. She read the label.

"Ethereum," Hazel said.

"Yes," Marie-Anne replied. "The Edinburgh dodge, they call it. Puts a patient to sleep so they don't feel the pain. Of course, there's always the risk they won't wake up again, but for severe cases—"

"I know," Hazel said. "I once saw a demonstration of it at the Anatomists' Society in Edinburgh." She had met Jack that day. He spirited her down a dark passage and they'd watched Dr. Beecham press a cloth soaked in ethereum up against a man's face before he cut his leg off. It was a lifetime ago. Back when Jack was just a stranger, and not the boy whose pale skin she had touched every inch of, in the barn at Hawthornden, when it was dark and raining out and the world was just the two of them for a few hours.

"I won't be needing any of that," Mr. Lewis said, bringing Hazel back to reality. He started unwrapping his hand again. It was a terrible sight. The index and middle fingers were both bruised and swollen—shrapnel was indeed embedded in them—but the index finger was crooked at an impossible angle besides. Hazel examined it: the bone was broken, but it had also been separated from his hand once and never properly reattached. The stitching at his knuckle was frayed and falling apart, the tendons and veins ragged and visible at the separation.

"I can get the shrapnel out," Hazel said, "but I don't know what I can do with the index finger. I'm going to have to remove it, and see if I can reattach it again."

Lewis sat very still on the bench while Hazel unrolled her canvas and lifted her scalpel. "Could I have a basin of clean water, please?" she asked Marie-Anne.

Marie-Anne returned with the water and a small vial of something yellow-gold. "For reattachments," she said, handing it to Hazel. "It helps the body accept the transplacement."

"Beecham used that too!" Hazel blurted out. "But not

when he was reattaching limbs . . . when he was attaching . . . new parts."

"Yes," Marie-Anne said. "We are well aware of the *work* Dr. Beecham conducted using this." She held it up to the light, which filtered through the gold liquid, making it shimmer. "Cruel, illegal work. But the dilution works just as well on one's own limbs as it does on the body parts stolen from the poor."

"Terrible," Mr. Lewis said through gritted teeth.

"Mr. Lewis and the Whigs work in behalf of the people, and not just the wealthy," Marie-Anne said to Hazel.

"Though the Regent seems keen to sabotage us at every turn!" Lewis said. "Two decades ago, he was a staunch Whig himself—progressive, idealistic. Willing and ready to move this nation into the nineteenth century! And then he becomes Regent and suddenly he's a staunch monarchist and all that goes with it. Defending antique and crumbling institutions while his people suffer."

"Yes, yes, Mr. Lewis," Marie-Anne said. "Don't get excited or Miss Sinnett will have trouble removing the shrapnel."

Hazel smiled gratefully and finished her work cleaning Lewis's wounds.

"Did you hear he died?" Lewis said, trying to keep his hand as still as possible. "Beecham. Or 'died' in inverted commas, I suppose. Read the obituary in the evening paper."

"I wonder if he wrote it himself this time like he did before," Marie-Anne said.

"Didn't pretend to have a son, did he?" Lewis said. "Who's he going to pretend to reappear as next?"

"Oh, a distant nephew maybe. Whoever knows," Marie-Anne replied.

"He'll have to go to the Continent this time," Lewis said, wincing slightly as Hazel pulled bits of gravel and metal from his fingers. "Everyone in London and Edinburgh already knows him."

"Or America," Hazel said. She was often thinking of America these days.

"America! Our government could take some notes from their founding documents, I will say that," Lewis said, looking everywhere but his left hand, where Hazel was performing surgery. He began pontificating on the merits of a constitutional democracy while Hazel worked, and she let him, happy the man could distract himself.

Hazel held her breath as she used her scalpel to slice through the thin tissue and thread holding Lewis's index finger to the rest of his hand.

The finger, sitting in her palm, was broken and misshapen, but she examined its root: the major blood vessels were still there. "I think I might be able to reattach," Hazel said.

"Just a moment, Miss Sinnett," Marie-Anne said, and she approached a locked chest near her store of medicine. From her breast, she withdrew a key and unlocked the doors with a satisfying click. The cabinet was full of small glass vials containing ink-colored liquid, which seemed to swirl even as it remained completely still. *Tincture*, Hazel thought.

On the lower rack of the shelves sat a row of bottles lighter in color, yellow, and almost glittering when it caught the light. Marie-Anne ran her fingers across that row and selected one. She examined its label approvingly and then returned to Hazel and Mr. Lewis.

"Allow me," Marie-Anne said, and she deposited a few drops of the gold-yellow liquid from the vial onto Lewis's mangled hand. "A little dilution. It will need it, if this reattachment is going to work at all."

"Is that what this is, then?" Hazel asked, staring at the liquid. "A dilution? A dilution of the . . . Tincture?"

"Yes. *Heavily* diluted, but still operating by the same general principle," Marie-Anne said. "Compounds oxygenated and then electrified. Beecham and I had developed it together, before we even realized the Tincture itself would be possible. We were attempting to create something with the ability to preserve the life of an isolated body part before it could be rejoined to a body."

"And it works?" Hazel asked.

"Indeed," Marie-Anne said. "Beecham and I had to make sure of it. Especially after we took the Tincture and our mortality became stronger than our physical forms."

She walked over to her husband, Antoine, who finally lifted his attention from his experiment. With gentle fingers, Marie-Anne lowered her husband's collar, and Hazel gasped.

Antoine's head was stitched to his neck.

The stitches were neat but thick and dark. The effect was nightmarish, a head attached to a body the way one might sew a patch onto a shirt.

"Couldn't manage the vocal cords," Marie-Anne said. "But the rest seemed to work the way it should." She kissed her husband's cheek gently and released his collar, hiding the scar and stitches again. Antoine returned to his work.

"During the Revolution," she explained. "A brilliant mind made to roll through the filthy streets. Power might belong in the hands of the people, Miss Sinnett, but that doesn't mean mobs are always wise. People need leaders. Good men like Mr. Lewis here."

Lewis held up his left hand, which had only two fingers and a thumb. "Fingerless as he may be," he said.

"Well, hold still," Hazel said. "Let me try to give you one more back at least."

It took an hour of intricate stitching, but eventually Hazel reattached Lewis's left index finger, and, no doubt thanks to the few drops of diluted Tincture, he was able to move it as if it had never left his hand.

"Remarkable," he said, bending and straightening the finger. "And such neat stitching!"

"You might not even need gloves to go to the commodore's ball next week," Marie-Anne said approvingly.

Lewis was already pulling on his gloves. Hazel noticed that the pinkie finger of the left hand was stuffed, so that a stranger wouldn't even know it was missing. "Now, I don't know about that, Madame Lavoisier." He winked at Hazel. "Ladies will be present."

The London Herald, Evening Edition

3 July 1818

WILLIAM BEECHAM, SURGEON AND GRANDSON OF ANATOMICAL PIONEER, DEAD IN EDINBURGH

William Beecham III, the head of the Royal Anatomists' Society and chief surgeon at the University of Edinburgh, is dead after an undisclosed illness. Beecham is best known as the grandson of Sir William Beecham I, Baronet, founder of the Royal Anatomists' Society and author of *Dr. Beecham's Treatise on Anatomy; or, The Prevention and Cure of Modern Diseases*, the foundational text that re-defined the study of Anatomy for the 19th century.

But Beecham was a celebrated physician in many regards as well, beloved by members of the medical community around the world. He was known for especially quick surgery with low mortality rates, and introduced the use of ethereum (also known as 'the Edinburgh dodge') in order to anæsthetize patients before surgery, though some other physicians in the field question its safety and it has not become widespread practice.

His body will be interred at the family crypt in Glasgow, and all funeral proceedings will be private. Beecham leaves no next of kin.

20

SINCE NAPOLEON'S DEFEAT, GREAT BRITAIN HAD been at peace, but that didn't mean the people of London lost their taste for a military parade. Sir Robert Mends had been the captain of a ship stationed off the west coast of Africa with the goal of intercepting slavers, but as he was returning to port in England, his ship had been boarded by French privateers. Mends and his men not only successfully fought off the privateers but actually claimed *their* ship in turn.

Now they were returning to London as heroes, Mends rewarded with a promotion to commodore and his entire crew rewarded with as many free pints as they could drink at any bar in the city for having played even a small part in an operation that led to France being humiliated.

Hazel was on a morning walk, and the crowds had begun to line the streets in the summer heat, waving small flags in eager anticipation of the spectacle to come. It would be an entire weekend of festivities—Hazel overheard Charlotte complaining to Eliza about how many dull events would require her presence while the two were getting dressed the day before.

"That's all they want me to do! That's all I *can* do: Curtsy, smile. Curtsy, smile. I wonder whether my cheeks or knees will give out first."

Eliza had been fastening the Princess's stays. "Most people in the country would envy a position that involves nothing more than dressing up and attending events with the finest food and drink, ma'am."

Charlotte caught Eliza's eye. "Yes, Eliza. I know. I'm *grateful* and all that, you know I am. This country needs a princess doll to dress up and play with, and it's my miserable luck to fill the brief. And 'toy doll' is a very well-paid position."

"Lady-in-waiting to toy doll could probably be paid a little better," Eliza added slyly.

"As if you're not weeks away from getting married to an officer with a *very healthy* annual income, Eliza—*yes, I do* make inquiries occasionally. First lieutenant, family estate. All very respectable."

Eliza's fingers lost their place on the ties of Charlotte's dress, and for the first time, Hazel saw that Eliza was at a loss for words.

"I *was* going to tell you, ma'am," Eliza said finally. "That I formally accepted his offer, I mean."

"No need," Charlotte said coolly. She pulled away and finished tying the ribbon around her waist herself. "A princess hears of these things. It's not as though I was expecting you to remain at my side, tying my dresses for all eternity. After all"—and here Charlotte turned to look at Hazel— "my health is beginning to return to me. Time marches on, no matter how long we stay in bed hiding from the world.

Sooner or later, I was going to need to become the princess the nation requires of me, and you were going to need to become a married woman. It seems our friend Dr. Sinnett here is the only woman of my acquaintance who has been able to escape the clutches of expectations. Is that all we need to do, learn how to sew a suture or remove a limb, and then we can be our own women?"

"I think you'll find, Your Royal Highness," Hazel said, and thought with a shiver of what it had felt like, in the infirmary, with Simon's lips against hers, "that even doctors are occasionally victim to the constraints of our social positions."

In the days since she and Simon shared that kiss, she hadn't been alone with him, even as she found herself finding more and more frequent excuses to linger around Kew. Twice she met Gaspar for tea in the gardens because she thought that Simon might pass by—on the second day he did, but as he strolled into the Palace, he was deep in conversation with one of King George's ministers and offered Hazel and Gaspar only a nod and wave from afar.

In theory, Hazel knew that she should have been terrified about the possible scandal of the kiss; Hazel's position as personal physician to the Princess was not one that offered unlimited grace, especially when it came to dalliances with the opposite sex. With the Princess's future marriage still undetermined, her reputation when it came to chastity (and thus the reputations of everyone who associated with her) was too valuable to besmirch.

But instead, Hazel found that her fears had become humiliatingly mundane, the type of mooning that she once mocked Iona for back at Hawthornden when the girl swooned over Hazel's older brother. Hazel would be reading a journal article and find herself scanning the same paragraph again and again, realizing each time she got to the end that she had failed to absorb even a single sentence. She would start the paragraph over, just to repeat the entire exercise because she hadn't been thinking about proper ethereum dosage at all; she was thinking about Simon. She was thinking of Simon and *worrying* like a silly girl of ten with a crush, about whether *he* was thinking of her. Maybe he went around kissing girls constantly. Maybe Hazel was just a curiosity to him, the way she was to so many people—a *female* surgeon, a fascinating specimen to add to his collection, to *boast* about. Hazel didn't know *anything* about Simon, not really. He might be engaged to a woman in Sweden, for all she knew. He could be *married* and keeping it secret during his time in London so he could go around *kissing strangers*! (It was around this time in the thought process that Hazel would chastise herself to focus again and return to her reading.)

The fantasy of *marrying* Simon was a foolish one that Hazel dismissed as soon as it dared make a cautious foray into her thoughts. Men like Simon von Ferris married dull, pretty girls trained to adequately maintain and run a household while he was working. His position would require frequent social engagements. His wife would be hosting dinner parties and salons to keep her husband in the good graces of the London ton. It would be all the better for Simon if his bride happened to be an heiress.

Hazel descended from a noble lineage—but there was nobility and *nobility*. Hazel had understood that her entire life: her family was respectable, but not particularly wealthy. Her father had set aside a reasonable dowry for her, but once he passed away, the entirety of the Sinnett estate would belong to

Hazel's little brother, Percy. Hazel knew deep in her bones, with the certainty that came only after hardship, that she would never be happy as a married woman. She would rather suffer the challenges of providing a meager existence for herself as a working surgeon than recline in comfort as someone's wife. And eventually, Simon von Ferris would need a wife.

It had been easy for Hazel, accepting that she would be alone. Now Simon had come in and kissed her and ruined it. Because now she would be alone and *distracted*. (*Prying. Jealous. Vain.*) Affection was poisoning her, taking over her brain and her thoughts like a growing weed.

Hazel managed to push her way through the throng of people and back to her apartments before the parade began, but she could hear them from her window: the cheers as the men from HMS *Iphigenia* rode by on horseback, and then the ecstatic *roars* from the crowd when Princess Charlotte passed by in her open-topped carriage. The cheers for Charlotte were ten times louder than the polite clapping for the Prince Regent in his carriage. No wonder he was eager for Princess Charlotte to get married and leave the country, Hazel thought as she washed her hair in the bath. The Prince Regent would only ever be half a ruler: he ruled now, but on behalf of his mad father, and when he *did* become King in earnest, the public would just see him as a temporary but necessary time-wasting prerequisite before their beloved Charlotte took the throne.

Hazel didn't have any new dresses; she would have to wear something old, an outfit she had brought from Edinburgh. Perhaps the green gown, even if it had gotten a little short in the sleeves, and even though there was a small bloodstain near the hem, on the back. (Hazel hadn't cleaned the legs of her bench after an operation and brushed against it later, forgetting that some of the blood on the wood might be wet.)

"Oh, please don't wear an old dress!" Eliza had moaned when Hazel showed her the green gown in her bedroom. "Those sleeves look ancient. No one is wearing long sleeves anymore."

"They're . . . classic," Hazel protested.

Eliza was digging through Hazel's trunk, trying to find something newer, when the maid knocked on the door. "A letter for you, miss," she said.

Eliza leapt to her feet. "A love letter!" she said, and snatched it from the maid's tray. "Oh, boo. It's from a solicitor."

Hazel grabbed the letter from Eliza's hands. She didn't recognize the name: a Mr. Samuel Eastman, Esq., located at 128 Chalton Street. Hazel used her scalpel as a letter opener.

It was a notice of inheritance.

Dr. Beecham, in his will, had left Hazel a thousand pounds, which she was at liberty to collect whenever it was convenient for her.

Maybe he really was dead after all.

Hazel folded the letter and put it into her trunk.

"Well?" Eliza said. "What was it? A love letter *from* a solicitor?"

"No," Hazel said, shaking her head and trying to banish the strange feeling that had lodged itself there. "Someone I used to know in Edinburgh died. He left me something in his will."

"I hope it's enough to buy a new dress," Eliza said. "I'm sorry, was that awful of me? I'm trying to learn to be less awful."

"I'm wearing the green dress," Hazel said. "And you should

consider it a favor, because imagine how fashionable you'll look in comparison next to me."

The truth was, Hazel liked the green dress. She liked the way the color brought out the peach tones in her skin, which looked so sallow most of the time.

As she held it up in the light on the morning of the ball, Hazel had wondered whether Simon might like her in green—and then in an instant, she felt mortified by her fixation on the young doctor.

Banishing Simon from her mind, she put on the dress and pulled her hair neatly back, covering it with a feathered hat of her mother's that had somehow found itself among Hazel's possessions to be sent down to London. There. She looked . . . Fine. Presentable. Pretty enough. There was no need to make a fuss; the party wasn't for her, after all. She was a physician, and she had done her job making Charlotte well enough to attend (even if Charlotte hadn't really required medical treatment in the conventional sense), and that was all. It didn't matter to Hazel what Simon thought of her dress. It was an *old* dress and her mother's hat—if she *did* actually care what Simon thought, she would have made more of an effort. Because she hadn't, Hazel reasoned, clearly neither Simon nor his attention meant that much to her. *Quod erat demonstrandum. QED.*

That was what she told herself as she entered the carriage to head to the party that evening, which was being held at the Regent's private residence, Carlton House.

Still, as soon as she arrived, Hazel found herself scanning the crowd for a tall, blond head. It seemed Simon hadn't arrived yet.

But Princess Charlotte was there, just as promised, her

first public appearance in weeks, and she looked resplendent in a rosy pink gown with floral embroidery at the sleeves and hem. Ostrich feathers were stuck in her hair. But more noticeable than her clothing, at least to Hazel, was how *healthy* the Princess looked. Though she couldn't pretend she was *pleased* to be there—the smiles were small and forced—there was, at least, unmistakable color in Princess Charlotte's cheeks.

From across the ballroom, the Prince Regent spotted Hazel and left his conversation mid-sentence to march over to her, practically bowling people over as he walked. (Gaspar was at his elbow, making apologies in His Royal Highness's wake.)

"Miss Sinnett," the Regent said, glancing at Gaspar to confirm that he'd stated Hazel's name correctly. (Gaspar nodded discreetly.) "It seems as though you have done it. My commendations to you. The Princess is here, as promised, in as good health as I've seen her in weeks. Now, tell me: What was it? Misalignment of the humors? Influenza? Spit it out, now. Come on!"

"A rare influenza, Your Royal Highness," Hazel fibbed. "One that seems to come and go for no clear reason."

The Regent continued talking, as though Hazel hadn't said anything. "I have to say, seems like the sort of thing that took care of itself, does it not? I wonder how much doctoring you really would have had to do if the Princess only took my advice: bed rest and vigorous exercise! Lots of rest, and lots of walking and sport! That's the cure for this sort of ailment! Every time. Mark it."

It was pompous nonsense. How could one's treatment be *both* rest and exercise? Besides, the Regent didn't even know *what* "sort of ailment" the Princess was suffering from to begin with. Hazel and Gaspar exchanged a small look of understanding.

"The Princess will, of course, be well enough to travel now, am I correct?" the Prince asked suddenly.

"I . . . I can't say for certain, sir."

"What sort of influenza becomes *worse* on boats?! The bracing sea air is good for one's health! Everyone knows that!" he said, loud enough for several people nearby to turn their heads.

"It's a very tricky case, sir," Hazel said. "But I think, in due time, she'll be well enough. It's always best not to rush these things. Just in case."

"Just in case," the Regent echoed, as if he'd thought of it himself.

"We both only want what's best for the Princess, of course," Hazel couldn't help but add. Gaspar glared at her. The Regent ignored her, and bounded away to corner another guest.

Word of Hazel's miracle treatment of Princess Charlotte seemed to have made its way around court. Stranger after stranger came up to Hazel to give her their most sincere thanks with an earnestness that Hazel found almost unsettling.

"I was beside myself when the Princess had the Roman fever," said an older woman with black feathers in her hair. "Like my own child was ill. I don't know what we would have done if we had lost her this time."

A man bowed so low to Hazel that his nose nearly touched the ground. "Thank the Lord you arrived to court, Dr. Sinnett. You're an angel from heaven."

"Just Miss Sinnett, please," Hazel said, unable to stop the blush creeping up from her neck.

The Princess *was* beloved, almost beyond belief, Hazel realized. Years ago, the nation had been helpless when Princess Charlotte suffered from a near-fatal case of the Roman fever; it must have been horrifying to hear that she was once again confined to her bed with a mysterious illness that no one was able to treat. And it wasn't just the common people who loved the Princess, the ones who lined up outside Warwick House with their well-wishes, but members of the court as well. (Of course, Hazel thought, they were the people who had to suffer the Prince Regent's arrogance and insufferable self-absorption most often.) Princess Charlotte was a breath of fresh air, a reminder of hope for the future.

But, Hazel thought, as she watched the Princess, who with a fixed smile and glazed eyes was greeting the next in an increasingly long receiving line, *it must be hard to exist as both a symbol and a person.*

The dancing wouldn't begin until after HMS *Iphigenia* arrived at the conclusion of their parade through London, and so Hazel waited, drinking a glass that appeared on a servant's tray at her side. Without trying to eavesdrop, she found herself caught up in the conversation between two mustachioed men to her left.

". . . the King in a terrible way . . ."

"More delusional by the day, I heard."

"Apparently that Swedish doctor hasn't left his side for three days straight. Some good it does. Just listening to him rant, I suppose."

So that was that. Simon wouldn't be coming tonight. Hazel was surprised at how disappointed it made her. She had been looking forward to seeing him, to teasing out whether anything about their dynamic had changed since their kiss.

"If I was the Regent," one of the mustachioed men said to his friend, "I would smother him myself."

"Martin!" the other chastised with mock outrage. "Treason, and within the walls of the *palace*, of all places."

"Oh, come off it, Frampton." The other man slurred a little. The wine splashed from the side of his glass. The two men laughed, guttural and convivial.

From the hall's entrance, horns began to bellow, announcing the arrival of the guests of honor. A herald stood beside the double doors. "Introducing Sir Robert Mends and the men of HMS *Iphigenia!*"

The doors swung open and the men entered in time to the crescendo of the band. Mends himself, leading the pack, was a handsome man in middle age, in a light blue jacket decorated with medals and gilded epaulettes on its shoulders. He had a full head of pepper-gray hair, that either the parade or decades of sea wind had swept into disarray. He grinned as he entered, clearly unaccustomed to the attention, but enjoying it all the same.

After making it through a gauntlet of royal guards, he knelt before the Prince Regent. As soon as he was in position, Gaspar gingerly handed the Regent a thin sword. "Arise," the Regent said after gently tapping Mends on each shoulder with the blade, "*Commodore* Robert Mends."

A cheer erupted through the room. Now the party could begin in earnest.

The women in the room *swarmed* the naval men, all wearing tight trousers and handsome dark blue double-breasted jackets with high collars and glittering brass buttons.

Eliza was on the arm of her lieutenant, Otto. They made a handsome couple, Hazel thought. Both young, and attractive, and adept at dealing with the rules and rituals of a life at court. Beside them, the handsome Prussian prince, Frederick Augustus, stood with a sour-faced woman who Hazel could only assume was his own fiancée.

Hazel saw the way that Princess Charlotte's eye kept going back to them.

She wondered at the full extent of the relationship between Frederick Augustus and Charlotte. Had they flirted? Almost certainly. (From afar, the prince appeared to flirt with everyone.) Had they exchanged love letters? Met in the middle of the night without anyone knowing? Had he made promises that he knew he couldn't keep? Had she?

It was painful, no matter what, Hazel knew, to have to see the one you love on someone else's arm. To see them smiling at someone else, fetching someone else's drinks, kissing their cheek. No wonder the Princess confined herself to bed.

A dance began, and Hazel was excusing herself from the dance floor—she had no intention of dancing tonight, and she was contemplating calling her carriage to take her home—when a sailor with dark, messy hair turned and Hazel saw his face.

It was Jack.

Jack.

Not a figment of her imagination or a fantasy, but *Jack*, here, and *alive*. He wore the navy blue jacket of the British Royal Navy, and a scar ran across his face, pink at its edges and white and shiny at its center. The scar ran from his forehead, across his nose, and down his lip, and where it should have passed his eye, it was hidden beneath a black patch.

Every memory of every moment they had spent together came flooding back in a single rush: the smell of him, the feel of his skin, the pace of his heartbeat. *My heart is yours, beating or still.* Hazel was back in the passage beneath the Anatomists' Society and in the kirkyard near Hawthornden and on the back of horses and in the barn looking at the night sky. She was watching his body, supine and bleeding, with Dr. Beecham holding a scalpel above it. She was pressing her hand against the bars of the cell where he was being kept, and handing over the small vial of Tincture.

And she was here, in this ballroom, staring at Jack Currer from across the room, looking into his one good eye when he looked back and saw her.

Jack Currer, the boy Hazel had loved and lost, made eye contact from across the room.

And he fled the ballroom in the other direction.

21

"EY!"

Hazel's feet were moving before her mind knew what she was doing. The universe was spinning around her, but all she allowed herself to focus on was the back of the man she was following out of the ballroom. He was halfway down a hallway before she finally caught up with him. Hazel managed to get a hand on his shoulder, and the man spun back.

It was him.

It was Jack.

The same narrow chin and long nose. The same curve of the cheekbone. And in his one good eye, Hazel saw the colors she had been dreaming about for months: gray and blue so light it was like the sky if you were trying to look straight at the sun on an overcast day. Seeing his face again made Hazel melt like candle wax.

Jack stared at her, unblinking. He looked as though he were questioning his own sanity, as if Hazel were a cruel prank or an apparition or a ghost.

"Jack," Hazel said finally. "It's me."

Like a curtain dropping, the shock on his face trans-formed suddenly into pain, and then fear. Jack clenched his jaw and he blinked his one good eye fast. He looked like a caged animal, ready to run again at any moment.

Should she embrace him? Kiss him? Her brain was telling her to do a million things at once, and so instead of doing anything, Hazel stood, paralyzed, staring at the face she had drawn in her dreams a thousand times. Here. Scratched and bruised and missing an eye, but here.

Jack seemed to be struggling against the muscles in his own face. His lip twitched, and then finally, voice tight as a bowstring, Jack spoke: "Are you having a pleasant evening, Miss Sinnett?"

Hazel didn't even realize she had slapped him until her palm was smarting from the force of it.

"'A pleasant evening'? 'Miss Sinnett'?" she hissed. "What are you *doing*? Why did you run away from me?" Her ears were burning and the sting from the slap was spreading up through her wrist.

Jack swallowed hard, and rubbed his cheekbone where Hazel's hand had made contact. He opened and closed his jaw slowly, making sure it wasn't broken. "For a moment, I admit I didn't think it was possible that it was really you. And now I have no doubt."

"Why wouldn't it be me?" Hazel spat. "Who else would it be?"

Jack looked around. He was breathing fast. "London, of all places. In a royal palace. There were rumors of a female physician treating the Princess that reached us even on the boat. I should have known then."

"You knew I might be here? And you didn't—didn't come?"

Jack didn't answer. He was stiff, treating her like a stranger, standing at attention like a soldier and not like the boy who had held her in his arms in stables while the rain came down back in Edinburgh.

"Jack," Hazel said. "What are you doing here? Why—why didn't you write to me?"

Hazel couldn't stop the pleading note that crept into her voice, and she felt the hot pinpricks of tears tickling at her eyes.

He had opened his mouth to say something when a pair of revelers from the party came giggling down the hall, two men carrying whole flagons of wine. A servant passed in the other direction.

"We can't talk about this here," Jack said quietly. "You shouldn't be alone with me at all in a hallway at a party where people can see us. That's the sort of thing they ruin a lady's reputation about here."

"Since when do you care about a lady's reputation?" Hazel said. She meant it as a joke, but the two of them had lost that rhythm. It came out harsher than she intended, and Jack looked at the floor. There was too much to say and Hazel couldn't figure out the right way to say it. "What are you *doing* here?" Hazel managed to ask again.

From the entryway to the ballroom, another sailor in a naval jacket was swaying slightly from too much drink. "Come on, Ellis!" he called. "Leave the lady alone!"

"Ellis?" Hazel asked. "Is that what you go by now?"

"Couldn't go by the name of a dead man, could I?" Jack said, and he smiled. A small smile, and just for a moment, but *his* smile. It was devastating, a smile that somehow felt completely familiar even though she hadn't seen it in months.

Had Hazel forgotten the way a dimple appeared on his left cheek and on his chin? In that moment, Hazel felt sure that if she let him leave her sight, this would all turn out to have been a dream and she would never see that smile again.

"I'll call on you," Jack said as if he could read her mind. "You're treating the Princess at Warwick House?"

"No," Hazel said. "I mean, yes, I am—but, no. I waited for you for months, Jack, I'm not going to let you run away from me again with a vague promise. I'm staying at Number 3, Stafford Street, in London, not far from St. James's Park. Come see me tomorrow."

"Aye," Jack said, his brows knitted together. "I will come see you tomorrow, Number 3 Stafford Street."

"Early in the day," Hazel said.

"Dawn," Jack said.

The drunk sailor back in the ballroom called out loudly, "Jack Ellis, get your one-eyed arse back in here!"

Jack gave Hazel an apologetic look. "Just a minute, Karrelsby!"

"I just can't believe you're here," Hazel said in a whisper.

"I'll see you tomorrow," Jack said. "I promise."

His eye traveled from Hazel's eyes to her lips, and for a moment he seemed to want to kiss her. For a moment he looked at her like he used to look at her, and the life came back into his features. But then he just gave a small bow and loped away, toward his friend, leaving Hazel alone in the hallway, feeling both empty and full, somehow at once drunk and completely alert.

She had *seen* Jack again. He was *alive* and he was here, and the strangest thing about all of it was the way that he had almost felt like a stranger.

22

S PROMISED, JACK ARRIVED AT HAZEL'S apartments first thing in the morning, just as the nearby church bells were ringing six o'clock. Hazel had barely slept all night. She spent an hour lying on the bed after the party, still in her evening gown, thinking about everything that had happened, everything they had said.

Jack was alive, in London.

The maid had opened the door for Jack, and he was standing awkwardly in the entryway, shuffling his feet and staring at the floor. He was no longer in the blue jacket and white trousers he had been wearing the previous evening; instead, he wore simple black trousers and a white tunic that had been heavily patched in multiple places.

When Hazel came down the stairs to greet him, he seemed uncertain as to whether they should embrace. He bowed his head slightly and then fumbled for Hazel's hand to kiss it. "Miss Sinnett," he said stiffly.

Hazel had already opened her arms to embrace him, but

she was left standing in place, like a dancer before a waltz who had lost their partner.

"You smell like you," Hazel blurted out. "I'm sorry. That's a strange thing to say."

"Do I?" Jack said. "What do I smell like?"

A little self-consciously, Hazel leaned toward Jack's neck and breathed him in. The fine hairs on her forearms rose. He smelled like himself. Like a musk she hadn't smelled anywhere else, and the woods, and dirt, and the tannic, metallic smell of blood; and also new smells, a starch in the fabric of his shirt, and salt from the sea in his hair.

"You smell a little like a sailor," Hazel said.

"Aye, and having spent the last two months with sailors, I know that to be an insult."

"In a good way!" Hazel said.

The maid cleared her throat. "Might I call for tea, miss?" she said.

"Yes, please, thank you." Hazel gestured for Jack to follow her into the small sitting room. "Please, follow me," she said, formal as if she had been reciting lines from a play. "I suppose when a man calls on a lady, even a lady who lives alone and works as a physician, certain rituals are still meant to be followed."

Jack had already removed his hat and coat and hung them on the wall. "Thank you, Miss Sinnett," he said.

"Hazel," she replied. "Surely you can call me Hazel."

"If you insist, miss," Jack said. He sank into a chair in Hazel's sitting room with his back straight as the mast of a ship. He crossed his legs. Had he always crossed his legs like that? Hazel wondered. Even his casual gestures seemed unfamiliar and formal.

Hazel managed to wait until the tea was poured before she began to ask all the questions she wanted answers to: How had he survived his hanging? When did he leave Edinburgh? Why didn't he go to America? How did he end up in the Royal Navy?

"Well, I'm not in the Royal Navy," Jack said. "Not really. I served on the ship while we were in the Atlantic, and when we returned to port, I would formally enlist and begin my service. Least, that's what they expect me to do."

"But you're not going to?" Hazel asked.

"Oh," Jack said. "I don't know yet. I'm not sure I know about anything I'm going to do until I do it."

"How did you lose your eye?" Hazel asked. Jack stiffened as she reached out toward him, and she pulled her hand back. "I'm sorry," Hazel said. "I know this is . . . strange."

"I never thought I would see you again," Jack said to the floor. "It would have been easier if I were dead to you."

"What do you mean, 'easier'?" Hazel asked. "What *happened*? Why did you leave Edinburgh?"

"I thought it would be easier," Jack said again, but he still wasn't looking at Hazel.

"You can at least tell me what happened," Hazel said.

Jack tried to take a sip of his tea, but he was so insistent on not looking at Hazel that he somehow missed his mouth, and tea dribbled onto his shirt. Hazel and Jack both smiled, and for an instant, something seemed to thaw between them.

"Just tell me what happened," Hazel said again. "Please?"

Jack put the tea down carefully. "Aye," he said. "Fine, then. I'll start from the beginning, and maybe we can go from there."

JACK WOKE UP SOMEWHERE UNDERGROUND, THE smell of rotting death everywhere around him. At first, he thought he must have been buried alive; in a way, he was. There was total darkness, and Jack's next thought was that he was dead, that this was the afterlife, and the potion Hazel had passed to him through the cell bars didn't work after all. But then his hand wrapped around another human hand, and even in the dark, Jack knew where he was.

He was in a pile of bodies.

He tried to force himself to the surface; a dozen corpses—naked and cold, some still dripping with blood or something worse—pressed up against him. The bodies had gone hard with the rigor of death; he heard the sound of snapping echoing in the darkness as he forced his way toward escape. His neck burned, but he would deal with that later. All he needed to do right now was get out.

Finally, he did—falling to the floor beside the mound of corpses onto a freezing-cold stone floor. A stone ceiling arched above him, and Jack muttered a thankful half prayer at knowing where they had brought him: he was in the basement of the University of Edinburgh Medical School. For years, he had delivered bodies to this very place, where students—or professors, more often—paid a handful of coins for fresh corpses fit to be dissected.

Hanged bodies were among the few legal sources of cadavers for doctors. After his hanging, no doubt there was a small crowd of boys elbowing each other for the chance to claim his corpse and sell it. Jack probably would have known every single one of those boys. He had been one of them. He hoped whoever had managed to get his body was offered a good price for it.

His neck ached. It wasn't just the rope burn—though that stung hot under his hand when he tried to touch the skin. There was also a deep ache going down his spine from the base of his skull.

He knew the way out of here—there were two ascending stairwells. The one at the south end of the basement went up to a classroom, but the one at the northern end of the basement would take Jack straight into an alley that fed onto Forrest Road. The boys' school, George Heriot's, would be on the left, and the gates of Greyfriars Kirkyard would be visible ahead of him. It was a pathway he had taken many, many times. Usually in the dark, and usually managing a wooden cart that carried the naked, dead body he had just dug up.

Hands out and taking small steps while his eyes adjusted to the dim light, Jack walked slowly toward the staircase, unable to focus on much except the ache that seemed to radiate outward from every bone in his body and the sharp pain in his neck. The steps were there, just as he remembered, thank the Lord, and though no one seemed to be around, Jack still winced at the creak of the wooden stairs. He held his breath and pressed the door open, not sure whether it would be day or night in the outside world. Fortunately, the alleyway was secluded—the purchasing of resurrected bodies was illegal, after all—and Jack was confident that even if it was high noon, he would be able to slip away without being seen.

Except the staircase hadn't led outside at all.

He had opened a door directly into a classroom full of medical students, all of whom were looking directly at him.

It was just then that Jack realized he wasn't wearing any clothes.

He ran.

He ran straight through the classroom, the professor gaping at the chalkboard, too stunned to say anything. He ran as fast as he could, past the rows and rows of wooden chairs, past tables with what looked like human brains splayed wet and open upon them. He managed to grab a cloak that was hanging on a hook by the door before fleeing, the sound of laughter and some scattered applause coming from the classroom behind him.

Jack escaped from the University of Edinburgh Medical School like a cork blasting from a shaken bottle and raced down the nearest side street he saw, pulling from a clothesline as he ran what he would later discover to be a woman's chemise and a pair of trousers several sizes too big. Still, it would serve for now, he thought, pulling the chemise over his head and tucking the excess fabric into the trousers.

And now it was time to go to Hawthornden Castle. He would finally be able to reunite with Hazel.

He briefly wondered whether his room in the attic of the theater he used to work at would have been raided after his arrest. The theater was closed down owing to the spread of the Roman fever, and Jack imagined that it all would have been picked over, at first by people stripping the seats of their velvet fabric to sell for pennies, but then by people who'd heard about Jack Currer, hanged mass murderer, and wanted trinkets to sell, worth more for their very association with him. Edinburgh was a city that lived with death in its veins and embraced it with a grimace and a grin. There were certain closes off High Street where locks of hair from a killer or their victim could be bought and sold like treasure.

Still, there was a chance that some of his belongings remained hidden away—there was a small box he kept tucked into the rafters of the theater with a handful of coins, a clean shirt, and a pocket watch he could neither repair nor bring himself to sell, and he doubted even an intrepid thief would have managed to find it.

But as Jack crossed the main road, he glimpsed the evening broadsheet waving like a flag in the hand of a young paper-seller. Even from several meters away, he could make out the headline above an ink drawing that even Jack had to admit was a pretty good likeness: KIRKYARD KILLER HANGED. Jack cursed under his breath. He hadn't done the killings, obviously, but none of the murders had even been done in kirkyards! The victims had been killed in operating rooms for parts, cut up and discarded by the wealthy elite. And then they had blamed it all on Jack to cover it up.

It was almost as if the people of the city didn't want to know about the searing injustices happening beneath their noses on a daily basis, the cruelty and greed of the people in power. That was the sort of rotting corruption that threatened the basic structure of ordinary life. But people had to keep living, didn't they? They had to keep waking up, and feeding their children, and cleaning their clothes, and preparing simple meals to eat. A "kirkyard killer" made a far more agreeable story—easy to understand, easy to fix with a single simple hanging. It was the type of scandal people could gossip about over pints—the resurrection man killing people in cold blood, to save himself the trouble of digging them up—a tale that would become legend soon enough, titillating but no longer scary.

There was no hope arguing with a lie people wanted to believe.

Jack Currer was going to be the Kirkyard Killer forever.

The more immediate problem, of course, was that his face was stamped all over the city. And in his mismatched clothes, he had no hope of avoiding attention. There was no way he would be able to make it back to the theater, in the heart of the city, to scrounge for meaningless possessions that were probably gone anyway.

Already, people on the street were eyeing him strangely. He pulled the collar of the cloak up to block his face and headed away from the city center, toward the place where he knew he would be safe: Hawthornden . . . and Hazel.

It was a long walk to get to the castle through the woods, and longer because Jack wouldn't be taking the main roads. He probably wouldn't even make it by nightfall, he thought as he elbowed his way through the woods and tripped over heavy underbrush. He would be lucky if he reached Hawthornden by sunrise.

By the time he finally crossed an empty field and turned the corner where the trees grew tall along the ridge, and the castle became visible in the distance, Jack was exhausted and aching. The pain along his spine had only worsened, and he could feel bruises blossoming across his legs. Hawthornden looked conjured from a dream, its lantern glow blurry in the mist, as if the entire castle were a reflection in a lake. He would knock on the door, and Hazel would open the door— and they would embrace again and he would fall asleep in her bed and she would treat his wounds in the morning and he would cook her eggs and sausage for breakfast, and then . . .

And then . . . what?

Hazel would continue her studies to become a physician; she couldn't be associated with a murderer. *Jack* couldn't be seen anywhere near Scotland, anywhere near Great Britain, with the way salacious news liked to travel. What would happen if they found him, discovered he had escaped the noose, so to speak? No . . . he would have to stay in hiding.

He could live at Hawthornden while Hazel went out in the world, becoming a surgeon just as she always wanted, being celebrated the way she deserved. Coming home to Jack at night with stories of places he couldn't see and people he couldn't meet.

And what about when her father returned from his posting abroad, or her mother returned from England? Where would Jack hide then? Hazel would probably find him some cottage somewhere, some apartment where she would pay the landlord—how could Jack get a job anywhere near here when anyone who saw his face might recognize him? And Hazel would have to pay extra for the landlord's discretion.

Perhaps the news would fade. Maybe after a time, people would forget the Kirkyard Killer and Jack could get some work, make an honest living for the first time in his life, and not be a burden.

And then what?

Would a lady like Hazel ever be allowed to marry someone like him? A man with no past and no name and no future? She would be expected to marry a wealthy gentleman who could *provide* for her, who could give her a home, a *great house* and a place in society. Children, maybe. A family. It was going to be hard enough for her to become a surgeon like she wanted, being a woman. She shouldn't have to be shackled to the shadows with him.

And, a nagging voice reminded him, there was also the matter of the potion. The thing he drank that made him survive the hanging. It had tasted like licorice and a grassy, oily herb, and something sharp and bitter. Would it really make him live forever? Or had he used up its power in the hanging? Jack didn't know, and he didn't know whom he was supposed to ask. (He would cut out his own heart now before going to Beecham for anything—and God help the man if he ever found himself near Jack again.) But if it really was true . . . if he really was immortal . . . then there was even less of a life for Hazel with him around.

But still, he had to see her.

Jack knew the way up to Hawthornden Castle by heart, the way the path was lined with bluebells and curved through a copse of ash trees, and he was able to make it even in the dark. Now that he was closer, he could see that lanterns were lit in the windows of the library and Hazel's bedroom.

There she was.

Even through the distortion of thick, mottled glass, Jack could make out Hazel's look of concentration as she flipped the pages of a book on her desk, a candle burning close.

A horse gave a loud whinny from the stable nearby but Jack continued to stare, a part of him desperate to knock on the door and kiss her again, but another, confused part somehow unable to disturb her.

And so he watched. He watched as she turned the pages,

as her expression changed ever so slightly from confusion to frustration to satisfaction and then pride.

Her maid—Iona—came in with a tray of tea. Hazel was home here. She was happy. And she had everything she needed.

He had told himself that Hazel deserved someone to grow old with, and he did believe that to be true, but there was also a tightening fear in Jack's belly that cut through everything else: he had already said goodbye to Hazel once, and the thought of ever having to do it again scared him. He knew, as he regarded her through her window, that he would never be capable of watching Hazel Sinnett die.

The sound of crunching leaves and the squeak of carriage wheels ripped through the quiet evening. They were still in the distance, but Jack bristled; it was a carriage, and it was coming closer. Anyone who saw him would know his face. Anyone could send him back to prison . . . or worse. Jack didn't know what they would do to him if they discovered the hanging didn't take, and he didn't want to find out.

A horse in the nearby stable gave another whinny, and the sound of carriage wheels was getting louder.

Jack needed to run.

It was warmer in the stable than outside, where the biting night wind chapped at Jack's wrists and neck, which his cloak didn't cover. The horses whinnied and stamped at the human intruder. "Shhhh," Jack said, running his hand along the nose of the black horse—Betelgeuse, his name was. Jack learned to ride on this horse—Hazel had taught him. "We're mates, ain't we? You and me, Betelgeuse." The horse gave a sharp exhale through his nose and then seemed to relax.

Jack saddled the horse and looked around. There were

some riding clothes and boots covered in dried mud over by a corner. They were men's clothes, and in his size. Jack was confused for a moment. Did Hazel *leave* the clothes here for him to find? But then, no, he remembered how Hazel often wore her brother's clothes out riding.

He changed outfits as fast as he could, stuffing the chemise and ill-fitting pants in a saddlebag, figuring he might be able to sell them when he got to the coast. He still wore the cloak he had stolen from a befuddled medical student; it was slightly short in the sleeves, but he liked it anyway.

"Be good for me, now," Jack whispered to the horse, and hoisted himself into the saddle.

Mercifully, the horse had stopped whinnying. Betelgeuse just tossed his head as if to say, *Now what?*

Now, Jack thought, *we leave.*

He didn't let himself feel the aching that transformed into deep, sharp pain as he rode through the night. At first, he was just riding as fast as he could, but as the hours passed, he allowed the murky outline of a plan to take shape in his mind. He was riding west, away from the rising sun, toward the coast, where he could get on a boat and sail away from Scotland, to America. Where he could start a new life.

He stopped at an inn only when he was so tired he worried he might fall off the horse while they were moving, and traded the chemise and trousers for a bowl of lukewarm stew and a bag of feed for Betelgeuse. "Not bad, not bad," the old woman behind the counter had mumbled over and over, running the gauzy white fabric of the undershirt between her thumb and forefinger. "Not bad." Miraculously, the pocket of the stolen coat contained a few coins, and Jack offered several of them in exchange for a night's sleep in a bed that smelled like mold. The old woman's eyes were milky and white, but Jack still prayed silently when she seemed to squint at his face in recognition.

It took another full day of riding before Jack reached the town of Greenock, where a wide, curved river emptied into the glittering sea. Ships swayed gently in the harbor, and Jack's stomach leapt into his chest. This was the place. The last of Scotland he would ever see.

Paying the fare would prove to be an obstacle—Jack couldn't bring himself to sell Betelgeuse, who didn't belong to him, and so he just released him in the woods when he'd arrived at the outskirts of the port city. (Betelgeuse, for his part, did not even hesitate before trotting off happily into the trees, as if he had always believed he belonged to no master but nature.)

There seemed to be more ships in the harbor than anyone could keep track of; Jack had spent a lifetime working at being invisible, and so he passed an afternoon half-hidden behind a stack of crates and a coil of rope the size of a large man, eavesdropping on the various transactions happening on the docks and adjusting to the new rhythms of their accents. He hadn't realized just how *English* his Edinburgh Scots accent was until he listened to these Greenockians, who swallowed their consonants and spat out vowels like chicken bones.

The men shouted destinations at each other, most of which Jack had never even heard of. Places that sounded distant and exotic. But he had made up his mind, deciding—perhaps arbitrarily—on America, and so he waited until he overheard a gruff shout that sounded like, *"Virginia!"* and he scrambled toward the voice of a man directing a large shipment of crates onto a small but handsome vessel at the edge of the pier.

Jack offhandedly wondered what the punishment for a stowaway might be, but he didn't let himself linger too long on worrying. A life on the streets had taught him the importance of action versus foresight. *Steal now, if you have to, face the consequences later—at least you'll be alive when you do. Besides*, he thought, *it's not like they can kill me.*

But as Jack was eyeing the possible methods of slipping up the gangplank undetected (could he fit himself inside a crate and be *loaded* onto the boat with its cargo?), he realized getting on the ship might be easier than he anticipated.

"Deck crew! Seamen! One pound, ten shillings a month, plus one ration a day. Looking for strong young men, shove off tonight!"

Already a group of boys Jack's age and older were congregated around the recruiter. Jack joined the queue.

"Name?"

"Jack C— Uh, Ellis."

"Well, which is it, then?"

"That's my name. Jack Ellis." The made-up name came to him in the moment, so there it was. He was Jack Ellis now, easy as that.

"Well, Jack Ellis, you been on a ship before?"

"Aye. Loads of times. Worked at the docks in Leith outside Edinburgh," Jack lied.

The man eyed him, not entirely convinced by the lie, but not willing to go through the trouble to challenge him. The life had returned to Jack's body—in the time since he woke up in the university basement, his skin had slowly gone from gray to pink, but Jack was still aware he didn't look *good*. He was bruised, with scratches crawling their way up every one of his limbs. He was too skinny and overtired. The man probably thought he was a thief.

"Why'd ye leave Edinburgh, then?"

"Got in a spot of trouble," Jack answered, figuring that getting as close to the truth as possible would be his best bet.

To his relief, the man chuckled. "Good strong arms, at least," he said approvingly. "Be back at six, ship shoves off at seven, and we don't come back for stragglers. No thieving on the ship, and no trouble."

"And the ship is going to Virginia, right? America?" Jack asked.

"Aye, Norfolk. In America. Delivering cargo. But don't be getting any thoughts about acting like a passenger on a luxury voyage! You go where the ship goes and you're grateful for the work!"

Jack hurried off. He *was* grateful for the work. He would arrive in America with a few extra coins, having had a place to sleep and food to eat. For much of his life, he'd been much worse off.

He had nothing to do in Greenock, nor any money to do it with. And he was still wary about being recognized given the speed with which news might have traveled across Scotland. And so, Jack spent the next several hours wandering past the small houses, weaving among the chickens and firepits on the outskirts of town. From a scarecrow, he stole a large vicar's hat, battered down by rain and weather to the point where its formerly black fabric was now dull and colorless and the brim sagged helpfully, hiding his face.

At the pub, Jack sat with a pint and a piece of parchment covered in scratched-out sentences. He had started a letter to

Hazel a dozen times, but with each attempt, his words seemed either trivial or stupid or cruel. How could he explain everything in words—that he *couldn't* see her, because he couldn't see a life with her? Just thinking of Hazel made Jack's heart ache. But how could he leave without saying anything at all?

Maybe in America, he could build a new life for both of them. He would become successful, buy land, become respected. No one would know about the hangings or Beecham or anything. Maybe in America, Hazel could even work as a surgeon openly. They could live in a house together as man and wife, and he could kiss her eyelids every morning before she woke up.

No.

Even if it was possible, that fantasy was a lifetime away. How could he ask Hazel to wait so long for him? Maybe it would be easier for her if she just thought he was gone. Hope was a dangerous thing. Most of the pain in the world, Jack had learned, was because of hope.

In the end, he was only able to come up with a single sentence that he felt conveyed everything: his love, his apology, his hope for the future. *I'll be waiting for you,* he wrote. And if she wanted to believe that he was dead, well, she still could.

Jack made it back to the dock an hour early and waited, watching the sun set red-orange over the port and the ship that would take him to his new life. It had two tall masts meant to be square-rigged with billowing sails. Jack would later learn that this type of ship was called a brig. The vessel's name was written on the hull in peeling white paint: AURORA.

"Oi!"

A man as tall and wide as a door bumped Jack's shoulder when he was walking up the gangplank. "Careful there," the man said with a nasty grin. He had a silver tooth that glinted in the fading sunlight. The man stared at Jack's face for a moment too long, lowering his own head to try to see under the brim of Jack's hat. When Jack tried to pass him, he jostled the gangplank, making Jack stumble. Jack just pulled his hat lower over his face and continued on belowdecks where the crew were instructed to hang their hammocks.

He had dealt with this sort before—if you couldn't take them out in a single punch (and looking at this gurk, Jack was almost certain he couldn't), the best thing to do was ignore them. The social hierarchy aboard the ship would settle; Jack never worried about making friends. The broad man with the silver tooth wouldn't have any actual power over him. (If he'd known then how wrong he was, he might have taken a job on a different ship. But how was he to know?)

The man's name was Smeaten, and as Jack would soon discover, he was the ship's boatswain, in charge of the deck crew. He was the miserable sort of man who took pride in an ability to make others feel as small as possible. Every morning, he swaggered out of the captain's quarters with a smirk at a private joke that he wouldn't be sharing and barked out assignments. "Muldon—rigging! McGinley, in the galley! Potter, tea for the captain. And *Ellis*." Hulking over to Jack, Smeaten would stand so close that Jack would need to arch his back to look him in the face. "Think you're capable of swabbing the deck, Ellis?"

"Aye, sir," Jack said.

"Louder," Smeaten said.

"Aye, sir," Jack said, louder, through his teeth.

Smeaten would then spend the rest of the morning watching Jack, commenting on his work ("You want those strokes to be even! What are you, some sort of idiot? What sort of idiot doesn't even know how to clean a floor?"), and stomping with relish whenever he could ruin what Jack had already cleaned. Smeaten was a bully to all the seamen, but for Jack he reserved a specific pocket of his vitriol and venom.

At the end of the first month, Jack and the other men lined up before the ship's purser, who gave them each a handful of coins for their wages. Smeaten cornered Jack before he made it back to his hammock. Before Jack could wriggle away, the man had his massive meaty forearm pinning him to a bulkhead. With his other hand, Smeaten ripped Jack's hat off. "Why ye always wearing that hat?" he said, his foul breath warm on Jack's face. "Some'in to hide, is it?" Smeaten smiled wide enough for Jack to see his silver tooth. "A handsome face like that," he continued. "Not one to hide. Memorable face, innit. Just the right sort of face for the papers." He ran a filthy finger across the scar on Jack's neck, and Jack's insides turned to ice.

He knew him. He recognized him.

Smeaten lifted his forearm and Jack was released from the bulkhead, but he knew there was nowhere for him to go.

"I 'ave a sister out in Edinburgh. Tells me loads about the goings-on. Shows me broadsheets too. Knew you from the first instant I saw you. *Kirkyard Killer.*"

"You're mistaken," Jack said, but he knew with a sinking feeling that Smeaten wouldn't believe him.

"Ought to tell the captain right here and now," Smeaten said, raising his voice a little and making Jack cringe. "Bet the captain wouldn't be too pleased with an escaped killer on ship. Somehow escaped the noose, eh? Wonder if you'd have better luck at the bottom of the sea."

Jack didn't know what to say and so he didn't say anything, mentally running through possibilities for ways to escape Smeaten and this ship. There didn't seem to be very many of them.

Smeaten grabbed Jack's wrist and pried his fingers open. "I think I'll be taking these," he said, pulling the coins from Jack's palm. "And I think I'll be taking these every month. Unless, of course, you want the whole ship to know they have a murderer on board. Course, I might just tell him anyway when we land. Just the lawful thing to do, serving King and Country. And I am the lawful sort."

"If I am a murderer," Jack said, "you'd think you'd be more careful about making me your enemy."

Smeaten just sniggered. "You're the dirt on my shoe, *boy*. And I'm gonnae be smiling real big when they take you back to hang again. I'm gonnae watch, and make sure you're good and dead."

He ambled off, jostling Jack's coins in his hand as he went, and Jack sank to the deck. The dizziness he felt wasn't due to the rocking ship. He was trapped.

The same situation repeated itself four weeks later: Jack was paid, and Smeaten demanded his full payment in order to keep his *silence*. The humiliation of it burned as badly as the lost wages. The other sailors began keeping their distance from Jack, unable to get a read on him, confused by the way Smeaten chose to call him out and toy with him specifically. There seemed to be a universal understanding that Jack was somehow toxic, and associating with him would only make things harder for you.

Jack needed a miracle, some way out of a situation that was taking him ever closer to true capture. Instead, *Aurora* got a disaster.

The storm was like nothing Jack had ever seen before. It had rained in Edinburgh, of course; it rained almost constantly some weeks. But at sea, the rain was *everywhere*. It seemed to come from every direction at once, whipping and biting at skin, soaking through fabric in an instant. It hit without warning after what had been a fine and easy day of sailing. Jack and the crew were awakened by the ship's violent lurching and the shouting that came from above, on the main deck. They sprang into action, hauling on buntlines, and Jack joined the topmen in climbing the masts in order to secure the sails once they were furled, before the wind could pull them beneath the waves.

One of the sailors on the mast below Jack fell from where he was climbing. The boy hit the side of the ship with a sickening crunch and then disappeared overboard.

The wind was impossibly strong; shouts were swallowed the second they left someone's mouth. When the big wave approached, tall as three ships stacked on top of one another, no one screamed. Or maybe it was just that Jack wasn't able to hear them.

The last thing Jack ever saw out of his right eye was a broken piece of the wooden rig whizzing right at him.

THERE WAS NOTHING. NOT EVEN BLACKNESS. A void so dark Jack didn't have a word for it. And then came the taste of salt, and the glug of the water that had filled his lungs and belly. He was holding on to a floating piece of wood, something he would later realize was part of the ship's hull, soaking wet and clinging to the surface with shaking fingers. HMS *Aurora* was gone, pulled into a thousand pieces by the storm, and every soul on board had perished. Jack had died too. Or rather, he *would* have died.

Instead, he was adrift at sea: starving but unable to die from hunger, thirsty beyond all imagining but unable to die from thirst. He was blind in one eye—a piece of wood remained sticking out of his socket, straight as a flagpole. Jack remembered enough from his time with Hazel to know that if you couldn't patch a wound, removing whatever was stabbing you would make things worse, and so he left it in. One of his legs was broken, twisted beneath his body at an angle that made him vomit seawater and bile.

By the time HMS *Iphigenia* passed by and spotted him, Jack's body had gone tomato-red and peeling from the sun, and he had lost so much weight each of his ribs and the curve of the cage beneath them was visible. If he wasn't immortal, he would have died ten times over.

So, Jack thought, *I really will live forever.*

The *Iphigenia* was a thirty-six-gun frigate, with three tall masts and a British flag waving proudly. The naval surgeon aboard had been astonished that Jack was still alive. "The blood loss alone," he murmured, examining the wooden stake that was still embedded in Jack's eye. Jack winced when the surgeon, an older man with a shock of white hair thin and fluffy as pulled cotton, prodded at him. Jack was given a strip of leather to bite down on while the surgeon went to work with a small scalpel.

"Best not to look under there," he warned Jack, who was recovering in the infirmary bed with a brand-new eyepatch. (Eventually, Jack would find it impossible to resist, and he would gasp at the empty socket, purple and wet.)

It took two weeks for Jack to regain enough strength to move about the ship, albeit limping on the broken leg that the surgeon had set. To the lieutenant on board, Jack had again given the name Jack Ellis. He said that he was the boatswain aboard the *Aurora*.

"And before that? That's an Edinburgh accent, isn't it?"

"Yes, sir," Jack said. "Worked as a . . . valet, sir. Personal valet to a noble family in Edinburgh."

"*Which* family?" the officer asked. His mustache bristled.

Jack swallowed hard, but the answer came to him in an instant: "Captain and Lady Sinnett. At Hawthornden Castle."

The first officer seemed pleased enough, and when Jack had recovered enough to leave the infirmary, he set Jack to work as a mess cook. The ship was headed south, toward the blockade along the western coast of Africa, with the aim of interdicting slave ships, and they weren't going to change course for a castaway. And so for the rest of the voyage, Jack would exist in a nether space, neither crew nor guest.

But the English sailors he shared a cabin with were affable—if a little too amused by Jack's Scots lilt. And Jack understood that the best way to secure a safe place for himself here would be to make himself invaluable. And so, he woke up before anyone else and helped to swab the deck and peel potatoes in the galley before changing into the livery they set aside for him to serve meals to the officers.

It was hard work, but work that Jack understood quickly enough. The rules on board a Royal Navy ship were clear and defined, and the rhythms were comforting in that way.

"What's that ship over there?" Jack asked one afternoon to a young English boy named Thomas whom he had become friendly with. Thomas was nineteen, but still had the face and voice of a child; he was proudly cultivating a mustache that looked to Jack like nothing more than peach fuzz.

Thomas squinted at the sails in the distance. "French ship, by the look of it," he declared. "Probably merchants. Though"— he rubbed his nonexistent mustache thoughtfully—"you don't often see a merchant ship with that many cannon."

The French ship was getting closer and closer; every time Jack's chores had him return to the deck, its hull was becoming larger on the horizon.

"S'nothing to worry about!" Thomas had shouted down to Jack. (Thomas was securing the rigging of the sails to the mast.) "We're at peace with France, but that doesn't mean they don't want to play a game of chicken."

It was at that moment the French ship fired upon them, while simultaneously raising a black flag. "Pirates!" the first officer cried.

In an instant, the ship's captain, Robert Mends, was standing on deck, wearing his full naval uniform, a sword at his hip. "To the cannon, lads!" he cried. "Swing wide round portside!"

The pirates' cannon fire had sent the *Iphigenia* rolling. Jack looked up: Thomas was clinging to the mast by his fingertips.

Jack didn't think. He was immortal, wasn't he? He grabbed a rope, looped it around his shoulder, and began to climb. "No!" the first officer called when he saw what Jack was doing.

"Too late!" Jack shouted down. He climbed as fast as he could while the ship rocked violently and dropped out from beneath him, making it to the mast, where Thomas's fingers were beginning to slip.

"There you are," Jack said, pulling him up onto the rigging. He gave Thomas the rope. "Use this to climb down."

"You don't need it?" Thomas asked, teeth chattering. He

had told Jack a few evenings before that this was his first voyage after joining the Royal Navy. Jack had pretended not to notice the sounds of Thomas being sick in the night.

"No," Jack said. "I'll stay up here."

And when the French ship struck the side of the *Iphegenia*, and the pirates, knives in their teeth and guns at their belts, swung across on ropes, Jack was stationed above, shouting down their every movement to the first officer and to Captain Mends. "Three of them still on the ship, sir! 'Bout to fire the cannon!"

Mends roared for a group of sailors to fire first, and the French pirates didn't get a chance.

Jack watched as one of the pirates across the deck cocked a pistol aimed at the captain. He acted before his brain realized what he was doing, leaping down and dragging a knife through the canvas sail to slow his fall.

"Best think twice about that," he said, landing with his knife at the neck of the pirate with the pistol. "Hand it over here."

Jack roughly tied the pirate's hands behind his back, tight enough to leave red marks, and then winked at him. "Thanks for the pistol," he said, and sprang back into battle.

In the end, HMS *Iphigenia* didn't lose a single man, and they made short work of boarding the privateers' ship—a sleek but sturdy gun-brig called the *Maria*—and claiming her.

"Excellent work," Captain Mends said to Jack as they were tying the hostages together.

"Jack, sir. Jack Ellis."

"Ellis, yes. The castaway from Scotland. There are career Royal Navy men who wouldn't have been as brave in the fight as you were."

"Thank you, sir."

Mends turned to the first officer. "Let's put Smithee on the *Maria* to take her back to London, and let's make Jack here my personal steward on the *Iphigenia*." To Jack he added, "And I hope once we go back ashore, you might consider formally joining our ranks."

From that day on, Jack served as the captain's personal steward, and when the ship docked in London, he was part of the crew that were given a hero's welcome: the group of English sailors who not only fought off French pirates without a single casualty but claimed one of their ships as well.

AZEL DIDN'T EVEN NOTICE THAT HER TEA HAD gone cold. She had been staring at Jack as he recounted how he'd spent the time apart since they last saw each other. Her heart was expanding through her chest. For months, she had thought that if she saw Jack again, she would throw her arms around him so tightly there wouldn't be an inch between them. And now they were here, sitting across from each other, drinking tea while trying to remember how to make conversation.

"Does it still hurt?" Hazel said, gesturing toward his right eye.

Jack raised his hand to it reflexively. He nodded. "Probably would have healed better if you had been the one doing the surgery. The doctor was old—his hands kept shaking. He kept saying it was the movement of the ship. He didn't have any of that—any of that stuff Beecham gave to people before his surgeries. The drops of the magic stuff."

Hazel smiled weakly.

"I guess it doesn't really make a difference," Jack said. "I got the big dose, didn't I."

They looked at each other, and Hazel wondered if Jack was as afraid as she was, or whether she was just seeing her own fear reflecting back at her.

"How long are you going to stay in London, then?" Hazel said.

"I don't know," Jack answered. "I hadn't really planned on joining the Royal Navy."

"I was going to say," Hazel said, "I wouldn't have imagined you living a life as a naval man. Saluting on cue."

"When it comes down to it, I'm terrible at following the rules," Jack said, and he smiled wide enough for the first time all morning for his long dogteeth to become visible.

"Oh?" Hazel said, her heart beginning to pound.

"Terrible," Jack repeated. He gingerly put his cup of tea down in his saucer. "I can fool them for a little while. But eventually?"

They were still sitting across from each other, but Hazel felt a heaviness between her legs, and she watched Jack's good eye flicker toward her lips.

A knock on the door brought Hazel back into her body. "I should get that," she whispered.

"Should you?"

The maid appeared in the doorway of the sitting room. "Miss, a Mr. Simon von Ferris is at the door for you," she said, averting her eyes from the sight of Hazel and Jack sitting so close together that anyone from society might have made the sign of the cross.

Jack crossed his legs again the other way. "Go on, then," he said. "It's okay. I'll finish my tea."

Head still spinning, Hazel followed the maid out to the front door, where Simon was waiting on the stoop with a handful of daffodils.

"Good morning, Miss Sinnett," he said, kissing her hand dryly. The bags under his eyes were as dark as Hazel had ever seen them, swollen and purple. And Simon's eyes were bloodshot and wet. He looked like he had been up all night— after not having slept in a week.

Hazel glanced down at the flowers in his hand, and Simon followed her gaze. He seemed surprised to remember he was holding them. "For you," he said, offering the daffodils, as if they had merely been waiting for her on the doorstep already and he had picked them up to make things easier.

Daffodils. Hazel knew what they symbolized: high regard, and respect. "They're beautiful, Dr. Ferris, thank you." As she spoke, she could sense Jack staring at the closed sitting room door, listening to everything they were saying.

"You can call me Simon, you know, Miss Sinnett," he said quietly.

"And yet you still call me Miss Sinnett."

Simon smiled, but he looked pained. The exhaustion settled over his features.

"Are you quite well, Simon von Ferris?" Hazel said. "Can I offer you anything? Tea?" She mentally cursed herself for the hospitality—she couldn't sit with Simon for tea when Jack was already in the sitting room, ear pressed against the keyhole, no doubt.

"No, thank you," Simon said. "I have spent the past few

days in the infirmary, working, and I recalled reading that fresh air might be conducive to mood and quality of thinking. I thought perhaps you might be interested in joining me in a brief stroll through St. James's Park."

"Oh, I—" Hazel said, and before she could stop herself, she instinctively glanced back at the sitting room door.

Simon's eyes followed, and then caught on something: Jack's coat, hanging by the entryway.

"Ah," Simon said. "I see you already have company. Forgive my intrusion, Miss Sinnett."

"It's no intrusion at all," Hazel said.

Simon lifted a hand. "It was a foolish outing regardless. I should get back to His Royal Majesty anyway."

"How is he, then?" Hazel asked, relieved to have found a way to shift the conversation back toward solid ground.

"His condition is only worsening. And nothing—*nothing* I do is even coming *close* to helping and . . ." He pulled his hands into fists but then relaxed with a long exhale. "Pardon me. I forget myself."

"You don't," Hazel said. "Maybe I can help you."

"Some problems," Simon said sadly, "are not to be solved. They're merely meant to be borne. Have a pleasant morning, Miss Sinnett." He bowed and turned on his heel and left before Hazel could say another word.

23

ACK WAS SITTING IN AN ARMCHAIR, STARING into the middle distance with a blank expression. His tea sat on the table, no longer steaming.

"I should go," he said.

"What?" Hazel said. "Why?"

"I'm tired," Jack said. "The work on the ship is hard and we're given very few days of leave."

"I— Yes, of course," Hazel said.

He stood and straightened his shirt. "Thank you for the tea, Miss Sinnett."

"Jack—Jack, wait a moment. What are you doing? Why are we . . . Why are we acting like strangers?"

Jack didn't turn to look at her. "What am I doing here?" he said quietly.

"Jack. It's me. I'm here. I missed you so much." Hazel heard her words as they left her mouth; they felt trite and flat.

"I should return to the ship," Jack said. "It was really nice to see you again, Hazel." He said her name like a prayer.

No.

She couldn't just let him walk away.

There had to be more. The thought of Jack leaving her life and disappearing again was a dagger, a knife wound, a twisting in her heart that no stitches would ever be able to secure.

There had to be something she was forgetting. Jack wasn't looking at her, and he was walking toward the door. She followed him.

"What are you going to do, then?" Hazel said. "Where are you going to go? What's your plan for the future?"

"I suppose I might as well do a tour with the *Iphigenia*, then," Jack said to the floor. "Get some money. Make a name for myself. And then, I can't tell you where I'll go. First, because I'm not certain myself. And second, because if I were, you're stubborn enough that I believe you'd try to track me down."

"How long before the *Iphigenia* leaves?"

"S'meant to shove off to the western coast on the first of September."

"September," Hazel said. "That's something." And then, all at once, she knew what to do. "Jack! Tonight!"

He paused in the doorway, confused.

Hazel blinked away the excitement of her brilliant idea and continued. "I mean, *tonight*, come with me. There are people *like you*. Immortal people. A society, called the Companions to the Death. They're brilliant, Jack. Brilliant chemists and writers, and—and it's not a 'curse,' and they'll prove that to you!" She couldn't believe she hadn't thought of it earlier. The Companions would meet Jack, and they would adore him. And Jack would see that he didn't always need to be alone.

Jack tilted his head and raised a hand to smooth his hair. Hazel had seen that gesture hundreds of times. It was a reflex on Jack's part, and never did it do anything close to making his hair look neat. Her heart leapt at seeing it again, now, here.

"I don't know if a place like that is my sort of scene," Jack said. "Fancy club with a fancy name."

"They'll love you," Hazel said. "You're *immortal*. You took the Tincture! You're already one of them."

Jack looked unconvinced, but he wasn't leaving. "I don't usually socialize with many chemists."

Hazel grinned. "Surgeon isn't that different from chemist. And we get on, don't we?"

For the first time since she had returned to the sitting room, Jack smiled back at her. "Aye," he said. "I suppose we do."

They stood there for a moment, two brown eyes looking into one blue-gray. "I really should head back to the ship," Jack said finally. "Before the boatswain has me flogged for abandoning my post."

"Do you know where the Seven Dials is?"

"I can find it."

"Meet me there tonight," Hazel said. "We'll go together. I'll introduce you."

"What time?"

"Eight?"

Jack nodded. "All right, then. I'll meet you at eight o'clock tonight."

"Don't run away again," Hazel said. "I mean it. Promise me."

Jack shrugged on his jacket and settled his hat on his head. "I can survive a hanging and a stabbing and shipwreck and starvation," he said. "And I still wouldn't ever dare to do anything as foolish as standing up Hazel Sinnett."

HE WAS EARLY, WAITING AT THE CORNER NEAR Seven Dials before the church bells rang eight o'clock. Seeing him standing there before he noticed her—*real*, shifting his weight from leg to leg, nodding at the shopkeepers closing up and heading home—made Hazel smile.

"You came," she said.

"I told you I would," he said, and smiled, but the smile didn't reach his eyes.

"Come on."

Hazel grabbed Jack's elbow and directed him toward the small door hidden beneath the swinging wooden sign with a brain on it. "Have you been bumping into things?" Hazel asked after knocking. "With only one good eye, I mean."

"No," Jack said. "I got used to it faster than I thought I would. Stumble a bit going down stairs sometimes if it's dim, but aside from that, I dunno. Don't think about it much."

"I think you look sort of dashing," Hazel said. "Swash-buckling."

"You think? I will say, it makes it easier to wink," Jack said, and his smile felt real this time.

If only, Hazel thought, she could spend the rest of her life trying to make Jack Currer smile.

The club room was only half-filled that evening. Byron was smoking something out of a pipe near the fireplace, with a man in a plaid vest Hazel didn't recognize, and Mrs. Thire, Marie-Anne, and Banneker were playing cards at the table. They all stood when Hazel and Jack entered.

"Miss Sinnett," Marie-Anne said. Her eyes widened in surprise. "You brought a . . . guest."

"She knows the Companions is invite only, doesn't she?" Byron called from his chair. "This is a *club*, not a public park."

"I know," Hazel said quickly. "This is Jack Cu— Jack Ellis. He's . . . like you. He was given the Tincture back in Edinburgh. It was from Dr. Beecham."

They all stood there, mouths open. It was the first time Hazel had ever seen a look of surprise on Marie-Anne Lavoisier's face. But almost instantly, she composed her features.

"Well," said the Frenchwoman. "In that case, I'm glad you brought him to us. Mr. Ellis, how long have you been . . . in your current state?"

"Immortal, you mean?" Jack said, and Marie-Anne bristled at his directness. "Since last winter, I suppose. Felt like ice and fire in my veins at the same time. And then"—he pulled the collar of his shirt aside to show the rope marks on his neck—"I survived a hanging." Every single member of the Companions to the Death was looking at Jack as though he were a strange animal that had wandered in off the street.

"Charming," Mrs. Thire said dryly.

"So they're letting horse thieves become immortal now, are they?" Byron said. He turned to his companion. "Brown, I'm sorry I voted against your little friend the other week. Clearly our standards have slipped and no one told me."

"It wasn't horse thieving," Jack said. "It was murder." Byron cocked an eyebrow. "I didn't do it, though!" Jack added quickly.

Byron smirked and turned back to the man in the vest. "How is your friend, anyway?"

Brown pulled his eyes from Jack and back to Byron,

crossing his legs. "We managed to raise enough funds to get him to go to Rome. Hopefully he'll recover his health there."

"Or not," Byron said. "Best thing that can happen to a poet is dying young, I've always thought that. Not letting what-was-his-name—*Keats*—into the Companions is going to be a blessing, Brown, you listen to me."

Brown just took a sip of tea.

Marie-Anne approached Jack uneasily, and Jack, sensing there was something he should do, bowed low. Hazel blushed and looked away. It had been an awkward bow, too formal and unsophisticated at once.

"Jack Ellis, ma'am," he said as introduction.

"Marie-Anne Lavoisier," she said. "Please, sit for a cup of tea. Miss Sinnett, I wondered whether I might trouble you for a quick repair on my shoulder. The muscles seemed to be fraying."

"Certainly," Hazel said.

"Make yourself comfortable, Mr. Ellis," Marie-Anne said. "We'll be upstairs for just a moment."

Hazel looked back at Jack apologetically while she followed Marie-Anne up the rear stairs. Jack stood, unsure where to sit with the cup of tea and saucer he was holding in his hands. He hadn't worn his one nice jacket: he was in a frayed white shirt and britches, and surrounded by the oil paintings and candlelit opulence of the Companions, he couldn't have looked more out of place. Seeing him here brought to mind the image of a street dog, fur matted and thin, sitting on a brocade pillow.

He gave Hazel a silent look back, as if to say *I'll be fine*, and

Hazel disappeared into the laboratory to do Marie-Anne's surgery.

Antoine was already upstairs, fiddling with some glass tubing being heated above an open flame.

"Good evening, Monsieur Lavoisier," Hazel said. He smiled back.

Marie-Anne removed her jacket and began unwinding the lacing on the back of her dress. "It's my left arm," she said to Hazel. "I can already feel it coming loose."

"Not a problem," Hazel replied. "I'll get it sewn up in no time at all."

Marie-Anne had been right: the arm *was* loose. If she had gone a few more days, it might have come off at the shoulder completely. Pink muscle was visible where the flesh had completely torn away, but there was already so much scarring there that the wound barely bled.

"Wear and tear," Marie-Anne said thoughtfully, even as she winced in pain. "The price of a body lasting longer than a body should."

"Have you ever thought of a way of . . . reversing the Tincture?" Hazel said, trying to make her voice sound light.

Marie-Anne blinked. "No. Of course not. Whatever for?"

"Just academically, I mean," Hazel said. "Is it possible?" She could feel Antoine's eyes on her as she finished threading her surgical needle.

"No," Marie-Anne said. "It isn't."

Hazel finished sewing up her arm, and Marie-Anne made a few exploratory circles with her shoulder. "Wonderful work," she murmured. "Best we've had since this whole exercise began. Wouldn't you agree, Antoine?"

Antoine raised a glass of bright orange liquid in confirmation.

"Now," Marie-Anne said, shrugging her jacket back on, "shall we return to your friend?"

Downstairs, Jack was sitting next to Lord Byron and his mate, Brown.

"Mind if I join you?" Hazel said, sliding into an empty seat beside Jack. Brown and Byron stood as Hazel was sitting down, the courtesy automatic. Jack scrambled to get out of his chair in time.

"I don't know if we've had the pleasure yet," Brown said, returning to his seat. "Charles Armitage Brown."

"Hazel Sinnett. Pleasure," said Hazel.

"I've heard you're quite the surgeon. I've been having problems with my bladder recently—*black urine*. And an awful stench. Can I ask you to get me on the table, say, next week? I'll want to be completely asleep. All the ethereum you can manage."

"What can she possibly do for your *urine*?" Jack said with mild horror.

"It's probably a problem with the bladder," Hazel said. "I'd be happy to take a look. In fact, I just finished a chapter on the bladder for the book I'm working on."

"Not a poetry book, I hope," Byron said into his glass.

"A treatise on anatomy and medicine," Hazel said. "A household guide straightforward enough so that even men—or women—who can't attend university can still learn."

"I think it sounds wonderful," Jack said.

"Do you know how to read, Jack?" Byron said.

"Aye," Jack replied. "I do."

Hazel glared at Byron, who returned his attention to his whisky.

"I think the book sounds wonderful," Charles Brown said. "In fact, I have *several* friends in London publishing who I think might find it of particular interest. If you would fancy an introduction—"

"Yes!" Hazel said, unable to conceal her excitement. "Mr. Brown, that would be wonderful. Thank you so much. It's nearly done. I'm just finishing a few final notes."

"My good friend Thomas Clout might be a good fit if you wish to engage a printer. Always looking for this sort of thing. I'll make some inquiries—"

"I think I'm going to need another repair on this foot, Sinnett," Byron said loudly, interrupting. "It's better, but still not *right*. I don't want to walk with a limp."

"If you were *half* as vain as you are, Byron," Brown said, "I think you'd be twice as good of a poet."

Byron sighed dramatically. "The only reason I'm *any* good as a poet is because I'm vain. If I cannot make myself more handsome, I can make my words more beautiful."

Brown rolled his eyes. "I'm remembering now why I seldom come down to London from the Heath. Your company is best in small doses."

Byron waggled his eyebrows. "That's not what your wife thinks."

Brown's nose went red. "I'm not married!" he said, and though he and Byron held each other's gaze for a moment in challenge, a second later they had both burst into laughter. Hazel joined them; even Jack cracked a smile.

Several drinks later, the conversation had transitioned

somehow to politics. Banneker and Mr. Lewis were playing darts nearby, listening intently.

"The Prince Regent was a Whig too," Brown was saying. "That is, until he became the Regent."

"Of course," Byron said. "He was all for the power of the people, for the Parliament, *against* the antiquated rule of a monarch, until *he* became the monarch. Same story as always: they're liberal until they're old and rich and scared."

"Well said," called Mr. Lewis from the bar, where he was pouring himself a large glass of a brown liquid.

"We thought the Prince would be easier to control because he's, well, idiotic," Byron was saying. "But turns out true stupidity is *believing* you're secretly brilliant."

"That last mistress had been a good influence on him at least," Brown added. "The Catholic one. At least she had some common sense."

"The quicker Charlotte becomes Queen, the better," Byron said. He drained his own glass. "Then we have a chance at some real change."

"Won't the same thing happen?" Jack said.

Byron and Brown stared at him, as if just remembering that he was sitting there. "She's a Whig now," Jack continued. "Right? But as soon as she's the one in power, who's to say she won't become a Tory like her father?"

The two men stared at him some more. "What was your name again?" Byron asked.

"Ellis. Jack Ellis."

"Cambridge man, Jack Ellis? Or was it Oxford where you read for politics?"

"Byron, don't be cruel to the boy," Banneker mumbled from the dartboard.

"No, no, I'm actually curious! Let me guess: King's College, Oxford! I've known plenty of Scots who read at King's."

"I didn't go to university," Jack said.

Byron made a face in mock shock. "And yet we clearly have a political scholar in our midst! Tell me, Ellis, have you read any of the poetry of Keats? Our friend Charles Brown here tried to put him up for admission to our little club, but we voted against him. Do you have an opinion on his use of metaphor? Of imagery. Personally, I found his work a little trite, but Brown disagrees. Break our tie."

"I haven't read him," Jack admitted.

"Pity," Byron said.

"Tell me," Hazel said, louder than she meant to. "Was it Cambridge where they taught you your manners, then, Lord Byron?"

Byron rolled his eyes. "I'm just trying to figure out what Beecham saw in him. What he was contributing to humanity that was so important that it should continue forever."

"He didn't," Jack said. "I mean, he gave the bottle of the stuff to Hazel. She gave it to me."

"Ah!" Byron said, with a playful lilt in his voice. "Now I see. The *brilliant* female surgeon who fell in *love* with a common criminal! It's charming!"

"That's enough, Byron," Brown said.

Byron smirked and refilled his glass from a decanter at his elbow. "If you say so, Charles. Did any of you read Beecham's obituary? I wonder if he wrote it himself, it was so fawning."

"Beecham is dead?" Jack said. "When? *How?* How did he die?"

Byron scoffed, but before he could say anything, Hazel interrupted. "They say he's dead. But since he took the Tincture, too, he's probably just biding his time to become someone else."

"Do we know who he is this time?" Banneker said. "Is anyone still in touch with him?"

"No," Marie-Anne said. "And it doesn't matter."

Jack cleared his throat. "Well, if none of you know who he's pretending to be now, how do you know he's not dead for real this time? That he didn't figure out a way to end this for good?"

The others went silent. The crackling of the candles was the only sound in the room, until Marie-Anne took a step forward.

"Mr. Ellis," she said. "I spent decades unraveling the precious secrets of human animation and formulating the Tincture to preserve life. It defies aging, loss of blood. It can overcome hanging and beheading. I could cut open your belly and remove every one of your organs one by one, and though you would writhe in agony, and though the normal functions of your flesh would cease, the eternal and holy spark of your existence would never cease to be."

Jack straightened his eye patch. "If there's a—Tincture or whatever that can make someone live forever, I don't see why Beecham wouldn't be able to make another one that would make him mortal again."

Marie-Anne smiled, not a cruel smile, but not a kind one either. "I assume, Mr. Ellis, that you haven't read my husband Antoine's discovery from 1789 proving that mass can be neither created nor destroyed in chemical reactions. Forgive me for my condescension, but the matter is a little more complex than a lever that one can flip back and forth at will."

She lifted a glass of wine and swirled it in her hand. She

emptied the remaining wine into a vase of flowers, and then, without warning, she dropped the glass to the ground, where it instantly shattered into thousands of pieces.

"In theory, we could find every one of the pieces and glue them back together exactly as we found it, and we would have a glass capable of holding wine again. But it wouldn't be quite the same glass again, would it? No. Some pieces are lost forever, too small to be seen by the human eye." She stepped on the pieces of glass with a sickening crunch. "Some of the glass has already become dust. And some of what was holding the glass together has become something else entirely. Heat. The sound of the crunch when it fell. The glass, Mr. Ellis, is *gone*. You cannot simply glue the pieces back together."

"People aren't wineglasses," Jack said quietly.

"Precisely," Marie-Anne said. "They're far more complicated."

Hazel was burning with humiliation, but she wasn't sure whether it was for Jack or for the Companions. The entire evening had become a runaway carriage, and the horses were now running too fast and too wild for Hazel to know how to get them trotting back on the road again.

"He's right, though, isn't he?" Hazel said. Her voice sounded strange in her own ears. "We wouldn't have known that immortality was even possible until you and Monsieur Lavoisier and Dr. Beecham managed it. None of you have heard from Dr. Beecham. None of us know where he went if he did go to reinvent himself. Maybe he *is* gone. He left me an inheritance, for God's sake. Through a solicitor and everything. Maybe Beecham *did* find a way to undo it, and you and I just can't see how he did it yet."

"How much did he leave you?" Byron asked.

"We have solved the secrets of life, Miss Sinnett," Marie-Anne said stiffly, ignoring Byron. "Though we might continue to work on labeling and measuring the world, the nature of the world itself is already known. It's solved. A pity for future generations, in that sense."

"I think I disagree," Hazel said. "I mean, I don't know if it *can* be done, but I don't think it's right to assume it can't. Surely there are things we don't know yet."

Hazel was aware that the entire room was staring at her. Banneker was standing with a dart in his hand that he had forgotten to throw.

"Science is not poetry," Marie-Anne said. "At a certain point, Miss Sinnett, it *is* knowable."

"Why would anyone *want* to reverse it, anyway?" Byron said. "To change back from a god to a man on *purpose?*"

"To grow old with someone?" Jack said quietly. "To not remain the same while the people they love change and die around them?"

Before anyone could respond, he slid his chair back.

"Excuse me," Jack said. "Thank you for having me at your club. Thank you, Miss Sinnett, for inviting me." And he pulled his jacket on and left up the stairs back to the street.

Hazel ran after him. "You can't keep doing this to me!" she shouted when they reached the street. "You can't keep running from me, Jack!"

It was dark, but lanterns flickered in the distance, illuminating Jack when he spun back to her, with his eye wide. His expression so haunted that in that instant, it broke Hazel's heart. "There is no future with me, Hazel!" he said.

Hazel tried to force herself to smile, hoping he would

smile back and bring their conversation toward levity. "You're immortal," she said. "You have nothing but future."

Jack's face grew hard and impassive. The blue had drained out of his one good eye; it was cold and gray. "What are you going to do, be penniless with me?" he said. "Age and grow while I remain this—*nothing*—forever?"

Hazel's mind reeled, trying to pluck at threads of his argument that she could challenge. "You're not nothing. You've never been nothing. You're in the Royal Navy!"

Jack laughed, one cold bark. "A castaway. A nobody."

"You don't have to be. You can enlist."

"No name," Jack said. "No money. No prospects."

Hazel reached forward and pulled his hands into hers. "That doesn't matter, Jack," she said, not even sure as she said the words whether she believed them herself.

Jack pulled his hands away and walked toward the end of the block, toward a damp corner where a dingy brick building stood with boarded-up windows. When Hazel managed to turn him around, she saw that he was crying. His nose had gone red and blotchy, and he rubbed with his fists at his one good eye.

He swallowed hard. "You—the Beecham potion, Tincture, whatever it was—you gave me life, and I'm grateful for it, Hazel, I am. But listen to me. I have thought about this for a long time. You need to listen to me. I am going to live *forever*. Do you hear me? I will never age. I will need to run away *forever* and start again every generation. There is no life for us while you're mortal, and I'm . . . cursed."

Someone far away shouted. There was the sound of a carriage door closing, and women singing a bawdy song. "I can't be with you now, Hazel," Jack said. "Because I can't bear to say goodbye to you."

"You won't have to say goodbye to me," Hazel said, her voice tightening in her throat.

"Yes," Jack said, "eventually, I will."

"What if there's a way to undo it?" Hazel said. "What if Beecham figured it out, and there's a way to make you mortal again?"

Jack paused, his eyebrows rising imperceptibly. "Is there?" he asked.

Hazel's heart sank. "I don't know," she said quietly.

"I would pray for that day, Hazel Sinnett," Jack said. "But until then, every time I look at you, it feels like the rip in my heart is getting bigger. *Give me up*, Hazel. Turn me into a good memory. It's what I did with you a long time ago."

He put his hands in his pockets and walked away.

"You're being cruel!" Hazel shouted after him. "The Jack that I knew was never cruel!"

Jack didn't turn, and he continued on, becoming smaller in the distance. "The Jack that you knew died," he said without looking back. "For everyone's sake, I wish he had stayed dead."

24

THE SUMMER HAD BECOME SWELTERING, AND Hazel could feel the sweat pooling beneath her arms and at her thighs while she was sitting in Charlotte's bedroom, reading a book while Eliza was doing needlepoint. Princess Charlotte was feeding bites of cake to her dog, Edwina, who was panting with her tongue out, pooled out in a puddle on the floor like a melted storm cloud.

Everything was making Hazel unhappy and uncomfortable. Her chemise was bunching uncomfortably under her stays. Her sleeves were too tight on her upper arm. Her feet were sweating. The room was too hot. (Charlotte had even made the rare concession of not lighting her fireplace that morning.)

Hazel had half expected Jack to arrive at her door with an apology the morning after their argument. She wondered whether *she* should have gone to the ship where he was sleeping and demanded—*something* from him. Just more to the conversation. The fact that he had simply walked away was infuriating. It turned Hazel tense and anxious. She was flipping the pages of her book violently, as if the unsheathing sound of each page was a meticulously crafted comment she was directing toward Jack. There was so much she *should* have said last night, and instead he had walked away and robbed her of the chance. That night, before she went to bed, she had started a letter to Jack, but as she wrote, she kept coming up with different things she wanted to say and crossing out what had come before until she was looking at a full sheet of parchment of almost entirely scratched-out ink. Eventually, she had burned the entire exercise and stared at the ceiling while waiting for sleep to come. How had he been so *cool*, so sure? So ready to leave her.

She was the one left stewing for days, wallowing in discomfort at the inadequacy of the interaction. And it was too hot out.

"You're in a mood," Eliza said to Hazel. "You've barely said a word since you got here."

"I don't know what you mean," Hazel lied. "I'm completely fine. I'm just reading,"

The Princess sat up. "You *are* upset. It's obvious. And I don't know what your excuse is," Charlotte said. "If anyone here is going to be miserable, it's me."

A few days before, Charlotte had finally agreed to marry William, Hereditary Prince of Orange. The Prince Regent had been thrilled.

"At least you still get the summer at home, ma'am," Eliza said.

Charlotte sighed exaggeratedly and tickled Edwina beneath her chin. Part of the arrangement in agreeing to marry William was that she wouldn't have to do it until September, and she would be allowed to remain in London until then.

Once she was married, she would be spending half her time in the Netherlands.

"It could be worse," Eliza continued. "He's actually very nice if you give him a chance. Not a terrible dresser."

"Wonderful," Charlotte replied. "How delightful it will be to spend the rest of my life and become mother to the heirs of a man who is not a terrible dresser." She sighed. "I suppose not all of us can be as lucky in love as our little Miss Sinnett here."

Hazel jerked her head from her book. "What could you possibly mean, ma'am?" she snapped.

Charlotte's lip curled, choosing to ignore Hazel's tone. "The entire ton is talking about your little flirtation."

In an instant, Hazel's sweat turned cold. How had people found out about her and Jack so quickly?

"It's nothing," Hazel said. "He's not interested in a future with me."

"Really?" Eliza said. "From what I've heard, the good doctor is absolutely besotted. He was practically drooling at you at the Regent's ball."

Simon. They're talking about Simon.

"Oh," Hazel said. "I don't know. I mean, he did bring me flowers, but—"

"He brought you flowers?" Eliza said. "Oh, Hazel, that means he's days from proposing. Everyone knows that's how men work."

"Well *done*," Princess Charlotte said. "He's tall. Wealthy. *Famous.* And they say he's brilliant, which probably matters to you. Tall is good, though. It means you'll have tall children."

"He's a catch," Eliza added. "Penelope Smythe had her

beady little eyes on him all season, and he barely gave her a second glance."

"Just be sure not to chase him," Charlotte added. "Men despise women who chase them. They want women who *want* them but pretend not to in order to give them the dignity of a hunt that seems worthwhile. There's nothing impressive about catching a rabbit that runs straight to you."

"Are women the rabbits in this metaphor?" Hazel asked.

"Yes," Eliza and Charlotte answered in unison.

"Well, anyway, I don't think he's going to propose," Hazel said, trying to turn her attention back to her book. "Not many men would want a wife who works as a surgeon."

Eliza and Charlotte contemplated that for a moment. "Maybe it doesn't matter to him," Eliza said lightly. "Things are different on the Continent. Maybe they have female physicians already working in Denmark."

"Sweden," Hazel said.

"Look at that," Charlotte said. "*Sweden.* She's already smitten, Eliza. Shall we be clearing our calendars for an autumn wedding? Maybe I can put off going to The Hague until afterward. Schedule it late, Hazel. How's Christmas work for you? You wouldn't get married in Scotland, would you?"

"I'm not getting married anywhere, ma'am," Hazel said.

Charlotte and Eliza exchanged a knowing glance. "If you say so," Charlotte replied. "Oh, a favor: Would you mind terribly if we have the illness return for a brief bout? My father is doing an evening of Handel music next week, and I cannot think of anything I would rather do less than keep myself awake while trying to make conversation with the Earl of Liverpool."

"More like the Earl of Liver Spot," Eliza said into her stitching.

"I don't know if that's necessarily a wise decision, ma'am," Hazel said.

"*Pleeease?* It's not as if I'm *not* going to marry Orange. I'm doing exactly what my father wants. I'm just going to be spending one of my few remaining evenings of freedom in my own house." While she was speaking, Edwina leapt from the Princess's lap and onto the side table, where what remained of the piece of cake sat on an elegant china plate. Edwina snatched it in her mouth and ran under the bed. Charlotte either didn't notice or didn't care.

"Perhaps we can tell your father that you're suffering from a headache," Hazel reasoned. In spite of herself, she felt her bad mood lifting at the prospect of helping Charlotte. "And a stomachache. And because we'll want you to be fit for travel in the autumn, I'll recommend bed rest to be safe."

"*Thank you,*" Charlotte said. "Now, perk up, will you? That gloomy face is making this entire day more unpleasant."

IT WAS COOLER IN THE INFIRMARY AT KEW, AND Hazel exhaled deeply when she arrived, ready to spend the evening finishing—*finally finishing!*—her treatise. Charles Brown had sent along a note to his friend the printer, who had replied instantly with tremendous interest and a request that Hazel submit a sample to him as quickly as possible.

The book itself was almost done: Hazel had meticulously cataloged a variety of the most common ailments and their treatments, but she had also included diagrams of every part of the inside of the human body. Musculature, circulatory system, nerves, and organs. They all came together, piece by piece, to create something greater than the sum of their parts.

How peculiar, she had realized one afternoon while drawing the stomach, that the vast majority of people would go their entire lives without an understanding of what was happening beneath their skin. So few people could attend anatomy lectures or have access to dead bodies to dissect—even if they did, Hazel thought, even fewer would have the tools to actually understand what they were looking at. Hazel tried to make her diagrams as clear as possible, so a person without any formal education or experience might be able to see what Hazel already knew: that the human body was a miracle, complicated and simple at once, an odd machine that defied easy understanding but which, if you were patient and studious, would reveal its strange logic.

Hazel had finished the final drawing, the foot, after resewing Lord Byron's onto his ankle the other day. The foot had been decaying, its skin graying and the stiff joints gone knobby.

"I can keep it from, you know, falling off," Hazel had said as she was sewing the extremity back on. "But I'm not sure if I can get the blood flowing back to the toes."

Marie-Anne was nearby, examining a purple gas expanding and swirling in a glass canister. "Some of the dilute Tincture will help," she said, passing Hazel a small vial.

Just as Marie-Anne promised, as soon as Hazel added a few drops of the liquid into the incision, the poet's foot began to regain color.

"It's amazing," Hazel said. "Just brilliant." She still could not wrap her head around it; it was unlike any science she had seen before. Marie-Anne gave a humble smile. "And another thing," Hazel added, "thanks to this little reattachment, I'm going to be able to complete a diagram of the anklebone for my treatise."

Byron was making circles with his newly attached foot. "How bully for you," he said sarcastically. "So happy to help."

"I *am* happy for you, Miss Sinnett," Marie-Anne said. "Completing your first work to be published is a major accomplishment. First of many, I imagine. Have you thought about what name you'll put it under?"

Hazel was rerolling her surgical equipment into canvas and looked up. "What do you mean? I thought—I mean, I assumed it would be under my name. Hazel Sinnett."

Marie-Anne looked a little sad. "It's still not considered appropriate for a woman to be publishing under her own name. Especially for a work on science. Even novels! Poor Jane is still publishing as 'A Lady.'"

"Jane?"

Marie-Anne dismissed the inquiry with a wave of her hand. "For much of my research," she said, "I worked alongside my husband. I conducted the experiments, took the measurements, had the ideas, even. Our research is published under one name. His."

Hazel tried to think back on the papers she had read by the Lavoisiers. She always knew that the pair of them had worked in concert, but all the published work had been credited to Antoine. "I just assumed—"

"Of course," Marie-Anne said smoothy. "Everyone assumes. Part of the sacrifice of being a woman who wants to contribute something to the world is understanding that sometimes, in order to get the message out, the correct messenger is needed. People are more willing to accept new ideas coming from a man. It's simple, and it's unfortunate."

"But," Hazel said. "Don't you want *credit*? Don't you want the world to know what you've come up with?"

"Of course," Marie-Anne said evenly. "A part of me does. A part of me wants to be celebrated. A part of me wanted every award, every royal appointment, every university honor that Antoine was given for the work we did together. But it was vanity, and pride. And more important than that, to me, was that our work was reaching others. That we were changing the world. The greater good was greater than my pride, I suppose. And in the end, it was Antoine beheaded on the guillotine when the French people rose up and, in their anger, confused violence for power. There are always women behind the scenes, pulling the strings, Hazel. We are invisible to history, but we also survive."

Marie-Anne's words replayed in Hazel's head over and over as Hazel sat at her bench in Kew, making the final adjustments and edits to her manuscript. The title page had said *A Work by Hazel Sinnett*, but now Hazel's pen hovered above her name. Hazel had done all the work. She *wanted* the credit. But maybe Marie-Anne was right. Hazel's goal wasn't to aggrandize herself; it was to help as many people learn as possible. Regardless of the quality of the writing or the work Hazel had put into making the diagrams clear and meticulous, it was true: if there was a man's name on the cover, more people would buy her book. More people would read her book, and trust it.

A drop of ink fell from her pen's nib right beside the *H* for Hazel when she felt the air shift in the room.

"I'm sorry," said a voice behind her. "Am I disturbing you?" It was Simon. Still looking tired, but also, Hazel had to admit, very handsome in a well-pressed jacket, his hair combed and his trousers tucked into high boots. He was also carrying a large box in his arms.

"Not at all," Hazel said. "I was just finishing. Besides, this is your infirmary."

"I like to think of it as our infirmary," Simon said. "I admit, even when you're not here, I enjoy seeing your notes and papers on the bench. Treating the King has been a lonely business; it's nice to imagine that I am not always working alone. That we work side by side."

Hazel smiled. The question of authorship could wait for another day. "I'm finished, you know," she said, racking the hefty stack of parchment on the bench and straightening the edges. Her treatise had somehow swollen to hundreds of pages, and Hazel knew that even if her name wouldn't be on its final form, she *was* proud of it. It was the first time she had said out loud that she was finished, and she realized, as she said it, how glad she was to be sharing that with Simon.

"That's tremendous," Simon said, his accent catching on the vowel sounds. He put the box he was holding on the bench beside Hazel and leaned over to read the title page. Hazel could feel his breath on her neck. "What an achievement. Will you publish, then?"

Hazel nodded. "I was just contemplating whether or not to use my real name."

Simon looked confused. "Do you have another?"

"No," Hazel said. "I mean, whether to use my name because I'm a woman. And people will be more willing to accept a medical text written by a man."

Simon scoffed. "Who cares?" he said. "You wrote it, did you not?"

"Aye," Hazel said. "I did. I'm not entirely certain it's that simple, though."

Simon shrugged. "I'll read it. As a matter of fact, I can't wait to read it. Is there a chapter on madness? I'm afraid my treatments are no longer effective. At this point, all we are doing is making the King comfortable." Simon gave Hazel a conspiratorial look. "The Prince seems to have given up all hope that his father will ever be well again," he said sarcastically. "And as you can imagine, he's heartbroken about it."

"Yes," Hazel said back. "He probably *hates* being the acting monarch. Ruling the Kingdom. Spending however he wants." The two shared their tiny moment of harmless treason for a moment before Hazel pulled away. "Unfortunately, the chapter on madness is a little limited," she admitted. "But what are the symptoms? Maybe I can offer a fresh perspective."

"Babbling," Simon said. "Constant babbling. Forgetting where he is. *Who* he is. When he's not talking, he's sleeping. Sometimes he complains of a headache."

"Fever?" Hazel asked.

"Almost never."

"The urine?"

"Strangely colored. Sometimes inky, sometimes bloodied."

"Hmm," Hazel said. "It sounds like poisoning, but—"

"Impossible," Simon said. "I began overseeing his diet personally. We eat the same meals, off the same plates sometimes. He's not poisoned. It's just something I've never seen before."

"There are still mysteries, then," Hazel said.

"Indeed."

Hazel turned her attention to the box that Simon had set down on the table. "What's the box for? Is it a gift for me?" she joked.

Simon looked down at the package and blinked, as if he had forgotten he brought it. "Oh," he said. "Yes, it is."

Hazel pulled it across the table. "Well then," she said, removing the lid.

Hazel gasped.

Inside was the most beautiful medical bag she had ever seen.

The clasps were gleaming; the leather was black and deliciously soft. Hazel's hands moved of their own accord; she stood and pulled it from the box and swung it gently at her hips, relishing in the weight and size of it. It was *perfect*—far better than the old medical bag that had been ruined with mildew—something exquisite and probably shockingly expensive. "I can't accept this," Hazel said, knowing that she was supposed to say that, but unable to take her eyes off the bag.

Simon chuckled. "You have to. It's personalized, see?" And he flipped the bag to show Hazel that near the handle on the far side, it was embossed with the letters *H.S.* "I didn't know your middle initial. Or if you have one. Not everyone does, I suppose," he said. "I noticed that you've been carrying your tools—well, really my tools—around in a bit of canvas, and I thought you deserved a real medical bag."

Hazel was awestruck. She immediately unrolled her fraying canvas and began depositing her equipment into the new bag. "It's perfect," she said. "Thank you, Dr. Ferris."

"Simon, please."

"Thank you, Simon."

And even though an image of Jack flashed in Hazel's head, it was pushed away almost immediately by how badly she wanted to kiss Simon von Ferris and the thought of what he would look like under his clothing.

"I was surprised to see a doctor without a medical bag," Simon said, pulling Hazel back from her fantasy.

"Oh," she said. "I had one. But it was ruined on the trip from Edinburgh to London. Soaked in water somewhere along the way and became covered in mold. The *smell* when it finally arrived—it was awful, like . . ." Hazel stopped. The smell of the mold of her old medical bag *had* been awful. It had been overpowering. It seemed to lodge itself in the front of her brain between her eyes. It lingered in the walls even after the bag had been disposed of.

Hazel retrieved the scalpel she had just placed in the medical bag.

"I need to see the King's room," she said, already walking toward the door.

Simon trailed after her. "With a *scalpel*? Miss Sinnett— Hazel!"

"Just trust me!" Hazel called, veering down the hallway.

Simon's legs were twice as long as hers, and he caught up in a few lengthy strides. "It's this way," he said.

The room was as oppressively warm as Hazel remembered, with a fire still blazing in the hearth and the windows closed against the suggestion of a breeze. And just as Hazel remembered, its smell was overpowering, a stench of human filth and mildew. King George III was a small, shriveled figure in the center of his large canopied bed, wearing a simple white dressing gown. His lips were moving, but no sound came out.

"Your Majesty," Hazel said quickly, before lifting the scalpel.

Two guards moved to stop her, but Simon raised his arms. "Let her work," he said, only a small note of fear creeping into his voice.

With the knife raised, Hazel turned away from the King and toward one of the walls. One of the beautiful walls, with intricate wallpaper in a green so vivid it made Hazel blink. With a single, confident motion, she swiped across the wallpaper (one of the guards shouted) and pulled it away.

The wall itself was black and green, fuzzy and wet to the touch.

"Mold," Hazel said. She ripped off a piece of the green wallpaper and smelled it. "Do you think they used arsenic in the wallpaper?" she asked Simon.

He felt the fabric in his fingers. "Possibly," he said. "But it wouldn't be a significant enough amount to cause poisoning. Arsenic paint is harmless. It's used in dyes all the time."

Hazel gestured to the wall. "The mold," she said. "The dampness. It could be allowing the arsenic to get in the air."

Simon was breathing fast. Hazel could practically feel his mind working. "Get the King out of here," he said to the guards. When they hesitated, he shouted: "Now!"

The guards sprang into action. The King was pulled from his bed and led carefully out of the room.

Simon and Hazel began ripping more and more of the wallpaper from the walls. They both covered their mouths with their sleeves. Simon flung the window open. A gentle breeze sighed into the room. The smell of death and decay began to dissipate.

"I can't believe it," Simon said. "I can't believe it."

"It might not be the only thing contributing to the King's condition," Hazel said, pulling down a large swatch of the arsenic-green wallpaper with a satisfying rip.

"Well, it's certainly something," Simon said. "It's something." And then again, as they revealed more and more of the bare walls the color of ill-healing bruises, he kept repeating, "I just can't believe it."

Gaspar arrived at the door to the King's chamber, distracted by some notice of business in his hands. He kept walking, head down, until he was already in the room, at which time he looked up, saw that Hazel and Simon had destroyed the King's chambers, and stood with his mouth open, gaping like a fish.

"I . . . I . . . I . . . Miss Sinnett!" he finally managed. He stared at the ruined walls and sputtered several more nonsensical syllables before he accomplished the phrase: "Where is the King?"

"It's all fine, Gaspar, my friend," Simon said. "Miss Sinnett discovered mold in the walls making the arsenic in the wallpaper poisonous. She saved the King."

Gaspar blinked, still befuddled. "But . . . but the King's chambers . . . ," he said.

"The King is no longer to sleep in this room, do you understand me?" Simon said. "In fact, I don't think he should be sleeping in this palace at all. Put him in Buckingham, with the Queen. Keep the windows open. Get him plenty of fresh air."

Gaspar finally understood. He sped away down the hall to

find the King, clutching at his wig as he walked so it wouldn't fall off.

"Gaspar is a good man," Simon said. "He'll help see that the King is taken care of. In the meantime"—he slapped his hands together to get the dust off them—"I think celebration is in order. I have a bottle of wine some lord or another brought me from Paris last year that I had been saving for a special occasion. I think this qualifies."

Hazel thought about sitting across from Simon, drinking a glass of wine, and then another, celebrating their momentous day. Hazel couldn't recall the last time she had felt so elated, so proud of her own abilities, her reasoning, her instincts. She had wanted to be a physician because she loved anatomy and the study of natural science, but it was an almost inexplicable feeling, like warm tea with honey settling in her stomach, to feel that it wasn't just that she had an interest: She had actual *ability*. She was *good* at this. Qualified to do what she always wanted to do.

She remembered the feeling last year, the giddy excitement of buying her first dead body from Jack and knowing that the entire universe was going to be expanding for her. The memory of Jack tightened her stomach. She didn't owe him anything, not when Simon was right here, ready to *be* with her, and Jack was God knew where. Simon was looking at her expectantly, and when Hazel finally answered him, it was to say, "It's been a long day, I'm afraid. I think I'd better get some rest."

He looked disappointed. "I'd better check on Gaspar and the King, then," he said. He kissed her on the hand and bade her a good evening before he left.

Hazel wasn't tired. She didn't know why she said that.

Perhaps it had been the knowledge, certain as death, that if she went to drink a bottle of wine with Simon, she would be thinking of Jack the entire time.

Hazel decided to walk home. The sun was setting and Hazel decided to take the long way back to her apartments so that she would see the streetlamps being lit.

She wasn't making a mistake, she told herself as she walked. The feelings that she was having for Simon were a momentary distraction, and spending more time with him would only complicate things. In the end, she would feel about Simon the way she was feeling about Jack now: preoccupied, and miserable, waiting for him to write her. Better to just enjoy the night alone, celebrate her victory with King George and finishing her treatise by spending the evening walking through London. She missed Edinburgh, the romantic crags and castles and the twisting streets, but as she strolled, she admitted to herself that London had its own beauty. It was an overwhelming place, with too many streets and vast sweeping parks, but in the evenings, when the light was fading and reflecting on the stone buildings and the rain made the cobblestones shine, London was also beautiful.

In the middle of the street, Hazel saw a familiar pair of eyes staring back at her.

"Well, hello, what are you doing here?" she said.

It was Edwina, the Princess's small gray lapdog, lying on her belly as if the cobblestoned lane was her own personal pillow. "How did you get away from home?"

Edwina didn't protest as Hazel lifted her into her arms; she gave a small contented chirp and almost immediately relaxed, boneless, so that Hazel then felt as though she were carrying not a dog but a fur muff.

Hazel could see Warwick House glittering in the distance thanks to the gaslight of Pall Mall. There were still lanterns lit upstairs, in the Princess's bedroom. She was awake; probably calling for Edwina and searching for her under the mountain of pillows on her bed.

"Evening, Martin," Hazel said to the footman who opened the door.

He saw the dog already asleep in Hazel's arms. "She'll be looking for that!" he said.

The doors to the Princess's room were closed, but Hazel saw light through the doorframe and heard movement inside. There was the muffled sound of something like laughter; Eliza was in, too, it seemed. Perhaps they were playing cards and hadn't even noticed that Edwina had run away. Hazel extricated a free hand from beneath Edwina's bottom and knocked gingerly on the door. "Your Royal Highness?" she said. "I have something for you."

Hazel should have waited for an answer. In fact, she shouldn't have gone up to the Princess's room at all. She should have left the dog with the footman and gone home. But instead, Hazel, still heady with excitement from the victory with Simon, simply opened the door expecting to greet her friends.

Princess Charlotte and Eliza were both in the room. They were on the Princess's bed, their dresses pulled down to their waists, exposing their bare chests. Their arms were wrapped around each other, their hair was loose and down, and they were kissing.

Hazel froze, and Edwina leapt from her arms. The Princess and Eliza turned to stare at her.

"I found Edwina. On the street," Hazel said, blinking and averting her eyes. "I'm so sorry. I'm just going to . . . go now."

And Hazel, with her eyes covered, bumped into the doors twice before managing to successfully escape into the hall-way.

25

"AIT! HAZEL, WAIT!"

Eliza was chasing after her. Her dress was pulled back on, but she was still fumbling with her shoes as she ran. "Hazel, come back!"

"I'm so sorry!" Hazel shouted back to her. "Pretend I was never here! I didn't see anything."

Eliza was small, but she was surprisingly fast, and she reached her arm out to Hazel's shoulder. "It's fine. It's okay. But you should come talk for a minute."

"Is Her Royal Highness going to have me beheaded?" Hazel asked, only half joking.

"Possibly," Eliza responded.

Charlotte was sitting on her bed, fully dressed (Edwina lounging happily in her lap now). "Please, sit," she said.

Hazel obliged.

"So," the Princess began. "Please—just, please don't tell anyone about this. It's—"

"—nothing," Eliza finished.

"Well, not nothing," Charlotte said. "But nothing that will

matter in the long run, as they say. Eliza will marry Otto. I'm going to marry the Prince of Orange." She spoke as if trying to convince herself as much as she was convincing Hazel.

How had Hazel missed this? *Of course.* The Princess had never been in love with Frederick Augustus of Prussia or *any* prince. No wonder she so dreaded the thought of getting married; she would be saddled with a man, and she would be separated from Eliza.

Hazel tried to remember every interaction the three of them had shared together. Had she missed glances? Flirtation? More? She had spent months with these two women and didn't think for a moment that their close friendship might be romantic. But now it seemed obvious. Hazel recalled moments of lingering touch, of gentle hands on bare arms. She was so focused on a treatment for her mysterious illness that she had missed the larger picture.

"Well?" Eliza said, her jaw tight and eyes narrowed. "Say something, Hazel."

"I just can't believe I didn't realize," Hazel said.

Charlotte and Eliza visibly relaxed at Hazel's response. Perhaps they had expected disgust or anger. That surprised Hazel more than anything, that the pair of them had become, in their moment of discovery and the quiet afterward, as afraid as Hazel had ever seen them. "I won't tell anyone anything," Hazel added.

"Not that they would even believe you," Charlotte said. "But rumors are dangerous as anything else these days. And imagine the filthy drawings they would do in the broadsheets. Imagine my father's reaction. Heaven forbid the Regent's daughter is in love with a woman."

"Love?" Hazel said. "You're . . . in love?"

Charlotte and Eliza glanced at each other. They each gave an imperceptible nod.

"But it doesn't matter," Eliza said. "We will get married. The Princess will do her duty. We had love for a time, which is more than most get."

"I thought you were in love with Frederick Augustus," Hazel said.

Charlotte giggled. "That mindless bore?! Oh, Hazel, you think too little of me."

"It's not my fault!" Hazel protested, laughing. "You were always looking over at him, looking so sad whenever they talked about him leaving."

The Princess blinked and lowered her eyes. "When Prince Frederick Augustus of Prussia leaves, his first lieutenant leaves as well," she said. "And the first lieutenant's bride-to-be."

"It's fine," Eliza said, comforting the Princess. The world narrowed to the two of them. "We will write. Constantly." Charlotte hid her face in the hollow between Eliza's chest and shoulder. "I will always be yours, Lottie," Eliza whispered. "Always yours, no one else."

"No one else," Charlotte echoed back, her words quiet but filled with tenderness. And then she lifted her head, surprised to see Hazel there. "Well, there you are," she said to her. "Now you know the full diagnosis. You know, you really are a good doctor, Hazel. If I really had been ill, I would have wanted you treating me."

She looked at the two of them, limbs intertwined as easily as if they shared their bodies as one, so comfortable with each other and so obviously in love, Hazel cursed herself again for having missed it. "You're the Princess of Wales," Hazel said. "Future Queen of England."

"That's what they tell me," Charlotte said.

"Surely, *surely* if any woman has the power to live independently, without marriage to a husband, to share a home with the person she loves—surely, it's you," Hazel said.

"Hah!" Charlotte snorted. "It's quite the opposite, I'm afraid. I am the only woman in the country whose future marriage and children are a national concern. My union will require the approval of the monarch and Parliament. Parliament determines my annual income. My very *existence* is contained within the prison of my privilege. I wake, walk, sit, sleep, at the discretion of the country. The less of a person I am, the better monarch. I am a clockwork doll told to smile and wave and wear expensive clothing that someone else picks out for me. I shall marry whom they tell me to marry, and I shall have children for the Regent and for Parliament to raise on my behalf. Every decision made for me, every act of my existence dictated by Parliament or my husband and *his* country's parliament. And I shall become smaller and smaller, more invisible even as I wear larger gowns and more expensive jewels. And then one day, I shall cease to be Charlotte altogether."

Eliza's hand was on top of Charlotte's and she gently moved her thumb across the back of it. "You will always be Charlotte," she murmured. "Perhaps I should go to a nunnery. Leave the country. Live in the estate you bought me in Bavaria and grow old as a spinster."

"I bought that estate for you as an early wedding gift," Charlotte said. "Besides, you'd be miserable away from society. Otto is kind enough."

"He has bad breath," Eliza said. "And he licks his thumbs when he turns the pages of a book. It will drive me mad."

"You will spend as little time with him as you can," Charlotte said. "And as a married woman, you shall throw the most wonderful parties."

Hazel's mind raced. She thought about Jack, and Simon, and the way that Charlotte and Eliza were looking at each other. "There has to be another way," Hazel said. "You only get one lifetime. You can't waste it away from each other."

Charlotte smiled sadly. "Like I said, you are a very good doctor, Hazel. But you can't save my life this time, I'm afraid. I might not have ever had one to begin with."

NEWS OF THE KING'S IMPROVED CONDITION WAS all anyone in London was talking about. Gleeful shouts and patriotic songs carried on the summer breeze; even Hazel felt her spirits buoyed by the joy around her.

She and Eliza had arrived to the concerto that night at St. James's Palace together, Eliza in a new dress, purple with organza sleeves, and Hazel wearing one of the old dresses she had received from Edinburgh.

"I can't see why you couldn't have bought a new dress," Eliza had chastised. (Hazel did at least submit to Eliza fixing her hair.)

"Because it doesn't matter," Hazel said. "No one is going to be looking at me tonight anyway."

"No," Eliza agreed. "No one is going to be looking at anyone but the King. The Princess couldn't have chosen a better night to play hooky."

Eliza was right. Gaspar had barely blinked earlier that afternoon when Hazel had found him at Kew and told him that the Princess wasn't feeling herself and wouldn't be able to attend the concerto.

"What? Oh, yes, fine, fine," Gaspar had said, straightening his cuffs. He was directing the setting up of the King's new bedchamber and removing furniture from the old rooms. "No, no!" he shouted to two footmen struggling with the weight of a large golden chair. "The one with the red cushion! The King prefers the red cushion! Leave that one!"

Eliza grabbed two glasses of wine from a passing man who may not have actually been a servant, and gave one to Hazel. "Still, you're telling me there's *no one* here you would want to wear a new dress to impress?" Hazel followed her eyes and landed on Simon.

He stood a head taller than the gaggle of men surrounding him, looking so dashing in a well-tailored jacket that it made Hazel's breath catch. The memory of kissing him, how his body had felt pressed up against hers, how his tongue had felt in her mouth, flooded her mind like syrup on a hot day.

He felt her staring.

"There she is!" he called, and he strode over to her, parting the men in his wake. "Miss Hazel Sinnett. The brilliant surgeon who discovered the cause of the King's condition."

"Dr. Ferris is too modest," Hazel said. "He recognized the symptoms—I just helped."

Simon slid his hand behind Hazel's back. "I couldn't have done it without her," he said to the men, and then he looked down toward her with a twinkling smile. His amber eyes really were perfect. Warm and intelligent and challenging.

"And she was the one who cured Princess Charlotte, was she not?" one of the men said.

"Yes," Hazel answered. "I was."

Simon lifted his glass of wine. "To Hazel Sinnett."

"*To Hazel Sinnett!*"

Everyone was happy, everyone pretending that they alone had been the only one with faith that the King's condition would be temporary. Everyone was happy, that is, except the Prince Regent. His face was painted with his usual powder, but it looked uneven, blotched by sweat. His shirt was too small, and buttoned incorrectly. He stood in the corner of the room, sulking, the edges of his mouth turned down to his chin. "What am I supposed to do *now?*" Hazel overheard him say.

And strangely, Marie-Anne Lavoisier was also muted in her mood.

"Madame Lavoisier!" Hazel had shouted, seeing the chemist across the room.

The Frenchwoman, in a dark brown dress that was almost black, glided across the floor. "Miss Sinnett. Dr. Ferris," she said, lowering into a small curtsy. "Congratulations, monsieur, on your tremendous accomplishment."

"If anyone deserves the credit, it's Miss Sinnett," Simon said.

Marie-Anne's lips were tight. "Indeed," she said.

When she had left to greet another friend, Simon turned to Hazel. "Is she not pleased the King is becoming well again?"

"She's a woman of science," Hazel countered. "Maybe she feels that she'll believe it when she sees it."

It wasn't until everyone was seated and the orchestra had lifted their instruments, ready to play, that horns from the other room blasted out a call. "*The King is coming!*" a herald shouted.

Everyone rose, and the double doors at the back of the room burst open.

King George III, wearing a bright red coat festooned with medals and ribbons, strode into the room with his wife, Queen Charlotte, at his elbow. She had been summoned back to London from her summer retreat with the good news of her husband's return to health; it was her first public appearance in months.

The King's face was stern and serious, but the Queen, her hair high and with a curl cascading down her shoulder, was beaming.

When the King reached the front of the room, the herald banged a scepter on the marble floor for silence.

The King cleared his throat. "I just must say," he said slowly, sounding out each syllable carefully. "How g-grateful I am, for the treatment of my physicians, and the patience of my country." He wasn't strong yet—Hazel saw the way that he held on to his wife, the way his knees bent and shook slightly. But as the King spoke, his words became more fluent. "I will continue to serve as your devoted King. And that is enough now from me, I think. Let us hear some music, no? What, what!"

There was a collective exhale in the room, the tension that had been building up until that moment bursting at once like water through a dam. People had heard that the King was improved, but actually *seeing* him, being present for the King's first public appearance in nearly a decade—well, it felt like a miracle.

Simon was sitting a few rows away from Hazel. He caught her eye through the bobbing heads and applause and winked. She winked back.

"I saw that," Eliza said. Hazel ignored her.

The concert was magnificent; the royal musicians seemed to feed off the energy and excitement in the room, playing Handel with as much vigor and joy as Hazel had ever heard. Hazel's hands hurt from clapping by the end of the third ovation. And then the King and Queen rose from their seats and stood at the front of the room, and the crowd cheered for them. The King whispered something private to the Queen. From where Hazel was sitting, it looked as if he'd said, "I love you."

"A real love match," Eliza said to Hazel, leaning over and raising her voice above the applause. "Married almost sixty years. Sixty. Can you believe it?"

Hazel looked at the King, the man who had been lost for so long and who now, finally, was able to attend a concert with his wife.

"It's beautiful," Hazel said.

"Fifteen children," Eliza said. "Charlotte's the only *legitimate* grandchild, but they've had fifteen children. They say he never took a mistress. They say he loved only the Queen for his entire life."

The royal couple stood at the front of the room, arm in arm, basking in the applause from their court. (Even the Regent was bringing his hands together, albeit rather languidly.)

And in that moment, when Hazel was seeing a couple who had survived madness and power and loneliness and decades and fifteen children together, she didn't think of Simon. She thought of Jack.

She turned to Eliza. "Do you really love her?" she asked quietly. "Really, really love her?"

Eliza knew immediately whom she was referring to. She nodded.

"Would you be willing to give up everything for her?" Hazel asked.

"What do you mean?"

"Or rather," Hazel said, "I mean, would you still love her if she wasn't the Princess?"

"Of course," Eliza said. "I love her for Lottie."

"Do you think she would be willing to give everything up for you? And not be the Princess any longer?"

Eliza took a deep breath. "It's all we've fantasized about for a decade. Our dream of running away together and just being Lottie and Eliza and nothing else. But it's not real. She's the only legitimate grandchild. She has no choice."

The applause died down, but not before Hazel was able to whisper to Eliza: "I have an idea."

26

AZEL WAITED FOR AN HOUR AT THE HARBOR where the *Iphigenia* was docked, watching the seabirds dive into the waves and listening to the endless song of merchants and seamen calling back and forth. She was dressed as a man; she had learned long ago that if she wanted to travel alone, she would attract less attention if she did so in trousers, with her hair tucked into a hat and the hat's brim pulled over her face.

Finally, just as the sun was becoming orange over the water, Hazel saw him: Jack, walking in his blue coat with a group of fellow sailors, sharing pieces of a Cornish pasty.

"Hey!"

The men turned quizzically. Jack recognized Hazel immediately and turned to his friends. "Thom, Weymouth, you go on ahead. I'll meet you." To Hazel, he said, "Look, I don't know why you came, but I—"

"I need your help."

Jack paused and scratched at the bridge of his nose, where

his eyepatch was leaving a pink groove in the flesh. "With what?"

"Do you still remember how to dig up a body?"

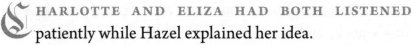

HARLOTTE AND ELIZA HAD BOTH LISTENED patiently while Hazel explained her idea.

"There will be no going back," Hazel said, trying to convey the gravity of the situation through her words. "If you do this, this is the end."

Eliza and Charlotte were holding hands: just passively keeping their arms intertwined, a casual show of intimacy they were now able to do because Hazel knew their secret. Edwina hopped onto the bed and nuzzled her way into her mother's lap and promptly fell asleep.

"It's your choice, Lottie," Eliza said. "You're the one who'll be dying."

"Not *actually* dying," Hazel corrected. "Nothing is actually going to happen to you. That's why I'm going to dig up a corpse that looks enough like you—"

"—to fool people from far enough away. To fool people during a procession and royal funeral," Charlotte said. She knitted her eyebrows together. "I think it will work. If we style its hair like mine, and dress her in my clothes and jewels. If we say whatever disease I died from is contagious enough, no one will get too close."

"We're faking your death, but you *will* be dying, in a sense," Hazel said. "To the entire world, *Princess Charlotte of Wales* will be dead. You will have to start again, somewhere else. *Become* someone else. With none of the privileges that come from your position. I just want to make sure you understand entirely what you'll be sacrificing if you go through with this."

Eliza squeezed Charlotte's hand.

"I know," the Princess said. "But the truth is, if I stay the Princess of Wales, I won't even have a life at all. I don't want to be a symbol any longer. I want to be a person. And I want to be with Eliza." Eliza rested her head in the crook of Charlotte's neck, and the two shared a quick, sweet kiss. "The problem will be Edwina," she said. The small dog was snoring on a silk pillow in the corner of the room. "She's never been anything but the darling puppy of the Princess of Wales. I don't know if she'll be able to adjust to life where her meals aren't served to her on silver trays."

"I love you," Eliza said.

"You have to love me," Charlotte teased. "It's your patriotic duty."

"Not for long," Eliza said with a smile.

The decision was made: Hazel Sinnett would kill Princess Charlotte in order to save her life.

JACK LISTENED AS HAZEL EXPLAINED EXACTLY what she wanted them to do. "It's love, Jack," she said. "She doesn't want to live a life if she has to marry a stranger and she can't be with Eliza, and I don't think she should have to."

Jack still had the crumbs of the pasty clinging to the scruff of his chin. Hazel had to force herself to resist the urge to reach out and brush them away, to remind herself that they were no longer so intimately acquainted as they once were.

"So," Jack said. "We dig up a body that looks enough like

the Princess that people believe it when you say she died of some . . . mysterious new disease or another. While the *real* Princess, completely unharmed, runs away with her friend to live happily ever after with no money and nowhere to go."

"Well, not *no* money," Hazel said. "She has jewels and a hefty allowance that she can take out in gold. And she's given a lot of her money over to Eliza. And a manor house. She bought Eliza an estate in Bavaria as a wedding gift. I think it actually might even be more of a castle, come to think of it."

"A wedding gift for a wedding between Eliza and . . ."

"A Prussian man named Otto. The wedding's not important. That wedding's not going to happen. Eliza is going to be so heartbroken after Princess Charlotte's death that she'll remove herself from London society, break her engagement, and run away to Bavaria. With *her* servant."

". . . Who will be the *real* Princess Charlotte."

"Charlotte, yes, but not actually really a princess anymore, if you're thinking philosophically about it."

"Because she faked her own death, using a corpse that we dug up."

"Yes," Hazel said. "Simple, really. It sounds as if you understand."

"It sounds," Jack said, "absolutely mad."

"I can't do it without you," Hazel said, and she meant it. Digging up a dead body was a two-person job, and even then it was risky when both of them were experienced grave robbers. Hazel had managed to resurrect corpses with Jack in Edinburgh only because Jack knew what he was doing—and even then, those were familiar kirkyards. The graveyards in London were strange and new: neither of them knew the schedules of the guards, or whether there were patrolmen working nearby.

It was incredibly risky, and if they got caught, the price would be not only their reputations but possibly their lives. Even immortals could spend years in prison, Hazel thought. The memory of her time in Calton Gaol bubbled up like bile, and she forced herself to banish it so she wouldn't be frightened for her own sake. "Please, Jack," Hazel said. "For me."

Jack smiled and Hazel's heart beat faster. It was as if Jack's smile had the power to send the blood rushing through Hazel's body in the wrong direction at will.

"You're not going to take no for an answer, are you, Hazel Sinnett?" Jack said.

"Never," Hazel said.

"I'm still leaving," Jack said, quieter. "I told the captain I would be on the crew of the *Iphigenia* when they set sail for the west coast of Africa."

"One last dig, then," Hazel said. "Just me and you."

"One last dig it is," Jack replied. "For old times' sake."

They decided on the burial ground of Bunhill Fields, an hour by foot to the east of Pall Mall, where the Princess's residence was located. Jack would bring the spades and rope, and Hazel had purchased a cart using a handful of coins the Princess had given her. "Try to find a body that's attractive," Charlotte had said, handing Hazel the coins. "I want people to remember me as pretty."

They would take the dark streets back, keeping the body in the cart, covered with a thick woolen blanket. To anyone who saw them, they should look like merchants trying to transport their wares across town by first morning light for a market.

They agreed to meet at two in the morning, and when Hazel arrived with the cart, just as the bells were tolling, she saw Jack already at the gates of the cemetery, carrying two wooden spades and a dark lantern. "Remember how to do this?" he said, handing her a spade.

"How could I forget."

"The problem," Jack said, "is usually we'd just go for whichever grave looked freshest and closest to the wall. But we're looking for something very specific now."

"A young woman," Hazel said. "Aged twenty to twenty-five."

Hazel and Jack gazed out onto the field of graves before them. A handful of them looked freshly dug, the dirt loose and wet-smelling in the damp night air.

Hazel wished she had brought a dark lantern as Jack had—his had a cover that slid closed and blocked the candle flame whenever he wanted to make himself invisible in the darkness. Hazel tried to keep the light of her own lantern small and contained against her body as she examined the headstones one by one: Humbert Beille (man), Arthur Gordon (man), Emily Clark Archdull (died at fifty-six), Eleanora Northwick (died at sixty-five), Lander Symondes (man, and died at eighty-one). Finally: "Jack! Jack, I think I found one!" Hazel whispered through the darkness. It was a fresh grave, dug within the past few days, for a woman named Lucretia Wilkes. BELOVED WIFE AND DAUGHTER, DEAD IN CHILDBIRTH, 1797–1818. "Twenty-one years old?" Hazel said, quickly doing the math.

Jack lifted his spade. "Let's hope she was a brunette."

The sound of the digging took on a soothing rhythm, a sound like cloth ripping or sea waves shredding against sand. Hazel found herself becoming pleasantly warm; even in the chill of the night, sweat prickled at her underarms and forehead. Jack's face, too, was sweating—he lifted his eye patch more than once to wipe the sweat away. They worked efficiently, without speaking except to occasionally comment, "On your left," or "A little deeper here, I think." The night was mercifully dead and quiet, but the sound of every errant twig snapping put Hazel on edge. At one point, Hazel had blown out her lantern in a panic only to discover it was merely a stray dog trotting past.

Jack stood in the hole they dug; Hazel was waiting on the grass, ready to help lift the body to the surface after Jack stripped it naked and tied a rope around the neck. He had taken off his jacket, and pushed the sleeves of his shirt up; Hazel had to avert her eyes so she was not staring at the way the veins popped against the skin of his forearms, how his muscles were visible even by the dim glow of his half-covered lantern.

Jack inhaled sharply, and brought his wooden spade down on the coffin lid. Hazel braced herself against the snap.

"Wait a moment," Hazel whispered. "I think I hear something."

She turned to look around, but when she did, her footing slipped on the damp grass and she slid into the narrow hole, directly into Jack's arms.

The loose dirt tumbled on the top of their heads like hail. The two were less than an inch apart, and it was dark, and it was *Jack*, and Hazel knew she shouldn't kiss him, because he wasn't going to stay with her, but she knew that she wanted to.

"Will you help me back up?" she whispered.

Before she had even finished the question, Jack pressed his mouth against hers.

Hazel dropped her spade and threw her arms around

him. They were *kissing*, and clamoring for each other, their limbs like hungry animals, holding each other close. Hazel wrapped one leg and then the other around Jack's waist; Jack pushed her back against the dirt wall of the hole they had dug and pinned her there, kissing her lips and then kissing her neck, sucking and biting at it hard enough that Hazel knew he would leave a mark.

"I have wanted you so badly," he breathed into her. "I have missed you so much."

Hazel didn't respond, she just kissed him deeper, so hard she could feel his teeth and the thick muscle of his tongue against hers. His arms were sinewy and strong, holding her up against the side of the grave without any sign of exertion. She wanted to be here with him forever, to stay in this moment, in the dark, where time didn't exist. *Nothing* existed beyond them, the entire universe contained in the space of their skins.

"Jack," Hazel breathed. "I love you."

Jack hesitated, pulling away slightly, just a millimeter. "I'm still immortal," he said. "I won't be able to give you the life you deserve. The life you *want*."

Hazel ran her hands through his hair. The smell of his skin was familiar and intoxicating. It was the smell of the woods after it had rained and the ground was misted with steam and dew, and the smell of a fresh pot of ink, and the oil that remained under her fingernails after she peeled an orange rind.

"You are the only life I want, Jack."

He kissed her again, but Hazel pulled away because she still had more to say: "Princess Charlotte is willing to give up her entire *country* for Eliza. Her entire identity. Her title, her privileges, her family. That's how I feel about you, Jack. I would give up anything for a life I was allowed to build anew with you. In a heartbeat."

"In a heartbeat," Jack said. Even in the dark, she could feel him grinning.

"I know I will grow old," Hazel said. "And perhaps a grave isn't the best place to talk about this, but I have been thinking about this a lot." Jack laughed, kissing her between words as Hazel tried to get the rest of her speech out: "There's a *chance*—a real chance—that I can figure out how to undo the Tincture. I don't know how yet, but only because I haven't examined the Tincture. If I can get a sample from Seven Dials . . . Because maybe Beecham *did* do it, and—"

"Hazel?" Jack said.

"Yes?"

"If anyone in the world would be able to figure out how to undo the Tincture, it would be you." He ran his hand so gently along the side of her face that it made Hazel want to cry. The lantern beam flickered in Jack's eye: the perfect gray color of a morning sky in Edinburgh.

"But . . . I'm really more of a surgeon than a chemist and—"

"Hazel?"

"Yes?"

"Just kiss me."

And she did.

TIME MELTED AND EXPANDED. HOURS AND MOMENTS were passing at the same time, at the same speed. Nothing outside the two of them mattered. Still, at some point, Hazel became aware that before long, the sun would come up.

She cursed herself even as she said it, but she managed to pull away from Jack's lips just long enough to murmur, "We need to get back to Warwick House."

Jack groaned softly, but released Hazel, and the two re-oriented themselves, remembering why they were there in the first place. Hazel, still feeling her heart beating in private, hidden places on her body, climbed back onto the grass to help complete the mission.

It was still dark, thankfully, but the sky was beginning to lighten in the east. They needed to work fast.

In a single, confident motion, Jack lifted the broken piece of the coffin lid and threw it to the surface.

"What is it?" Hazel called down. "How does she look?"

"Um," Jack replied.

Hazel lifted the lantern and looked down at the body they had just uncovered: it *was* a young woman, but she was entirely wrong. She was blond—her curls tangled around a face that was nothing at all like the Princess's. Charlotte had a round face and a small, beaklike nose. Lucretia Wilkes's face was long as a horse's, with large, wide-set eyes and a mouth straight and thin as a knife wound.

"Maybe she can wear a wig," Jack whispered.

Hazel shook her head. It wouldn't work. It was impossible. They would need to start again, to dig up another body. But how many freshly buried young women could there be in London graveyards? What were the odds that *any of them* resembled Charlotte enough to pass as a double? And even if they did try again (and again), how long would that game of roulette take? Their odds of getting caught became higher with every excursion.

Hazel had let excitement and optimism cloud her logic. She had gone about this all wrong. "Get out," she told Jack. "We can't take her."

Jack was already pulling himself onto the grass, and with a sigh, he began refilling the hole. It took only a few moments.

"Should we try another?" he whispered. "We have a few hours before it's light." He was being polite; Hazel knew there was no way they would have enough time to dig up another grave and make it back to Warwick House without being detected.

"No," Hazel said. She had already started back toward the cemetery gate with the empty cart. "I think I actually might have a better idea to find a body. Quicker, and more efficient than digging."

"Oh?" Jack said.

"You wouldn't need to come," Hazel added quickly. "It would be incredibly risky. I don't want to put you in any un-necessary danger."

"Incredibly risky, eh?" Jack said, wiping the dust from his hands onto his trousers. "In that case, I'm in."

27

IMON WAS CUTTING BANDAGES IN THE INFIRMARY
at Kew when Hazel and Jack arrived.

"Thank God you're here," Hazel remarked when
she saw him at his workbench. "I realized on the way over
that if you *weren't* here, I would have no idea where to find
you."

"I live here," Simon said.

Hazel smirked.

"No, I mean it," Simon said. "In apartments upstairs. I
was given rooms at Kew while I was treating the King. They
wanted me close."

"Of course," Hazel said. "That . . . makes sense. And how is
the King's condition?"

"Much improved. Thanks to you, Miss Sinnett. He's speaking like his old self again. Of course, he still will require significant time to regain his full physical power, but I think
treatment is off to a wonderful start."

"Well, he has a wonderful doctor," Hazel said.

Jack, behind her, cleared his throat.

"Oh!" Hazel said. "Forgive me. Dr. Ferris, this is my friend, Jack Cu— Ellis. Jack, this is Dr. Simon von Ferris, personal physician to King George."

"I've heard of you," Jack said.

"Pleasure to meet you, Mr. Kellis."

"*Ellis*," Jack corrected. Neither man shook the other's hand.

Hazel broke the awkward silence. "Simo— Dr. Ferris, do you happen to be a member of the Royal College of Surgeons?"

"A fellow. Yes, I am." His eyes went from Hazel to Jack, and then back again.

"In Edinburgh, there was a room at the university—I heard, from a friend—below the medical school, where bodies were kept for students and surgeons to dissect. Is there—?"

"Yes. There's a room of bodies available for the Fellows of the College in London. Very much the same, I imagine."

Hazel glanced at Jack before returning her attention to Simon. "I can't tell you why. I wish I could, but I can't."

"What do you need, Miss Sinnett?" Simon asked. He looked more concerned than anything else, as if he was genuinely worried that Hazel might have found herself in trouble.

"We need your help to steal a body."

Simon thought for a moment, folding the bandage he was cutting neatly and adding it to the pile. "Does the body have to be stolen?" he asked cautiously. "I'm a Fellow of the Royal College. The bodies are available for my use. For purchase."

"Oh," Hazel said. She raised her eyebrows. "No. That . . . that would work. We can just . . . purchase a body."

"Perhaps they weren't procured *by* the Royal College legally, but I believe they prefer a system where the physicians and surgeons turn a blind eye, so to speak. Does that make things better?"

"Yes," Hazel said. "No, I mean. It doesn't have to be stolen at all."

"Wonderful," Simon said. "I can take you this afternoon. Mr. Ellis is, of course, welcome to accompany us if he would like, but I believe we would attract less attention if it were just the two of us. If this is something of a secret task you're occupied with."

"That's fine," Jack said. "I can wait back at Warwick House."

"Wonderful," Simon said again.

HAZEL COULDN'T BELIEVE IT COULD BE THAT easy. After spending months in Edinburgh procuring bodies illicitly, in the darkness of night, terrified that policemen or robbers might happen on them, pulling naked corpses from broken coffins, she hadn't conceived of a world in which power and esteem could afford one to just . . . *get* what they needed, without fuss or fear.

Simon and Hazel rode together in a carriage to the Royal College of Surgeons, which was located at the public square of Lincoln's Inn Fields. It was a beautiful and imposing building, gleaming white stone with stairs leading up to an entrance defended by six Ionic columns: a temple to science and the men who upheld it. "Hello, Fred," Simon greeted the uniformed man at the door, who doffed his cap.

"Dr. Ferris."

Simon led Hazel through a room with neck-achingly high

ceilings, stacked on every side with bookshelves, where men were smoking pipes and sitting in red velvet chairs while they read. Simon greeted a few of them casually as they passed, but he was keeping a quick gait, and Hazel was grateful for it; the faster they were in and out, the better. The room let out into a winding hallway.

"This way," Simon said to Hazel, and he pressed through a nondescript white door and began down a flight of stairs. The temperature dropped as they went farther into the ground (to help keep bodies cool, Hazel thought), and then, before they had even reached the next door, Hazel smelled it: the stench of death and decay, of rotting flesh gone rigid and then soft again. It was a smell she knew now as well as the perfume her mother used to wear.

"Are you looking for any sort of body in particular?" Simon asked, eyebrow arched. An attendant stood by a door on the other side of the room, coughing into a soiled handkerchief.

"Young," Hazel replied. "Female. Mid-twenties or so?"

The corpses were lying horizontally on the floor. It took Hazel only a few minutes to find one that was almost a perfect match for the Princess—curved nose, brown curls, soft figure. In the dim light of the basement room, Hazel thought that she could have been, if not the Princess's twin, then at least her sister. "That one," Hazel said.

Simon walked swiftly to the attendant, and passed a few words quietly. When he returned to Hazel, he wrapped the body she had selected in a sheet and then hoisted it up over his shoulder as if it weighed no more than a sack of flour. "Okay. It's done. Let's take it out the door to the street this way. We can put a cart behind the carriage."

"Wait," Hazel said. She fumbled in her pocket for her purse. "I didn't pay yet. How much do I owe that man?"

"I took care of it."

"Simon, no. This is my body. Please. How much do I owe you, then?" Her fingers found the coins, and she thrust a handful of them toward Simon.

He waved her off. "It's nothing. I owe you this much and more for your help with the arsenic and mold in the King's bedchamber."

"I insist," Hazel said.

Simon was already halfway across the room again, almost at the back exit. "And I," he said, "refuse. To Warwick House, then. Come along."

Hazel and Simon made it back into the carriage together with their new cargo safely secured behind them. Their knees touched as the carriage jostled down the road.

"So," Simon said when they had been driving for a few minutes in silence, "I assume the body is not for you to dissect and study, then." He spoke, as he almost always did, in declarative statements.

"No," Hazel assented.

"And I assume as well that you're not going to tell me what the body is for?"

"Also correct." There was a beat of silence, and another bump in the cobblestone street, and then Hazel added: "I want to. I mean, I *would* want to, but no good would come of it. It's . . . dangerous."

"Dangerous," Simon echoed softly. "Well, then I am glad you came to me and did not attempt to steal a body from the Royal College without any reason to."

Hazel was aware that their legs were still touching, that

his hand was resting on his thigh, and if she wanted to, she could reach over and grab it by just lifting her fingers. "Thank you," Hazel said. "Truly, thank you."

Simon didn't reply, but then he said, not as a question but as a statement: "You are in love with the Scottish sailor."

The carriage gave a hideous jolt and Hazel nearly hit her head on the roof. A thousand different responses filled her brain at once, and when she finally regained control of her tongue, she said, "He's not even really a sailor."

"But you are in love with him." There was no cruelty in Simon's words, no jealousy or malice. There wasn't even sadness; it was just a man of science stating a simple fact that he formed based on observation.

"Yes," Hazel said. She couldn't lie to him. He was sitting there, his face so placid, lit by the afternoon sun streaming in the window. "I still don't actually know if we can be together," she added quietly.

"Hmm," Simon said.

"It's true," Hazel said. "There's a possibility that he might—that I *might* not be able to do . . . what I need to do for us to have a life together. And if I can't . . . I think I'll just spend my life alone. Because being a surgeon is all I ever wanted, and it's okay if I have to be alone to do it." It felt good to say it out loud. Hazel hadn't even realized that she was keeping those feelings corked tight inside her.

"You shouldn't be alone," Simon said. "You should marry me."

He said it so matter-of-factly that it took several seconds for Hazel to realize that he had just proposed to her.

Simon registered the shock on her face and said, "Perhaps you might not love me as you love your sailor. But I believe that a marriage can be built on more than that. It can be mutual respect. The decision to share a life together. To support and care for one another. Conversation. Companionship."

"You're—you're *proposing* to me?"

"Proposing marriage, yes."

Hazel laughed; she couldn't help it. It wasn't funny, but laughter seemed to be the only reaction her body was capable of in that moment.

"What is so funny?" Simon said, smiling, even as he didn't understand.

"I can't get married!" Hazel said. "I want to be a surgeon, not a wife."

"I want you to be a surgeon as well," Simon said, as if it were the most obvious thing in the world. "We would work together, as we already do so well. Practice medicine side by side."

Hazel saw it then, his beautiful vision: the two of them in a London town house with their apartments upstairs and a laboratory downstairs, treating patients who arrived to the door. He would kiss her on the forehead as she worked, and she would pour him tea when he was up too late, and maybe children, with blond hair and eyes the color of honey on toast, would run around their feet, giggling and trying to steal glass bottles from the shelves. Hazel and Simon would grow old by each other's sides, seeing the lines deepen in each other's faces like a mirror. His hair would go from blond to white, and their children would grow up to have children of their own. He would show her Sweden and she would show him Edinburgh, and they would be famous. Acclaimed, celebrated, and maybe even in love. It was possible, wasn't it?

But in every imagining, there was a phantom in the corner

of the room, a figure with dark hair and a smile that made Hazel's stomach turn in on itself. Hazel desperately wished that she were the type of person who could have accepted that beautiful future with Simon von Ferris. But Jack would always have her heart. And so, when the carriage rattled to a stop at the end of Pall Mall, Hazel turned to Simon, and he knew her answer before she even said a word.

"I understand," he said. "Love is hard to unknot."

"Yes," Hazel said. "It is."

They sat inside the carriage.

"Wait," Simon said, and Hazel's heart pounded in her chest even though she wasn't sure what she wanted him to say. "If what you're doing is secret—with the body—it would be foolish to walk up to the door. We should disguise it. Perhaps purchase a rug to roll around the body."

He was right. Simon gave a quick word to the coachman, and just a few minutes later, Hazel was at a market, paying for a rather ugly ornate rug that she wouldn't feel was wasted when it was ruining with the fluids and bile of a decomposing body.

Simon helped Hazel wrap the body inside the rug when they reached their destination for a second time. "This was a really good idea," Hazel said. Sure, they could have waited until evening, or sneaked in through a servant's entrance, but Pall Mall was lit with gas lamps throughout the night, and it would have taken only one errant resident glancing out their window to note something suspicious. This merely looked like the Princess had purchased a piece of furniture.

"I know," Simon said.

Jack was already at Warwick House, standing on the stoop, cupping his brow with a hand to block the sun and watch Hazel and Simon as they were preparing the body for delivery.

"You are a very talented surgeon and physician," Simon said. "I hope whatever you are doing with this body works out the way you plan."

"Thank you, Simon."

He kissed Hazel on both cheeks.

Jack took the rug inside, and Hazel waited on the stairs to Warwick House while Simon rode off in the carriage back to Kew. She half expected him to turn back and watch her, or to call out from the window of the coach, but he never did.

"Come on," Jack said finally, returning to the door after he had dropped the body off on Charlotte's bed. "We're all inside."

PRINCESS CHARLOTTE LEANED IN CLOSE TO HER dead double, which was lying flat on her bed, wearing one of her dresses. "Her eye color is wrong." She held open her own eye to demonstrate: "See? Mine are blue. Hers are brown."

"I can sew the eyes shut," Hazel said. "A hidden stitch. No one will even know."

The Princess nodded her assent and continued her intimate examination. "Good limbs—perhaps a little narrower than mine, but maybe I became slenderer in my illness." She circled the bed. "Her feet are big." It was true: the dead woman's feet were several inches larger than Princess Charlotte's. They had selected a pair of Charlotte's softest slippers, and Hazel and Jack spent several sweaty minutes trying to squeeze the feet into the fabric without causing the shoes to flip off. "But aside from that," the Princess said, "a remarkable likeness."

Eliza had styled the dead woman's hair in the curls the Princess was best known for, and applied cosmetics on her face the same way the Princess wore it. From far enough away, it would be almost impossible to distinguish the two; up close, they still looked remarkably alike—certainly convincing if you believed that the Princess had suffered from a strange, slightly distorting illness.

The Princess had already changed into a simple black shift dress, a servant's dress. She would be posing as Eliza's servant while they traveled across the Channel to France, and then through the Netherlands and Prussia to Bavaria. She had dismissed all her own servants at Warwick House the previous evening, and Hazel had strategically whispered to the kitchen maid she knew was the fondest of gossiping that the Princess was highly contagious.

"Well," Charlotte said. "I suppose that's that, then."

She had already packed her valise with the few most precious things she owned, along with a hefty collection of banknotes she would use to travel. As soon as they had settled on the plan, the Princess began loudly gifting jewels to Eliza and Hazel so that no one would raise an alarm when they were missing.

There was no one else for the Princess to say goodbye to: Hazel knew, as the entire country did, that the contentious marriage between the Regent and his wife had meant that Charlotte's mother, Princess Caroline of Brunswick, had absconded to Italy a few years ago to cavort with a cadre of lovers, all but abandoning her only daughter. "If you could mail this letter, Miss Sinnett?" Charlotte said, extending a note toward Hazel that was addressed in beautiful script to the Queen, Charlotte's grandmother. "It's just a short note. I figured that if I were actually close to death, I would tell my grandmother that I loved her."

Eliza squeezed Charlotte's hand. "She knows you love her."

Suddenly, the Princess wrapped her arms around Hazel and hugged her tight. "Thank you, Hazel," she said. "Thank you for saving my life."

"Now we just have to hope this works," Eliza said.

"It will work," Charlotte replied. "I know it will."

She scooped up Edwina and held the small dog close to her chest. "Come on, little one," she sang. "It's time to go on an adventure."

HAZEL AND JACK RETURNED TO HER APARTMENTS together. The next morning, Hazel would "discover" the Princess, and then there would be no going back.

When they were in Hazel's room, Jack unlaced the back of Hazel's dress. She was wearing only her stays and stockings, and her skin prickled where the breeze from the open window touched it. Jack ran his hands over both her shoulders and down her back. His hands were firm and rough with calluses, but he touched her so gently it was almost enough to make her cry. He buried his head into her hair and the nape of her neck from behind while he pulled her chemise down her shoulders. His breath was hot with wanting.

Jack had gotten stronger in his time away from her: his arms, once slender, were now taut with muscle, like rope.

Scratches and shiny white burns marred his skin like tattoos; Hazel wanted to know him again, every part of him, the way she once did. She would put her lips to every new scar.

When Hazel reclined onto the bed, her naked skin glowing in the candlelight, Jack pulled himself on top of her. He made her feel small then, wrapping her into his arms, and Hazel raked her fingers through his thick black hair and pressed herself even farther up against him. He breathed her name over and over again, until it became a chant, just sounds, beyond meaning, in time with the one-two beating of his heart. *Hazel. Hazel. Hay-zel. Haze-el.*

Before they fell asleep, Jack curled his body around Hazel's in bed, spooning her from behind and breathing into her hair. "Haze," he said. "Have you thought about what's going to happen?"

Hazel turned to face him, and knocked her pillow out of the way so that she could see him better. "Of course," she said. "I've thought about every aspect of this plan. The Princess is right. It's going to work."

"No," Jack said. "I mean, what's going to happen to *you.* With the Princess dead . . . I just mean, she's so beloved, right? People will be upset. You're her doctor."

Hazel swallowed. It was the aspect of the entire endeavor that left a lump in her throat. Jack was correct: people would be despairing at the Princess's death. She was their young, beautiful, liberal hope for the future. Who knew what the future would hold, who the next heir to the throne would even be? Despair would turn into anger, and much of it would be channeled toward Hazel, the physician who let her die. It would permanently tarnish Hazel's reputation, completely dispel the glow of respect and esteem that had surrounded her after she "cured" the Princess the first time and helped Simon treat the King.

After tomorrow, Hazel would no longer be a medical celebrity; she might even be a pariah.

"Charlotte is a person," Hazel said finally, as much to herself as to Jack. "She deserves a life with the person she loves. A life that belongs to her. This is the right thing to do. Besides, I managed to get this far, didn't I? No matter what happens, I'll figure something out. I always do."

Jack brushed a stray hair from her face and tucked it behind her ear. "Have I told you today," Jack said, "that you are so beautiful?"

His stomach was bare and uncovered, his ribs and muscles ridged under his skin. There were bruises and scars across his body, new ones that Hazel hadn't seen since they were last together.

"Will you still love me even if all of England despises me?" Hazel said.

"We're Scots, Hazel," Jack said, a smile extending across his face. "If England hates you, we can hate them right back."

Hazel knew if Jack hadn't been there with her that night, she wouldn't have been able to sleep at all. But somehow, in his arms, she drifted off sometime after midnight, awaiting the morning that would change the world.

The London Morning Chronicle

27 August 1818

DEMISE OF HER ROYAL HIGHNESS
THE PRINCESS CHARLOTTE

It is this day our melancholy duty to make known to our Readers, the demise of Her Royal Highness the Princess Charlotte. This young, beautiful, and interesting Princess survived bouts of Roman fever in previous years only to succumb to a mysterious illness which has afflicted her of recent months.

The shock which this unexpected and afflicting event gave this morning to the loyal and affectionate inhabitants of the Metropolis cannot be adequately described, and it will be equally felt throughout every part of His Majesty's Dominions. Her amiable virtues—the bright promise of her early life—her soon-to-be connubial happiness with the Hereditary Prince of Orange—the edifying picture of exemplary benevolence which she held out—her well-known constitutional principles, as well as the high political considerations dependent on her life, all combine to render the event of her premature death a calamity that must involve the Empire in universal gloom. Every heart partakes in the suffering of her inconsolable Husband-to-be, whose agonies are now unutterable. Her Royal Father is also, we learn, sunk into the deepest affliction.

The Princess had been treated by the Female surgeon Hazel Sinnett, who discovered her body this morning at seven o'clock and who then sent word to inform His Royal Highness the Prince Regent on this most lamentable tragedy.

(CONT.)

The dejection and sorrow universally expressed in the countenances of all were the best testimony to the character of the deceased. The influence of the event was felt at the Stock Exchange, where it was considered as likely to affect national prosperity, and the funds suffered a sensible depression. Shops were everywhere voluntarily shut and all business was suspended, except, we are sorry to say, that of vending newspapers by horn-boys in the streets—a scandal that was generally reprobated. The melancholy news was calculated to fly fast enough, without such indecent clamour.

The order of succession to the Crown is now by her death disturbed; and from the age of the Princes in the order of succession, and the state of the illustrious family, apprehensions will occur to every loyal mind. It will be the earnest prayer of the nation, that an early alliance of one of the unmarried Princes may forthwith be settled.

28

 T TOOK ONLY AN HOUR FOR THE ENTIRE CITY
to be enveloped in black. Hazel went to Warwick
House at seven in the morning and sent word to
Carlton House and Buckingham that the Princess was dead.
By ten o'clock, every house on the street had a length of black
cloth extending from the window. By noon, drapers and dress-
makers across London were reporting that they were sold out
of mourning fabric. Weeping was audible in the streets, as
were the barks of the young boys selling hastily printed newspapers, the ink still wet and staining their fingers.

Hazel remained at Warwick House, greeting and soothing the various members of the extended royal family and
Parliament who arrived to pay their respects. Charlotte's fiancé, the Hereditary Prince of Orange, was present, holding
court and talking loudly about the beautiful Princess's virtues. Hazel glanced at the clock on the wall: if all had gone
according to plan, Eliza and the real Charlotte were already
on board a ship at Dover bound for Calais.

No one was allowed into the Princess's bedroom until the

Prince Regent arrived. He was in all black, his head low. He had seemingly aged a decade overnight: his face, normally powdered and rouged, was bare, and his hair looked thin and uncombed. He ignored the members of court who bowed low when he entered, who attempted to touch his shoulder or speak to him. Instead, the Regent walked directly to Hazel Sinnett—so quickly the private secretary walking a pace behind him stumbled, trying to keep up. "Show me the Princess," the Prince Regent said.

Hazel took him into the room. She had purposely kept the lighting low, candles placed around the bed but no lamps— but she hadn't needed to: the body was swelling and bruising, in the state of normal decomposition more than a day after death, contorting her face. Wearing the Princess's dress and jewels, it was impossible to imagine that even the real Charlotte would have looked much different had she actually been deceased. The Prince extended his hand, as if to touch her face, but then he turned away. "My only daughter," the Regent said quietly. "My beautiful daughter."

His private secretary had slipped in the door behind the Regent. He turned on his heels toward Hazel, his eyes narrowed with malice, and hissed: "This is *your fault. You killed the Princess!*"

"I'm sure she did as well as she could, Hornsby," the Regent mumbled. "Perhaps it's my fault, for hiring a female surgeon at all."

"*Never* your fault, Your Royal Highness," the private secretary cooed. "How were you to know that she would be an *incompetent?*"

Hazel opened her mouth as if to protest, unsure of what exactly she would say, when there was a gentle knocking on the door.

"Finally!" the private secretary sighed.

Simon von Ferris entered the room slowly, as if afraid he would spook a frightened animal on the other side. "Your Royal Highness," he said, bowing to the Regent. "And Miss Sinnett."

To Hazel, the Regent said, "I thought we might bring Dr. Ferris in to examine the Princess. Examine the . . . body. See if he might be able to discover how she . . . how she . . ." A silent sob seized him.

The private secretary looked as though he would have given anything in the world to be allowed to comfort him, but of course, touching a royal would be strictly forbidden. And so, instead, he just continued to glare at Hazel.

"Yes, certainly, sir," Simon said, and he approached the dead woman lying on the bed. Every muscle in Hazel's body tensed at once; she tried to relax her face, to look natural. Simon took his time. He prodded at the woman's eyes (surely he could tell that they were sewn shut?) and felt for swelling at her neck. He gently raised her hand, and then lowered it. He walked around the bed to the other side and repeated the process again. There was no way Simon didn't recognize the body he had purchased himself and personally helped deliver to Warwick House.

"Well?" the Regent asked. "What's your determination?"

Simon's eyes barely flicked to Hazel before they returned to the Regent. "The Princess is dead," he said.

"Well, we *know* she's dead!" spat the private secretary. "What did she die of?!"

This time, Simon's eyes lingered on Hazel's. She tried to silently beg for help.

"My estimation? Alpine blood disease. Incredibly rare. Yes, in fact, I'm certain of it. The Princess died of Alpine blood disease. The signs are abundantly clear."

"Alpine blood disease?" the Regent said. "I've never heard of it."

Neither had Hazel. She had made it her mission, over the past year, to read every single medical textbook she could get her hands on, and not one of them had ever mentioned, or even alluded to, Alpine blood *anything*. Simon had made something up. *Thank you*, she mouthed silently to him.

"What's that?!" the private secretary said, pointing to a large scar running along the fake Princess's right hand. It looked like the scar from a knife injury. Hazel hadn't noticed it. *How did they not notice it?* "The Princess had never been scarred or maimed!"

"Oh," Simon said, speaking slowly, giving his brain time to fill in the blanks of the sentence as he was forming it. "Scarring is, actually, the most common effect of Alpine blood disorder. They just . . . appear. Very normal for the body—after death—to have some strange and unusual markings of this sort."

The private secretary sighed loudly. "What *I* would like to know," he said, "is how *Miss Sinnett* failed to recognize such an easily identifiable disease. Her lack of proper care is responsible for the death of the Princess. If Her Royal Highness had been treated by Dr. Ferris or another suitable *male* doctor, I find it difficult to believe that she wouldn't be with us today, mere days from celebrating her wedding!"

Hazel began to speak but she was interrupted by Simon. "Actually," Simon said, "Miss Sinnett and I worked closely on the treatment for the Princess, as we worked closely on the treatment for His Majesty the King. Miss Sinnett suggested that the Princess was suffering from Alpine blood disease weeks ago, but I dismissed her theory. Incorrectly, as it turns out."

"Ah," the private secretary said. "Well, nevertheless—"

"Thank you," the Regent said to Hazel. "And to you, Dr. Ferris, for your time. I do not blame you for the unknowable workings of God and the tragedies he chooses us to suffer. If you will excuse me, I would like to go home now."

Hazel and Simon both bowed as the Prince Regent left, his private secretary scrambling behind him, looking like there was still more he was desperate to say but no longer having an excuse to do so.

"Simon," Hazel said when the door had shut behind them and Hazel and Simon were alone in the bedchamber. "Thank you. *Thank you.* You didn't need to do that! Your reputation—"

"—will be fine. And is less fragile than the reputation of the first and only female surgeon with a royal appointment." Simon lingered at the Princess's desk, picking up and rolling one of her pens in his fingers. "I wasn't trying to be kind. If they blamed you, it would set back the hundreds of young women who want to follow in your path in the medical field. Your success is their success, and your failure their failure. You are greater than yourself now. It's not fair to be a symbol, Miss Sinnett, when it is so much easier to be a person."

"No," Hazel said. "It's not."

"And," Simon said, placing the pen back where it belonged. "You and I both well know you were not to blame for the Princess's untimely, very tragic death."

"Thank you," she said again, and she meant it. She was more grateful to him than he could possibly know.

"Besides," Simon said, "I'm planning on returning to Sweden. It matters not to me what these Englishmen think of me any longer. I miss my family. My brothers are becoming men without me."

"I'm sure they miss you too," Hazel said.

"They do. And I miss the cold. Too rainy here. Too much gloom. The cold is bracing, and when the sun reflects on the snow, it is the most beautiful sight in the world." Simon straightened his posture and fixed a piece of hair that had fallen into his face. "I do not know where your journey will take you, Miss Sinnett, but if you find yourself in Stockholm, please say hello."

"I will," Hazel said.

"I believe you shall do great things." He said it like he said almost everything, just a statement of fact. There was no condescension, or even flirtation. It was just Simon saying what he believed to be true.

"Well, I think I have to," Hazel said. She pulled her medical bag off the table and held it facing Simon, the initials *H.S.* visible on its leather surface. "I feel it's my duty to do this bag proud."

Simon kissed Hazel on the cheeks and squeezed her hands in his. "I hope your love for the sailor is always enough for you," he said. "And I hope you are happy."

"Is anyone actually happy?" Hazel asked.

"People like you and me? Very intelligent people? Almost never. But who knows? Perhaps we will be the exceptions." He winked, his brown eyes twinkling, and Hazel knew that one day he would make a wonderful husband for someone else. "Very difficult to treat Alpine blood disease, you know," Simon said as he was leaving.

"Yes," Hazel replied. "Almost impossible. But I've read that the cure might be a quiet life spent in Bavaria."

"Hm," Simon said, nodding contemplatively. "Yes, I think that just might do it."

And he disappeared through the door, vanishing in his black medical coat into the throng of mourners outside.

**Excerpt from Childe Harold's Pilgrimage,
canto 4, stanzas 167–168,
"Death of the Princess Charlotte," by Lord Byron**

HARK! *forth from the abyss a voice proceeds,
A long low distant murmur of dread sound,
Such as arises when a nation bleeds
With some deep and immedicable wound;
Through storm and darkness yawns the rending ground,
The gulf is thick with phantoms, but the chief
Seems royal still, though with her head discrown'd,
And pale, but lovely, with woeful grief
She held to her betrothed, but his love yielded no relief.*

*Scion of chiefs and monarchs, where art thou?
Fond hope of many nations, art thou dead?
Could not the grave forget thee, and lay low
Some less majestic, less beloved head?*

29

THE DREARY MOOD HAD PERVADED LONDON and permeated the Companions to the Death in their den at Seven Dials. In the fireplace, the embers burned low and miserable, more ash and smoke than flame. Mrs. Thire, draped in a sheer black veil that extended to her ankles, was sipping tea from a tiny china cup; Banneker was staring in the middle distance, his head resting in his hands; Charles Armitage Brown was reading and rereading a newspaper, as if he might, by examining it closely enough, be able to unlock an alternative version of events, in which the Princess might still be alive, or else discover that the entire thing had been a cruel prank.

Byron sat sideways on a chair, both legs hoisted onto its arms, his brow furrowed. "Miserable," he said. "Our beautiful romantic dream, *over*! *What hope have the Whigs now?*"

Marie-Anne had been writing in a large ledger book, but she looked up at Byron's lament. "We shall do as we always do," she said.

"And what's that?" said Byron. "Write poetry? I've been doing that."

"Look to the future, of course," Marie-Anne said. Her voice was light and musical, almost singing. "The Princess is dead. The Prince Regent—or I suppose, he might just be the Prince again now—will become King as he was always going to. And now, one of his younger siblings shall have to marry and have a legitimate child who will one day be King or Queen in turn. Maybe the Duke of Clarence will give us an heir. Or Cambridge. Or Kent. Patience, George. Things are complicated now, but they are not over."

"But how long will that take?" Byron said.

"As long as it takes," Marie-Anne replied.

When Hazel arrived, the entire room had turned to stare at her. No one said a word. The silence lasted so long and was so thick in the air that Hazel awkwardly cleared her throat. "I—I wish I had been able to do more," she said finally. "I'm . . . so sorry."

It was Banneker who rose and clapped her on the shoulder. "We're sure you did everything you could," he said quietly, but he didn't make eye contact.

Byron scoffed.

Hazel approached Marie-Anne Lavoisier, walking softly. She was careful not to let her voice get much louder than a whisper, afraid to disrupt the room more than she already had. "I was wondering if I might be allowed to use some of the equipment in the laboratory upstairs for some of my own research."

"Yes," Marie-Anne said. "I think that would be all right."

"Too late to find a cure!" Byron called from the far side of the room. Hazel ignored him.

"I was also wondering," she said, her heart pounding, "whether I might be able to get a sample of the Tincture to work with."

Marie-Anne cleaned the nib of her pen and placed it beside her book. "Miss Sinnett," she said, "glad as I am of your passion for research, Antoine and I have made it an unbreakable law between us that we will neither teach nor share the formulation of the Tincture. So, if you have hopes of replicating it—"

"No," Hazel said quickly. "It's not like that. I want to undo it."

"The sailor," Marie-Anne said.

There was no use in lying. "Yes."

If Hazel had access to the Tincture, if she could understand, if not how to *make* it, then at least how it functioned, then she would have a chance of understanding how to undo it. Months had passed since Beecham's apparent death, and there wasn't a whisper of another Beecham relative appearing in Europe, or a young surgeon emerging out of obscurity with skills surpassing his alleged experience. Hazel was finding it easier and easier to convince herself that he really was gone. And if Beecham was able to end his immortality and his life, Hazel could make Jack mortal again.

Marie-Anne rose. "I suppose, as a member of the Companions of the Death, even in part, you're entitled to a vial, to do with as you please." She pulled the key from beneath her chemise, where it hung on a chain around her neck. "I shall unlock the cabinet."

Hazel followed the chemist up the creaking stairs to the laboratory. She wondered whether Marie-Anne, too, resented her for the death of the Princess, blamed her for failing to treat her correctly, even though the news had somehow come out that the "Alpine blood disease" was such a rare and fatal disorder no treatment would have been effective. Or maybe Marie-Anne knew something was wrong with the story. With every step up the back staircase, Hazel somehow had the sense that she was walking into a trap.

But, no, the laboratory was empty: not even Antoine was there. His experiments were neatly put away, and the tables were clean and the sun was streaming in clear and bright through the curved glass of the windows. The room was warm; the glass containing the heat like a greenhouse.

The cabinet was a large, imposing thing, black wood and taller than both Hazel and Marie-Anne Lavoisier. Its lock was tarnished brass, mottled and green with patina. Marie-Anne inserted the key and snapped it to the side.

There they were: a dozen vials of the Tincture. Hazel had seen it now many times, but she never ceased to be fascinated by its impossible color, black and gold at the same time. It was a liquid, but it seemed to swirl like gas. It left a milky sheen on the sides of the vial.

There were other shelves in the cabinet: an entire bottom row was dedicated to the yellow-gold diluted Tincture in vials with droppers atop them, the formula that allowed dead limbs to be reattached.

And then there were rows of drawers, small as an apothecary's, neatly labeled with a handwriting that Hazel now recognized as Marie-Anne's. Hazel took a step closer. There was a smell, a familiar scent of earth and decay coming from the cabinet, a smell made stronger by the summer's heat.

"Here you are," Marie-Anne said, plucking a vial of the Tincture from her cabinet and holding it out to Hazel. Its lid was sealed with black wax. "Yours to do with as you wish. Even if you wish to waste it in experimentation that will only come to naught."

But Hazel was distracted. The smell was so familiar, like a forgotten dream, but she couldn't place it. And it was coming from one of the cabinet's tiny drawers. "What do you keep in there?" Hazel asked.

Marie-Anne blinked. "Various chemicals for our experiments. Liniments. Herbs. Minerals. My husband and I are chemists, Miss Sinnett."

Hazel couldn't help herself. The smell was getting stronger, buzzing in the front of her brain like a siren, and as if in a dream, she felt herself reaching toward one of the small wooden drawers before Marie-Anne could protest, and she pulled it open.

It was mold. Fuzzy spores in acid green and black, clinging to every surface of the inside of the drawer. It was mold, alive and *breathing*, noxious and pungent, and at once Hazel knew where she had smelled it before. The answer was written on the label on the front of the drawer in Marie-Anne Lavoisier's perfect, elegant script: *Kew.*

"You," Hazel said, pulling the drawer out completely and letting it clatter to the ground. Mold bounced out and scattered onto the floor. "You . . . were poisoning the King. You were making him mad."

"Don't be silly, Miss Sinnett," Marie-Anne said, but her expression held no indication of a joke being told.

"You put the mold in his walls. You knew what would happen with the arsenic in the wallpaper. *Of course* you did. You probably put the wallpaper in his bedchamber! You, or another of your . . . your *Companions.*"

Marie-Anne sighed. She stooped, gathered the fallen mold spores back into their drawer with her fingers, and returned the drawer to its empty square in the cabinet, where it belonged. Hazel took a step back while Marie-Anne placidly patted the dust and debris from her hands.

"Allow me to explain something to you," Marie-Anne said. "In the beginning, when the Revolution started in France in 1789, Antoine and I were excited. We were seeing change happen all around us. It would be a new era of reason, and science! We saw the fishwives march on Versailles with their pikes; the heads of royal guards dripping blood on the happy masses below, and even then, we thought that the anger of the people was justified, that the king and the elite had abused their power and taken too much from the country who were now demanding something back.

"There was a time, in 1791 or 1792, before what they now call the Reign of Terror, when Antoine and I could have fled the country. King Louis and Marie Antoinette were prisoners then, in Paris, but they were alive. The people were negotiating a new way of government, a new France, born of the Enlightenment. And we knew people were angry at those who had benefited from the Old Regime, people like Antoine and me. But Antoine was a member of the Académie des Sciences—the Academy of Sciences. He wanted to protect what he had built, do you see? He was a servant, not of the king but of the people.

"They came for him in the spring in 1794. There were narcissi and daffodils, I remember that, in Paris, blooming on the day they came for him. They took him, and my father, and twenty other men and cut their heads off in the street and cheered. They cheered, Miss Sinnett, when my Antoine's head fell.

"I respect the people," Marie-Anne said. "A nation must be in service of its people, and its government must represent them. Our country should not, as the Tories choose to believe, be led by a despot. They believe a king's strong fist will lead to safety and order. I have seen firsthand that that is not the case."

"So, you tried to kill King George?" Hazel said. "Because you hate the monarchy?"

Marie-Anne looked at Hazel with tender concern. "No," she cooed. "Of course not. If we wanted King George dead, he would be dead. We wanted him . . . controlled. It is a precise and delicate balance, you see. A king too strong, and the people fight back. A king fully overthrown . . . And chaos reigns. A nation needs a leader, but it also needs to be controlled, by those with vision, and intelligence. The Prince is a buffoon—you know this. Unpopular and unloved. But easy to control, and easy to manage. And"—she ran her finger along the edge of a scalpel—"after the Prince, we would have had Charlotte. Poor, brilliant, *doomed* Charlotte. Raised to understand the role of a monarch in a modern world. To serve the people."

Marie-Anne picked up the scalpel and examined its sharp edge. "A long life gives one perspective, Miss Sinnett. Things look . . . smaller. We can see the entire tapestry while the stitches are being sewn, do you understand? And so, with that particular power comes a very specific duty. The Companions to the Death have an aim: to steer the nation—gently, mind you—but to steer it, the way a coachman would a spirited horse. For horses to progress down the correct road, they require reins, and command."

Marie-Anne closed the distance between herself and Hazel, still holding the scalpel. "What a pity that England lost the Princess. What a *shame*," she said, enunciating each syllable. Her tongue flicked over her words. "'Alpine blood disease,' was it?"

"That's what they say," Hazel said, forcing herself not to look nervous, to keep her posture straight. Hazel's heartbeat was so loud; she wondered if Marie-Anne could hear it. She wondered if Marie-Anne could see the lie in her eyes, the dilation of her pupils, the rapid blinking.

And then Marie-Anne's left hand was around Hazel's neck.

She *squeezed*.

Hazel gasped. Her face was hot and red; the tendons of her neck strained against Marie-Anne's grip. She tried to pry Marie-Anne's hand away but all her strength had left her. She was fumbling ineffectually and she was choking to death. There was a glint in the corner of her field of vision: Marie-Anne was still holding that scalpel in her other hand.

"Where is Princess Charlotte?" Marie-Anne hissed through clenched teeth. *"What did you do?"*

An ugly gulp squeezed its way out of Hazel's throat, and Hazel's voice was hoarse and thin when she said, *"Dead."*

Hazel flailed, and there was the sound of glass shattering: she had broken the vials in the cabinet. Vials were rolling, draining their liquid onto the wooden shelves and the floor, but Marie-Anne paid them no mind. Her grip tightened on Hazel's neck. "Do not take me for a fool, Miss Sinnett. We *welcomed* you here. I invited you in. *Bring. The. Princess. Back.*" The world went dark at the edges. A dull ache was blossoming across the front of Hazel's skull, and her mouth was gaping open and shut like a fish on land. "I will *ruin* you. There is too much at stake here for reckless *children!*"

Hazel had to do *something*. The hand on her throat was only becoming tighter, Marie-Anne's thumb and three fingers pressing into Hazel's flesh; she had no air now, no air, and when she blinked, the blackness was taking longer and longer to recede. She had sewn the very arm now squeezing the life from her. She had ensured that the muscles were properly attached and the ligaments were in place and that blood would flow to each and every finger. She had stitched that shoulder all the way around using strong, neat, invisible sutures.

It was reflex, an unthinking instinct, the way an animal lashed out against a predator: Hazel extended her own arm with what little strength she had left, and when her fingernails were directly above where she thought the stitches might be on Marie-Anne's shoulder, she clawed down as hard as she could.

Marie-Anne screamed.

Her grip slacked, and Hazel gasped in a deep breath of air. Now she could see: she had pulled apart the seam where Marie-Anne's arm was attached to the rest of her body, and the edges of the black thread were dangling from it.

Once more, Hazel yanked.

Marie-Anne's left arm fell to the ground with a wet splatter, with a sound like an overripe orange falling from a great height.

Hazel blinked the oxygen back to her brain. Blood was pooling, bright red, across the floor. Hazel managed to pull up her leather medical bag before the puddle reached it. Marie-Anne was clutching at her empty shoulder—gasping, shouting, wailing. And then she fell silent—it was either the shock or the blood loss.

In a moment, the rest of the Companions would be thundering up the stairs to see what had happened—only a few seconds to get out.

Marie-Anne's detached arm twitched on the floor like an insect. All four of its fingers shivered. A few inches away, rolling in the blood, was a single intact vial with a black wax stopper. Hazel snatched it from the floor, and then she ran.

When Hazel made it back to her own apartments, she closed and bolted the locks. She panted, sliding down the door. How far did Marie-Anne Lavoisier's strings extend? How much did she know? The Companions seemed all-knowing; they had once delivered invitations directly onto Hazel's pillow. It had seemed charming at the time; now it made her blood run cold. Who knew what the Companions were capable of?

Perhaps a part of her had always known what the Companions were doing. A month ago, Hazel had been enthralled by the notion that there was a secret room of influential, brilliant people planning and strategizing. It was wonderful—comforting, even!—to learn that such a cabal of power existed, that the fate of the country was not entirely in the hands of a clownish Regent who dressed like a Macaroni and gambled his way into heavy debt. To know that Britain was not a dinghy adrift at sea. It seemed *noble*, Hazel thought, to imagine philosophers at work, hidden beneath the surface, acting as a rudder.

It had taken just a small drawer full of mold for Hazel to realize that the Companions that existed in her mind were a fantasy. Godlike power had reduced humanity to a game for them. It had made them cruel. Hazel promised herself, as she sat against that door, that her mission as a doctor would always be to help people. She would never negotiate compromises or plots if the cost was human suffering. There would be no shortcuts for her, no grand visions of impossible plans to fix society as a whole. Her work would be slow and long and deliberate: person to person, as many individuals as she could serve. It would not be glamorous. There might no longer be French champagne or Italian wine or evenings rubbing elbows with royals or celebrities. But she would be doing what was right.

Hazel Sinnett had made her choice. She would never let herself turn into the type of creature Marie-Anne Lavoisier had become. She would leave London, the city that worshipped fame and nobility and money—and the power conferred by all three in turn.

It was time to move on.

30

I T WAS GASPAR WHO HAD ARRIVED AT HAZEL'S apartments, in all black but still wearing his old-fashioned wig, to inform her that since the Princess was deceased, Hazel's service as a royal physician had officially concluded. "I'm sure I can arrange a carriage to take you back to Edinburgh, if you wish, Miss Sinnett," Gaspar added, and Hazel had the sense that the royal family did not instruct him to make that accommodation.

"That's quite all right, Gaspar," Hazel had said. She was already folding her dresses and packing them into her trunk. Only a few were worth saving. (She could hear Eliza in her head, remarking that she should probably just get rid of *all* of them.)

The midnight-blue dress made by Mrs. Thire was the nicest one that Hazel had ever known, but now just looking at it reminded her of the Companions. She smelled mold and madness on it, and felt Marie-Anne Lavoisier's dead fingers curled around her neck. She would leave the dress behind for the maid to keep or sell. "I do not know if I'm actually going back to Edinburgh."

"But whyever not?" asked Gaspar.

The real answer was Jack: Hazel knew that Jack would never be able to return to Edinburgh, a city where his face had been plastered on the front of newspapers for weeks. Where he had friends and enemies who knew his real name. Where he was supposed to be dead. Hazel didn't know when she would be able to see Hawthornden again—to sleep in her own bed, to work in the laboratory she had built for herself in the dungeon below the hill, to stand at the balcony off her bedroom and stare into the green clefted creek that ran below the castle. She didn't know whether she would *ever* get to see Hawthornden again. But she knew that she didn't want to be without Jack. She would rather be with Jack in a strange, new city than spend her life in the numbing cocoon of the comforting and familiar.

"My mother and younger brother are in Windsor," Hazel said. "He's at Eton. I thought perhaps I would see them." She didn't add that from there, she and Jack would travel farther: west to Bristol, or south to Portsmouth. Somewhere they could get on a ship.

Her entire time in London fit into a single trunk. Besides a few old dresses, a pair of drawers that the Princess had given her (Charlotte had sworn, through a fit of giggles, that they would be the most comfortable thing Hazel could wear under her dresses), her medical bag, and the pages of her treatise, though heaven knew now, without the connections and influence of the Companions, whether Hazel would ever be able to get it published.

And there was the vial of Tincture, still stoppered. The

blood on it had dried and coagulated, the ridges of her fingertips gummy and brown on the glass, clouding the liquid inside. Still, when she turned it at particular angles, she could see it: inky black, shimmering, and viscous.

Wherever Hazel and Jack made their home, Hazel would make it her mission to study and understand the liquid contained in the vial. She would learn how the rules of immortality worked, and she would discover how it might be undone.

"I don't blame you, you know," Gaspar said as he was leaving. "For what it's worth. God chooses when to take us all. And I think you're a wonderful doctor, Miss Sinnett."

"Thank you, Gaspar," Hazel said. "For everything."

He kissed her hand, and closed the door so softly it didn't make a sound.

There was one more thing she needed to do before she would hire a carriage and meet Jack at the docks.

She held the letter in her hand from Mr. Eastman, Esq., the executor of Dr. Beecham's will, which had given an address on Chalton Street. It was finally time to pick up the respectable amount of money Dr. Beecham had left for her. She and Jack would use it to begin their future together.

Number 128 Chalton Street was located in the middle-class development of Sommers Town, near the development of town houses known as "the Polygon." The Polygon was uncompleted; though it had been originally planned as a structure with five sides, surrounding a shared park-garden in the middle, the builders went broke partway through the construction, and now the Polygon was just two sides of row houses set at an angle, apartments surrounded by fields and occupied by the type of artists and working people who could never hope to afford the far more fashionable, urban addresses in the heart of London to the south.

There was no plaque for Mr. Samuel Eastman, but after glancing down to check the address on the envelope she had been given to confirm she was at the right place, Hazel rang the bell. An ancient maid opened the door, with blind milky eyes and a face soft as mashed potatoes. She ushered Hazel through the door without a word.

Mr. Eastman was sitting at his desk in an office with almost no other furniture, reading a report of some sort. The shelves were less than half-filled with books. There was no chair for Hazel to sit in across from the lawyer. His papers appeared disorganized, strewn about and expanding beyond the desktop to the floor. Hazel wondered how Dr. Beecham could have possibly entrusted his estate to a solicitor like this, but then Mr. Eastman looked up from his report and Hazel didn't wonder any longer.

Dr. Beecham was not dead.

He was posing as his own solicitor.

"Miss Sinnett," he said pleasantly, "I was wondering when I might be seeing you."

The realization kept pouring over Hazel like cold water: Beecham wasn't dead.

Until that moment, when she felt the disappointment curdle in her belly, Hazel hadn't realized how much hope she was hanging on the notion that the doctor had figured out a way to end it, that the Tincture *wasn't* permanent, and that one day she and Jack would be able to live a normal life together. Somehow, it had just become an indisputable fact in her own mind: eventually, she and Jack would figure it out. Eventually, things would work out the way they were supposed to.

Now here was Beecham in front of her. Breathing, shuffling papers around, as alive as he had been the last time she saw him, months ago. His death had been a charade, as false as the future she had once imagined possible.

"You," Hazel said. "You—you're not dead."

Dr. Beecham rose. His hair had grown out slightly since she saw him last, but aside from that, he was unaged. Unharmed. He was still wearing black leather gloves.

"Yes, Miss Sinnett," he said, the way one might talk to a confused child. "Yes, of course I am."

"I just thought—"

"Ah." Beecham gathered some papers on the table. "Yes. The inheritance. Death requires a certain commitment, I've discovered. Paperwork. Finances. Dull matters that I have found I prefer to handle myself. Hence, a nom de guerre. Simpler. But the money I promised in the will is very much real. What did the letter say—a thousand pounds? Give me a few moments, I have the banknotes here somewhere."

"I don't care about the money!" Hazel said, loud enough that the brass lanterns mounted on the wall vibrated. "You're— I thought you had died."

"No," Beecham said gently. "Just starting over. Perhaps in Philadelphia this time, I was thinking. Have you been?"

"What? Philadelphia? No," Hazel said. She wished there was a chair for her to sit in. She paced in a small circle. "I thought there was a way to fix it. To undo it."

Beecham gestured, offering her his desk chair, but Hazel waved it off.

"I should go," Hazel said. "I don't want your money."

He found the banknotes and held them out in his gloved fingers. "It's yours. Less than I owe you for everything that happened, I'm sure."

Hazel's fists tightened into knots. She could feel her nails pressing half-moons on her palm. "You killed him. You framed Jack Currer for murder and he was hanged. You've killed so many people and you—"

"—Mrs. Parker? Could you send for tea?" Beecham turned his attention back to Hazel. "I've found that long conversations are always more manageable with a cup of tea."

The elderly maid arrived with a tray wiggling in her grip. "Thank you, Mrs. Parker," Beecham said. "Now, Miss Sinnett, do you take sugar?"

Hazel didn't reply. "You let him hang for the things you did."

Beecham sighed. "Live long enough and the past becomes an endless parade of mistakes and things that might have been done better or differently. What can we do but continue on, and try again?" He took a sip of tea. "Besides, I think we're both aware that the hanging was only a, shall we say, temporary inconvenience for our friend Mr. Currer."

Hazel didn't accept the cup of tea he poured for her, pushing it across the desk.

"Ah," Beecham said. "I think I better understand your interest in remaking one's mortality."

"It's useless now," Hazel said. "It doesn't matter. You aren't dead."

"No," Beecham replied. "I'm not."

The steam from the tea swirled into circles and tendrils.

It reminded Hazel of the way the Tincture behaved inside its vial. "Is it even possible, then?" Hazel asked. "To undo it?" Even if he had offered her a chair, she wouldn't have sat. She wanted his opinion on the science, and then she would leave.

Beecham was in no such rush. He poured his own cup of tea. "Look in the cup, Miss Sinnett," he said.

She did. Leaves of black tea were staining the water. The threads of transparent auburns and browns wove together in the cup.

Then Beecham took the milk and added a quick splash. He stirred it once, twice, and then three times with the small spoon, and Hazel watched as the color went from translucent to opaque. "There is much about the world of science that we still don't understand," Beecham said. "But the Tincture to a soul is like milk into tea: you can stir it in, but no matter how vigorously you stir in the other direction, the milk will never separate. The tea is changed, fundamentally. And the process of sifting or boiling and condensing that we *might* do to try to separate the tea and the milk would never again be able to give us the same cup of tea we had before we chose to add the milk."

"Marie-Anne Lavoisier said something similar to me," Hazel said.

"She and Antoine and I created something miraculous together," Beecham said. "That's not to say another miracle cannot be created. But as I get older, I admit, mortality is something I find myself dwelling on. Reminiscing about. Becoming nostalgic for. And I will say, I have yet to come up with a way in which undoing the milk in the tea would become possible."

Hazel's heart sank. She would meet Jack later at the dock, and his face would be bright and full of hope. And she would have to tell him that she had no answers. That she had nothing.

"Please," Beecham said. "Take the banknotes. Mr. Eastman would be a terrible solicitor if he couldn't execute the terms of a simple will."

Hazel took the bills numbly. "I wish you well in Philadelphia, then, *Mr. Eastman*," she said. She left her cup of tea on the desk beside his. One with milk and one without, both becoming stronger and darker with each passing second as the tea leaves continued to steep.

31

ACK WAS WAITING AT THE HARBOR, WEARING his blue jacket with its buttons undone, hanging open, a cutlass at his hip. When he saw Hazel approach in the carriage, he smiled as wide as Hazel had ever seen. She leapt—*flew*—from the seat of the carriage and into his arms, and he lifted her feet from the ground and spun her around. Her life was packed in the trunk at the back of the carriage; he had officially been given leave from his position on the *Iphigenia*.

Hazel wanted to get away from all of it: the royal family, the Companions, powerful people with terrible schemes. She was finally free, and finally with Jack.

When he put her down, and Hazel let the dizziness settle, she realized that Jack was holding out something small.

"It's not much. But I figured I should get you something."

He was holding a silver ring. The metal was coiled like a snake, without coming to a complete closed circle. As Hazel looked closer, she realized it was a ring made from a needle, its eye on one side and its sharpened point on the other. "I got a surgeon's needle from the ship. Bent it into the right shape myself.

It's silly I know, but I thought maybe you might like it." He slid it onto Hazel's finger. "I know I can't promise you much, Hazel, but I can promise you'll have me, for as long as you want me. I will be by your side for your entire life. I will give you everything I am. If you find a . . . a cure, or if you don't—there is no world in which I want to be apart from you ever again."

She kissed him there on the docks with sellers and sailors jeering, but she didn't care. He helped her back into the carriage, and they set out together toward the small church Hazel had found on the far side of town. She hadn't ever meant for them to get married, but Jack insisted. "Let me make this promise to you, Hazel Sinnett," he said, kissing her neck. "Let me tell the world that I am yours and you are mine. Until death do us part."

Saint Pancras was a squat stone church with a weathervane making lazy circles at the top of its tower. There was no one inside on that Wednesday morning, save a drunk in the back pew and the young vicar, no older than thirty but already losing his hair. He agreed to the marriage even without a special license, in part because Jack had buttoned his coat and looked every bit a naval man, and because Hazel had passed along a sizable donation (which the vicar rather embarrassedly put into his pocket before they began). The vicar's wife, a beady-eyed woman who stared pointedly at Hazel's belly while trying to gauge whether she was pregnant, agreed to bear witness for an additional donation.

Hazel and Jack knelt before the pew while the vicar peeled open *The Book of Common Prayer*. Hazel could not remember the last time she had been to church, but she remembered the rhythm of the words nonetheless; they came back to her, familiar as an old song. The morning light came in through the stained glass, and the room was warm and drowsy. Hazel glanced over at Jack from the corner of her eye as the vicar spoke, and Jack looked back. And then he winked and Hazel knew that she would spend the rest of her life loving him, with or without the word of the church.

"Jack Ellis," the vicar said. "Wilt thou have this Woman to thy wedded Wife, to live together after God's ordinance in the holy estate of Matrimony, as long as ye both shall live?"

"I will," Jack said.

"And Hazel Almont Sinnett: Wilt thou have this Man to thy wedded Husband, to live together after God's ordinance in the holy estate of Matrimony, as long as ye both shall live?"

"I will," Hazel said.

The vicar cleared his throat. "Who giveth this Woman— er—well, you, then. Take her by your hand. Is there wine? Did you bring the wine?"

"Yes," Hazel said. "Sorry, just a moment." She rose and went to her medical bag, where she had placed the wine in a small flagon. The vicar gestured, indicating that she should hand it to him.

"Just a moment," Hazel said. "I would prefer to pour it myself."

Turning away from Jack and the vicar, she carefully poured the wine into two glasses, one for Jack and one that was meant only for her.

She was careful not to spill a drop as she brought both glasses back and returned to kneeling.

"Well, then," the vicar said. "Take a sip."

Hazel did. It was strong and strange—tannic, bitter, biting all at once. Jack followed.

"May your life be fruitful and sweet as the wine the Lord

gives us," the vicar said. "And now . . . You didn't bring a ring, did you?" He didn't sound hopeful.

Hazel pulled the sewing needle ring off her finger and handed it to Jack so he could give it back to her. The vicar looked away and pretended he didn't see.

"With this ring," Jack said. "I thee wed."

"I thee wed," Hazel echoed.

The vicar's palms were clammy, and he clutched Hazel's and Jack's hands together. "By joining of hands," he said, his voice rising with a dramatic flair that Hazel suspected came from a thwarted dream of performing on the stage. "I pronounce that they be Man and Wife together, In the Name of the Father, and of the Son, and of the Holy Ghost. Amen."

Hazel and Jack rose, still holding hands. "My wife," Jack said.

"My love," said Hazel, and squeezed his hand in hers. She could feel his pulse through his palm, the beat of his heart through his skin into hers. She didn't really *feel* different, as they left the church and walked across the dry, browning grass of late summer back toward their carriage, as she had thought she would. It was as if she and Jack had always been bound together, that the word of a nervous vicar was merely a small, tedious ritual they must endure before embarking on their life together. The wine swirled in her belly, but perhaps that was just her imagination.

Hazel had procured two horses for their carriage, a small, two-wheeled curricle that they would drive themselves without a coachman. It would take them to Windsor, where Hazel would be able to say a proper goodbye to her mother and Percy, and then it would take them to the coast, where Hazel and Jack would find a boat bound for America.

They had agreed on New York, the site of King's College

in Manhattan, the first medical school in America granting the Doctor of Medicine degree. When Hazel had told Jack they didn't accept female students, he scoffed.

"But they haven't met Hazel Sinnett, have they? I bet you know more than the teachers there all put together. Wait till they see you, *then* we'll see if they'll say they don't take female students, all right."

She leaned her head against him as their carriage took them through the city. She could see the points of Westminster Abbey and the roof of St. James's Palace in the distance. Somewhere beyond the horizon was Pall Mall, where the Princess's remaining possessions were being packed and brought back to her father. Somewhere even farther away, Charlotte and Eliza were together. Hopefully safe, and hopefully happy. "And they say there are theaters in Manhattan that put Le Grand Leon to shame," Jack said. "I can build sets."

"There will be a world of things we'll be able to do," Hazel said. "And no shortage of time to figure these sorts of things out."

The horses continued on as the pavement became bumpier and narrower. Trees edged closer to the road, and London was becoming smaller behind them. Only a few carriages passed in either direction; Hazel and Jack were taking a leisurely pace, not to tire their horses out before they knew where they would be able to find a place to rest.

Hazel was just nodding off to sleep under the warmth of the afternoon sun when she was jolted awake by a horse's shriek. The carriage rattled; one of the horses had bucked.

Their path was being blocked by a black horse ridden by a rider in trousers and a black jacket. Jack extended a protective hand over Hazel. "Highwayman," he whispered, and pulled his cutlass from beneath his jacket.

And then Hazel realized that the highwayman's left jacket arm dangled loose and empty.

Marie-Anne Lavoisier slid down from her saddle and walked toward Hazel and Jack, her face a mask of fury. "Leaving town like a coward," she said. "I thought more of you, Miss Sinnett."

"I don't owe you anything," Hazel said. "We're leaving in peace."

Marie-Anne laughed a cruel and crazed laugh. "Peace! You destroy *years* of work, undermine *everything* I have worked for, for the *good of this nation*, and now you leave in a carriage with a *man* of no better standing than a common street sweeper. If I hadn't known you to be so capable, I really would think that you're a madwoman. It's madness, is what it is. Throwing away your entire future. An invitation to live at the heart of British society, to help serve humanity. And instead, you have chosen to run off with"—she gestured toward Jack—"a lover?"

"A husband," Hazel said.

"Then you truly are a fool, Miss Sinnett." She twitched her tongue over her lips. "He's taken the Tincture, so I won't waste a bullet on him."

And then, before either Hazel or Jack could react, Marie-Anne Lavoisier pulled a pistol from beneath her coat. To Jack, she said, "It'll be simpler for you if you say it was a robbery. Fewer questions."

Several things happened at once: Jack jumped from the carriage with his knife, Hazel shouted, and Marie-Anne Lavoisier fired her pistol directly into Hazel's chest.

There was smoke, and the smell of gunpowder. And shouting—more shouting.

And then Hazel's world went black.

32

HERE WAS A GAPING WOUND IN HER CHEST, A hole the width of her finger with ragged, fluted edges like the petals of an iris. It was wet, and when Hazel pulled her fingers away, she was vaguely aware, somewhere in the back of her mind, that they were covered in blood.

Jack's face was inches above hers, she could feel his breath, and he was saying something. His mouth was moving, and his eye was wide with fear, and he held on to one of her hands. "Hazel," he was saying, "Hazel, Hazel."

She swallowed. That worked at least. There was enough life in her that she could push the thick saliva that had gathered on her tongue down her throat. She sat up. The pain wasn't here yet, but she knew there would be pain.

They were on a road by a field, edged on both sides by trees. A road leading out of London—oh, yes, they had been in a carriage, but now they were on the ground. Hazel's palms were pockmarked from being pressed onto the pebbles of the road.

"Hazel," Jack said. "Hazel, can you hear me?"

Her medical bag had fallen in the chaos, her instruments and herbs scattered in the dust. No one had noticed the empty vial with a broken wax stopper roll beneath the carriage.

"I think there's a bullet in my heart," Hazel said.

She could feel the muscles straining, trying to pump blood in vain while it drained away through the hole left by the small lead ball. Her face was numb, and the pain was starting—yes, there it was—a horrible, sharp cramping that began at her chest and moved outward so that even her toes clenched in their shoes.

Jack's eye was wet; he was crying. And he was covered in blood. His chest, his trousers, his jacket. *That can't all be from me*, Hazel thought.

"I have an extractor for removing bullets. In my bag," Hazel said. "I wonder if I could remove it myself. It would probably make things worse. Leave a bigger hole. If I am immortal, it's probably just as well to leave it in."

Her heart was beating now, but still irregularly, a *thump* and then two smaller flutters and then another *thump*. And then it stopped. And started again. "How odd," Hazel said.

"You're alive," Jack breathed. "You took it— You drank it."

"There was wine at the wedding," Hazel said. "It was a pledge of 'as long as we both shall live.' It seemed only fair."

He was angry. Was he angry? It was hard to tell. The air came out of his nose fast and strong, and he swallowed hard. "How could you do that, Hazel?" he said, his face wet with tears. He kissed her hard, like he wanted to make sure she was still there. "How could you do that? You were going to fix it. You were going to fix it for both of us."

"I still can," Hazel said. "But now, I won't grow old without you."

Jack kissed her again, so hard she felt his teeth. He was crying while he kissed her, and Hazel could taste the salt of his tears.

Marie-Anne and her horse were gone. Jack would later tell Hazel that after Marie-Anne shot at her, he had attacked her with his knife, cutting off as much flesh as he could. He got both arms, and one of her legs, and slashed through a good section of her torso before she had time to reload her pistol.

"The closest anyone could have come to killing her, I figure," Jack said. "More pieces than person now."

Jack stayed by Hazel at the side of the road while she performed surgery on herself to close and bandage her wound. She had never done it before; now that she had taken the Tincture, she imagined she might start needing to.

The bullet was too deep; it was embedded within the muscle of her heart, and her immortal heart had already begun to beat around it, like the trunk of a tree growing up and around a nearby object. The stitches were uneven and larger than normal, but she had just died, and so Hazel forgave herself. When the wound was closed, Jack pressed his hand against her chest and pulled Hazel's hand to his. "My heart is yours," he said. "Beating or still."

"I might still find a cure, you know," Hazel said. "We might grow old together."

"And when we tire of this world, I will gladly drink it," Jack said. "But looking at you now, I can't imagine ever tiring of living with you by my side."

"Let's start with a hundred years," Hazel said, "and decide again then."

"Two hundred."

"All right," Hazel said. "In two hundred years. In the year

of our Lord two thousand and eighteen, when we all live beneath the sea, or in flying machines in the air, we can decide whether we want to continue on an immortal life together."

Jack lifted Hazel into the carriage and set her down gently so that she could lie with her head in his lap as he drove down the road, toward the sunset. He laced his fingers into her hair and played with it gently as she watched the world pass overhead, tree branches and sunlight and sky. And every now and then, Jack would look down and smile at her, and Hazel wondered whether eternity would even be long enough.

ON CHRISTMAS DAY, AT THE END OF THE YEAR 1818, two women arrived at a small town named Riedenburg, on the river Altmühl. They were wearing mourning clothes, but they didn't seem unhappy. In fact, they were giddy with the spirit of the holiday, and as they walked through the town, which had been dusted with snow the evening before, they laughed and smiled, walking a small gray dog on a leash. One of the women knew how to speak German; the other would soon. There was a Christmas market in town, and the smell of roasted chestnuts pervaded the air. The man who sold them a mug of hot mulled wine pointed them in the direction of the estate toward which they were heading. Widows, he thought. How lucky that they found each other. Their new home was a medieval castle, with a stone tower and a red roof built onto the side of a limestone cliff, surrounded by trees in every direction. It was just a short walk to town, but entirely private. A place to live one's own life.

ON THE FIRST FLOOR OF A BUILDING IN SEVEN Dials in London, a man with stitches around the center of his neck was holding a book and turning the pages. At first glance, it would seem he was reading to himself. But he was not alone in the room.

There was a head beside him, sitting on a counter.

A woman's head, blinking and breathing. Undying, but just a head nonetheless.

They had attempted to sew her head back onto her body—it was limbless and torn, but still a body—but the efforts had been useless. Their stores of Tincture had been destroyed; there wasn't time to make more before the body began to decompose past the point of repair. Though the cheeks retained their color and the eyes remained bright, the torso beneath became pale and white and bloated with death. Eventually, the choice was made to amputate again.

But still, *she* was alive, as much as one could be. A brilliant mind, trapped in a head with no body below. She and her husband would continue to entertain, hosting a select few friends, all esteemed artists and members of high society, to share their wine and their evenings together, talking about philosophy and literature and ways in which the world might be twisted into a more suitable direction.

THERE WAS A MARRIED COUPLE STANDING AT the bow of a boat, heading toward America. The man was steady on his feet, rocking easily with the movement of the waves. He laughed as his wife retched, and patted her back, and petted her hair. They spoke and laughed in Scots accents. Over the course of the long sea journey, the woman would deliver two infants. The husband and wife would never call themselves Americans, unlike so many of the other immigrants who were eager to leave behind the people they had been. They were Scots and they knew it, and no amount of time in Manhattan would ever dull their accents, which remained sharp as a scalpel.

The man would get a job at the Park Theatre on Chatham Street, and his eye patch would give him an air of mystique that would lead the young actors to come to revere him as a sort of legend. She would enroll at the medical school of King's College in Manhattan. They had turned her down a dozen times but she continued to show up, waiting in the offices of administrators and professors and visiting surgeons for hours, with an embossed medical bag and a treatise she had written in her lap. Her dresses covered the scar, shiny and white, that ran down her chest, the length of a fist.

She would wait for as long as it took, she would say. She had time.

Excerpt from A Treatise on Modern Medicine
(1822) by Hazel Sinnett-Ellis

ALPINE BLOOD DISORDER—is an extremely rare illness whose exact provenance is unknown. Symptoms include extreme drowsiness, fatigue, unexplained scarring and bruising, and swollen feet. Alpine blood disorder is deadly, and no treatment exists. However, it is so rare and unlikely an affliction that physicians reading this Treatise are advised not to frighten their patients with a possible diagnosis.

notes and acknowledgments

Immortality: A Love Story is a work of fiction, and though I pulled from real-world history, part of the joy of writing a novel is getting to bend and stretch that history to suit my narrative purpose. Perhaps most obviously, the Roman fever is a fictional plague, though it bears some similarity to scarlet fever. (Actually, the most obvious change is that, to the best of my knowledge, no one has created a tincture that makes someone capable of living forever.)

In the real world, Princess Charlotte died in childbirth in 1817, a year after her wedding. In this universe, I imagine that her having suffered from a bout of Roman fever meant that her marriage was put off for several years, allowing the events of the novel to take place. A few other changes are small: Sir Robert Mends was only given his position as commodore in 1821, three years after this novel takes place. In our world, anesthesia was first used in surgery by William Morton in Boston in 1846. During a demonstration in the United Kingdom, it was referred to as the "Yankee dodge." In the universe of the book, Dr. Beecham invented his own anesthesia several decades earlier, and so it becomes known as the "Edinburgh dodge" instead.

I hope this novel inspires you to explore the real history of the figures and locations I used for fun and fiction, and if you're mad about anything I got wrong, feel free to send me an email, even though I can't promise I'll actually read it.

This book is possible only because of the tremendous amount of work and dedication of the incredible people who helped its predecessor, *Anatomy: A Love Story*, find its audience. Thank you, of course, to my agent, Dan Mandel, who always answers my frantic emails and who understands that I need more encouragement than a self-respecting adult really should. The entire team at Wednesday Books is wonderful, and I owe my thanks to my fearless and incredibly patient editor, Sara Goodman, and to Alexis Neuville, Mary Moates, and Rivka Holler. Thank you so much to the brilliant copy editor Eliani Torres for her detailed and patient work. I also owe special gratitude to Kerri Resnick and Zack Meyer for their work on creating two such beautiful, captivating covers. I really do think any success these books have is really thanks to *how good* these covers are, and I'm allowed to say that because that's the part of this book that I had really nothing to do with.

Thank you so much to the team at Reese's Book Club, and to Reese Witherspoon for selecting *Anatomy: A Love Story*, which changed my life, and also for *Legally Blonde*, which also changed my life but in a different, more subtle way.

The first and only person to read early drafts of this book was my sister, Caroline Schwartz, who knows exactly what readers want. Thank you for reading quickly, talking me off ledges, and giving me the exactly correct ratio of validation to actually useful feedback. This book is so much better because of you.

Thank you to Stories Books & Cafe in Echo Park, where I wrote almost the entire second half of this book while drinking your very good drip coffee with oat milk.

Katie Donahoe, you were my cheerleader through this entire process, and I am so lucky for your friendship. Thank you for believing I could actually write this book, even when I was complaining the entire time.

Thank you to the cats, Eddie and Beetlejuice, for permission to use their likenesses.

To my husband, Ian Karmel, I am so lucky that I found you. Everything I do is better because I get to do it with you. I love you so much.